Henry A. Wise

**Seven Decades of the Union**

The humanities and materialism

Henry A. Wise

**Seven Decades of the Union**
*The humanities and materialism*

ISBN/EAN: 9783337362379

Printed in Europe, USA, Canada, Australia, Japan

Cover: Foto ©Andreas Hilbeck / pixelio.de

More available books at **www.hansebooks.com**

# SEVEN DECADES

OF

# THE UNION.

## THE HUMANITIES AND MATERIALISM,

ILLUSTRATED BY

## A MEMOIR OF JOHN TYLER,

WITH

### Reminiscences of Some of his Great Cotemporaries.

### THE TRANSITION STATE OF THIS NATION—ITS DANGERS AND THEIR REMEDY.

## By HENRY A. WISE.

"'Tis Liberty, or 'tis Death!'
LOGAN: *Runnymede.*

"Give me Liberty, or give me *Death!*"
PATRICK HENRY,
*at the "Old Raleigh," Williamsburg Va.*

PHILADELPHIA:
J. B. LIPPINCOTT & CO.
1872.

# DEDICATION.

To the rector, board of visitors, faculty, alumni, and students of the College of William and Mary, I dedicate this memoir of her late rector and chancellor, John Tyler, the tenth President of the United States of America; prepared for the archives of his Alma Mater, in obedience to her resolves and orders, at intervals snatched from professional business, and from household hinderances and cares, since the meeting of the rector, board, and faculty in the year 1868.

It has been to me a task of tears, dashed with some sacred joy,—a tale of sadness cheered and lightened by some exultant songs of triumphant reminiscence.

Mr. Tyler's life ran through seven decades, from 1790 to 1862; it is full of the themes of many and mighty events and thoughts; it has a divine moral in its teachings, and lessons for the deepest study of mankind.

Humbled by attempting the performance of this task, I profess only a "joy of grief,"—no talents for the volume of its labors. To bring that volume within readable compass, I have sketched a memoir, not altogether a biography, and not at all a history,—an outline not wholly filled up,—a drawing somewhat colored and shaded, but foreshortened to delineate salient points and parts in the important and impressive life and action of a good and great man.

I glance, first, at the results of history just before his birth, up to the time when he took part in events; and then follow them until he finished his course on earth; leaving his country, in the midst of a revolution, the beginning of which he saw and took part in, but the witnessing of the end of which he was graciously spared.

I have treated of measures and men mostly affecting him, but have made free to indulge in episodes touching causes and effects affecting the nation during his time, and describing some of the men who were his cotemporaries.

I make no apologies to the public for the work. It was written at the request of William and Mary, and has grown into its present proportions and form, to gratify my own affections, and to perform a duty of gratitude to a good, true, and faithful friend, who was much maligned in life, and who is now far above all praise.

The writing of it has soothed some aching agonies of my own; and my only wish or prayer about it is, that it may do good to others, and especially aid in reviving the hopes of constitutional liberty in a land which is still, thank God, the asylum of the free. Its aim is to direct the attention of a republic back to the "Humanities," from the "material and the physical," which now preponderate and prevail too much over the moral elements of government and of society.

The attempt is itself laudable, whatever may be the failure of the performance. If it is not thought well, nor grouped well, nor written well, it may perchance suggest something worth weighing to those who can think and group and write; and with that I will be content.

With the highest reverence and respect, I am

Your obedient servant,

HENRY A. WISE.

# CONTENTS.

( v )

## CHAPTER VIII.

### THE FIFTH DECADE, FROM 1830 TO 1840.

## CHAPTER IX.

### THE SIXTH DECADE, FROM 1840 TO 1850.

## CHAPTER X.

### THE SIXTH DECADE, FROM 1840 TO 1850.

# SEVEN DECADES OF THE UNION.

## CHAPTER I.

### THE FIRST DECADE FROM 1700 TO 1801.

The American Revolution—The Effect of the Reformation—The First Administration under the Constitution of the United States, during which Mr. Tyler was born—The Second Administration, and its Revolution of Parties in 1801—Mr. Tyler's Lineage, and the Peninsula on which he was born and raised.

> "THE dust on antique time would lie unswept,
> And mountainous error be too highly heap'd
> For truth to overpeer,"

had not Heaven's messengers of the Reformation, in the latter end of the sixteenth and the beginning of the seventeenth centuries, broken its thick crust of ages. The smouldering fires of accumulated wrongs burst forth in Europe with more than volcanic force, shaking and scorching the Absolutism of the Old World, and setting human intellects free.

Wickliffe, Calvin, Luther, Melanchthon, Cromwell were not the only ones thinking and daring and doing, but hosts of mightiest minds, in every department of knowledge and of truth, were scattering lights abroad to illumine the darkness. The closets of the Vatican were thrown open; the secrets of the Schoolmen were revealed; the stools of Dogmas and the thrones of Despotism were thrown down. Powers and Principalities were subdued to become the Protestant pupils of a divine faith of "good will to men," and were themselves made to question

( 11 )

and confront Absolutism defiantly, with the cross of suffering and of martyrdom, for the sake of Truth.

This shock of old things, thought to be firmly established because simply hoary, and having custom without law, had its ample course. Students of the laws of God and of the rights of man were in the laboratories of the great school of the Humanities, and the Humanities were made ready for the occasion of their uses. Earth was crying for them, and they went forth to the call. Philology, Grammar, the Hebrew, Latin, and Greek languages, Logic, Poetry, History, Metaphysics, and the Divine Philosophy of Christianity found the Printing-Press ready to give them the wings of the morning, and Columbus had already sailed over the seas and found a New World for their theater. Here, in North America, they found a huge, rude, barbaric continent, lying prone in a state of nature, ample for the fires and the blasts of all their mighty furnaces, forges, and foundries.

In the mean time, Bacon had been at his inductions; Oxford was teaching; the divines were translating and publishing the Bible; Milton was singing; and by the time America was ready for her first Revolution Burke had generalized the philosophy of human government; Bourbons and Stuarts of old dynasties had been beheaded; Hampdens and Sydneys had asserted rights and been martyred; the Publicists had codified international law, and the convulsions of England had settled some ideas of Magna Charta for domestic government. The people of England had learned to rehearse the noble Baron's chant of Liberty:

> "Let every Briton, as his mind, be free.
> His person safe, his property secure;
> His house as sacred as the fane of heaven;
> Watching unseen, his ever-open door,
> Watching the realm, the spirit of the laws;
> His fate determined by the rules of right;
> His voice enacted in the common voice,
> And general suffrage of the assembled realm
> No hand invisible to write his doom;
> No demon starting at the midnight hour,

To draw his curtain, or to drag him down
To mansions of despair.  Wide to the world
Disclose the secrets of the prison walls,
And bid the groanings of the dungeon strike
The public ear.  Inviolable preserve
The sacred shield that covers all the land,
The Heaven-conferred palladium of the Isle,
To Britain's sons, the judgment of their peers.
On these great pillars, freedom of the Mind,
Freedom of Speech, and freedom of the Pen,
Forever changing, yet forever sure,
The base of Britain rests!"

These were the mighty throes making grand preparation for the working of new ideas.

The American Revolution breaking out in 1765, and brought to a denouement in '76, germinated thoughts which will never cease growing, until they cover the whole earth with the ægis of *laws made for the sake of liberty, not of liberty only to make laws.*

1st. The right of self-government, in all separate communities defined into *distinct peoples*, requiring separate and different laws, and capable of either separate or *confederate nationality.*

2dly. *Self-government, guarded in law-making and in law-administering power by limitations of authority in* WRITTEN *constitutions of government.*

3dly. *The demolition of colonial and provincial States dependent on central sovereignties.*

4thly. *Freedom, equality, and source of sovereignty in the governed, and responsibility and accountability in the governors of men.*

5thly. *Sovereignty in the constituency or source, and not in the mere municipality of government.*

These were the five cardinal points of the North American system of constitutional republicanism.

The forest-born Demosthenes did not catch songs of liberty from the birds of the trees in the wilderness.  Old Logan had written his poem, and Runnymede was read in the forests where Henry hunted; and it was thus that the orator's thunders caught the notes of the poet's soul-music; the one singing, "'Tis Liberty or Death!" and the other singing, "Give me Liberty or give me Death!"

It was about this period of liberty brooding over States which had just ceased to be colonies of America, and germinating these indestructible thoughts in mighty men, that John Tyler was born. It was the age of heroes and of sages, and of battles, too,—battles of which those of the sword were only heroic, while those of the souls and minds of men were spiritual and immortal. It was the age which gave the world a Washington; and the shrine of Mount Vernon is sacred to all men, next only to the unapproachable shrine of Mount Nebo. The Moses of the New World inducted these new ideas into the government of men. The novelty of this new government was the least difficulty in the wondrous work of its establishment. Its magnitude was immense, and yet all its parts were aptly fitted together, and appropriate to all its far-reaching ends. The administration of the Father of his Country gave it at the beginning its true form and expression.

His wisdom settled foreign relations on the surest foundations of peace and justice with all nations, and entangling alliances with none; he firmly guarded neutrality; he organized the executive departments.

During his term were founded the judiciary, the land ordinances, the Indian policy, the laws of immigration and naturalization, a navy and military system opposed to standing armies; and he so ordered the public fisc as to frown down the bad faith of repudiating the public debt, and assumed the States' debts incurred in the Revolution. He restored the national credit, revived trade, and provided ample revenue; he protected the frontier against Indian depredations. He resisted Jacobinism from abroad, and, above all, taught us the application of the Constitution and laws to cases of rebellion and treason, using the military force as ancillary only to the civil power. In a word, under the auspices of the administration of the first President, grace, dignity, decorum, order, and power were imparted to the government of the United States; and it

was made to give assurance to the hope of permanent and perpetual civil liberty, and commanded the highest respect of the
nations of the earth. But there was one canker in its bud
which needed to be dreaded, and has since proved to be destructive to its bloom and beauty,—not yet, I hope, to all its
fruits. It was the *canker of construction.*

All then admitted that all the powers granted in the Constitution were guarded by limitations; but two schools existed as
to the extent and application of limitations. Jefferson at the
head of one, Hamilton at the head of the other school, both
of the first Cabinet, came into serious conflict first upon the
construction of the words "*necessary* and *proper*," as to the
power of Congress to create a national bank. The strict school
contended that the power was not granted, and was, therefore,
reserved to the States or the people.

The school of broader construction resorted to the *incidental
powers.*

Mr. Hamilton admitted all the granted powers were strictly
limited, and that the *granted* powers only could be exercised;
but that all powers "necessary and proper" to carry the expressed powers into execution were granted and could be exercised; though he admitted that they were restrained and
limited in extent and purpose by their relation to the powers
expressed.

Neither contended that either the expressed or the necessary
and properly relative or incidental powers were unlimited and
unrestrained; but, as we shall see, this memorable start of construction soon passed beyond all bounds of either expressed or
necessary and proper incidental powers.

The history of construction shows that in less than a quarter
of a century the incidental powers, restrained at first by the
ends and extent of the expressed powers, were carried far beyond the expressed powers themselves, which limited and restrained them. And here commenced the first struggle between
what then began to be called the Federal and Democratic
Republican parties.

Well for us all would it be, at this day, if construction had not carried incidental power further than it was carried by Mr. Hamilton, in his masterly argument, which won the mind of Washington on the Bank question. But the Federal party, under his august influence, succeeded in electing his immediate successor; and the second administration met the portentous obstacle of a threatened war with France.

The crushing conflicts of England and France for universal supremacy assailed the neutral rights of our country, and a provisional army had to be raised. Genet, the French minister in this country, had outraged our internal sovereignty, and the elder Adams recommended measures which were defended under the pretext of the imminency of war. His party started the doctrine that even *threatened war* set aside the checks, balances, and limitations of the Constitution, and justified the passage of the acts of the Alien and of the Sedition laws,—the one act to remove aliens suspected of hostility, and the other to punish sedition, in forms violating the freedom of speech and of the press. It was then that the Virginia Legislature resolved: "That the powers not delegated by the Constitution to the United States, nor prohibited by it to the States, are reserved to the States or to the people; and, therefore, the exercise of the powers not enumerated in the grant by the United States, is an usurpation of the authority of the States or of the people."

This was in turn met by the Federal party assuming that whilst the States and the people of the States were originally the sources of sovereignty, yet they had delegated that sovereignty to the Federal government of the Union, and that the Congress of the United States had, by the Constitution, become invested with the national sovereignty, and might exercise its powers and dominions over any and every subject of the "general welfare."

The Democracy insisted that the national sovereignty could not be delegated, and could not exist in any one or all of the mere municipal departments of government, either executive, judicial, or legislative,—that sovereignty could exist alone in its *source*, the States, and that the people could act only through the organism of the States; and that its very nature, under our system of republican constitutional freedom, was *conventional*, and not *municipal;* that the mere municipal functionaries of the Federal government were but creatures of sovereignty, and its mere trustees, servants, and agents, to do the biddings of the conventional power of the States and the people as expressed and limited by the Constitution; that the Constitution itself was but the creature of the sovereignty of the States or the people, and was made by it the guide, and standard, and rule of legislative, executive, and judicial authority and functions, and that the Presidency, the Congress, and the Supreme Court each and all were but creatures of the Constitution. They were creatures not in the first, but in the second degree from sovereignty, and could pretend neither to be the sovereignty itself nor to have delegated to them its absolute powers, that the conventional powers of the States or their people alone could exercise absolute and unlimited power, and that all questions of doubtful or disputed power by the mere municipal Federal government, and either or all of its departments, had of right to be referred to the conventional power of the States or of the people, in their separate State organizations. Thus began the discord of State rights and of Federal absolutism. The Alien and Sedition laws were passed, the provisional army was provided, a regular army created, Democratic members of the House of Representatives were insulted in the theater for words spoken against standing armies in the House. Mr. Jefferson, then Vice-President, had to be guarded by his friends from his presiding chair in the Senate to his boarding-house and back; the judiciary had, both in the case of Jay and of Marshall, become officially conjoined with the executive, mixing the chief justiceship in the same person with the secretaryship of state and the office of a foreign minister; and some of the inferior Federal judges had played the Jeffries-scenes over again so rampant that the whole judiciary was very much lowered in dignity, and finally Chase was impeached.

The excesses of the second administration became odious to the States and the people, and the Federal party was overthrown in the memorable political revolution of 1801, when the great apostle of liberty and author of the Declaration of Independence was elected the President. For a study of this era we refer to Wharton's "State Trials," and particularly to his able, philosophical, beautiful, and just preface.

Besides the canker of construction, other causes showed themselves during the first administration which brooded mischief, and from the beginning foreshadowed the danger of dissolution of the Union, by reason of infractions of the Constitution and of infringement of the rights of the States to domestic and internal self-government.

On the 12th February, 1790, the first petition was presented to Congress for the emancipation of slaves. It was signed by Dr. Franklin, President of the Society for the Abolition of Slavery. He was a philosopher "wise as a serpent," but not "as harmless as the dove." He had been chiefly instrumental as a pacificator in the convention which framed the Constitution of the United States on the question of the apportionment of representatives between the free and the slave States; but it seems that he was wily enough to resort to a more effectual mode of assailing the property in slaves and the power of the States which held them in bondage. Whether he foresaw that the dragon's teeth which he was sowing would sprout armed warriors or not, is not for us to say; but he was either not wise in not foreseeing the consequences of his movement, or he was fanatically heedless of the consequences themselves which followed. It irritated sectional antagonism, aroused religious antipathies, fomented jealousies and discord, disturbed the legislation of Congress, and finally caused civil war. So much for the motives and action of the highest human wisdom. He was doubtless a man of peace, but was blind to the mode of preserving it.

The Congress of 1790 was wiser than Franklin, more faithful to the Constitution of the United States, and resolved: "That Congress have no authority to interfere in the emancipation of slaves, or in the treatment of them in any of the States." And the territory south of the Ohio was accepted without excluding slavery. What a contrast this is with the executive and congressional action in 1862, when civil war was made the pretext for violating the Constitution !

Another cloud, not larger at first than the palm of a man's hand, formed another prognostic of coming wars. The territory ceded by North Carolina, out of which the new State was formed, was what is now included in the State of Tennessee. That territory was ceded by North Carolina in a deed executed by her senators under her laws, in December, 1789, and was accepted by act of Congress passed April 2d, 1790, just fourteen days after the birth of John Tyler. The cession was forced upon North Carolina by the acts of rebels to her jurisdiction, countenanced by Congress. The history of this territory shows the first and only instance of *de facto* "squatter sovereignty" known in the United States prior to the period of the Mormon monstrosities in Utah, and it was the first instance of nullification.

The settlers in the then State of North Carolina west of the Stone Mountain, complaining that they were not afforded due protection by the parent State, declared their independence, and set up against both State and Federal sovereignty a sovereignty of their own, called "the State of Franklin." They organized a State government, with all the municipal departments. They practically nullified in their limits both the laws of North Carolina and of the Federal government. They established a currency of peltry, and the then governor, General Sevier, complained that he was cheated grievously in the payment of his salary, by having put upon him opossum-skins with raccoon-tails sewed on to them.

They contended that his story was absurd, because if they had the *raccoon-tails*, they would have the *raccoon-skins*, too ; but he convicted them of using the same tails for numerous different payments, and of stealing the tails again for the repayments.

The United States, under Washington's administration, did not deem it a duty or a necessity to use force against this grotesque but flagrant rebellion ; but compensated North Carolina

and pacified the rebels by admitting the Territory or State of
Franklin into the Union as the State of Tennessee.  But it
must not be forgotten that by *rebellion* that *State gained* admission instead of *losing* its place in the Union; and *secession*
and *nullification* were both sanctioned by the then Congress of
the United States of America.  Such, then, was the jealous
regard paid by all to the right of independent self-government.
And this, too, was a precedent sanctioned by both State and
Federal authority, which fixed a habitude of thought and feeling
and action on the very first settlers of this country, engrafting
in them a ruling sense of the right of self-government against
any power which either oppressed or failed to protect them.
If it was not taught them by precedent sanctioned by Congress, its spirit was caught by them, assuredly, from the colonies, especially from Massachusetts and all New England and
Virginia.

It was in this decade, beginning with the first under Washington and ending with the second administration, under the
elder Adams, that John Tyler's childhood played.  He drew
his first breath in the atmosphere of the wisdom of Washington, and his mind was imbued from his cradle with the spirit of
the age of reformation, resulting in the men and the events of
the American Revolution.

He was at his grammar-school just at the moment when the
doctrines of State and popular sovereignty began to be successfully taught, and became triumphant for half a century of the
future from that time.  He was taught and trained in the school
of strict construction of the Constitution and of the sovereignty
of the States or the people, and in the principles of the school
of Democracy,—a school which never sought to lower itself in
the mud of manners and morals, and to pull all men down to
the depth of vulgar mobocracy; but one which, like a mighty
charity, sought to build up a broad platform high as kings'
crowns, to reach down the strong arm of popular sovereignty
to raise all men, the least and lowest, up to that exalted level;
ay, as high as possible, near to God!

He was thoroughly and fully imbued by birth, by education, by the men and events around him, with the spirit and the truths of times resorting to revolution and reform for liberty.

His father's residence at the time was at Greenway, near Charles City Court House. His cradle was rocked there, and all his childhood was nurtured at that locality. For his parentage and family history, we condense a statement prepared by his son, John Tyler, Jr., Esq. He says that he was born at Greenway, on the twenty-ninth day of March, A.D. 1790. In the paternal line he was the fifth in descent from the first in Virginia bearing the same name, who, together with his brother Henry, came at an early period to the colony at Jamestown; and eventually, in the year 1636, established themselves in the Middle Plantations, intermediate between the settlements at Jamestown and Yorktown, embracing the present city of Williamsburg and its adjacent country. Henry located himself on the spot where Williamsburg was laid out, in 1690; and the lands upon which the palace of the royal governor was erected, together with those upon which the college itself was built, were acquired from his estate.

John located himself four miles from the present site of Williamsburg, where the round brick house constructed for his residence still stands,—now called Warburton's, in the county of James City.

These brothers, John and Henry Tyler, were younger members of the ancient Shropshire family, originally from Wales, recently and at present represented in Great Britain, in the elder line, by the late Sir William and the present Sir Charles of the Parliament and the Admiralty. They were of orginal Norman and Welsh extraction.

Who the first John Tyler of Virginia married, is unknown, the records of James City County having been repeatedly destroyed. They were destroyed in Bacon's Rebellion, in 1676. Again when the old capitol was burnt, and again during the late war of secession. What remained at Williamsburg were transferred to Richmond, and they were burnt in the conflagration of that city in 1865; and most family records of the peninsula of York and James Rivers were destroyed in the wars of 1776, of 1812, and of 1861.

The son of the first John Tyler was known as John Tyler, Esq. He was a man of note in his day, and married his cousin, Elizabeth Tyler. His son John, the third John Tyler, was, by royal appointment, marshal of the colony. John Tyler, the marshal, married Anne Contesse, the daughter of Dr. Lewis Contesse, a French Huguenot of nerve and character.

He left several daughters, and two sons, John and Lewis. John, the elder, and the father of President Tyler, lived to attain high honors. He was a distinguished Revolutionary patriot, and a zealous leader in the cause of the American colonies. He was an eminent jurist, and as judge of admiralty he decided the first prize case which occurred after independence was declared, holding his court under a large golden willow, which stood in the yard at Greenway. He was the bosom friend of Thomas Jefferson. After independence was achieved, he was speaker of the House of Burgesses, and was a judge of the State District Court; was governor of the State from 1808 to 1811, and ultimately judge of the United States District Court until he died.

Many rare and rich anecdotes are told of his life. At the christening of his first-born son, when the name of the child was announced,—" Wat Henry Tyler,"—Mr. Henry being present and somewhat surprised, nervously asked "why that name was selected." The mother replied, " We have so named him, sir, after the two greatest British rebels, Wat Tyler and Patrick Henry." And the watch-seal which he wore when he died was presented to him by Mr. Jefferson, with the initials " T. J." engraved on its face, reading forward " Thomas Jefferson," and backward " John Tyler."

In Abell's " Life of President Tyler," we have a sweet story of his saving Patrick Henry from an awful repulse by a hostess, who, when told that they were members of the House of Burgesses flying before Arnold's invasion, was indignant that they were running away when her husband had just left her to meet the invader. He had to vouch for Mr. Henry's being himself; and when convinced of that fact, such was her confidence in him that if *he* ran away, all was right; it obtained for them shelter and food for the night.

Another anecdote illustrative of the man, and not yet written, was related by the late General M. Pitts, the father of Judge E. P. Pitts, late of the Norfolk Circuit. He was a student of law in the office of John Wise, on the Eastern Shore of Virginia, and when he was ready to apply for his license, Mr. Wise gave him a letter to Judge Tyler, then of the District Court, residing at Norfolk. He was a young man of great promise, and afterwards distinguished in his profession, but was exceedingly diffident and awkward. He reached Norfolk, and easily found the judge's office, but the judge was not in. His clerk received young Pitts politely, took his letter of introduction, and invited him to await the judge's return, expected every moment. He sat down, anxiously awaiting the awful appearance of the strange judge. Suddenly a fine horse dashed up to the office door, mounted by a grand-looking, erect rider, venerable and commanding in his mien, with powdered hair neatly queued, wearing the shad-cut coat with long-flap waistcoat, shirt ruffled at bosom and wristbands, with shorts and knee-buckles and white topboots. He dismounted abruptly, stalked in, dashed off his buck-skin gauntlets, threw his whip on the table, and began to walk and talk to himself, violently exclaiming, "Yes! I will teach the upstart what the rights of land proprietors are! He is so little of a gentleman, and so much of an ignoramus, that he has no idea of land-titles or rights, or the laws which protect them!"

The truth was he had had a hot collision with the "supervisor" of the streets, who had encroached, as he thought, on his lot, and he had returned to his office before his passion was cool, and neither his clerk nor Pitts knew what the soliloquy was about. He had entered without noticing young Pitts, and continued soliloquizing aloud as he stalked the room, swearing not a little, and commenting in such a mood that the clerk did not venture to present the letter of young Pitts, who sat trembling with apprehension. " Was ever judge in such a humor wooed for a law license ?"

At last the clerk caught a lull in the storm, and handed him the letter. Pitts timidly rose, and the judge, holding the letter, read it, and exclaimed, " Young gentleman, my friend John Wise, Esq., tells me you wish to be a lawyer."

" Yes, sir," replied Pitts, "if you will be pleased to sign my license ; but—but—I can come at another time, if it please you, sir, better." He hoped to be let off from the hour of wrath and bad omens for lenity in the examination.

The judge exclaimed, " No, young gentleman ; I can tell now by a single question whether you are fit to be a lawyer or not." Then raising his voice to a higher pitch, he asked, " Can you tell me the meaning of the word ' *supervisor ?*' "

Pitts was overwhelmed : he thought there was a "catch" in the word ; perplexed, he looked down, tasted his lips for a reply, the judge's eye glaring on him bewildered. At last, hesitatingly and half choked, he muttered, " Judge, I—I hardly—know—any technical—meaning,—but—suppose—its common meaning is—' super'—' over'—and ' video' to see—the noun—' overseer !' "

Eagerly the judge exclaimed, " Yes, young man, you have hit it exactly. He is on the stilts of ' *supervisor,*' just as if he was lord of the manors and of all the owners, and all the time he is nothing but a d—d vulgar ' *overseer.*' You know the meaning of words, sir, and interpret truly, and are fit to be a lawyer. Give me your license, and I will sign it with pleasure.'

In a moment he was calm, signed the license, pressed upon young Pitts every kindness, and sent him back home rejoicing !

December 11th, 1808, in a note dated at Greenway, he accepted the office of governor of Virginia, and he filled that office with distinguished vigor of intellect and nerve for about three years, resigning to accept the office of judge of the District Court of the United States, which office he honored until his death in 1813.

One has but to read his messages whilst governor to see the intellect, the integrity, the courage, the patriotic fervor, the pure and stern republicanism, and the prophetic power of a watchful, jealous lover of popular liberty. In his message of December 3d, 1810, denouncing the effects of foreign influence and commerce upon our country and its destiny, he said : "It produces also what is called in polite circles citizens of the world,—the worst citizens in the world, who, having no attachments to any country, make to themselves wings to fly away with from impending dangers." Again, speaking of the Court of Appeals, he denounced its example and habit of relying so much upon British cases as precedents, applying to cases under American institutions. He seems to have had an instinctive perception of the danger of citing the maxims of British monarchy, and the doctrines and dogmas laid down by Blackstone, and by judges who were keepers of a king's conscience.

He was afraid of the effect which he foresaw it would have, and has had, in gradually undermining republican ideas and overthrowing the sovereignty of the people. He accused the highest court and the bar of British "case mania," and of subserviency to their lordships and barons of British courts. He urged the duty of revising and codifying the common law, selecting only such of its maxims and such of its popular principles as suited our system of democracy, taking its maxims without its cases; proving propositions by the maxims, not proving the maxims by the propositions; and ends by saying: "Shall we forever administer our free republican government on principles of rigid high-toned monarchy? I almost blush for my country when I think of these things!"

January 15th, 1811, he notified the legislature that he had accepted the judgeship of the United States District Court of Virginia; and he was succeeded in the office of governor by James Monroe. He was a noble specimen of the "booted and spurred cavalier" of colonial times,—a ruffled gentleman of great learning and mental force, and a man of unspotted name for honor, truth, integrity, and pluck. He was universally known, respected, and loved throughout the State,—so much so that, though in the midst of the war when he died, in

1813, the General Assembly paid his remains and memory unusual honors, such as have never been paid to those of any man, except the Father of his Country, before or since.

The maternal line of President Tyler was not less distinguished. His mother was Mary Armistead, of Buck Rowe, in the county of Elizabeth City, on the Back River, looking out upon the Chesapeake Bay, and in sight of now Fortress Monroe.

The Armisteads, of Buck Rowe, and those of Hesse, in Matthews, formerly a part of Gloucester, in Virginia, sprang from the Hesse Armistead family in Germany. The propositus of this family came from England in the seventeenth century, and fixed his residence at Hesse, in the county of what was then called Gloucester, on the south bank, and near the mouth, of Piankatank River. The daughters of this family have been strikingly remarkable for their strength of character and beauty of person, and the continuous line of male descendants has marked the name of hero after hero on the tablets of their country's history. The "Star-Spangled Banner" is blended with the name of Colonel George Armistead, the defender of Fort McHenry in the war of 1812. He was fighting the invader while Francis Key was writing the anthem, "our flag is still there!" His brother, General Walker Armistead, won his laurels and lost an arm in the same brilliant battle. Two other brothers lost their lives in the assault upon Fort Erie, in the war of 1812; and he who was lately killed at Gettysburg, leading a Confederate division against "certain death," was the son of General Walker Armistead. Armistead T. Mason, senator of the United States, through his mother; and Cary and William Selden, through their mother; and General Robert E. Lee, through his ancestress, Judith Armistead; and President John Tyler, through his mother, Mary Armistead, all alike in the maternal line sprang from the root of the same family tree.

But no matter what her blood, or whether she could trace a title from what is now derisively called the F. F. V.'s or not, she was Mary Armistead, of Buck Rowe, instinct with life, beauty, and virtue; and we emphatically pronounce, from all that is

known and can be gathered from tradition, that one of the prevailing causes of the greatness of the men of that period, was
the lovely and noble character of the mothers of the men of
that day.

They were eminently strong, and yet pure, refined, chaste,
delicate, and modest, given to household cares, frugal, practical,
and compelled to be heedful of the life and its events around
them, challenging the practice of wisdom and virtue, and demanding every effort of body and mind.

Mary Armistead, like most other ladies of her day, was,—

> "One
> Not learned, save in gracious household ways;
> Not perfect, nay, but full of tender wants;
> No angel, but a dearer being, all dipt
> In angel instincts, breathing Paradise,
> Interpreter between the gods and men;
> Who looked all native to her place, and yet
> On tiptoe seemed to touch upon a sphere
> Too gross to tread, and all male minds perforce
> Swayed to her from their orbits as they moved,
> And girdled her with music. Happy he
> With such a mother! faith in womankind
> Beats with his blood, and trust in all things high
> Comes easy to him, and though he trip and fall
> He shall not blind his soul with clay."

Woman, as well as man, had her part in the great dramas
then acted, and her part required great naturalness as well as
romance, and uncommon grace as well as a capacity for great
uses, in her acting. The women at that day were principally
formed by education *at home.* There was no meretricious training of misses at the domestic schools where mother was mistress. Rarely a few "finished" at some such school as Mrs.
Davenport's, at Williamsburg. We remember well the cramped,
Italian-like chirography of the last of the pupils of that school.

These pupils were bland in their tone as the proudest dames
of court when the colony had a palace; and yet they were
taught to cut out and cure hams of cherry-red juices sweeter
than the "Be-kan"-raised of Westphalia; they could arrange

the warping-bars, turn the spindles, wind the skein, darn the
stockings, and, walking over the floors of waxen cleanness, see
to pantry and laundry.   And oh, what sweet charities their
perfumed presence shed around home, husband, and children,
guests, servants, the poor, and the church!  Physicians and
nurses skilled in every balmy herb and soothing salve, at home
and in the neighborhood around, blessing and blessed by all,
they could not but be fresh and fair, and happy as beautiful.
One supreme duty marked these mothers.  All had to work,
and the lessons of the children must be gotten, come what
would.   Even war did not more than stay that duty; and the
long winter nights were the happiest hours for the homestead
tasks.   Feast and frolic made the house warm and bright for
children and servants when the tasks were done.  Sons and
daughters at all odds, even amidst the whirring of spindles and
the rumbling of warping-bars for woof and web to clothe families in domestic fine linen, had to study their lessons until the
tasks were relieved by waiters full of nuts and cakes and taffy,
brought in as signals of fun and tale-telling, and chitchat bois-
terous with glee, until the hour of rest, when all tiptoed to bed.

These were no rude scenes of peasantry or yeomanry.  Gentle
manners, grace, order, and decorum, presided in stately form,
but bright and cheerful.  The mother of these domestic scenes,
when an affair of state came on, was a queenly woman,—high,
commanding, stately, whether at the table or in the saloon, at
the dinner or in the dance ; she could talk of stately matters
with bewitching wisdom, or play her smiling, classic wit or
humor like a fairy, and command men to do her homage, due
only to dignity, sense, sweetness, and grace.  And when the
season of chirping spring would come, flowers of sweetness
and of taste bloomed around her; midsummer's harvest was
made to smile with her bounty, and autumn's fruits were preserved by her,—thoughtful provisions for coming winter.  She
made home happy and healthful as it was hospitable, without
stint, or sham, or seeming.  To guest and family alike it was a
warm home of unaffected, liberal, wooing welcome.  There was
no place on earth where the word "domesticity"—sacred to the

household gods—meant more than it did then at such homes as Greenway and Buck Rowe, in the plantations of all the peninsulas of the Chesapeake Bay of Virginia.

The homes of Greenway and Buck Rowe were made one house by the marriage of John Tyler and Mary Armistead, the father and mother of John Tyler, Jr. And we should omit a pertinent and poetic theme in its story if we did not sketch at least a description of the Peninsula and the population in which these homes flourished and bore such precious fruits in their day and generation.

Greenway and Warburton are in a section of the Peninsula between the historical, majestic James and the consecrated banks of the York River. They are not far from the old 'Capitol, and the old Raleigh, and the powder-magazine at Williamsburg, or from the old redoubts at Yorktown; and the first and last events of the Revolution of '76 have there, at these spots, and all around them, their local habitations and their names; every turf is a soldier's sepulchre, and every hall was the scene of some sayings or doings of sages and heroes who set the first ball of the Revolution in motion. After it had bowled over the Atlantic slope,—at Lexington and Boston Harbor and Bunker Hill, at Princeton and Trenton and Germantown, at Monmouth Court House and Chadd's Ford and Stony Point and Ticonderoga, at King's Mountain and Guilford and Eutaw and Camden and Charleston, at the Great Bridge and Hicksford,—it ricocheted back again, and was spent at Cornwallis's surrender at Yorktown, within twelve miles of where it started, at the powder-magazine in Williamsburg. And that powder-magazine is still standing; and now,—oh, shame to this old city's corporate authorities!—after being used as a temple of the living God, it has been sold by the corporation of Williamsburg, and converted by the purchaser into a horse-stable,—a monument of the contrast of the present with the past.

This Peninsula was thus the Alpha and Omega of the scenes of the American Revolution. It is a land of genial climate, of generous soil, of majestic rivers, of fruitful fertility of fields, and of forests of richest frondage,—above all distinguished for its men and women. It was settled by a race, or rather stock, of families, the like of which will rarely be seen again,—so manly, so refined, so intelligent, so spirited, proud, self-reliant, independent, strong, so fresh and so free. The family names of this Peninsula known to honor and to fame are countless,—the Armisteads, Bollings, Byrds, Blairs, Burwells, Amblers, Carters, Cloptons, Christians, Carys, Dandridges, Digges, Fontaines, Gregorys, Harrisons, Coles, Inneses, Mallorys, Nicholsons and Nicholases, Randolphs, Pages, Nelsons, Kennons, Griffins, Barrons, Sclaters, Shields, Dudleys, Tuckers, Tylers, Tabbs, Tazewells, Wallers, Peachys, Saunders, Wythes, Lightfoots, Semples, Bassetts, and others no less known, from whom have sprung names of note in every Southern and Western State, as well as in other parts of Virginia.

Many heads of these families were themselves educated in the schools of the old country, and they employed tutors in their households, who were scholars of no mean grade, from the Universities of Oxford and Glasgow and Dublin. They lived neighborly in peace and plenty, "guided by law and bound by duty." Owning boundless broad acres, fair and fertile, without wants which they could not supply by home-made, of plain habits, genial in intercourse, and profuse in hospitality, every manor was one of gentle graces and of manly bearing. The sons and the Di Vernon daughters had their packs of hounds and bugles for the horn-music of frosty mornings, and duck and plover, bounding deer and wild turkey, partridge and woodcock and snipe, rabbit and coon and opossum, were their game and sport.

Every boy had his horse, and lived in the saddle: there were riders in those days. Thus minds and bodies of men and women were trained to the nerve-tunes of health and strength and burly freshness; and manners and morals were brought up in all gentleness and grace to make a glad, social, and glorious political state. The times taught them wisdom, and to practice vigilance, prudence, endurance, industry, self-denial, and patriotic devotion. Masters, tutors, teachers, of the schools of

Europe, were residing in every neighborhood throughout all the peninsulas of Virginia, and they prepared the knights and ladies at home for graduation at the principal schools of William and Mary and of Mrs. Davenport's in Williamsburg. They were all proficients in the Humanities, and trained the generation which immediately succeeded the Fathers of the Revolution, and which was so distinguished in state papers and in the debates on law and politics.

We once had a conversation with Benjamin Watkins Leigh, at Callaghan's, in the mountains. He was speaking of thorough teaching.

" Why, sir," said he, " the people nowadays can't spell and can't accentuate. Editors of the newspapers spell 'expense' with a 'c;' and no one nowadays pronounces 'a-c-c-e-p-t-a-b-l-e' correctly."

" Well, Mr. Leigh, how do you pronounce it ?"

" I pronounce it *ac'ceptable*, of course," said he.

" But Johnson and Walker pronounce it either 'ac'ceptable' or 'accept'able.' "

" And who looks to Johnson, or Walker, or any mere lexicographer," he replied, " for accent or pronunciation ?"

" We look to good lexicographers for reputable use."

" And who cares for ' reputable use' when it is against the laws of grammar ?" said he.

" And who taught you the laws of grammar ?"

" I was taught my lessons of the laws of grammar by Needler Robinson, in the parish of Dale, in the county of Chesterfield."

"And who was Needler Robinson ?"

He looked at his collocutor with surprise which expressed that he must be himself unknown, never to have heard of Needler Robinson.

" Needler Robinson was a Scotch scholar, the friend of my father, the parson of the parish, and he was my teacher. It was the joy of my boyhood to sit at Robinson's knee and listen to his conversations with my father and John Randolph's mother, who then lived at Mattoax. The world thought her son spake as never man spake, but she could charm a bird out of the tree by the music of her tongue; and Needler Robinson taught us all, young and old. He taught me the laws of my mother tongue."

And what Needler Robinson was to Benjamin Watkins Leigh in Chesterfield, a Mr. McMurdo, another Scotchman, was to John Tyler and his schoolmates in Charles City. Both Leigh and Tyler were alumni of William and Mary, and in after-life brought home to their Alma Mater their sheaves of distinction and honors for her training.

Those old Scotch schoolmasters were awfully severe, and McMurdo's harshness to a certain good-natured Luke Lubin, of his pupils, caused a rebellion in the school to mob the master, in which the boy John Tyler was a rebel leader.

This was hardly to be expected from his nature. He was a slender child, of silken hair, with a twinkling bright eye, and genial smile; a singular face, with a very prominent, thin Roman nose, which gave exaggerated expression to his look of comic goodness.

His face of manhood was not unlike the pictures of Charles the First of England, especially that picture of the monarch when the mob made him drink a cup of wine. His expression was that of playful, soft, bland mildness. He was a delicate boy, no pupil of Zeno, and no Centaur; rather effeminate, imaginative, flexile, versatile, and mercurial as a girl; sincere, frank, affectionate, benevolent and generous, gleeful and social, seeking innocent sports among the young, but preferring and delighting in a reverential companionship with his seniors in age and experience. An eminent trait in his character was reverence. His intercourse with the sages around him always struck him with awe and inspiration, and thus he was teachable more by association with his betters than by much reading of books; but his ambition was healthful, and kept him posted in letters, and he had quick perception and great power of appropriating what he heard or read. At about the age of thirteen, in the year 1803, he was sent by his father to reside with Judge James Semple, at Williamsburg, and entered the grammar-school of William and Mary. In a year or two he entered the college,—perhaps in 1804, though his name does not appear in the college-rolls before 1806. He was then in a class with John J. Crittenden of Kentucky, William S. Archer, Linn Banks, William Crump of Powhatan, John F. May, and others afterwards distinguished in life. His room-mate was Judge Briscoe G. Baldwin, of Staunton, whom he loved and honored much, though their names were enrolled in different years in the catalogue.

He graduated in 1807, at seventeen years of age, showing that his progress was rapid and his development precocious. He was a pet of Bishop Madison, then presiding, and always spoke of him as the father of his instruction.

To show how he could win men in spite of their prejudices, he was in the convention of 1861, which passed the ordinances of secession. Colonel John B. Baldwin, the son of Judge Briscoe G. Baldwin, was a member. His politics differed widely from Mr. Tyler's. Mr. Tyler from his youth up was a Democrat of the order of Jefferson, whilst Judge Baldwin had educated his son in the ultra school of Alexander Hamilton. He abided not any school or schoolmen of Democracy; was opposed to secession; was for peace, or prevention of war, on almost any terms; made a speech for which he was crowned by a Boston woman with flowery wreaths, as the champion of the Union in the convention; and uttered sentiments and arguments which bound him, it was thought, on principle, to unite himself with the Northern cause against his native valley land of Virginia. He especially opposed Mr. Tyler's views on the report of the Commissioners of Virginia respecting the results of the Peace Conference at Washington. His Whig prejudices, indeed, against Mr. Tyler, for long-past bitterness of his party, for reason of his bank vetoes, and other matters of difference, kept him aloof from his society. He had avoided personal contact with him. But at last the ladies of the two houses met at the hotel where they messed, and brought them together. Mr. Tyler had observed Colonel Baldwin's avoidance of him, if not his aversion to him; and one morning he walked up to him, and drew a paper from his bosom and asked him to read it. It was a letter to Mr. Tyler from Colonel Baldwin's father, written late in life. It proved that Judge Briscoe G. Baldwin knew, loved, and honored John Tyler, and it subdued the son's aversion, and made him honor and respect the man of whom his honored father was proud to be a friend.

# CHAPTER II.

THE SECOND DECADE, FROM 1800 TO 1810.

The Aggressions of England and France upon Neutrals, and the Rejection of the American Mission by France—Commencement of the American Navy—The Effect of the Alien and Sedition Laws, causing the Kentucky and Virginia Resolutions of 1798—The Presidential Election in 1800, overthrowing the Federal Party, and dividing the Democratic by the Contest of Burr for the First Place on the Ticket—Peace with the First Consul, and the Acquisition of Louisiana—Disunion Sentiments in the North in 1803, on account of the Treaty with France—The Lewis and Clarke Expedition—The Orders in Council, and the Imperial Decrees—The Attack of the Leopard on the Chesapeake—The Embargo Act—Preparations for War—The War turned over to the Madison Term—What Mr. Jefferson did for Science.

THE election of Jefferson and Burr in the year 1800 was not more a revolution of parties than of principles and measures of administration.

The mission of the United States to France, consisting of John Marshall, Elbridge Gerry, and Charles Cotesworth Pinckney, was repulsed at court with contumely, and withdrew, Pinckney declaring the noble sentiment which became a motto in the war with France on the ocean, and afterwards in the war with England on sea and land,—"Millions for defense; not a cent for tribute."

The first regular navy was begun by building the two illustrious frigates, in 1798, the "Constitution" and the "United States;" and Decatur in the "Delaware," and Truxton in the "Constellation," and numerous prizes of our privateers, proved that we were more than a match for Frenchmen, and trained our seamen somewhat for meeting the British navy afterwards on the high seas.

Before the twelfth amendment of the Constitution, in 1804, the President and Vice-President were voted for indiscriminately on the same ticket, and, Thomas Jefferson and Aaron Burr receiving an equal number of votes on the same ticket in 1800, the House of Representatives had to choose by ballot which should be President, and which Vice-President, of the United States. To determine the choice there were thirty-six ballots. The Federalists united with a minority of the Democrats upon Burr, and this struggle added much to the acrimony of party spirit at the time. Mr. Jefferson was finally chosen, on the 17th of February, 1801.

Napoleon Bonaparte, then First Consul of France, seeing how Canada and all the French possessions in America had been wrested from him by the superior naval and merchant marine of Great Britain, and needing money for the schemes of his boundless ambition on the continent of Europe, made peace with the United States, and ceded the whole territory of Louisiana to them in April, 1803, for the sum of fifteen millions of dollars.

This was a bold and immense measure of administration for so young a nation, and changed at once the whole horoscope of its future. It bore immediately, and has ever since continuously borne, upon the destiny of the United States with more incalculable effect than any other stroke of policy ever did, or probably ever can. It extended our boundary to the Pacific, and gave to us the whole valley of the Mississippi, and the jurisdiction of its mouth. It was the first acquisition of territory by the Federal Union under the Constitution of 1787, otherwise than by cessions of the States. This territory, ceded by France to Spain in 1764, was on the 1st of October, 1800, by the treaty concluded at St. Ildefonso, retroceded to France; and its boundaries had been determined by the treaty of San Lorenzo between the United States and Spain, made by Thomas Pinckney and the Prince of Peace, on the 27th of October, 1795. It was ceded by France to the United States with the same extent which it had when in the possession of Spain.

This first and sudden leap of the United States to so vast an empire laid the foundation for a permanent and progressive change of policy and of destiny for the infant giant,—yet an infant nation, made at once a giant by this *immense acquisition of territory, inviting an immense immigration,* and rousing the most rankling sectional jealousies and strifes.

Here was indeed a cause, commencing with the beginning of the first century after the birth of the nation, for a thorough revolution and reformation of policy and of political parties and principles. The Federalists at once attacked the measure, and the northern and non-slaveholding section of the country was startled and alarmed by its adoption.

The struggle at once commenced as to whether the acquired territory should be "free soil" or not. The Federalists, the most latitudinarian in the construction of the Constitution,— those even who advocated the charter of a national bank, and justified the enactment of the Alien and Sedition laws,—suddenly became strict constructionists, and assailed the acquisition as unconstitutional.

And New England was suspicious of Mr. Jefferson's motives, thinking that his aim was to make the measure kick the beam of power in favor of his own slaveholding section.

The North, having the shipping of the country, and most intercourse with and transportation to and from Europe, looked at once to immigration for the control of the settlements of the newly-acquired territory. They ought to have foreseen that it, more than any other cause, would increase their preponderance in the Union; but they feared its effect upon their relative political strength, and blindly, without cause, manifested a strong disposition and made some concealed movements for a dissolution of the Union and a separation from the Southern States. This, long afterwards, was exposed by Mr. John Q. Adams, and is now being more fully revealed by sundry publications and books of biography reviewed lately by Professor Bledsoe, of the *Baltimore Southern Review.*

This suspicion of Mr. Jefferson and jealousy of the South were both unfounded. In the first place, they forgot that he was among the first emancipationists of the country; that when Virginia ceded her Northwest Territory to the Union, he incorporated in the deed of cession the inviolable condition that involuntary slavery, except for crime, should not be permitted in the ceded territory. And in the second place, they ought to have known that all the settlers from immigration, or from their own hive of white and free population, would have more political influence than any number of slaves carried to the new lands could possibly have.

Mr. Jefferson was fully justified in the measure, as national necessities have since developed. There is nothing in the Constitution which forbids the act, and everything in the importance of the territory to demand the acquisition. New States might be admitted into the Union, and it was absurd to deny that the United States might acquire territory by arms or by purchase, as well as any other external sovereignty on earth. France would never have sold it but for the fear that it would be conquered by Great Britain, as Canada had been, by a superior naval force and power of transporting troops across the ocean; and the apprehensions of France might well be those of the United States in a greater degree. A European power already held it in perfect obstruction to the march of empire westward, and another was seeking to snatch it from a weaker power who could not hold it, and Louisiana added to Canada would have placed a cincture by land and sea around the boundaries of the United States, which would, in the naval grasp of Great Britain, have been a constrictor about our very life as a nation. We could not have existed, much less have expanded, in such boundaries. The separate States could not acquire the territory, and, if the United States could not, the progress of popular liberty would have been constrained and stopped, if not destroyed, within our infant dominions.

The very water-shed of the continent argued the necessity of the case, and flowed to the conclusion of the legitimacy as well as the expediency of the purchase. Every river on the continent, except the New River, the Monongahela, and the Shenandoah,—all three in Virginia,—flows from north to south. The Mississippi, commencing near the Lake of the Woods and emptying into the Gulf of Mexico, is the great artery of the continent. In the hands of Great Britain, sovereign of Canada, it would have been to that power, in case of war, what it was to the Northern States in the late war with the Confederacy, an anaconda, and the United States would have been what the Confederacy was, a Laocoon !

Mr. Jefferson would have proved himself to be without foresight or patriotism not to have made the purchase. The tide of immigration was setting in, and every inch of fertile soil was needed to the Pacific and to the limits of the territory of the Hudson Bay Company to form the requisite asylum for the oppressed of the Old World escaping to the New. There was no limit to the treaty-making power, but the discussion arose upon the question of the power of the House of Representatives to make the appropriation. And there was a problem in this which the war of 1812 was necessary to solve.

Party spirit never raged more rabid than during the presidential terms of the elder Adams and of Mr. Jefferson. The feuds became more complicated during the latter term, owing to the course of Aaron Burr in the election of Mr. Jefferson. Whilst Vice-President during Mr. Jefferson's first term, he was a candidate for the chief magistracy of the State of New York, and was defeated by the partisans of Mr. Hamilton, though they had done their utmost to elect him in the House of Representatives to the Presidency of the United States over Mr. Jefferson, against the true intent and meaning of the people at the polls. He was good enough for the Presidency whilst used as a treacherous tool with which to defeat Democracy, but then he was thrown aside by the Federalists and denounced as unworthy of trust in the office of governor of a State.

The history of Mr. Burr is still involved in great mystery, and will never now be fully cleared of all cloud of doubt. He was an eminently able and bad man, brave beyond all question, but ambitious in the extreme, and unscrupulous in the means by which he aimed to climb the ladder of preferment. Yet he had some high qualities, and, doubtless, in some material respects was woefully wronged. Hamilton was incomparably his superior in character and intellect; but we are not convinced that Mr. Hamilton was not the wrong-doer to Burr, and to himself too, in the affair of their fatal and lamentable duel.

There were two very remarkable traits in Mr. Burr: first, he was never known to vituperate any rival or opponent in public, either by word spoken or written; and second, he made it a rule never to resort to the public prints to defend his reputation against any assault, whether true or false. It was not so with General Hamilton. He despised Burr, and openly denounced him as a *Catiline*. Burr actually declined to take any notice of the assault. The assault was not slight, as according to the general belief, but severe, pointed, and personal. Burr's friends demanded that he should notice it, coming, as it did, from authority so high as that of Hamilton. He then acquiesced in his friends' demand so far only as to call for explanations. He received from Mr. Hamilton the explanation that the name of Catiline was applied to him in no other but a political sense, describing the consequences and not the motives or intentions of his (Burr's) political opinions, and not imputing to him any personal, bad, vicious, or unpatriotic motives. This explanation Burr readily accepted as satisfactory, and Mr. Hamilton voluntarily pledged abstinence from all allusion to Mr. Burr again in any offensive and public way.

In a very short time afterwards, Mr. Hamilton alluded to him again in the same manner, and called him the same offensive name.

Mr. Burr's friends then demanded that he should challenge him. He did so; Hamilton accepted without offering other explanation, and, seemingly conscious of wrong, reserved his fire, exposed his own life, and would not endanger Burr's.

Of his intention not to aim at Burr's life, the latter was, of course, not informed, and Burr being the challenger, it was necessarily known that he would fire at Mr. Hamilton. By the laws of honor constraining gentlemen at that day, he was bound to challenge Hamilton, and was to be expected to shoot his adversary if he could, and was not bound to wait, in delivering his fire, until he could see whether his adversary was going to shoot at him or not. He had not time, and the risk was too great.

They both had been distinguished officers in the army, were

governed by its then code of responsibility to fight, and neither, it was thought, meant any child's play when they did resort to arms and fought.

On Burr's trial, no overt act of treason was proved, and it is far from being established that he had any intention of treason to the United States. It was fully declared, in his last moments, that his design was to enter Mexico with a considerable force of volunteers, and to establish a splendid empire there. And can any friend of civilization say that he would have done harm to humanity?

Certain it is that Mr. Jefferson was his avowed and active enemy, and all the power of the executive of the United States was brought to aid in the attempt to criminate him. He bore his trial with great coolness and fortitude, and was his own best counsel, though he had a John Wickham to defend him. He was never a desperate man; but calm, clear-headed, indifferent to all the decrees of fate. He was false to woman and to the Democratic party, wholly unscrupulous in his means and Lucifer-like in his designs, regardless of the judgment of mankind, and defiant of public opinion, put himself on a venture without a conscientious compunction, and was a horrible infidel; but the killing of Alexander Hamilton was according to the code of human honor in his day; and the worst that can be said of him is, that it was the least of his offenses against the laws of God.

He was not run a second time for the Presidency; Clinton's was substituted for his name, and Burr was no longer an actor in American affairs.

The Territory of Louisiana, beyond the Mississippi and to the Pacific, was explored by the expedition of Lewis and Clarke, in the year 1804, and the way was thus pioneered for emigrants.

And this brings us to another historic event of this decade, from 1800 to 1810, which met John Tyler at home, just as William and Mary gave him his diploma to begin active life, in his seventeenth or eighteenth year of age,—the daring outrage of the British frigate the Leopard, which pounced upon an American frigate, the Chesapeake, at the Capes of Vir-

ginia, when unprepared for action. This condition of the
Chesapeake was undoubtedly designed by the administration,
even at the sacrifice of as noble, brave, and competent a captain as ever was "monarch of the peopled deck" of a man-of-
war.    Mr. Jefferson's policy was to rouse the nation to a
declaration of war, and James Barron of Hampton, as gallant
a son of as gallant a sire, and brother of as brave a brother, as
ever honored Virginia by his birthright, was cruelly and treach-
erously made the victim of that Moloch policy.

The frigate Chesapeake was at anchor in the harbor of Norfolk, undergoing repairs, and her officers fitting her for sea;
storekeepers, ship-carpenters, riggers, ordnance officers, and
shore commanders were at work on her, and superintending
her preparations.    Her crew was just enlisted, unorganized,
strangers, undrilled, and consisted largely of foreigners. Knowing this, and bent on asserting the right of search for British
seamen, under the despotic maxim of Great Britain, "once a
citizen always a citizen," the Leopard was lying off and on,
just outside the Capes of Virginia, awaiting the sailing of the
Chesapeake, to board her, insult her flag, and seize such of her
crew as might be claimed as British subjects.    The Leopard's
commander had insolently warned the Chesapeake that such
was her domineering threat.

This was notorious to all Norfolk, and was communicated
officially by Captain Barron to the Navy Department; but he
was not allowed to prepare the ship he was to command.   Her
crew and munitions and stores were hurried on board, and with
cordage and spars lumbering her deck, and guns not mounted,
and useless for action, he was ordered to take command and
put out to sea immediately, in the then condition of the ship.
She had not cleared the marine league before the Leopard
made good her threat, bore down upon her, demanded the
delivery of a part of her crew, and the right of search.    All
that Barron could do was to refuse the demand, take the destructive broadside of the Leopard, return her shot, and surrender the Chesapeake as a prize of war.    That was what the
administration wished him to do, to rouse the national indigna-

tion ; but they had not so ordered or informed him, and immediately tried him for cowardice and neglect of duty, and suspended him from command. He was banished to Europe by his poverty, and this brought on the duel with Decatur, instigated by others whom Barron could never insult enough afterwards to make them fight. It was a sad thing that the gallant Decatur should have fallen in a combat which he was made to seek with the friend of his father, who led him, a dissipated youth of Philadelphia, to the quarter-deck of Barron's ship, and committed him to his care and training. Barron had treated him like a father, and taught him all he knew of seamanship ; and yet he was set up by the enemies of both to champion their diabolical design, to put out of the way of their promotion the senior officer of the navy.

Never, until Barron and Decatur were lying side by side on the gory sod of Bladensburg, did each, shot by the other, know the wanton wickedness of the fomenters of their duel. It was not until Decatur asked, "Now, Barron, tell me why you did not come home during the war," and Barron replied, "Ah, Decatur, why did you not ask me that before ?" and told him the reason, that he knew how he had wronged his father's friend, and his own patron and benefactor. Then he heaved a broken sigh, dropped a tear, grasped Barron's hand, and bade him farewell, —"God bless you"—for all of this life.

This episode is due to friends of old Elizabeth City, to that game-cock town of Hampton, which was never known to breed a coward, and to James Barron, who was ever the friend of John Tyler.

Great Britain and France were struggling for the destruction of each other, and for the mastery of the world, and both had grossly violated the neutral rights of the United States in almost every form of irritating insult and injury. The despotic maxim of "Once a citizen, always a citizen," fixing allegiance forever to the sovereignty of the place of birth, and the doctrine of "the right of search," dominating all the high seas, asserting that a British-born subject, though he had left his birthright, had quitted the limits of his parent country, had renounced his allegiance and quit claim to British protection, and had been domiciled and naturalized in another land; though he had taken the wings of the morning and flown to the uttermost parts of the earth, yet but drew a lengthening chain, and might be seized wherever found, and be impressed into the British service; and the "right to hail and heave to" a friendly or neutral flag and search all ships on the high seas, to find British subjects, drove the United States to the necessity of asserting the rights of neutrality, that free ships made free goods, and the rights of expatriation and of naturalization.

The United States first asserted to the world the true policy of peace, and that true allegiance was not a bondage; that the subjects of any sovereign might elect the place of their allegiance outside of the limits of the nation of their birth; that the high seas were free to the trade of every lawful power, and that every neutral flag was sacred, and intact from search.

After searching our merchant vessels, and filling the Dartmouth dungeons with sailors seized on board of our ships on the high seas, Great Britain sent her man-of-war the Leopard to the very pillars of Hercules at the Capes of Virginia, and at the front door of our Atlantic coast slapped the sovereignty of the United States in the face by capturing the frigate Chesapeake, in a helpless state, unprepared for action, and taking from her such of her crew as were arbitrarily claimed to be British-born subjects.

It was in vain that the United States urged their independence, and that all their population born before 1781 were British-born subjects, and might, under the same pretext, be searched for and seized, and impressed to fight against their own country, to the destruction of the freedom of our flag. This very argument was irritating to the national pride of Great Britain, and aggravated her soreness at our independence, and her jealousy of our rapidly-growing merchant and naval marine. The action of the State of Virginia against this insolent aggression was grand and glorious. The legislature passed a resolution couched in these burning words:

"At a moment when the rights of our country have been

assailed by the encroachments of foreign nations, whose conduct towards the United States has been regulated by *no law of nations* nor by any principle of justice; at a moment when our commerce is menaced by the iniquitous edicts of Great Britain and France, our flag insulted, the great highway of nations, which Nature and Nature's God have allotted for the use of all countries, has been actually turnpiked by the tolls and tribute of the British government for the benefit of the British exchequer; at a moment when it becomes every American to rally around the measures of his government, to vindicate the undoubted rights of his beloved country, and to declare for his country or against his country;

"*Resolved*, That a committee be appointed to prepare an address to the Congress and President of the United States, pledging every nerve and every exertion of this legislature to support the rights of the United States, to endure every privation and pain, and to perish upon the ruins of our country rather than abandon its rights, its honor, and its independence."

The committee appointed were Pope, Semple, Baker, Robertson of Amelia, W. Brokenborough, Preston, E. Watts, Wirt, Archer, Murdaugh, Graham, Peyton, and Strother.

President Tyler's father accepted the governorship of Virginia on the 11th of December, and this resolution was passed by the legislature on December 13, 1808. Soon after this the committee made their report on the affair of the Leopard and the Chesapeake, and their reported resolutions were adopted unanimously:

"That it is better for us to cease to exist as a nation than to exist under dishonor and violated rights.

"That the aggressions of Great Britain and France have infringed our honor; have violated our rights; have usurped upon our sovereignty as an independent nation.

"That we will stand by the government of our country, and that we will support them with the last cent of our treasure and the last drop of our blood, in every measure, either of defense or offense, which they may deem expedient to vindicate our injured honor and our violated rights."

These were finally adopted January 6, 1809; and let those of the present times who deny that national honor involves personal honor, and those who affect to deem him a mad martyr who devotes himself and all that he is and all that he has to patriotic sacrifice, read these resolutions, and drink in an inspiration which will elevate them to a nobler nature above the sordid selfishness which would price public honor and liberty by the calculations of a false and fatal expediency, and learn that where honor and freedom are seriously assailed, noble men and patriots count not the costs of contest.

The measure chiefly resorted to by Mr. Jefferson was the Non-Importation act; he ordered British war-vessels from our harbors, and Congress passed an embargo act forbidding the departure of vessels from American harbors. But these measures were worse than futile, for they only inflamed the commercial sections of the country, and formed a pretext for the treasonable resistance which culminated in the Hartford Convention.

The purchase of Louisiana, the admission of Ohio into the Union, the increase of the population to seven millions, and the flood of immigration, showed that the country was multiplying and magnifying into large proportions; and when, in 1807, Fulton applied steam to navigation, that mighty motor gave the first physical impulse to causes which have magnified and multiplied the United States into mammoth dimensions.

The mechanic began his great work of conquering time and space for settlement of virgin lands by one of the most irresistible powers of nature, and the age began to be "a fast age," running by the old mile-stones of the past too speedily to read the way-marks and figures inscribed on them, from causes growing out of the wars of Napoleon. Up to 1810 he had turned Europe topsy-turvy, not so much by arms as by the arts and physical sciences of the Polytechnics, which his armies and conquests demanded and developed. Chemistry, natural philosophy, mechanics, applied science, mathematics, and civil engineering advanced rapidly and rose highest in the studies of men; and they were all called for in turn by the new continent inviting the Old World to its rivers and forests, and craving for its crooked ways to be made straight and its rough places to be made smooth. Mountains had to be leveled, and valleys to be raised.

The wars of Europe, caused by Napoleon, from 1800 to 1815, had an immense influence upon immigration and settlement in the United States. And Mr. Jefferson, too, was a philosopher and a man of science. Not only was he the chief builder of the University of Virginia, but he ought to have had it also inscribed upon his tomb that he brought Hassler to the United States to lay the base-line of our surveys and triangulations. Hassler was a master of science, and should not be forgotten in our history.

Mr. Jefferson brought him to this country, and he repaid him by his weights and measures and his coast survey. He was a wonderful study in himself. An old man when we first knew him, with a head which phrenology would have instanced as a marked one and a sculptor would have chiseled as a model; an aquiline nose, thin and intellectual, and lips and chin which gave an expression of sweet manliness; a form erect and energetic; of an extreme nervousness, which made him unique and often grotesque; with a deep-set eye, sparkling, bright, and penetrating by a glance,—his appearance was attractively "game;" and it did not falsify his heart; he was afraid of nothing; no intellectual puzzle, no physical obstruction or obstacle, no fear of man, could make him hesitate in his pursuit and following straight after the truth.

We can never forget a scene between him and Mr. Woodbury, Secretary of the Treasury during Mr. Van Buren's administration. Whilst the most corrupt extravagance was indulged in for the patronage of partisans, the administration was urgent in recommendations of economy and of reduction of appropriations to the most important branches of the public service. The lighthouses, for example, it was proposed should be reduced in expenditure. This was met by the exclamation of the Opposition, in the House of Representatives, in behalf of the storm-distressed mariner, that it would be "putting out the eyes of the ocean!"   And the Coast Survey it was proposed should be reduced.   The salary of Mr. Hassler was eight thousand dollars, and that of his son three thousand dollars, per annum, and this was thought too much.   The old gentleman kept, at the expense of government, a singular sort of "Shandradan" vehicle, curiously slung on springs in a way not allowing of the least jar.   This was though to be unnecessary, and not in keeping with allowances to other branches of service of higher grade.   Mr. Woodbury sent for him to show cause why he should be allowed to keep his coach and pair at public expense.   He replied, with eagerness, " Oh, it is necessary for my *babies.*"

"Your BABIES, Mr. Hassler?—I did not know that you had any at your time of life!"

"Yes; as I get older they increase rapidly and become more and more tender and delicate, and require a carriage."

"But, Mr. Hassler, if that be so, the government must not pay for riding out your babies."

"Ah, it must not, say you, when they are the government's babies too?"

For the first time the secretary began to see that Hassler was speaking of his fine instruments, his theodolites, etc., used on the Coast Survey.

"Your instruments, you mean.   But you need not ride them out here; and when you go to the field of your work you can transport them by the railroad-cars better than in a carriage."

"No! no ! That jarring concussion makes them nervous, puts them out of order, and unfits them for exact use.   They shall not be vexed by the railroad-cars !"

"Well, then, your salary, Mr. Hassler, and that of your son, —you and he in one family receive eleven thousand dollars, whilst I, the Secretary of the Treasury, get but six thousand dollars for superintending the whole department !"

"Well, tarn it, tat is right !   A President of de United States can make a Secretary of de Treasury, but it took an Almighty God to make a Hassler !"

He was left undisturbed.

Some ignorant persons in New Jersey once had him imprisoned for trespassing on the lands, by cutting trees, etc., in the way of his triangulations, and he would make no concessions to the prosecution. The government had to relieve him. At one time an effort was made in the House of Representatives to curtail and change his elementary plan of survey, as too tedious and expensive. The substitute proposed was what is called the chronometric plan. It was our pleasure to be on the committee, and, siding with the old hero of science, to enjoy his collisions with some of the members who advocated the substitute. One and another annoyed him by repetition of the questions, " What was his system ? When would it be completed ? When would expenditures cease ? Would it ever be completed ?"

This would be answered by reference to his correspondence with Mr. Jefferson, by exposing what absurd expenditures were made when the work at one time was turned over to the Navy Department, by illustrating the necessity of a base-line and actual triangulation, and by referring to all his reports and manuscripts. He was told in reply that his explanations were unsatisfactory, and a brief exposé of the distinctive difference between his plan and the chronometric was required. Then he would turn again to two large baskets full of papers, showing his plan in general and in detail. Worried again and again by these examinations, at last he exclaimed, indignantly, " I am not paid to teach members of Congress mathematics !—tat is an impossible task ! And this committee would sit too long if it sits so long as it would take to complete tat task."

He was asked no more such questions, and the Coast Survey on Hassler's base was happily continued.

Not only the acquisition of territory, the immigration from Europe to settle it, Napoleon's wars and science, the genius of Hassler, and the application of steam, but our own preparations for war with either England or France or with both, gave great prominence and progress to the " physical and material" in the United States.

The war was not allowed to break out during Mr. Jefferson's administration. Pretexts for it were afforded, and preparations for it were made, but its declaration was withheld, and hostilities were actually restrained.

At the time of these events, John Tyler, Jr., had just been graduated, in the eighteenth year of his age, at William and Mary, in the year 1807. His seventeenth birthday was on the 29th day of March, 1807, and he took his degrees, it is said, in that year, the commencement occurring after his birthday. He commenced study of the law at once, first in the office of his father, and afterwards with the illustrious Edmund Randolph, the Attorney-General of the Washington administration, the chief draughtsman of the Constitution of the United States, and one of the ablest lawyers and statesmen of the convention which formed it, Hamilton, Madison, and Pinckney not excepted, and the cabinet officer whose correspondence with Governor Mifflin, of Pennsylvania, in '94, coupled with Hamilton's instructions to General Harry Lee, forms the true code of constitutional law governing cases of insurrection and rebellion. He obtained his license to practice his profession in the twentieth year of his age, having obtained a certificate without inquiry as to his age, and was at once engaged in a large and lucrative practice.

Mr. Jefferson's administration was to terminate in March, 1809, and on the 6th of February of that year the Legislature of Virginia passed their valedictory address to him, gratefully acknowledging the purity of his republican administration, thanking him for internal taxes abolished, for superfluous officers disbanded, for renouncing the monarchic maxim that "a national debt is a national blessing," for extinguishing the right of the Indians to one hundred millions of national domain, for the acquisition of Louisiana without guilt or calamity of conquest, for the preservation of peace amidst great and pressing difficulties, for cultivating and securing the good will of the aborigines and extending civilization to them, for the lesson taught to the Barbary powers, and for the preservation of the liberty of speech and of the press inviolate, without which genius and science are given to man in vain.

We cite this notation of the virtues and benefits of Mr. Jefferson's administration in order to compare what he did with what may proudly be claimed for Mr. Tyler's administration afterwards.

# CHAPTER III.

MR. JEFFERSON had the sagacity or the timidity, the prudence
or the selfishness, to turn the responsibility and the burden of
the war with Great Britain over to his successor, Mr. Madison,
whom General Jackson pronounced to be a President " not fit
for blood and carnage."

So it was that nearly five years elapsed from the time of the
outrage by the Leopard on the Chesapeake, in 1807, before the
Democracy ventured to make the declaration of war.   Mr.
Madison paused and parleyed for over three years, and it was
not without the most strenuous opposition that the war was
declared at last.   Mr. Tyler often jocularly said that the question was got at rather by "*spittoons*" than by "national *spirit*,"
and told an anecdote showing the spirit of the times in the
Congress of the United States.

Party spirit ran rankling to the most violent extremes.   Not
only was personal courtesy forgotten in partisan rudeness, but
measures were carried or defeated by means "*fas aut nefas.*"

( 52 )

On the question of "war or no war," the House of Representatives was kept in session several weeks, day and night, without recess or respite.

So determined was the Opposition that the Federal leaders, with an organized phalanx of debaters, got the floor, and held it by preconcerted signals, until the patience of their opponents was exhausted. The physical endurance of the Speaker was overcome; his sleep was not that of "tired Nature's sweet restorer," —it was not "balmy." An elderly gentleman from New England, with rather goggle-eyes, took the text of peace, and spun it out exceeding fine and broadly disquisitive, from point to point, each of infinite detail, like Captain Dalgetty's pious tormentor, far beyond "eighteenthly," and never towards "lastly," until Bellona, or some one else, resorted to most startling means of storming the tenure of the floor to get at the "previous question." The Speaker of the House and most of the members, making a bare quorum, were asleep, and there was nothing to disturb the solemn silence but the Dominie-like drawling of the member on the floor,—didactic, monotonous, and slow; the clerk's head bent low down upon the journal; when lo! sudden noises, rattling, dashing, bounding down the aisles, awoke and astonished Speaker's chair and clerk's desk; spittoons were bounding and leaping in the air, and, falling, reverberating their sounds like thunders among the crags of the Alps. "Order! order! order!" was the vociferated cry; but, in the midst of the slap-banging confusion of the no longer drowsy night, the humdrum debater who had the floor took his seat from fright, and a belligerent Democrat snatched the pause to move the "previous question," which was seconded, and the declaration of war against Great Britain was thus got at, and carried in the House of Representatives of the Congress of the United States in June, 1812.

Another of his stories about the times of this Congress, was an odd scene between the gallant Governor Wright, of Maryland, and Mr. Timothy Pickering. Mr. Randolph—John of Roanoke—had been riding out, and came to the door of the House, whip in hand, where he stopped and stood with a group around him, listening to his wizard words, when Governor Wright came passing in with a pile of books under each arm, as many as he could carry, and preventing him from using either hand for salutation.

"What does this mean, Governor Wright?" said Mr. Randolph.

"It means — for Timothy Pickering," replied Governor Wright,—"I will convict him of treason!"

Governor Wright was one of the warmest for the war, and Mr. Pickering was accused of being what was called a "Blue-Light Federalist,"—taking the Anglican side of the question.

"But, sir," said Mr. Randolph, "you do not mean to attack Mr. Pickering without a notice of your design?"

"Do you think etiquette demands that of me?" asked the governor, for he was the soul of chivalry and honor. And Mr. Randolph, who opposed the war with Great Britain, said,—

"I thought you were always for a declaration of war before beginning hostilities."

"Well, then," said the governor, "he shall have the notice at once." And, stalking down the aisle with his full armament of books under each arm, he went to the seat of Mr. Pickering, who was a gentleman of dignified mien and elegant appearance. Being unable to reach out a hand, the governor "nudged" him with his elbow.

"Look here," said he; "do you see that?" (pointing with the digit of the right hand to the books under the left arm.)

Mr. Pickering said, "Yes, sir."

Then, pointing with the digit of the left hand to the books under the right arm, he repeated,—

"Do you see that?"

Mr. Pickering, still wondering what was meant, again said,—
"Yes, sir."

And the governor notified him: "With these I mean to give you ——!"

Such was the spirit of party, and such were the manners of men, in those times of trial in the second war of the United States for independence.

The wrath against British outrages had been pent up for ten years, and it was bursting out at last, and the flame could not be repressed. The very moderation and delay of Mr. Jefferson and Mr. Madison had intensified the heat, and the war was absolutely necessary to the vitality of the United States as a nation. Without it the national character would have been debased. The country would have returned to a state of pupilage worse than the colonial. Its destinies would have been ignominiously subordinated to the caprices of Great Britain, without the care or the interest of a mother country to protect her colonial protégés. It was not waged promptly enough, with too little preparation, after the hesitation which rather cravenly delayed its declaration. But, once begun, it was fought gloriously, against immense odds; and its results were most beneficial to the United States, and to all the secondary and lesser powers of the globe.

1st. It established our navy and laid the keels of our merchant marine on a basis to enfranchise the highway of the ocean and to defend and guard for all future time the freedom of the seas.

2d. It made eventually a new code of neutrality. It established the rule of "Free ships, free goods," and lessened the little less than piratical barbarities of "search" and "impressment."

3d. It created anew a national spirit of independence, manifested by the motto of "Millions for defense, and not a cent for tribute."

4th. It forever annihilated the detestable maxim of tyranny,—"Once a citizen, always a citizen." It maintained the cause of freedom "once begun," without which the Revolution of 1776 would have been in vain,—the principle that all governments are intended, in the very nature of the only legitimate purpose of political power, for the good of the governed; and that whenever abuses of government become intolerable, the people governed may emigrate and renounce allegiance to tyrants; or the people or provinces governed may throw off the yoke of oppression within their own limits. It went further than the Revolution of '76, which asserted this right for colonies alone :

it asserted that the individual citizen might at will migrate, renounce allegiance, and choose another sovereignty and be naturalized, as if born its liege subject, and maintained the right of States to judge of remedies. By its other motto of "Free trade and sailors' rights" it meant nothing else than fealty to the freedom of the high seas, and that the poor British sailor, escaped from a press-gang, might be made a new citizen of a new sovereignty, and be naturalized, or born again from bondage, by a new birth of liberty, and might enlist to fight even the flag under which he was pressed and oppressed. The United States hailed all peoples with the grand hail of freedom, and called to them, saying, "Ho, every one that thirsteth for liberty, come unto us, and we will make you free!" They offered bounties of land, the richest of earth, to all subjects of all nations to renounce their native allegiance and assume a new and voluntary allegiance, which, in turn, might at will be renounced. It triumphantly asserted the individual right of man to choose his own sovereign. It set the down-trodden masses of the Old World free to leave "the land of memory" and come to "the land of hope."

5th. It gave a Christian chapter to the code of international law.

The second year after Mr. Tyler qualified in his profession, just twenty-one years of age the preceding spring, in December, 1811, he took his seat as a member of the House of Delegates of the General Assembly of the State of Virginia. Inheriting a hatred of British tyranny, he was filled with the "gaudia" of this contest, and urged and supported every measure of the administration to rouse the national spirit, to provide for the contingency of the war, and to maintain its declaration. He himself raised a company to help fight its battles. At the very first session of his service, his sagacity, eloquence, and winning address gave him a very high stand as a leader of the legislature for five successive years ; and in the session of 1811–12 he played a most important part, which ever since has borne testimony to his integrity and consistency in two most essential particulars of his public life. The legislature had instructed the senators of the State in Congress, Messrs. Giles and Brent, to vote against the charter of a United States Bank. The senators refused to obey the instructions of the legislature. Mr. Tyler moved a resolution of censure in the House, claiming the power and right of the legislature, as representing the constituency of senators in Congress, to instruct them, and asserting it to be the duty of senators to obey the instructions. He took two positions then from which he never departed afterwards:

1st. The unconstitutionality of a national bank.

2d. The right of a legislature to instruct their senators in Congress, and the duty of senators to obey the instructions of the legislature of their State.

The vicissitudes and changes of all life are strange and strangely contrasted; but none are so strange and so much in contrast as those of political life.

In 1811 the attempt was made to charter a Bank of the United States by Congress. Mr. Clay voted against the power as unconstitutional.

In 1812 Mr. Benjamin Watkins Leigh drew the resolutions of instructions to the senators of Virginia in Congress, requiring their obedience to them, to vote against the charter of the Bank of the United States, and Mr. Tyler introduced the resolution in 1812 to censure Messrs. Giles and Brent for their disobedience to Mr. Leigh's instructions.

Afterwards, in 1816, Mr. Clay voted for the charter of a Bank of the United States, notwithstanding his vote on the same subject for the opposite reasons in 1811; and in 1836 Mr. Leigh violated his own resolution of 1812 in respect to instructions, and refused to obey the instructions of the legislature to expunge a part of the journal of the Senate.

The one, Mr. Clay, contradicted himself within four years, in respect to the bank; and the other, Mr. Leigh, contradicted himself in respect to the right of instructing senators in Congress, in twenty-four years; whilst Mr. Tyler remained firm and uniform in his course upon both questions for a lifetime; and yet, afterwards, no two men of either party were so zealous, and strenuous, and bitter, in 1836 and in 1841, in denouncing Mr. Tyler for inconsistency on the very questions of instructions, of obedience to instructions, and of chartering a Bank of the United States, as were Henry Clay, of Kentucky, and Benjamin Watkins Leigh, of Virginia! And the sad but ludicrous absurdity of popular credulity, even among men of respectable information, is illustrated by the fact that Messrs. Clay and Leigh were regarded as paragons of uniform consistency, whilst Mr. Tyler was denounced as a traitor to his principles and to his party. But the Muse of History is now reviewing the lives of the men of that day, and her truth is slowly but surely lighting up with her torches the wreck of error long past, and will vindicate herself.

Mr. Tyler, from the beginning of his public life, was exceedingly popular, overwhelming all opponents. He was elected to the legislature five times in succession, first to the session of 1811–12, and last to the session of 1815–16; and during that of 1815–16, whilst a member of the House of Delegates, he was elected, by a large vote of the two houses, one of the Executive Council in Virginia. He continued to act in the Executive Council until November, 1816, when a vacancy occurred in the representation in Congress from the Richmond district, by the death of the Hon. John Clopton. Mr. Tyler and Andrew Stevenson, then Speaker of the House of Delegates, afterwards Speaker of the House of Representatives in Congress and Minister to England, were the candidates; both belonged to the same political party, the Democratic Republican, both were popular and powerful on the "stump" when the "stump" was a great moral and political monitor of the people and touchstone of candidates, each relied upon his personal influence, and Mr. Tyler, as usual, and as ever before and after, was successful. He had in March, 1816, reached the twenty-sixth year of his age, was elected at the first election after he was eligible, and took his seat in the Congress of the United States at the second session of the Fourteenth Congress, in December, 1816. His success at the commencement of his career was doubtless owing not only to the great influence of his own family, and especially of his father, and to his own genius and genial manners, but also to his happy early marriage, on the anniversary of his birth, the 29th of March, 1813, to Letitia Christian, the third daughter of Robert Christian, Esq., of Cedar Grove, in the county of New Kent, Virginia. This marriage united the House of Democracy, in the bridegroom, with the House of Federalism, in the bride. The father of the bridegroom was no less the friend and adherent of Thomas Jefferson, than the father of the bride was the friend and adherent of George Washington. Robert Christian was one of the main leaders of the Federal party, and was necessarily so from being the honored head of a name the most numerous on the peninsula of the James and the York.

During the late Confederate war, we were struck with the singular fact that almost every fifth white man we met in Charles City and New Kent was a *Christian*, and almost every other colored freeman we met was a *Charity*. On one occasion, we told the crowd in one of these counties that they were the most and best *Christians* and the most and worst *Charities* we had ever known ; but that was in the heat of war, when the free colored people were supposed to be our enemies and spies upon our struggle, and the Christians were all our friends and fellow-patriots.

Robert Christian was a gentleman and patriot, the father of the late Judge John B. Christian, and he and his brother were men of mark and influence. Letitia Christian is enrolled by Mrs. Holloway among the ladies of the White House as one of the sweetest matrons ever there. She was born in the same year with her husband, he in March, and she on the 12th of November, 1790, and proved, as a true woman can always prove, that a lady need not be so much the junior of her lord to hold his heart by a love-cord strong as life and lasting to the death. We knew her. She was a matron of gentle sweetness, such as could not but grow up lovely from a stock so strong, nurtured by parents so graceful, and cherished by a manly husband's love, to whom her love was ever fresh and youthful to the last. Her beauty budded forth in "piety and domestic virtues." Mr. Tyler's union with her in holy wedlock made him blessed of Heaven, happy in his home, and strong in the favor of men of both political parties. She bore him a houseful of children. His chivalrous homage to woman, and his delicate refinement of attentions to a wife, made her a devotee of home. He was extremely affectionate and indulgent to his children. The highest compliment he could pay them was to count upon them, as he did, with implicit confidence, and he gave them every opportunity to acquire all the cultivation necessary to enable them to excel. His daughters were tended and trained by a sweet, tender, mild, pious, discreet mother to all the duties and all the charms of that being described by but one word— *lady*. Mr. Tyler was proud of his children, and passionately fond of them, but his wife trembled and prayed for them. She was not exalted by her elevation to the White House, and sighed always for her happy home in Gloucester.

Married at the age of twenty-three, elected to Congress at the first election after he was eligible, his national career commenced just as Mr. Madison's administration closed and Mr. Monroe's commenced. The middle of this, his third decade in life, was a remarkable epoch in the history of the United States. The scenes of the war had been enacted. Its first baffling and futile measures had been abandoned, after causing what was denounced as treason and rebellion in the New England States. Its feeble negotiations at first had only irritated its causes. The doubtful affair of the Little Belt had occurred. British officers and agents had incited the Indians to war in the Northwest. The league of the Shawnee Prophet and Tecumseh with the Creeks, Choctaws, and Chickasaws of the South, had been broken by General Harrison at the junction of the Wabash and the Tippecanoe. The insult of the Leopard, five years before, had been repaired, but the orders in council remained, and, when revoked, the right of search and impressment was still claimed and persisted in.

The war had been at last hesitatingly proclaimed, under protest from the Federal opposition. The attempt to conquer Canada had failed, and our strength had been wasted in the effort. Queenstown Heights had been stormed. The New

York militia, in spite of all the brave Van Rensselaer could do, had refused to cross the Niagara. The only victories on land of the year 1812 had been won at Sackett's Harbor and Ogdensburg, and at the defense of Fort Wayne.

The massacre of the Pottowatomies had occurred at Fort Dearborn. The Essex had captured the Alert. The frigate Constitution had outmanœuvred a British squadron, and, in her escape, had captured the Guerriere. The Wasp had captured the Frolic; the United States the Macedonian; the Constitution the Java; and three hundred prizes, by our men-of-war and privateers, had been taken by the end of the year of the declaration of war. Madison had been re-elected President, and Gerry elected Vice-President in place of Clinton, who had died. The policy of reinvading Canada had been pursued in vain. The defeat of Winchester and the massacre at the river Raisin had disgraced the British arms. Harrison had been besieged at Fort Meigs by Proctor and Tecumseh. Croghan had gloriously defended Fort Stephenson. Pike had fallen in taking Toronto. Fort George had been stormed. Perry had won his victory on Lake Erie, and reported, "We have met the enemy, and they are ours." Harrison had conquered, and Tecumseh had fallen at the Thames. Fort Niagara and Lewistown had been sacked. Armstrong had failed egregiously against Montreal; and the American forces barely saved at Chrysler's Field. Wilkinson had been disgracefully repulsed at La Colle. The Hornet had captured the Peacock. The Shannon had captured the unlucky Chesapeake, and Lawrence had been killed giving his last order, " Don't give up the ship; fight her till she sinks." The whole of our coasts had been closely blockaded. The Constitution, the United States, and Macedonian frigates had been shut up in port. Decatur's attempt to get to sea had been betrayed by the blue-light signals to the enemy, and this had fixed the name of " Blue-Lights" on the Federalists. Cockburn had ravaged Lewistown, on the Delaware, and Frenchtown, Havre de Grace, Frederickton, and Georgetown, at the head of the Chesapeake Bay. General Robert Taylor had successfully and gallantly defended Norfolk, at Craney Island. Cockburn had not only ravaged but ravished Hampton, and his disgrace had been indelibly branded upon his brow by the pen of Taylor, which was sharp as his sword. The Creek war had burst out in the Southern Territory. The commerce and carrying trade of the United States had been nearly destroyed. Revenue had failed, taxes had been increased to such a burden that the opposition to the war grew so strong as to threaten its abandonment. The defeat of Napoleon, in April, 1814, had let the British forces in Europe loose upon America. Fort Mimms, on the Alabama River, had been captured by the Creek Indians, and the garrison and occupants been massacred. Jackson and Coffee had punished the Indians at Tallaschatche and Talladega, and Floyd had taken vengeance at Autosse. Claiborne had routed Weatherford at Eccamachea, and driven him over the perpendicular bluff into the flood below. Jackson and Coffee had burnt the Indians out at Topeka, or the Horse Shoe of Tallapoosa River. The Creeks had been crushed, and begged for peace. Weathersford had ridden into Jackson's camp and surrendered by a speech the most remarkable of any in the Indian tongues. A peace had been concluded with his nation in August, 1814. In the Northern campaign, on the St. Lawrence frontier, General Brown had crossed the Niagara and taken Fort Erie. General Scott had met Riall at Chippewa, and Riall and Drummond at Lundy's Lane; and Miller had won the sobriquet of " I'll try, sir." Ripley had repulsed the enemy at Fort Erie. General McComb and Commodore McDonough had won the victory at Plattsburg. Cochrane had been ordered to destroy the coast towns and ravage the country of the Chesapeake. Ross had captured the Capitol and ravaged Washington City, and plundered Alexandria. Eastport had been taken, Stonington bombarded, and Bangor plundered. Fort McHenry had defended Baltimore whilst the anthem of the " Star-Spangled Banner" was written.

The British had supplied the Creek Indians with arms from Pensacola, and Fort Bowyer had been invaded from that point, and the enemy repulsed. General Jackson had captured Pensacola, and gained the victory at New Orleans, and paid his fine for contempt of Judge Hall. Maritime commerce of the United States had been almost at an end; but the Essex had swept the ocean for prizes, and had been captured by the Phœbe and Cherub in bad faith. The Peacock had captured the Epervier. The President had been captured by five ships of the British blockading squadron, after crippling the Endymion. The Wasp had captured the Reindeer, and had made the Avon surrender. By the intermediation of Russia, peace at last was obliged to be made, and left the country exhausted, with one hundred millions of debt, and an empty treasury. Volunteering had ceased before the peace, and Massachusetts and Connecticut had refused to send their militia to the Northern frontier. The discontent in New England had increased. Massachusetts had called the Hartford Convention, which had clamored for alterations of the Constitution to limit the Federal authority.

At last the treaty of peace had been ratified, February 17, 1815, but no concession had been made of the American demands in regard to the right of search and impressment. To repair the damages of war, the tariff of duties was raised, protection was sought for the home manufacturers by heavy duties and imposts, and a national bank was established at Philadelphia the 4th of March, 1817, with the approval of President Madison. The Barbary powers of Algiers, Tunis, and Tripoli had been subdued. Louisiana and Indiana had been admitted into the Union. The Colonization Society had been formed, to provide a colony of civilized, liberated slaves, after much opposition in Congress, denying the power of the Federal government to interfere with the subject or to found the present Republic of Liberia. Mr. Monroe had succeeded Mr. Madison. Such was the course and state of events when Mr. Tyler entered Congress.

There was a pause in party strife,—a calm after the storm. It was ominous, and has never been correctly described. The hackneyed phrase, "We are all Democrats and all Federalists," does not give the sense or show the color of the times, or paint the era. It demanded a new observation, and required a new departure.  The thirteen *colonies* had grown into nineteen free, sovereign, and independent States, and by a severe contest in the second struggle with Great Britain had proved that they could and would fulfill a great and surprising destiny.  A new reckoning had to be taken after the storm, and it is wonderful to look back to the logarithms of history and see the complex calculations by which to reckon where the ship of state was, and whither she was tending.  Vast exchanges of positions were made by leading men.  Intrigues of peace succeeded and supplanted action in war.  The results of the war, the admission of six new States, the immense expanse of the eminent domain by the acquisition of Louisiana, and the lull of party strife in the election of Mr. Monroe, inaugurated a new epoch on the 4th of March, 1817.  It was the hour of transit from the Humanities to the material and physical.

Mr. Clay and Mr. Calhoun, the two Democratic leaders of the war party of 1812, changed their positions by becoming the leaders of the Federal party, in respect to the United States Bank charter, in 1816, voted for by Mr. Clay, and the great scheme of internal improvements by the Federal government, projected by the mighty mind of Mr. Calhoun in 1816–17.  Here is another popular error to be noted.  This generation generally takes it for granted that Mr. Clay was the author of the system of the national internal improvements.  Nothing is more incorrect.  Mr. Calhoun was its founder, on the broadest views of expediency, and Mr. Clay did not take it up until years after, when he embraced it in his grand policy of what was called his "American System," and then Mr. Calhoun gave up his own bantling, disowned it, changing on the question of the power in the Federal government to make internal improvements, just as Mr. Clay had changed on the question of the power of Congress to charter a United States Bank.  But Mr. Tyler, as we have said, held steady by the needle of the compass of Democracy, pointing to the star of strict construction.

On the famous Compensation Bill he again manfully maintained the right of the constituents to instruct their representatives, and the duty of the latter either to obey or resign.  He won a victory in debate on that question, at his first session of service, against two very able opponents, Mr. Grosvenor, of New York, and Mr. J. M. Clayton, of Delaware. He stood on the very ground he occupied in 1812, and this must be remembered by those who would censure his course of resigning afterwards, when he was instructed in 1836 to vote for the expunging resolutions of Mr. Benton.

At the first term, too, he opposed the bill of Mr. Calhoun to set apart for purposes of internal improvement the bonus and the government share of dividends of the Bank of the United States. Unfortunately, the doctrine of strict construction in respect to the powers of the general government to build roads and canals, was opposed to the genius of the continent, and to the irresistible force of coming causes, which have operated since with a certainty and rapidity beyond all human calculations.

The immense enlargement of the eminent domain, the rapid admission of new States, the flood of immigration, the innumerable wants and necessities of new settlers in the new States and Territories, and the tendency of steam, all demanded the exercise of the power to construct the national improvements. Had Mr. Calhoun adhered to his first foundations of the system, resting himself on the necessities and proper wants of our country's vast new settlements, he would probably have been the most influential public man of his day; he might have changed the destiny of the Southern section to which he belonged, and have made it keep pace with the progress of other sections of the country, which have since dwarfed it in the Union, and he might have preserved the popularity of the Democratic party and been promoted to the Presidency. The war, which he so ably supported, had shown the necessity for means and ways of transportation, and peace was the time to prepare for war. He foresaw much, but neither he nor any one else foresaw what was coming. The vastness of his own conceptions he himself did not seem fully to comprehend. Neither he nor any one else then conceived the extent of turnpikes and canals and railroads and steam transportation and telegraph lines that this continent would absolutely require in his day, much less how rapidly they would increase after his death.  Had they been begun in 1816–17, instead of being vetoed, and steadily pursued on a grand and impartial scale, extended equally to all sections, North and South, East and West, in forty years this Union would have been bound together too indissolubly by homogeneity of interest ever to have been threatened and actually marred by the sectional war of 1861.  Yes! even the mind of Mr. Calhoun erred lamentably in departing from that foundation, and the Democratic party erred in not following his lead on that question, whether he continued to lead or not.  The Constitution itself allows the "means necessary and proper," and internal improvements are both "necessary and proper" to this continent, so vast and various in its extent, superficies, topography, mineralogy, products, and population.  Time has proved that the necessity was the true law of that subject, and it was in *the letter of the Constitution* because it was in the *very land of the country.*

Mr. Clay afterwards took up "the wondrous tale" begun by Calhoun, and broke down the party of his first love by the power of that necessity.  Federalism laid hold of that necessity, and again the doctrine of the "general welfare" revived, and has increased until all the limitations of the Constitution are broken down, and merely incidental, and necessary and proper powers consistent and congruous with those granted have become primary, discretionary, and optional powers of legislation or congressional expediency.

But we must mark this period of a pause and change in politics as no negative epoch of individual men and parties.  It must be treated in a higher, holier light of Providence and of Philosophy.  We have said that at the beginning of the history of the United States the Humanities were called for by the continent of America; and they came, and did their work well in giving to man the best bills of rights, the best constitutions of government, ever known before; and they were first needed by the earlier settlers to establish the true, moral, social, and political codes for the government of men.  They gave our respective peoples municipalities for protection of their rights.

But the gigantic physique of the country required the physical sciences and works in turn, after the first works of the Humanities were laid to develop the mammoth materialism of this continent. Not only had the Reformers been at work, and centuries of work been done before the dawn of the Reformation, from the moment when the fountains of life were opened in the Temple by the divine disputation with the doctors; from the time when persecution made Christianity so strong as that its champions and martyrs proclaimed an emperor over the seven hills of Rome; when it had so governed the world as to give it the Justinian Code, when it had founded Cambridge and Oxford schools in England, and the University at Glasgow, in Scotland. Not only, we say, had the Humanities been working out their problems since the time of Christ, but the physical sciences, too, had their Columbus, Copernicus, Tycho Brahe, Kepler, Galileo, Newton, Franklin, Arkwright, Fulton, Watt, Herschel, La Place, Godfrey, Cartwright, Whitney, and other hosts of Titans at work; and then came the wars of Napoleon, ending in 1815, mightier than all, to develop the arts and to apply chemistry and mathematics and civil engineering.

All the results of physical science thus studied and developed and applied were called for by this continent. It was then a crude world, calling lustily, we say, for the combinations of applied science. We needed mathematics, natural philosophy, chemistry, mechanics, civil engineering, galvanism, and electricity,—and no one knew then that Morse was soon coming after, to course metallic wires with wings of messages swifter than the wings of Pegasus, through the air, and over the land, and under the "deep, deep sea!"

Physical science was to have its day begin after the close of the epoch of 1815. Thence the Humanities began to be neglected, and were left behind as too slow for the locomotion of the age. And therein is the moral of the loss of the reign of constitutional law, and the ascendency of materialism, and the ready question of the age as to anything, "Will it pay?" "Will it pay money?" "What is the per cent. of pecuniary profit?"

But we must ever guard against the mistake of placing the

moral in antagonism with the physical or material construction. That has ever been one of the grossest and most mischievous errors of the world in every period of history. We repeat, that the error of supposed antagonism between the Humanities and the Physiques of earth has led to some of the most wondrous discords of human imperfection. The divines once dreaded the sciences of mineralogy, geology, and astronomy as actual enemies of Revelation. What was material was looked on as the opposite of spiritual. But what a revelation of Nature has since been made, elucidating instead of contradicting the Word by the works of God, and proving that all human knowledge, spiritual and physical alike, comes from God's works harmonizing beautifully with God's Word and Spirit! The one is not more pure and ethereal of its kind than the other. Shakspeare's Ariel amid the flaming shrouds of shipwreck is not a proximate type even of the mysterious monads of matter which Chemistry, with more than magic power, puts in motion in the baking of a loaf of bread for man's wholesome nourishment. Behold Gravitation aplumbing his line of central attraction! Magnetism standing steady, pointing to a single star in the heavens! Heat and light expanding solids and liquids into vapor and air, with a power to conquer distance and time! Cold contracting oceans into crystal continents! Crystallization grouping its grotto of mysteries, and Electricity shooting nervous vitality through all agitated space!

Matter is not gross; it is subtle and sublime, and must be so to be the habitation and agent of mind and spirit. Spirit is not defiled by matter, but matter is sublimed by spirit! Events of the world from 1790 to 1815 showed how essential to human power and mental development matter in all its forms and combinations is. To be without form was to be void. Not only did the wars of Napoleon show this in being everything to the savans of science, but matter and morals were personified in the two Humboldts, Alexander and William. William communed with Goethe and Schiller, and drank from the Greek and Roman fountains which he found in Italy; this he did whilst the younger explorer was measuring the dragon-tree at

Teneriffe, and inscribing his name highest on Chimborazo. Alexander's Cosmos is wonderful; it has put scores of savans at work upon the filling of its outlines, and they have not yet exhausted his discoveries; but the "Cosmos" does not exceed, and hardly equals, the spiritual of his brother of the Humanities. The two noble brothers illustrate that the spiritual is the life of the physical. They show how spirit and matter not only harmonize with each other, but are necessary to each other in God's universe of spiritual and physical; how they sublimate into each other, and are nearer and nearer together, and become nearer and nearer the same, as they approach nearer and nearer in time and eternity to God, the Maker of both,—of that God who made the revelation of the Divine Nature tangible and comprehensible to the finite mind by making human flesh the temple of clay in which the Spirit of God is revealed! The spiritual and the physical are both essential to the life and well-being of men and of nations. Neither must be allowed to predominate, but each must be harmoniously equipoised by the other. And this is the great first lesson to be taught in the science of human government. Up to 1815 the moral and abstract school predominated in the American government, and then began the reign of the physical and concrete, disregarding too much the Humanities. Each in turn has predominated, and now the beam is kicked in favor of the physical. The Titanic school is now in vogue, and its first work was the national turnpike from Cumberland to Wheeling, with its monument on the wayside to Henry Clay, and now at its climax in California railways, in the Atlantic cable, —all resulting in expedient and practical,—and in the absolute war power of the supreme Congress!

We have not yet begun to discern that God's harmonizing government is the adjustment of the two parts of humanity,— the moral and physical, the mental and material. All now is physical force; and this is the dragon's tooth which sprouted the armed men of civil war, teaching us that the Humanities must be restored; that something better must be studied than the curriculum of West Point.

After the war of 1812, the rush of the crowds of emigrants from Europe to this country, seeking naturalization in this asylum of liberty, should have been appalling to tyrants only; but it begat a feeling of opposition from those in this country who dreaded the power of the democratic masses. The land laws came into play with magical effect, building settlements in a day. The navigation acts were reviewed, and commerce unfettered; "free trade" sprang forth, with no silken sails of Cleopatra, but with a canvas of cotton; and every day opened a new harvest-field in the Western forests and prairies. Congress had but to say, "Let there be Territories and new States," and there were Territories and new States. The wonder of the world was, not that their creation was so easy, but that they were all so consentaneously assimilated in the assertion of rights, and, above all, the rights of self-government. The "E Pluribus Unum" was a mystery evolved by America for the wonder of the Old World,—"One, as to the world besides; many among ourselves,"—the many growing out of and strengthened by each one, and the one fortified by the many. This was a union never known before,—stronger in its many parts by the parts making all one, by one law for the whole, and by the whole laws of the many. This was apparently a complete solution for a continent so vast, and the experiment so far seemed to succeed in making our country the theater for a new life and liberty for all mankind. But, alas! the States had hardly multiplied to the number of twenty-four when the canker of construction raged red again in the memorable Missouri question of 1820–21. This began a war of sections and of races, which ended in secession and in the sacrifice of civil liberty in men, and of sovereignty in States.

Mr. Tyler opposed the internal improvement policy of Mr. Calhoun, but ably supported all the great measures necessary to repair the breaches of the war; and in April, 1817, he was re-elected to the House of Representatives by an overwhelming popular majority. From 1817 to 1819 his action on the South American question, the recognition of the *de facto* independence of the colonies of Spain, upon the renewed question of internal improvements by the Federal government, upon the repeal of internal taxes, upon a uniform system of bankruptcy, and especially upon the inquiry whether the Bank of the United States had violated its charter, met with the approbation of his constituents, raised his reputation as an able statesman and debater, and proved the consistency of his course in after-life. He was on the committee with Messrs. J. C. Spencer, Lowndes, McLane, and Burwell, to investigate the affairs of the bank,— to determine the question whether its charter was forfeited. This committee acted, and reported during the Fifteenth Congress, from 1817 to 1819; and during the debate of that time, on the questions whether the charter had been violated so as to inure a forfeiture, and, if so, whether it was expedient to exact the forfeiture, he declared emphatically and argued strenuously to prove that the creation of the bank "was unconstitutional, and that he could not, without a violation of his oath, hesitate to repair the breach in the Constitution, when an opportunity presented itself of so doing without violating the public faith."

# CHAPTER IV.

## THE FOURTH DECADE, FROM 1820 TO 1830.

The Second Term of Mr. Monroe—The Debate on the Execution of Arbuthnot and Ambrister—The Presidential Election in 1824—General Jackson.

IN the debate in the House of Representatives during the first term of Mr. Monroe, Mr. Tyler took very strong and decided grounds in disapprobation of the proceedings of General Jackson in invading St. Marks and Pensacola and executing Arbuthnot and Ambrister. In after-time it cut him off from the favor of that great and powerful man, though Mr. Tyler supported his election to the Presidency, and mainly his administration. His speech on the limitation of military authority, involved in the resolution reported by Mr. Nelson, of Virginia, condemning the conduct of General Jackson, was one of the ablest and most eloquent he ever made. One of its passages ought to be repeated at this day, or at any other, when hero-worship becomes a besetting sin of the people. He said, "Your liberties cannot be preserved by the fame of any man. The triumph of the hero may swell the pride of your country, elevate you in the estimation of foreign nations, give to you a character for chivalry and valor; but recollect, I beseech you, that the sheet-anchor of our safety is *the Constitution of our country*. Say that you ornament these walls with the trophies of victory, that the flags of the conquered nations wave over your head,— what avail these symbols of your glory if the Constitution be destroyed? . . . Why do gentlemen point to the services of the hero in former wars? For his conduct there he has received a nation's plaudits and a nation's gratitude. We come to other acts. If just, we must look alone to the *act*, and not to the *actor*. A republic should act as in the case of the Roman Manlius, and disapprove the conduct of her dearest son, if that

( 72 )

son has erred. From what quarter do you expect your liberties to be invaded? Not from the man whom you despise: against him you are always on guard; his example will not be dangerous. You have more to fear from a nation's favorite; from him whose path has been a path of glory, who has won your gratitude and confidence; against his errors you have to guard, lest they should grow into precedents, and become in the end the law of the land. It is this consideration, and this *only*, which will induce me to disapprove the conduct of General Jackson."

But this disapproval, though thus courteously, kindly, and wisely couched, General Jackson remembered afterwards and did not forgive. John Quincy Adams, in the Cabinet of Monroe, sustained his invasion of Pensacola, and the thanks for his support he received afterwards from General Jackson when the issues of Texas were joined, which we will advert to again.

Mr. Calhoun's opposition to his proceedings in the Seminole campaign, in the same Cabinet where Adams sustained them, was made the groundwork afterwards of that estrangement between him and General Jackson which caused the great split of the State-Rights from the Locofoco faction of the Democratic party, and the election of Mr. Van Buren to the Presidency.

Mr. Tyler was re-elected to a seat in the House of Representatives of the Congress of the United States in the spring of 1819. Besides having to do with the questions of the tariff, and of protection to domestic manufactures, upon both of which he continued to prove his Democratic Republican orthodoxy of strict construction, he was brought to act on a question,—the admission of the State of Missouri into the Union, with conditions to exclude slavery from the new State,—directly involving slavery, containing the seeds of death, which ultimately, forty-one years thereafter, brought civil war and all our woe. The faith of strict construction, and limitation of the powers of the Federal government, had been contending first with "incidental power," then with the doctrine of "general welfare," and now was sown the germ of the fatal faith of the "higher law,"—that not only the Constitution was general and universal in all its granted and implied and incidental

powers, but its prohibitions were to be disregarded by the
majority if their religion required them to yield to what their
moral sense dictated to be the divine law and will. In a word,
the consciences and convictions of a majority of the States, or
people, were to be substituted for constitutional rule, and the
will of a majority was to be the Providence not of a confederate
but of a consolidated nation.

It is a wonder now that the restriction placed upon the territory, other than Missouri, north of 36° 30', in 1821, did not
then cause a dismemberment of the Union. *Then* forcible resistance to the breach of the Federal government would have
been effectual. But after destroying the equality of settling
Territories and forming new States, after the entire Northwest
had been filled with a powerful population, overwhelming in
the representation in Congress, it was too late to contend for a
restoration of the Constitution or a separation of the Union.
Slavery was then doomed. It is needless to say that Mr.
Tyler had always opposed the latitude of construction by which
the Missouri Compromise prevailed, and that he always foresaw
and predicted that the prohibition of slavery by Congress in any
of the Territories or new States would eventually abolish it in
all the States where it existed, by violent revolutionary means.
The line of 36° 30' was not a line saying, "Thus far shalt thou
go, and no farther," but it was a mark of the doom of slavery
on this continent, plainly proclaiming that it should not exist
anywhere at all.

Before the close of this signally fatal Congress he resigned
his seat in the House of Representatives, for reason of extreme
illness, which for a time threatened his life. He had been in
Congress five years, and made his mark firmly as a statesman,
as a consistent, strict Democrat of the school of Thomas Jefferson, and as a man who, by his talents, integrity, dignity and
urbanity, had won a most enviable influence and high reputation. Ten years' service—from his twenty-first to his thirty-
first year—had made him known to the nation and beloved by
his native State. He soon recovered his health, and in 1823
was urged again to become a member of the Virginia Legisla-

ture.  He served with eminent usefulness for two years, and in December, 1825, was elected by the General Assembly governor of the State, succeeding his Excellency James Pleasants.

We have adverted to the common saying that Mr. Monroe's time was a time of truce, if not of peace, between parties.  Pity it was seemingly so only.  In the delusive, treacherous calm of the times from 1817 to 1825, construction gained its most expansive latitude, rival factions brooded their worst mischiefs, leaders rose from every section, and theories of government began which could not but end in anarchy, or despotism, or war; and politicians "chasséd" into new Protean shapes for the best prospects of pay and promotion in the current revolution.  The star of the Great West had risen, the public lands were political prey and prize, and corruption had become a commerce.  The Cabinet of Mr. Monroe contained no less than three aspirants for the Presidency,—Mr. Crawford, an invalid, Mr. Adams, a latitudinarian and fanatical statesman of the highest training, learning, industry, and will, and Mr. Calhoun, a giant of intellect, who was a child in party tactics, and a founder of new political theories.  The invalid and the man whose mind was like " Michael Angelo's dome in the heavens, without scaffolding of thought," were from the extreme South; the fanatical scholar-statesman was from the North; and the Ohio Valley, then the center of the growing West, had two candidates outside of the Cabinet, who were more formidable than all,—Andrew Jackson, of Tennessee, and Henry Clay, of Kentucky.  Sections, as well as men, were rivals.  Such a time of complicated intrigue, still and lying in wait, was not favorable to the truths of the Constitution, and was disastrous to the federative principles of government.  They all tended to consolidation.  With the archbishop in Runnymede, we may say of America as he said of Great Britain :

> " If I judge aright,
> The voice of freedom is not a still, small voice;
> 'Tis in the fire, the thunder, and the storm
> The goddess Liberty delights to dwell.
> If I rightly foresee Britannia's fate,

\*     \*     \*     \*     \*     \*     \*

The hour of peril is the halcyon hour;
The shock of parties brings her best repose;
Like her wild waves when working in a storm,
That foam and war, and mingle earth and heaven,
Yet guard the island which they seem to shake."

The period of Mr. Monroe's administration was an hour of peril. So halcyon that it became stagnant, for want of the storm to purify its atmosphere; and it generated the political animalcula and fetor of bargain and corruption.

In 1824, the race of the five candidates for the Presidency was about to develop an entirely new state of parties and political relations, and a new influence of sections. The West was then felt distinctly for the first time to be a major estate in the empire. Which of the two old sections of the two old political parties—the New England or the Virginia school, the Federal or the Democratic Republican—was to have the alliance and the combined power of the West?

That was the problem to be solved,—the question to be answered.

The old Federal party had two factions,—the one of the anti-war school, called the "Blue-Lights," and the other consisting of such leaders as had strongly advocated the war and all its measures, but agreed with the "Blue-Lights" in the most latitudinous construction of the Constitution, claiming the strongest powers for the general government, and that it was national, not federative,—consolidated and sovereign over the States and the people. And this war faction of the Federalists had come out from among the Democracy of the administration of Mr. Madison since his term of office had expired. The coalition of these two factions assumed a new political name,—that of the "National Republicans." Aiming to catch the West, they contended for the largest latitude of construction, encouraging internal improvements and fostering immigration upon the most liberal terms to magnify and multiply the settlements of the new lands. To retain New England, they adopted the creed of protection to domestic manufactures, and gave fishing bounties and passed navigation acts to her content; and, touching the pocket-nerve of the people everywhere, in every section, they set up public credit upon the Bank of the United States as its pedestal of power. Mr. Clay headed the War and the West faction, and Mr. John Quincy Adams headed the Puritanism of New England of this coalition. The hobby of this party was, "the American System," which Mr. Adams, during his term, carried as high as "lighthouses in the skies."

And the Democratic party was likewise divided into factions. Mr. Crawford was the consistent representative man of the Jefferson school of strict construction in its purity. Mr. Calhoun had belonged to the same school; but he departed from its tenets as Secretary of War in the Cabinet of Mr. Monroe, and was the author of the system of internal improvement by the general government, but he still adhered to the Democratic party; and General Jackson, who had always been a Democrat, represented the *"juste-milieu"* faction between Mr. Crawford and Mr. Calhoun, and was justly classed with the Virginia school of Democracy of the type of the war and of Mr. Madison.

Perhaps one of the most graphic campaign papers ever published in this country was written by Thomas H. Fletcher, Esq., of Nashville, Tennessee, during that canvass for the Presidency. The title of the essay was "The Political Horse-Race." Each courser was minutely described, and each portrayed as he pranced or quietly walked upon the track. The prognostic of the jockey knowing one was all in favor of "Old Hickory," the most aged steed, who had seen most hard service; of long body, firm and steady step, clean legs, in hard, low, whip-cord condition, of powerful loin, rather lank in look, but fire in his eye; high in the withers, above a shoulder set at an angle of forty-five degrees; broad in the stifle, long in the thigh, with a wide overreach in footprints; hard hoofs, and cup-footed; round in the rib-barrel; deep in the chest, and nostrils like trumpet-nozzles; caprioling not at all, but erect and alive the moment mounted; the daybreak and all the signs were for him!

But his rival, Mr. Clay, in the same section of the West, did not so divine.   He dreaded most the man with whom he politically agreed, Mr. Adams.   He relied on the "American System" as strong enough to carry one or the other of its only two candidates, and his aim was to make himself the preferred of the two, Mr. Adams and himself.   The celebrated Amos Kendall, who afterwards became his bitterest enemy and the most devoted protégé of General Jackson, was then his leading editor in Kentucky.   The partisans of Mr. Clay, not as good jockeys as the author of "The Political Horse-Race," judged that General Jackson had but little chance of election, and that they could well afford to praise him while they detracted from Mr. Adams with every sort of vituperation.   They admitted General Jackson's patriotic life and services, acknowledged the national debt of gratitude due to him, but simply set him aside in the estimate of chances as a mere military man,—great as an Indian-fighter, and the most successful "Captain of cotton-bags," but he was a "Hickory," the best for *ramrods*, but not fit for "*cabinet-ware.*"   But as to Mr. Adams, the abler he was as a trained scholar and statesman, the more dangerous he was to the "Great West;" for they alleged that at Ghent he had offered to barter away the interests of the whole Mississippi Valley for the cod-fisheries of the Newfoundland Banks.   Mr. Adams had had a long and bitter controversial correspondence with Mr. Russell, one of his co-commissioners at Ghent, in which he had been signally victorious, and Mr. Clay, the other co-commissioner, had been neutral ; but now that this charge was made, openly assailing his course at Ghent, by Mr. Clay's leading journal and editor, on the tenderest point of popularity in the West, he caused Mr. Clay to be drawn out to say whether he indorsed the accusation against him, Mr. Adams, of betraying, or offering to betray, the interests of the Mississippi Valley.   Mr. Clay did, in effect, indorse the charge under his own signature in the public prints.   Mr. Adams met the indorsement with indignant denial, and demanded the proofs.   Mr. Clay very wisely declined to have such a controversy as Russell had experienced with so ready a writer and one who always took notes and kept memoranda of every event of his life, who was a

555

5555

555555

555555555

perfect "*vade-mecum*" of facts, and who never failed to use them with a precision and pungency fatal to his adversaries, and contented himself with an excuse as to the impropriety of such a time as a political canvass for the Presidency to have a controversy with a rival to the damage of both, for the benefit of other aspirants, and he adjourned the question of fact asserted on the one part and denied on the other, to a more auspicious period. Mr. Adams reiterated his denial, and threw the onus of proof upon Mr. Clay until such time as he might deem it necessary to redeem his veracity. This is what is called "the adjourned question of veracity" between these two champions of the same National Republican party and advocates of the same "American System" of politics.

In this state of quintuple canvass between parties and factions, the election of 1824 was held, and it resulted in General Jackson's receiving a plurality, but not a majority, of electoral votes, and this took the election into the House of Representatives. The House had to choose from three persons having the highest number of votes; the votes had to be taken by States, the representation from each State having but one vote, a majority of all the States being necessary to a choice. General Jackson, Mr. Adams, and Mr. Crawford were the three highest on the list of those voted for as President. Here was a struggle which gave the arch-enemy of the "federative principle" of the government all the advantages of its federative effect. It was an election by States, not numerically, according to the proportion of electors, but by States in their federative unities and identities. Each of the six New England States counted one for Mr. Adams, and gave him a certain considerable count at the first ballot. He ought to have remembered this forever after, whilst he was laboring a lifetime to show that State separate sovereignty was merged and consolidated into one nationality.

The events of this period were the first to attract our attention to public affairs and to the study of political life.

General Jackson, in the fall of 1824, was on his way to attend the Congress which was to decide the issue of his success or defeat in the election of the House of Representatives. He had come up the Ohio to Wheeling, and there, placing his family in his own private carriage, which he brought up with him, he mounted his saddle-horse and traveled the Cumberland road, *via* Washington, Pennsylvania, to the metropolis. He reached Washington, Pennsylvania, in the evening, and stopped for the night at the principal hotel. The populace flocked to see the hero, and among the hero-worshipers who crowded around him was the eminent and excellent Andrew Wylie, D.D., president of the college.

His presence immediately struck us by its majestic, commanding mien. He was about six feet high, slender in form, long and straight in limb, a little rounded in the shoulders, but stood gracefully erect. His hair, not then white, but venerably gray, stood more erect than his person; not long, but evenly cut, and each particular hair stood forth for itself a radius from a high and full-orbed head, chiseled with every mark of massive strength; his brow was deep, but not heavy, and underneath its porch of the cranium were deep-set, clear, small, blue eyes, which scintillated a light of quick perception like lightning, and then there was no fierceness in them. His cheek-bones were strong, and his jaw was rather "lantern;" the nose was straight, long, and Grecian; the upper lip the only heavy feature of his face, and his nasal muscle somewhat ghastly and ugly, but his mouth showed rocklike firmness, and his chin was manly as that of Mars. His teeth were long, as if the alveolar process had been absorbed, and were loose, and gave an ugly, ghastly expression to his nasal muscle. His chest was flat and broad. He was very unreserved in conversation, talked volubly and with animation, somewhat vehement and declamatory, though with perfect dignity and self-possession. He evidently wished to impress himself upon his visitors, but without any air of affectation, and his intent manner asserted his superiority. He hesitated not to dissent from any remark or opinion which called for contradiction; but was extremely polite, though positive in the extreme. He knew Dr. Wylie, and had the highest respect for his character and reverence for his religious profession of the Presbyterian faith. We were not awed by his presence, but intently studied him, and we augured his greatness from his looks and words, which drew us close up to him.

Dr. Wylie made the remark to him that he had no apprehension about the certainty of his being chosen by the House of Representatives, unless Congress was corrupted or beguiled by factious intrigues.

Immediately General Jackson replied, with flashing spirit, "Sir, no people ever lost their liberties unless they themselves first became corrupt. Our people are not yet, if they ever will be, corrupt; and the Congress dares not decide this election by the intrigues of corruption, for fear of their sovereigns, the people. The people are the safeguards of their own liberties, and I rely wholly on them to guard themselves. They will correct any outrage upon political purity by Congress; and if they do not, now and ever, then they will become the slaves of Congress and its political corruption."

This remark struck us then as indicating that he was fit to govern a republic, and it has come back to us a thousand times since with all the weight of truth and prophecy. He was our choice from that moment for the Presidency.

The next morning a select corps of students obtained leave to join his escort on horseback for miles on his way. He rode a splendid chestnut sorrel, the stock of his old racer, Pacolet, which he bought from William R. Johnson, in Virginia; and we can see him now, a model of grace in the saddle, whilst he chatted at ease as his horse kept the pace of a quick traveling walk. He saluted us with marked valediction when the students in escort drew up to return, and bade us accept his acknowledgment of our courtesy, and the advice from him "to study hard to fit ourselves for the service of our country."

We thus first knew Andrew Jackson, the greatest man, take him all in all, we have ever known among men.

The next time we saw him was on his return, by the same route, the next spring. He had been defeated by "bargain and corruption" in Congress. His wrath was tremendous; but he

6

seemed to be still more inspired by his unwavering faith in the people. He talked even more indignantly of the treatment of Mr. Calhoun, the Vice-President, than of that which he had received from Congress.

Ninian Edwards had charged Mr. Calhoun with corruption in the War Department, and had immediately gone westward to avoid the investigation which Mr. Calhoun had promptly demanded, and the sergeant-at-arms was in hot pursuit of him. Speaking of his own defeat, he hesitated not to declare his full conviction of the truth of the charge of "bargain and corruption" brought by his friends against Mr. Clay and Mr. Adams. He believed in its truth until the day of his death; but the version which he had received was not correct. The "old George Kremer" version was the vulgar one. That of Mr. Clay himself, repeatedly told by him, was, doubtless, the true one; but it did not clear his skirts, and certainly not those of his friends and of Mr. Adams, of guilt.

When the election came before the House of Representatives, Mr. Crawford could hardly be counted in the contest of the three rivals. His friends had endeavored to seclude him from the observation of visitors. He could with difficulty be seen. Many members preferred him to either General Jackson or Mr. Adams. They were doubtful only of his health, and this delayed their determination to vote for him. At last it became known that he was a paralytic, and the contest rested then, of course, between General Jackson and Mr. Adams. Mr. Clay, then, and his friends, had to decide between these two. They were in an awkward quandary. Mr. Clay had resolved to vote for Mr. Adams. His reason was avowedly placed on the ground that General Jackson was a mere military man, and one of very arbitrary will, and that he had not the civil training for the Presidency; but the better reason, doubtless, with him was that General Jackson had always belonged to the Democratic school of Mr. Jefferson, whilst Mr. Adams was thoroughly committed to Mr. Clay's American system. He urged his preference upon his friends, especially the members from Kentucky and Ohio. They reminded Mr. Clay of what had been insisted upon by him and by them during the canvass,—that Mr. Adams had been inimical to the interests of the valley of the Mississippi; and they could not see how they could reconcile their support of him then with their late denunciations of what they had termed his treachery to their constituents; their constituents could hardly be expected to understand or tolerate the inconsistency; and it was known that General Jackson was friendly to their interests; and, besides, they could not comprehend how Mr. Clay himself could support Mr. Adams while there was "an adjourned question of veracity" between them.

Mr. Clay admitted the embarrassing category in which he and his friends were placed, but pertinaciously insisted on their union with him in the support of Mr. Adams. At last his friends consented to unite with him, provided he would give their constituents a guarantee that Mr. Adams would not be inimical to the interest of their section, by Mr. Clay's becoming the premier of the Adams administration. They could then have it to say that the valley of the Mississippi would be represented and guarded if he would accept the place of Secretary of State in Mr. Adams's Cabinet. He earnestly protested against this condition; urged that it would impair his prospects for the future, and that his acceptance of office would be ascribed to corrupt motives. But his friends were inexorable; they insisted that if they were to follow him, he should make the sacrifice to guard their course, and they made this condition a *sine qua non.* He consented to make the sacrifice. The question then rose, how the matter was to be arranged with Mr. Adams. The mediators were selected, and they approached Mr. Adams without any further intervention by Mr. Clay. The negotiations were skillfully conducted, and soon reached a successful result.

Mr. Adams was in effect asked, "Was he then, or ever, really inimical to the interests of the valley of the Mississippi?" The answer was, "No, he was not then, and never had been; the accusation was false; he had denied it; had defied the proof of the charge; had called for it, and, as was well known, the question of veracity was adjourned, and he was still waiting for the proof."

This seemed sharp upon them and upon Mr. Clay; nevertheless, they steadily pursued their suit, and inquired further, " Whether, to manifest his sense of justice to their constituents, he would appoint his Secretary of State from the valley of the Mississippi ?"

He made no objection to select the Secretary of State from a section so important, and abounding, as it did, in men of the first rank of ability and experience. The next inquiry was, " Had he any personal animosity to Mr. Clay, on account of the question of 'adjourned veracity' between them ?" The answer was, " None whatever; he was content to leave Mr. Clay in that matter where he was until he made the proofs which he (Mr. A.) had challenged."

" Would he, then, appoint Mr. Clay ?"

He (Mr. Adams) knew of none abler or better qualified for the place in the valley of the Mississippi, and if the representatives of the valley preferred him, there was " no personal prejudice of his own in the way, and their preferences should prevail." Thus the bargain was made, in consideration of giving the appointment of State to Mr. Clay, against his personal wishes, but to carry out his individual views of policy. Mr. Adams, the minority candidate, was elected President of the United States by the vote of the House of Representatives, voting by States. The charge of bargain and corruption, as it was made, was promptly denied and easily refuted, that he (Mr. Clay) had ever approached Mr. Adams; but the truth fairly told leaves a case of casuistry still to be determined: Whether Mr. Clay's knowledge of, and consent to, the negotiation and its results was not a case of bargain for, and in consideration of, reciprocal offices, and whether that was or was not a case of corruption. It was certainly so thought at the time, and for years afterwards by the people of the United States.

It had defeated their will, it made General Jackson, the victim in their name, forever afterwards their favorite; and it embittered the contest of the National Democracy with the

National Republicans even more than the past contests had been between the Democratic Republicans and the Federalists. The administration of Mr. Adams proved rampant in pressing latitudinarianism to its ultimate extremes on the Bank and Manufactures and Public Lands and Foreign Relations, and his measures of internal improvements mounted to "lighthouses in the skies," and of the tariff of 1828, descended to a " Bill of Abominations," as they were called.

This united all the friends of Constitutional Limitations against him; and when he gave his "Ebony and Topaz" toast, which has never been understood to this day, he was set down as a visionary of some sort not to be trusted on the vital subject of the negro, and he and his party at the next election were crushed, as it was thought, forever. But time has shown that it was not to be so. His latitudinous and multitudinous works were continued by him to the day of his death in harness at the Capitol, and they now survive him in ascendant terrific form of death to the Constitution and civil liberty.

Mr. Tyler was engrossed in his office of Governor of Virginia, earnestly endeavoring to promote the prosperity of the State, when he was suddenly called on to do funeral honors to the remains of the immortal Jefferson. The elder Adams and the Great Apostle died on the same day, the 4th of July, 1826; and the governor pronounced, on the 11th of the same month, an oration on the life and death of the latter, which will compare favorably with any other composition of his life, and most favorably with the eulogium of General Harry Lee on Washington.

He was alike distinguished by his messages to the legislature, in the years 1826-27. The second time he was elected Governor of Virginia he was chosen unanimously. And then, the 13th of January, 1827, he was elected by the General Assembly to a seat in the Senate of the United States, to succeed the illustrious John Randolph of Roanoke.

This was the first contest of his life which involved any bitterness of feeling and brought upon him any denunciation or reproach. Mr. Randolph's term was to expire on the 4th of

March, 1827, and he was a candidate for re-election. He had
become utterly odious to the Adams party, called the National
Republicans, and obnoxious especially to the friends of Clay. He
had denounced the coalition of 1825 between Adams and Clay
as the union of the Puritan of New England and the blackleg
of Kentucky, and had met Mr. Clay on the duel-ground. His
"*longo emandacior*" speech, comparing Jackson and Adams
Knowledge and Wisdom, was fully written out by himself, and
is one of the most extraordinary productions of genius and eloquence which ever emanated from the mind of man. No other
man upon earth could have uttered it, in the same style and
vein of critical comparison. He was suffering very much with
sickness,—a chronic disease of the bowels,—and was exceedingly irritable and exacerbated ; he was *sui generis*, because no
other man had his inspiration, and no man ever spake as he did.
But he was often egregiously misrepresented. For example, he
had to drink "toast-and-water," for the charcoal effect on his
stomach, and, whilst speaking, often called for it : "*Tims, more
toast-and-water !*" And this was turned by malignant reporters
into "Tims, more *porter !*" And the rumor in this and innumerable other instances got out and ran wild that he drank deeply
and thus was betrayed into a maudlin invective. So it was
that whilst the *par-excellence* State-Rights faction adhered to
him, a large portion of the mass of the Democratic Republican
party became restive under what they called his "eccentricity,"
—a term with which didactic dolts, *common* enough in mere
routine to be justly enough said to have common, but no uncommon, sense, detract from their superiors in powers, acquisitions, and the gifts of genius. They united with the friends
of Adams, Clay, and Webster,—the National Republicans of
the day,—and elected Mr. Tyler, whilst Governor of Virginia in
his second term, over Mr. Randolph, by a vote of one hundred
and fifteen to one hundred and ten, on the 13th of January, 1827.
Mr. Tyler did not seek the nomination, and he always declared
that he was averse to it, preferring the honor of the office he
then held, and really preferring, too, that Mr. Randolph should
be chosen.

He declined to say that he would accept the place of senator. This he said to those inclined to support him; and when the peculiar friends of Mr. Randolph requested him "to say explicitly that he would not abandon the chair of state at that time to accept a seat in the Senate," he replied, " That propriety and due regard to consistency of deportment required him to decline an answer then;" adding, that " should the office, in *opposition to his wishes* (a result which he could not anticipate), be conferred upon him, he would then give to the expression of the legislative will such reflection, and pronounce such decision, as his sense of what was due to it might seem to require."

This was written on the day of the election, and was produced before the General Assembly, and yet he was elected " in opposition to his wishes." Mr. Randolph's friends rather assailed his personal independence before the ballot was brought to an issue, and their vindictiveness for reason of his not positively refusing to allow his name to be used, caused him, doubtless, in part, to accept the senatorship, which he did on the 18th of January, 1827. This lost him the personal and political friendship of all Mr. Randolph's warm friends in his own party, and gained him no adherents among the National Republicans, or the partisans of the Adams administration, and was the first impairment of his popularity. The then administration party had no desire to promote Mr. Tyler, but he was the only man with whom they could defeat Mr. Randolph. No two men of deserved eminence and influence could be more unlike than were Mr. Tyler and Mr. Randolph, — the one genial, gentle, and bland, the other acetic and bitter; the one less gifted in genius and acquirements, the other less winning and influential and useful; the one more inspired, more heliocentric in his views, the other more laborious to please, more practical, and always successful. It was difficult for him, or any man, to bear a contrast with Mr. Randolph as his successor; and it is the highest encomium upon his abilities to say that he lost nothing by the ordeal to which his defeat of Mr. Randolph exposed him. What he lacked in classic taste and power of utterance and wizard-like wisdom, be more than supplied by grace of manners, by sound judgment, and by a glowing goodness of heart.

Byron's description of Lara might well portray the character of Randolph:

> "A high demeanor, and a glance that took
> Their thoughts from others by a single look;
> And that sarcastic levity of tongue,
> The stinging of a heart the world hath stung,
> That darts in seeming playfulness around,
> And makes those feel that will not own the wound.
> \*   \*   \*   \*   \*   \*   \*
> In him inexplicably mixed appeared
> Much to be loved and hated, sought and feared.
> \*   \*   \*   \*   \*   \*   \*
> There was in him a vital scorn of all.
> \*   \*   \*   \*   \*   \*   \*
> He had (if t'were not nature's boon) an art
> Of fixing memory on another's heart;
> It was not love, perchance, nor hate, nor aught
> That words can image to express the thought;
> But they who saw him did not see in vain,
> And once beheld would ask of him again;
> And those to whom he spake remembered well,
> And on the words, however light, would dwell:
> None knew, nor how, nor why, but he entwined
> Himself perforce around the hearer's mind;
> There he was stamped, in liking or in hate,
> If greeted once; however brief the date,
> That friendship, pity, or aversion knew,
> Still there within the inmost thought he grew.
> You could not penetrate his soul, but found,
> Despite your wonder, to your own he wound;
> His presence haunted still; and from the breast
> He forced an all-unwilling interest;
> Vain was the struggle in that mental net,
> His spirit seemed to dare you to forget."

Soon after Mr. Tyler's election, he vindicated his course before a large assemblage of the members of the legislature and of citizens at Richmond. He indignantly repelled the charge of a lurking treachery, and called witnesses present to prove that if he had deceived any one, he had deceived some of his nearest personal friends, who would not have voted against his nomination if they had not been convinced by himself that he did not desire the senatorship. He had bowed simply, as a Democratic Republican should, to the will of the legislature. His fault, if any, was that; and he declared, with pointed significance, that, by accepting the appointment, while he interfered with the pretensions of no other citizen, he had acquitted himself of a sacred obligation. He was under no obligations to Mr. Randolph, and was not bound to forego any honor conferred upon him in deference to the wishes of his personal friends against the wishes of a majority of the legislature. He had formed no coalition with the party of the administration. On the contrary, all his hopes in the administration of Mr. Adams were withered by his "splendid message to Congress." He saw in it "an almost total disregard of the federative principle." He iterated his honest convictions that "the preservation of the federative principles of our government were inseparably connected with the perpetuation of liberty, and he cared not who should assail it, whether personal friend or personal foe, whether that or any subsequent administration, he would ever be ready to oppose such an attack with feelings of the most determined resistance." And in making these pledges, he combined prediction with promise when he uttered the words which he nobly redeemed in his very last days: "*When these banners which now float above us shall be made to lower on the embattled field, then I may abandon the doctrines of our fathers and forget my allegiance to the Constitution, but not before.*"

How truly and faithfully the burning patriot kept that "oath of the altar" we all know. God be praised! He loved him too well not to test his faith by seeing his State banners "flung out upon the battle-field," and too well to let him live to see those banners lower! He was spared the sight of hauling down the banners of State sovereignty and hoisting over them the ensigns of imperial consolidation! His toast in 1827 was, "The Federative System: in its simplicity there is grandeur; in its preservation, liberty; in its destruction, tyranny!"

What a truth! What a prophecy! What a verification!

# CHAPTER V.

"The Monroe Doctrine"—Northwestern Coast of America—The Tariff of 1828—
The Election of General Jackson—An Episode and Anecdote.

THE only memorable State measures of Mr. Monroe's administration were the organization of the War Department by
Mr. Calhoun, the recognition of the South American republics,
the assertion of what is called the "Monroe doctrine" of non-
interference by European powers with the affairs of North and
South America, and conventions with Great Britain and Russia
as to the northwestern coasts of America. Each one of these
subjects has had great influence in controlling the destiny of
the United States.

In connection with, and in aid of, his gigantic scheme of internal improvements and of the national defense, Mr. Calhoun
did all in his power, with the assistance of General Bernard, who
had come from the wars of Napoleon to introduce and apply
the polytechnics of France, and to build up the military school
of West Point. It has had a disastrous effect upon the system
of the republic. It has studied physics altogether, nothing
of the Humanities, has been taught servilely to "obey orders
and break owners," and has finally crushed eleven sovereign
States of the Union, overborne the Federal Constitution, and,
for the time, set up the oligarchic supremacy of Congress. First
came Hassler to survey the coast with his benign theodolite,
and then came Bernard with his polytechnics to set aside the
maxims of Washington, that standing armies are dangerous,
and that a well-regulated militia is the safe reliance of a republic, by the swords and bayonets, shot and shell, grades, titles,

( 90 )

and high pay of the cadets of West Point. It has proved no Pop Emmons argument to make Presidents:

> "Rumpsey, Dumpsey,
> Col. Johnson killed Tecumseh."

It has become the power of Parliament, and if it must and will enthrone a despot, God grant that he may be of the order and temper of Cromwell,—no Stuart, no Bourbon.

At a Grand Assembly held at James City the 10th of October, 1649, the colony of Virginia, by its first act, declared the decapitation of Charles the First treason, in denying the divine right of kings, and therefore enacted, that to defend the regicides by reasoning, discourse, or argument was to be accessory after the fact to the death of the king; that to asperse his memory should be punishable at the discretion of the governor (Sir William Berkeley) and the council; that to doubt the right of succession of Charles the Second should be deemed high treason; and that to propose a change of government should be equally high treason.

These were bold declarations, adhering bravely to the Second, after the execution of the First, Charles. Yet, notwithstanding this worse than outlawry of the Protector, when he sent commissioners to take the "surrender of the countrie" in 1651, he set an example by which republicans of the present hour may profit, by learning what the Humanities did at that day in contrast with what the physical force of this day has done to Virginia.

By "articles at the surrender of the countrie,—Articles agreed on, and concluded at, James Cittie, in Virginia, for the surrendering and settling of that plantation under the obedience and government of the Commonwealth of England by the Commissioners of the Council of State, by authority of the Parliament of England, and by the Grand Assembly of the Governor, Council, and Burgesses of that countrie:"

First. "It is agreed and consented that the plantation of Virginia, and all the inhabitants thereof, shall be and remaine in due obedience and subjection to the Commonwealth of England, according to the lawes there established. And that this submission and subscription be acknowledged a *voluntary act, not forced nor constrained by a conquest upon the countrie; and that they shall have and enjoy such freedomes and privileges as belong to the free-borne people of England."*

Thirdly. "That there shall be a full and totale remission and indemnities of all acts, words, or writings done or spoken against the Parliament of England in relation to the same."

Fourthly. "That Virginia shall have and enjoy the ancient bounds and limits granted by the charters of the former kings."

Seventhly. Free trade was granted Virginia.

Eighthly. "That she should be free from all taxes, and none to be imposed on her without consent of her Grand Assembly."

Tenthly. A year to remove, with their effects, out of Virginia was given to all malcontents.

Eleventhly. The use of the Common Prayer was allowed by Cromwell, "provided that those things which relate to kingshipp or that government be not used publiquely ; and the continuing of ministers in their places, they not misdemeaning themselves."

These were regularly signed and countersigned, and again other articles were agreed on :

First. "No oaths or engagements to the committee were required of the governor and council, and neither to be censured for praying for or speaking well of the king."

Ninthly. "Full indemnity to all persons in as clear terms as the learned in the law of arms can express."

Tenthly. An act of indemnity and oblivion was agreed on and passed.

How unlike this to the late Fourteenth Amendment, passed by Congress and enforced by West Point !

Mr. Monroe declared a doctrine of non-interference by Europe which has proved a *"brutum fulmen."* Where Europe has not interfered with American governments, the United States have, as with Mexico in the past and with St. Domingo in the present. And they allowed Europe to send an Austrian prince to be inaugurated Emperor of Mexico, and then to be deserted by

Louis Napoleon and to be shot like a felon, without a fault except that of filling a European mission; and they have allowed Europe to interfere in the affairs of the Isthmus to an extent of partial control. And the United States, barely recognizing the independence of the South American republics, gave them no material aid or guarantees, and again and again countenanced the interference of Europe in American affairs by themselves interfering in the affairs of Europe, as in the case of Greece. And we did not stand up to 54° 40' on the northwest coast. And here it must be noted that not the least cause of magnifying the physical and material elements over the Humanities has been and is the gold of California.

Mr. Tyler took his seat in the Senate of the United States December 3d, 1827, and continued steadfastly in opposition to the coalition of Adams and Clay. He took a conspicuous part in the question of the Panama mission, on the odious tariff of 1828, called the "Bill of Abominations," on the Cumberland road bill, and on other minor measures.

The personnel of the Opposition was too eminent in ability and power to be resisted. The leaders were men of the highest attainments, and combined all the factions of Democracy, consisting of the War party, the State Rights and Strict Construction school, the Free Trade and Valley of the Mississippi interests, and the Southern interests of slavery.

Party spirit raged with rancor, and the administration was shown no quarter on any subject at issue, and was crushed. General Jackson was elected in 1828 by a majority so overwhelming and so pointedly in reproof of "bargain and corruption," that it stigmatized Mr. Adams's defeat with ignominy. He and Mr. Clay were indignantly hurled out of office, and their party of National Republicans was so prostrated as never to assume its name again.

And here the author of these pages must be indulged in an episode which connects himself with the great men of this narrative and with events of importance in after-life. In the month of August, 1828, with a law license in hand, we left our native Eastern Shore of Virginia for Baltimore, on our

way to Nashville to be married and settled for life. We stopped
at Tangier Island, in the Chesapeake Bay, there to part with
kindred and friends who accompanied us to the island, where
was held the annual camp-meeting of the Methodist Episcopal
Church.    Love and plighted troth urged us to fly with swift
wings westward, and the "*amor loci*" drew us back to "Home
in Old Virginia."

Tangier is south of Smith's Island and southeast of the mouth
of the Potomac.   Its southern end was occupied during the war
of 1812 by the British fleet, under Cockburn, just fifteen miles
from the eastern main at Chesconessex Creek, where our childhood was spent during the war, and where the morning, noon,
and evening guns of the red-coated enemy taught us the signals
of horrid war and made us early familiar with dangers.   Sand
redoubts were thrown up on the island, and their faint outlines
still remain.   Before war made the island one of its sites, it
had, from the time of Asbury and Coke, and from a memorable date of persecution of the Methodists on the Eastern
Shore, been made a place of refuge for their religious worship
on the occasion of their great annual assemblages in camp-
meetings.   There, upon the bald sands of the beach, every year,
have the tents of worship, wooden and sail-cloth, been pitched
by piety, for now three-quarters of a century, to watch and
pray and preach for weeks at a time, in humiliation and homage
towards God, in the open air of heaven, by the bright waters
of the grandest, loveliest bay of old ocean's salt seas.

Healthful, refreshing, of clean shores, and abounding in fish-
eries, the population of cities, towns, and country on both sides
of the Chesapeake, from the mouth of the Susquehanna to the
Capes, congregate there at the wonted season of August.   It
is a yearly feast of fruits and fish as well as of "love," and re-
vivals of health as well as of "spirit."   There collect the great
campaigners of the pulpit, some of the greatest divines and
elders; there are fathers and mothers and sons and daughters
of the Church; there collect people of the world of every degree and dignity; there are hucksters and caterers for the
"multitude come not to be taught;" there whole families come

with household utensils and every appliance which tent can afford to table; some come in steamers from Baltimore, Annapolis, and Cambridge, Maryland, and from Norfolk and Fredericksburg and other towns in Virginia, and from both sides of the bay; and from every creek come vessels of all sizes, schooners, sloops, pungies, cats, canoes, and skiffs, loaded with people and provisions, until the island harbors are studded with shipping and a forest of masts, which gives the wharves and island the appearance of some considerable mart of commerce. The camp is regularly laid out in large squares, with wide streets; bowers are erected for the pulpit-stands, and for the "anxious benches," and broad planks are nailed horizontally across the tops of posts for sand whereon to kindle light-wood flambeaux to illumine the scenes at night. A police is carefully detailed of saintly watchmen, of pious pith and discretion, to keep order and to guard the camp, and the exercises are conducted under orders duly proclaimed by authority. No Salisbury Fair ever exceeded it in variety of strange scenes, grotesque and grave, ludicrous and sad, sacred and sinful, affected and real: here a powerful, learned man of God pouring out the word of truth in great volume of lungs and labor and love; there his contrast of a little exhorter; here prayer, and inward groaning of spirit struggling openly with conviction; there a loud-mouth braying of hymns sung by nasal Stentors of psalmody; here a "trance" of mute adoration, and there a cotillon of "*chasséing*" shouters, cutting in and out and grasping of brothers' and sisters' hands in a mazy dance of praise; here one "down" under weight of sin, and there another leaping for "joy" and crying out for "glory;" here a calm and solemn invocation to prayer, and there a stirring of anxious mourners; here a crowd of whites worshiping without noise, decently, and there a mass of blacks and whites preaching, praying, exhorting, singing, shouting, bawling, yelling, up and down, whirling around in perfect Bedlam time of "confusion worse confounded;" here the ministers of the Church winning souls away from Satan, and there the sons and daughters of vanity sipping the siren draught of sensual pleasure in all the ways of wanton delight; here, at night, the camp at rest, and all its suburbs drinking, fiddling, dancing, and doing worse, uproarious in shameful frolic until morning light.

The night is far spent, and at early dawn the horn is blown. The tents rise again to repeat the last day's scenes and exercises, and the sinners sink away to sleep until the curtain of the night falls again. Whilst goodness is dealing out "grace" at the table of the "love-feast," huckster and vender are selling chicken-pies, and barbecued, broiled, fried, and boiled fish, and peaches and melons and cantelopes, cider, crabs, and ginger-cakes, June apples, lemonade, and ice-cream; and, if you cannot find religion, you may—and if not always on guard, you will—lose your purse, for "camp-meetin' time" is always a time for stripping orchards and robbing hen-roosts, wherewith to make a penny to pay for expenses whilst on the lookout for the main chances of picking and stealing in the midst of the crowded camp and its concomitants.

An old physician complained to a sister who loved the camp-meeting where she had "got glory in her soul," that if he made a feast with every viand to tempt indulgence, he, though temperate himself and abstinent, might well be held responsible for all the excesses of his guests. The old lady replied that she was not responsible for the concomitants of sin around the table of the Lord; that if all even were to go to the "anxious benches" and kneel in sincerity and truth, there especially would the Evil One and Tempter be to beguile souls and take from them their heavenly food.

"Well, madam," he said, "while you were kneeling at the anxious bench, a thief stole my surgical instruments, which had been my companions for life, and with which I saved life and limb."

"Ah, doctor, where did you have those implements of pain? Somewhere, perhaps, where they ought not to have been?"

"On my honor, madam,—honestly, I was not bush-dodging!"

There are many salt-water bushes on the higher portions of the island off from the beach. The camp of 1828 was most numerously attended. We had started in a sail-vessel from a beautiful creek late in the evening, and when within about two miles of the beach the breeze died away, and we were helplessly becalmed. The sun set clear o'er the bay, smooth, rippleless, like a mirror of the Almighty; in a few moments the island was not to be seen, until the moon effulgent rose o'er the eastern land and lighted up the glassy waters, and she had not risen high when suddenly the light-wood flambeaux of the camp shot forth their beams, and the rows and avenues of hundreds of broad and high blazes were like supernatural lamps of the heavens; and soon the hymns of the multitude came softly stealing by moonlight o'er the mirrored bay, mellowed by distance, as if angel-voices were in choirs of melody coming from an island cloud! Oh, it was sweet beyond fancy's dreams!

We could not but exclaim, "That is the anthem of farewell to home and friends! and that is the cloud-music giving welcome to the West and to active life! Here is a start with good omens!" Tears both of joy and grief were wept. This is now told in the "sere and yellow leaf," because the memory is still refreshing and helps to renew life.

In a month or more we were at Nashville, and married the daughter of the Reverend Dr. O. Jennings, the Presbyterian pastor of Andrew Jackson, who honored him with tender reverence and respect. The general tendered his daughter the hospitalities of the Hermitage, and ordered our attendance there, the day after the wedding, to make his house the home of our honey-moon. The marriage was on the 8th of October, and our whole wedding-party was punctually at the Hermitage on the day appointed. We desired to study General Jackson in his slipshod ways at home. The weather had been wet, and the roads were exceedingly bad in that soil of unbroken limestone. The bridesmaids and groomsmen were on horseback, and the bride and groom rode in a gig which had been driven all the way from Baltimore, in a travel full of incidents, but without a serious accident. Escape from all disasters in a travel of eight hundred and fifty miles had made us too confident for a drive of only twelve miles, the distance to the Hermitage from Nashville. On the way out we noticed a narrow defile of rock and mud-holes on one side, and stumps on the Murfreesborough road on the other side of the track, which required a nice eye, good light, a steady rein, and a strong horse, quick to obey every touch of the rein.

We arrived at the Hermitage to dinner, and were shown to a bridal chamber magnificently furnished with articles which were the rich and costly presents of the city of New Orleans to its noble defender.

Had we not seen General Jackson before, we would have taken him for a visitor, not the host of the mansion. He greeted us cordially, and bade us feel at home, but gave us distinctly to understand that he took no trouble to look after any but his lady guests; as for the gentlemen, there were the parlor, the dining-room, the library, the sideboard and its refreshments; there were the servants, and, if anything was wanting, all that was necessary was to ring. He was as good as his word. He did not sit at the head of his table, but mingled with his guests, and always preferred a seat between two ladies, obviously seeking a chair between different ones at various times. He was very easy and graceful in his attentions; free, and often playful, but always dignified and earnest, in his conversation. He was quick to perceive every point of word or manner, was gracious in approval, but did not hesitate to dissent with courtesy when he differed. He obviously had a hidden vein of humor, loved aphorism, and could politely convey a sense of smart travesty. If put upon his mettle, he was very positive, but gravely respectful. He conversed freely, and seemed to be absorbed in attention to what the ladies were saying; but if a word of note was uttered at any distance from him audibly, he caught it by a quick and pertinent comment, without losing or leaving the subject about which he was talking to another person,—such was his case of sociability, without levity or lightness of activity, and without being oracular or heavy in his remarks. He had great power of attention and concentration, without being prying, curt, or brusque. Strong good sense and warm kindness of manner put every word of his pleasantly and pointedly in its right place. He conversed wonderfully well, but at times pronounced incorrectly and mis-used words; and it was remarkable, too, that when he did so it was with emphasis on the error of speech, and he would give it a marked prominence in diction.

To illustrate him in a scene: The Hermitage house was a solid, plain, substantial, commodious country mansion, built of brick, and two stories high. The front was south. You entered through a porch, a spacious hall, in which the stairs ascended, airy and well lighted. It contained four rooms on the lower floor, each entering the passage and each on either side opening into the one adjoining. The northwest room was the dining-room, the southeast and southwest rooms were sitting-rooms, and the northeast room had a door entering into the garden. The house was full of guests. There were visitors from all parts of the United States, numbering from twenty to fifty a day, constantly coming and going, all made welcome, and all well attended to.

The cost of the coming Presidency was even then very great and burdensome; but the general showed no signs of impa-tience, and was alive and active in his attentions to all comers and goers. He affected no style, and put on no airs of greatness, but was plainly and simply, though impulsively, polite to all. Besides his own family he had his wife's relatives, Mr. Stokely and Andrew J. Donelson, around him every day, and his adopted son, Andrew Jackson, relieved him of all the minuter attentions to guests.

Henry Lee, of Virginia, was, we may say, resident for the time with him, as he was engaged in writing for his election some of the finest campaign papers ever penned in this coun-try. One of Lee's fugitive pieces, on the death of an Indian youth, the son of a chief who was killed at the battle of the Horse-Shoe, whom the general had taken as godson, an orphan of one of his victories, is a precious pearl of poetry in prose.

He was not handsome as his half-brother, General Robert E. Lee, but rather ugly in face,—a mouth without a line of the bow of Diana about it, and nose not cut clean and classic, but rather meaty and, if we may make a word, "blood-beety;" but he was one of the most attractive men in conversation we ever listened to. Alas! alas! that such a man, so gifted, should have had to write as he did, long afterwards, from Paris, where he was not allowed to be consul, that "everything had turned to the bitterness of ashes on his taste." He, Harry Lee, who was so severe upon Mr. Jefferson and his writings because of his "Arcana" about his father, Light-Horse Harry Lee of the Revolution, was then, in fact, the entertaining host of the Hermitage, and attracted the crowd of visitors around his glowing words of commentary on the election.

The first or second evening of our stay, Mr. Lee had drawn around him his usual crowd of listeners; but we were the more special guests of Mrs. Jackson. She was a descendant of Colonel Charles Stokely, of our native county, Accomack, Virginia, and we had often seen his old mansion, an old Hanoverian hip-roofed house, standing on the seaside, not far above Metompkin; and she had often heard her mother talk of the old Assawaman Church, not very far above Colonel Stokely's house, pulled down long before our day, endowed with its silver communion-service by our great-grandfather, George Douglas, Esq., of Assawaman. Thus she was not only a good Presbyterian, whose pastor's daughter was the bride, and she a Presbyterian too, but the groom was from the county of her ancestors, in Virginia, and could tell her something about traditions she had heard of the family from which she sprung. With pious devotion to her mother's family, she desired to have a talk with us particularly, and formed a cosy group of quiet chat in the northeast corner room leading to the garden. The room had a north window, diagonal from the door leading to the garden. At this door her group was formed, fronting, in a semicircle, this north window of the room, the garden door on our right. First, on our right, next the window, was old Judge Overton, one of General Jackson's earliest and best friends. He was a man who had made his mark in law and politics, but was not pious, and was a queer-looking little old man. Small in stature, and cut into sharp angles at every salient point, a round, prominent, gourd-like, bald cranium, a peaked, Roman nose, a prominent, sharp, but manly chin, and he had lost his teeth and swallowed his lips. "There was danger," as Mr. Philip Doddridge once said of his own nose and chin, "of their coming together, for many sharp words had passed between them!" Next to him, on his left, sat General Jackson, his hair always standing straight up and out, but he in his mildest mood of social suavity; on his left the Reverend Dr. Jennings, one of the sweetest men in society, very distinguished as a lawyer first, and then as a divine, with a rare sense of humor which even his religious zeal could not always repress, and yet awfully earnest and severe against all levity; on his left was Mrs. Jackson, a lady who, doubtless, was once a form of rotund and rubicund beauty, but now was very plethoric and obese, and seemingly suffered from what was called phthisis, and talked low but quick, with a short and wheezing breath, the very personation of affable kindness and of a welcome as sincere and truthful as it was simple and tender; on her left was ourself, responding to her every inquiry about things her mother had handed down concerning the Stokely family. On our left sat Henry Baldwin, the son of Judge Baldwin, of the Supreme Court of the United States, one of the groomsmen, a gentleman of fine culture, good sense, and taste; and on his left was sweet Mary ——, one of the bridesmaids. Thus the *dramatis personæ* sat in the scene.

Judge Overton had thrown over his head a bandanna handkerchief, and sat all the time muttering or "mounching, mounching, mounching" on his toothless gums, looking like the Witch of Endor. His profile, to the eye, cut its outline clear upon the window-pane. He and General Jackson and Dr. Jennings, at first, were talking on the topics of the day. Mr. Baldwin was whispering to Mary ——, and Mrs. Jackson was for an hour or two questioning us about her people and their place in Accomack. We had just described to her, as nearly as we could recollect, one of the goblets of the plain plate of Assawaman Church, the only piece of it we had seen, in the house of a maternal great-uncle, when suddenly she seemed satisfied, or the subject was exhausted, and she turned to Dr. Jennings, saying, " Doctor, a short time ago I came near sending for you on a very important concern to me."

" Indeed, madam ! I should have been pleased to obey your call, and, duty permitting, would have come with pleasure to serve you in any way I could.  Pray, what was the occasion ?  Perhaps, if permitted, I may still render you a service."

" Oh, doctor ! at a time lately, but for a moment, I feared the general was giving way to the *Swedenborgian* doctrines.  I wished you to talk to him on the subject and to counsel me."

We looked at the general and closely watched his expression.  His eye was soft whenever he looked at his cherished wife ; and raising himself a little in the attitude of surprise, until he understood her sudden allusion to himself, but calm and composed, he said,—

" Pooh, pooh, madam ! your anxiety was vain.  I was in *no* danger of giving way to the *Swedenborgian doctrines ;* all I said was that some of Swedenborg's conceptions of Deity were the most soo-*blime* [pronouncing *sublime* as if spelt "*soo*," and emphasizing the first syllable] that tapped the drum ecclesiastic."

" What !" exclaimed the doctor of divinity, " do you pretend to compare the crudities of Swedenborg with the divine conceptions of David, or Job, or Isaiah ?"

" Yes," said the hero, for he had said it, and his whole mien changed to one of pious pugnacity.  " Yes, sir, Swedenborg's conceptions, by being among the most *sooblime*, only prove that the Almighty Creator has at all times, among all nations, inspired the souls of men with images of Himself, and the original inspirations are in some instances as *sooblime* as are the revelations of divinity : both come from God."

His positiveness appeared in his flashing eye, his erect form, his hair standing up and out, in his compressed lips, and in his upraised gesture with hand clinched.  There then was a theological fight.  It was exactly what we wanted to see : had he logic and metaphysics in him ?  The discussion which ensued was rich and rare.  It was the scimitar of Saladin against the battle-axe of Cœur de Lion !  The doctor exact, a fencer poised, quick, steady, skilled, with weapons keen enough to cut eider-down; he would seem to run in the Damascus blade and turn the point coolly to feel for the vital point, but Richard did not fall nor faint, but thrashed about him with his massive axe as a harvest-man would wield the flail! It was sharp science against a strong arm which wanted not natural " cunning."

Both forgot the witnesses of the single-handed struggle, and were too busy in the tight try of argument to notice any inter-polations of the listeners and lookers-on.

The Witch of Endor was not silent in the fray : "mumble, mumble, mumble" went his chin and nose, and, catching his own argument between two fingers and his thumb, he would try to push it in, but it always failed to enter the list, and stuck in the palm of his hand, he each time starting to say with a vim, " By G—d !" but turning that insult to the divine pres-ent into the words, " By G—Jupiter !" It was ludicrous, and we nearly clapped our hands with the *"gaudia certaminis,"* when suddenly Mrs. Jackson reached across our knees, and touched Mr. Baldwin, saying, "Mr. Baldwin, dear, you are sleepy !" The startled groomsman, broken down by his wait-ing on matrimony for two or three nights, suddenly opened his eyes from a nod, and rubbing them with his knuckles, protested that he was not at all sleepy, but wide awake and enjoying the discussion ! His protestations were all in vain. Up Mrs. Jackson would rise and ring the bell for servant and candle to light the dear child to bed ! This broke the discussion and separated the coterie for the night. As we rose to leave the room, Dr. Jennings touched me and said, *sotto voce*, " Henry, did you hear that poor old sinner turn 'By God' into 'By Jupiter' ?" " Yes, and it touched me as it did you, doctor; not only to shock my piety, but to shake my risibles."

After several days of delightful delay, we moved to leave the Hermitage, but day after day were detained by the entreaty of General Jackson and his lady. At last we were resolved positively to start; still, we were not allowed to leave until after dinner, and the hour for dining was as late as 4 P.M.

We apprehended anxiously the danger of the defile of stumps and mud-holes on the Murfreesborough road, on the way back to Nashville. The road then was not paved, and it would certainly be dark when we arrived at the point of danger. We urged this necessity for early departure, but in vain. After dinner the general insisted it was too late, but ordered the horses, and whilst awaiting their being brought to the door, he took his pipe, sat on the sill of the front door, and with a group in the porch around him, consisting of several of the family and guests, repeatedly warned us that it would be dark before we could travel half the way, that the road was unsafe, and that we would certainly meet with disaster. This led to tales by one and another of the group of "hairbreadth 'scapes." In every instance narrated of disaster we noticed that he pointedly and oracularly said, "Ah! young man, you did not trust in Providence." This was repeatedly said, adding, "Never encounter danger if you can avoid it: if inevitable, meet it more than half-way; but whether to avoid or encounter it, trust altogether in Providence." We were struck by his repeated remarks of this sort, so much so that we could not but think, "Is this real faith, or is it not like an affected Napoleonic belief and trust in Fate?"

The gig came up to the door. He rose to wait on the bride; and in handing her up the step, he said to her, "I have tried my best to protect you, madam, but your chosen one seems too self-reliant to heed your safety or my admonitions; I fear he don't trust in Providence, and will meet with disaster on the way. I shall be anxious until I meet you at church, safe in Nashville, Sabbath next. Trust in Providence, and you will not be hurt; and you have a goodly escort to help you in time of need. May Providence protect you!—it seems your husband thinks he can protect himself."

We drove off, and hurried on faster than the saddle-horses traveled, in order to reach the "stumps and holes" before dark; but darkness overtook us; and, on approaching the place, the road was scrutinized; we drove slowly and steadily, but vision was perfectly deceived. The wagon-wheels, daubed with the mortar of stiff clay, had to pass so close to an inclined stump that the dripping mud had fallen on the stump and colored it precisely like the bed of the road and the offal of the stump on the opposite side of the road looked black, and was taken for the stump itself; and this led the left wheel directly up and over it, overturning the gig to the right in the mortar of clay in the road. The horse was a generous lion of draught, and, though spirited, perfectly broken. The right shaft was broken, and the fragments pricked his right hind leg and made him restive; but we remained perfectly still, steadily grasping the reins until the bride could creep out into the road, and then, gradually relaxing the rein, we too crawled into the mud. The breeching and traces were immediately undone and slipped out, and we found a dry spot of leaves on the roadside to stand on. So far was the bride from being put out or frightened, that she joined in the proposition to tie the horse in the woods and hide ourselves behind a large tree until the cavalcade escort should come up. In a short time they arrived at the spot, and, finding the gig upset and broken in the road, and no sign of the horse, or harness, or ourselves, they set up a wail of agony most distressing. Dr. Thomas R. Jennings was so shocked that we could conceal ourselves no longer, but ran out and relieved the party. Fortunately a four-horse wagon soon drove up, and the driver having an axe and other tools with which to cut a pole and straps to lash on the broken shaft, it was repaired, and we reached Nashville safe, but very muddy, in the wedding fine clothes.

The next Sabbath General Jackson and his lady came into Mr. John C. McLemore's, and, calling at the house of Dr. Jennings, at once inquired for our safety; when told of our "escape" from hurt, again he repeated, "Ah! young man, you did not trust in Providence! You would not be advised to avoid danger when you could. But for your trusting wife, it would have been worse for both."

We then began to perceive what he meant by trusting in Providence. It was no inactive belief, no blind faith; but it was to do what was prudent, careful, and obviously most safe, and leave the "whole care" of the result to God. It was to do every little thing necessary to be observed by human foresight and precaution, however inapt, apparently, to the end, as the mother of Moses did with the preparation of bulrushes and slime and pitch, and then put the basket on the waters, however much exposed to the crocodile and the Nile, and leave the whole care for conjunction of causes and effects to the goodness and wisdom of God! Contrary to the general opinion of strangers concerning him, Jackson was an abundantly cautious man, and yet his exquisite tact often imposed upon the world by what he called "the policy of rashness,"—of doing what would be least expected of him under the circumstances by his enemies,—violating general rules to obtain the advantage of surprise. That, as well, was the very cunning of caution.

We heard numberless anecdotes of him illustrating the same characteristic of consummate tact. He knew that the world, or those who knew him least, counted him of a temperament weak, impassioned, impulsive, and inconsiderate in action; and he often turned this mistake as to his character into a large capital of advantage. He was a consummate actor, never stepped without knowing and marking his ground, but knew that most men thought he was not a man of calculations. This enabled him to blind them by his affectation of passion and impulse, and neither Talma, nor Garrick, nor Kemble, nor Kean could excel him in the "histrionics." Frequently, when strangers thought he was in a towering passion, his whole excitement was deliberately simulated for effect. For example, when bank committees would come from Philadelphia or elsewhere to overwhelm him with memorials upon the removal of the deposits, and to represent the crash of commercial credit by his anti-bank policy, he was fixed in his plans, and knew that they could not change his purpose, and that he could argue and remonstrate with them only in vain; and he would lay down his pipe, rise to his full height of stature and voice, and seem to foam at the mouth whilst declaiming vehemently against the dangers of a money monopoly: "Yes, he had rather be in the desert of Sahara, dying of thirst, than drink from such a fountain of corruption!"

The committees would retire in disgust, thinking they were leaving a madman, and as soon as they were gone he would resume his pipe, and, chuckling, say, "They thought I was mad!" and coolly comment on the policy of "never compromising a vital issue; one always lost friends and never appeased enemies." He was often derided for want of learning. He had read very few books, and he made his supposed ignorance an instrument of policy. To illustrate this: General Call and the Honorable Joseph L. White were rivals from Florida for his favor. White wanted a foreign mission. Call was one of the "braves" of the general's campaigns, and White was an accomplished scholar, lawyer, and courtier, but not of that tone which stamped a man with General Jackson. White was far the fitter of the two for diplomatic life; but General Jackson preferred sturdier stuff than mere manners and cultivation. He wished not to offend White, but was in favor of a pet comrade in arms, whose sense and courage he had tried. The delay of preference between them was long. At last an incident occurred which assured White that the beam would kick in his favor. The true boundary between Florida and Louisiana had long been hidden in a secret treaty between France and Spain. Both territories had been ceded to the United States, but the limits had not been accurately defined, and were so uncertain that numerous disputes as to land-titles had arisen on the borders of the State and Territory. To settle the line, and ascertain precisely where the French and where the Spanish laws furnished the rule of land-titles, a large fee was raised by the proprietors and claimants to send Mr. White to Europe to obtain the clause relating to boundary embraced in the secret treaty. The fee was deposited with Barings, at London, to be paid to Mr. White whenever he presented the copy of the clause of the secret treaty as to the boundary. Mr. White made due preparation, and among other credentials took letters to Lord Palmerston. He was received kindly by him, and told him his mission. He desired a favorable presentation to Prince Talleyrand, then envoy from France at the Court of St. James. Lord Palmerston told him that the most he could do was to give him opportunity with the prince. He would give a dinner, and place Mr. White's seat next to that of Prince Talleyrand, and he must then watch his chances and make his own approaches. There was no telling what tact to observe or what artifice to employ to obtain the patronage of Prince Talleyrand. The dinner-hour came, and White found his card on the plate next to that of the prince at table. During the dinner the prince questioned minutely on many American matters, and White was so obliging and satisfactory that the prince was caught in the humor to admit the opening of his budget.

"Yes, the boundaries between the French and Spanish territories had been fixed by a certain treaty which was secret; but that clause was no secret, and could be had at his order, and he would write for it to be copied in form, with a voucher to its being all cognate to the boundary."

Thus in a few days it was obtained under the proper seals and vouchers, and being placed in White's hands by Talleyrand, it was presented to the Barings, and White's fee for obtaining it was cashed by them. He immediately prepared for a continental tour. He purchased a rich English equipage, a "little moving England" of a coach, and a traveling "turn-out" of "bloods" for the route from Paris to Rome and Naples. He was "passported" and "couriered" as "the Hon. Jos. L. White, a Delegate in the House of Representatives, of the Congress of the United States of America, from Florida," and progressed in state grandly until he came into some one of the little states of Italy, when and where he was suddenly summoned to appear before his Highness the Prince. Aha! what had he done, omitted, said? Why summoned? Had he uttered aught against the Pope? Was he suspected? Of what?

Obeying the summons thus in doubt and distrust, what was his relief when he found himself received most graciously! He was "the Hon. Jos. L. White, a Delegate, etc. etc. etc., was he?" "Yes." Well, the duties of the Italian state had lately been changed so favorably to the commerce of the United States, and the port regulations so mitigated, that the prince was anxious to communicate intelligence thereof to the President of the United States, but he regretted that his Highness had no diplomatic correspondence or intercourse with Washington, and would the Hon. White, thus opportunely passing through his dominions, take dispatches to his Excellency General Jackson, the President of the United States?

Certainly, the Hon. Mr. White would do himself that honor, and wait on the prince at his pleasure. A messenger was called, and took memoranda of orders for the proper dispatches. He retired, when the prince seized his silver bell, and ringing to recall the messenger, said to the Hon. Mr. White, " We have not inquired in what language the dispatches shall be written. Which language, the Italian or French, does the President read or understand best ?"

The President read or understood neither; and with true diplomatic tact, White replied, " The one as well as the other, your Highness." The dispatches were then made out and given with many gracious thanks to the bearer, Mr. White. Mr. White was still more thankful for them. He was then, by accident, a diplomatic bearer of good news to General Jackson, and had beaten a Caulaincourt by his ready safeguard of General Jackson as a linguist.

If Jackson was a Napoleon, he would be made an envoy for that smart, Machiavellian answer.

He guarded the dispatches of the prince with the tenderest care, and when he got to Washington City, put on his best European costume, and waited on Old Hickory. He told his story of the travel and summons and alarm and relief, and all went smoothly until he came to what he imagined would be *" la crême de la crême"* of the adventure for the general. Without lying, he had not admitted that the President did not understand any but his own mother tongue of English, and had truthfully conveyed the meaning that as to the French or Italian he understood "the one as well as the other !"

The moment this was uttered, the general rose in his wrath, and let the Honorable Mr. White know " that he did not thank him for any such liberty with his name; he had suppressed the truth, and he would let him know and feel that he estimated himself as highly as if he read and spoke all the barbarous tongues. His name and character needed no such bolster of deception!"

This was what the court circle, who saw him only superficially, supposed was the weakness of pride and vanity and ignorance. Not so: he was going to prefer Call, and this was an opportunity to make a pretext for cutting White. It was cunning, not weakness; and, after White left, he laughed at the opportunity to make him quit courting for a diplomatic place. White thought it was weakness.

But, on another occasion, his ignorance of language did entangle him in a ridiculous mistake, and almost in a scrape. During his administration, whilst Mr. Louis McLane, of Delaware, was Secretary of State, France sent a certain dashing minister to Washington, a young man just elevated above the grade of chargé, whose passion was display. His outfit of equipage, grooms, postilions, and gold lace was magnificent. He called on the Secretary of State to appoint an audience with the President; and Mr. McLane, an accomplished, easy gentleman, begged him to call the next morning at ten o'clock at the State office, and he would accompany and present him to the President.

Monsieur le Ministre mistook as to the *place* of calling. He thought he was to call at the President's mansion at ten o'clock A.M. Accordingly, in full panoply of costume, in coach-and-four, with attendants, grooms, postilions, outriders, and footmen, at the hour appointed he drove up to the front door of the White House, instead of to the State Department, where Mr. McLane was awaiting his arrival.

At that time the President was served by a French cook, and the celebrated Irishman, Jemmy O'Neal, was General Jackson's petted major-domo. The hour was about the time of General Jackson's finishing puff of the pipe after breakfast, and he smoked, as he did everything else, with all his might! His mode was no Latakia curl, no dreamy, thready line, from barely-opened lips; but a full drawing and expanding

volume of white cloud, rising up whiff after whiff, puff after
puff, and bowl and stem and pipe all smoked as hard and fast
as they could, and the fire was red and the ashes hot, and
the whole room was so obfuscated that one could hardly breathe
its atmosphere or see. His usual mode of sitting while smoking was with his left leg thrown across the right, and the left
toe brought behind the right tendo-Achillis, and the long pipe-
stem resting in the fork or crotch of the two knees, and reaching nearly to the floor. He smoked the old Powhatan bowl,
with reed stem very long. In this attitude he was sitting
and smoking, whilst Mr. McLane was waiting at the State
office for Mr. Minister, and whilst Mr. Minister was riding up
to the presidential mansion. He arrived,—the French cook in
the kitchen, Jemmy O'Neal about his business, and General
Jackson alone in his office. A bustle was made, bells began to
ring, Jemmy was summoned to the door, and there presented
itself all this parade. The divil a word could Jemmy understand, and the best he could do was to run up-stairs to the
general and announce somebody very grand ; but Jemmy
winked that all didn't seem right, as there seemed too much
fuss for that soon in the morning, and it might be, after all,
an imposition :—"Och, there was no telling about the thing,
it was so unusual !" It might turn out what afterwards occurred,—a Lawrence affair ! The general quietly replied, "Oh,
Jemmy, show the stranger up,—we will see who it is." Jemmy
ran, and Jackson sat smoking, when presently the room-door
was thrown wide open, and a manikin of gold-lace entered,
cocked hat, with bullion and white feather, flourished in hand,
making a salaam to the right and a salaam to the left with
tremendous sweeps, whizzing and whirring French with vehement gesture, and approaching nearer and nearer ; it seemed
threatening in the extreme !

The President quit smoking, beat the bowl of his pipe in his
hand, rose quickly, took hold of the back of his chair, and
exclaimed, with strong voice, "By the eternal gods, Jemmy
O'Neal, who is this ?"

Jemmy, with eyes and ears open, and hands ready, was

amazedly looking on, when, fortunately, he bethought him of the French cook, and ran for him.  There was no time to be lost: so the French cook, with his shirt-sleeves rolled up to his shoulders, and just as he was, besprinkled white with flour, ran up with Jemmy, arriving just in time to save Mr. Minister's pate from being smashed by the chair in General Jackson's hands.

"Mon Dieu!" exclaimed the cook: "it is the grand minister of Louis Philippe!"

"Oh!" said the general: "walk in, sir; there is no ceremony here!"  And he was about taking the minister by both hands just as Mr. McLane entered to see the mistake, to witness the prevention of the catastrophe, and to enjoy the joke, which made him a thousand times afterwards "shake" with jollity "like a bowlful of jelly."

But we are anticipating events by painting, perhaps out of place, the private characteristics and traits of a very great man, whose name belongs only incidentally to this memoir of one of his successors.  General Jackson was elected President in the fall of 1828.  His domestic life had been scanned and scourged, and his beloved and honored wife had been most malignantly reviled and tortured, by the forked tongues of his political opponents.  She was happy in his love, and never aspired to the splendor of his fortune in life.  She had fled to his manhood for protection and peace, and had been sheltered and saved by his gallant championship of the cause of woman.  He, and he alone, was her all, and of him it may be truly said that, in respect to "wassail, wine, and woman," he was one of the purest men of his day, and that, too, in an age of rude habits and vulgar dissipation among the rough settlers of the West.  He was temperate in drink, abstemious in diet, simple in tastes, polished in manners, except when roused, and always preferred the society of ladies, with the most romantic, pure, and poetic devotion.  He was never accused of indulging in any of the grosser vices, except that in early life he swore, horse-raced, and attended cock-fights.  As for the wife of his bosom, she was a woman of spotless character, and an unassuming, consistent Christian: yet political rancor bitterly assailed her, and, not content with defamation, endeavored to belittle her by the contemptuous appellation of "Aunt Rachel," and held her up to ridicule for "smoking a corn-cob pipe." She did prefer that form, not for the pleasure of smoking, but because a pipe was prescribed by her physician for her phthisis; and she often rose in the night to smoke for relief. In a night of December, 1828, she rose to smoke, and caught cold whilst sitting in her nightclothes; and the story is that her system had been shocked by her over-hearing reproaches of herself whilst waiting in a parlor at the Nashville Inn. She had said to a friend, upon the election of her husband, "For Mr. Jackson's sake, I am glad; for my own part, I never wished it. I assure you I had rather be a door-keeper in the house of my God than to live in that palace in Washington." She was not allowed to live "in that palace in Washington." Before the day of her husband's inauguration at the White House she was taken by her God to that "house not made with hands, eternal in the heavens."

The 23d of December was the anniversary of General Jackson's greatest strategy in war. He had without means made preparations for the defense of New Orleans. He had arrested suspected persons by a strong arm; he had roused the populace of the city, of all races and colors, to seize arms for defense; he had seized cotton bales to make him a line of impenetrable ramparts from river to lagoon for miles; he had manned gun-boats to co-operate with the land forces; he had done wonders in making strongholds out of nothing for the last ditches of defense; but the *coup de main* was, after making his last hold as strong as he could, in leaving his intrenchments to attack the invading foe in full force at night, with a handful of men, under Coffee and Carroll, on the night of the 23d of December, and striking the enemy so hard a blow full in the face that he was staggered and made to hesitate and pause, giving Jackson sixteen days' time to recruit his forces and strengthen still more his defenses. Had the enemy marched directly upon New Orleans on the 23d or 24th of December, the "beauty and booty" of the city would have fallen a prey to his lust and rapine. But Jackson pursued his "policy of rashness,"

struck unexpected and unseen, saved the city, and won immortal laurels.

This, the 23d of December, 1814, not the 8th of January,
1815, he counted his day of victory. Strategy was the successful forerunner of courage and force.

Preparations were being made in Nashville to give him and
his lady a grand reception and celebration of the anniversary
of this his lucky day, and all eyes were bent towards the Hermitage to see the conquering hero, the then President, come,
with his cherished wife at his side, when, lo! a messenger on
"the White Horse" was seen, riding fast, to announce that his
partner was—dead. She was no longer the afflicted, deserted
one, whom he had championed and married and lived with in
holy and lawful wedlock. She was no longer his angel bosom
partner; she was no longer a target for this world's fiery darts
of detraction,—she was a saint. The day's gladness was turned
to earthly mourning, and the day of the funeral came instead
of the day of feasting.

. Dr. Heiskel, of Winchester, Virginia, was just starting as a
young physician in the neighborhood of the Hermitage, and
was the first to minister to her relief, and attended until two
eminent physicians were called in from Nashville. From him
we learned that she had caught cold, and pleuritic symptoms
supervened upon her constitutional nervous affections. She
was sitting smoking her corn-cob pipe when she caught her
last malady.

The day of burial came, and we witnessed the solemn scene.
This we can confidently testify, that more sincere homage was
done to her *dead* than was ever done to any woman in our day
and country *living*. Thousands from the city and from all
the country around flocked to her funeral. The poor white
people, the slaves of the Hermitage and adjoining plantations,
and the neighbors, crowded off the gentry of town and country, and filled the large garden in which the interment took
place. She had been a Hannah and Dorcas to every needy
household. She had been more than mistress, a mother to her
servants and dependents; and the richest and best were proud

of the privilege of her sincere and simple friendship. She was, without question, loved and honored by high and low, white and black, bond and free, rich and poor, and that love was so unaffect-edly expressed by a wail so loud and long that there was no mistaking its grief for the loss, not of the departed one, but of the living left behind her. From that same door of the northeast room of the house near which the happy bridal party sat but a few months before, her coffin was borne to the grave dug in the garden for her remains.

Following the pall-bearers came General Jackson, with his left hand in the arm of General Carroll, holding his cane in his right hand, not grasping it with the hand over the head, nor with the thumb up, but with the back of the hand up and hold-ing the point of the cane forward as he would have held a sword, and where he stopped at the pile of clay its point rested on the clods. Weeping and mourning were heard on every side; but at that moment of his coming up to that clod portal of clay a favorite old servant of Mrs. Jackson burst through the group around the pit and tried to get into the grave with the coffin. She was about sixty years of age, but robust and strong, and, falling near the brink, got both feet over the edge of the grave, when the sexton and others took hold of her and prevented her descending, and were trying to raise her up and remove her. Her cries were agonizing: "My mistress, my best friend, my love, my life, is gone,—I will go with her!"

This was but a moment; but, close to General Jackson, we watched him intently. Every muscle of his face was unmoved; steady as a rock, without a teardrop in his eye or a quaver in his voice, he quickly raised the point of his cane and said, "Let that faithful servant weep for her best friend and loved mistress; she has the right and cause to mourn for her loss, and her grief is sweet to me." The persons who had hold of her immediately released her, and left her sitting over the fresh clods, weeping; and there she remained, hindering the burial, until after awhile some of her friends persuaded her to leave the side of the grave and let the ceremony go on. The body was let down, "dust to dust" was said, the grave was filled up and shaped into the common mound which covers poor mortality, and General Jackson was led away by General Carroll back to the northeast room. The crowd followed, and we got in near to the chief mourner. Arriving fairly into the room, and pausing a few moments, he looked around him, and, raising his voice, said,—

"Friends and neighbors, I thank you for the honor you have done to the sainted one whose remains now repose in yonder grave. She is now in the bliss of heaven, and I know that she can suffer here no more on earth. That is enough for my consolation; my loss is her gain. But I am left without her to encounter the trials of life alone. I am now the President elect of the United States, and in a short time must take my way to the metropolis of my country; and, if it had been God's will, I would have been grateful for the privilege of taking her to my post of honor and seating her by my side; but Providence knew what was best for her. For myself, I bow to God's will, and go alone to the place of new and arduous duties, and I shall not go without friends to reward, and I pray God that I may not be allowed to have enemies to punish. I can forgive all who have wronged me, but will have fervently to pray that I may have grace to enable me to forget or forgive any enemy who has ever maligned that blessed one who is now safe from all suffering and sorrow, whom they tried to put to shame for my sake!"

This was uttered calmly, firmly, mournfully, and in such deep silence of the crowd that it was audible and distinct to every one in the room. We can never forget it. Could he? The answer to the question illustrates his leading trait of *the policy of pugnacity.*

In due time he went to Washington City, and was inaugurated President of the United States. He took up his abode in the White House. His bed was placed in the appropriate chamber. Prominent on the walls of that chamber, right opposite the pillow of the bed, was hung a picture of his wife,— placed there, as he himself said, so that it might be the first object to meet his eye when his lids opened in the morning, and the last for his gaze to leave when they closed in sleep at night.

And yet, soon after he was a lodger there, that room was the scene of his private conferences at night, in which Amos Kendall was his chief scribe and amanuensis, to write the broadside editorials of the *Globe* under his dictation and instruction, but not with his diction. He was a better thinker than his scribe, his scribe a better writer than he. He would lie down and smoke and dictate his ideas as well as he could express them, and Amos Kendall would write a paragraph and read it. That was not the thing; many times the scribe would write and rewrite again and again, and fail to "fetch a compass" of the meaning. At last, by alteration and correction, getting nearer and nearer to it, he would see it, and be himself astonished at its masterly power. General Jackson needed such an amanuensis, intelligent, learned, industrious as Mr. Kendall was. He could think, but could not write; he knew what nerve to touch, but he was no surgeon skilled in the instrument of dissection. Kendall was. But how came Amos Kendall there, in General Jackson's sanctum, where his saint's picture hung! She had been most maligned by Amos Kendall, the editor of Clay's leading journal in Kentucky, during the canvass. Kendall had called her "Aunt Rachel with the corn-cob pipe," and had exaggerated Robard's wrongs and Rachel's failings in every term of reproach and ridicule. There was the chief enemy who had maligned her, there hung the picture of the wounded saint, and there was the husband avenger who volunteered a vow at her grave! This was mighty strange! Not so, however, to those who knew General Jackson well. No man was cooler in his calculations than he was. He would sometimes seem to fight most rashly, but no one ever knew him to fight at all unless there was a stake up worth fighting for.

Kendall had been a poor Yankee schoolmaster, and was a protégé of Mr. Clay. He had been but a hireling, and was but a pen for the political malice of Mr. Clay's party.

What had he (President Jackson) to gain by fighting the pen, the mere amanuensis, when his aim was to slay the prompter of all his wrongs? Kendall, for cause, left the fallen house of Clay, and fled to the rock of power and strength. He knew much, could reveal much, could deliver up all the enemy's armory. He was indefatigable, unscrupulous, and able. He was the very weapon for a pugnacious patron to use, and could surest strike the arch-enemy,—he had been the arch enemy's own.

General Jackson then could throw away prejudice, passion, vengeance itself, and vows, and coolly take Amos to that chamber, in presence of that picture, though he had applied the "scavenger's daughter" of torture to "Aunt Rachel!" Amos Kendall was his man, and he could and did use him with tremendous effect to destroy his first patron, Mr. Clay.

Such was General Jackson, the man with whom Mr. Tyler and his compeers had to deal at the beginning of Mr. Tyler's career in the Senate of the United States. No two men were ever more unlike than Mr. Tyler and General Jackson. They were bred in totally different scenes and schools in life: the one a child of gentle people and brought up in ease, the other a poor boy of humble Irish extraction, orphaned and exiled by war and poverty to build his own fortunes in the western wilds of Tennessee; the one taught and trained by the best of teachers and books, the other a Hercules of action, without learning, except that which was self-taught; the one winning the stakes of life by gentleness and grace, the other taking them by main force and commanding success by seizing the prize he sought; the one a civilian and orator, the other a warrior always in the camp of life, a leader of men, and in every sense a tremendous actor. Mr. Tyler had touched him sorely in the tender point of Arbuthnot and Ambrister, and he remembered what he deemed an unkindness, and he showed no good opinion of, or favor to, any one who had censured his course in that affair. Finding that Mr. Calhoun had censured him in the Cabinet of Mr. Monroe, he separated from him, though they were elected on the same ticket in 1828. Thus Mr. Calhoun's friends, among whom was Mr. Tyler, were soon made to stand aloof from General Jackson; though in the main, as on the Maysville road bill, the States Rights party still maintained some of the leading measures of the administration.

# CHAPTER VI.

## THE FIFTH DECADE, FROM 1830 TO 1840.

Debates from 1831 to 1832—The Tariff of 1828 for Protection—The Compromise—Mr. Clay the Great Pacificator—South Carolina Ordinances and Force Bill—Mr. Tyler the real and only Peace-Maker—The Presidential Election of 1832—Democracy divided—Mr. Van Buren the Favorite—The Names of Factions—Mr. Tyler's Error of siding with Nullification—Difference between it and the Virginia Doctrines of Mr. Madison—The Conservative purpose and end of a Convention of the States for *Cases of last Resort.*

WE left Nashville and returned to Virginia in the fall of 1830, and began to take more note of public affairs, and more interest in public men. We had seen and scanned the Man of Iron Will, but, as yet, had never formed the personal acquaintance of Mr. Tyler. In 1831–32, he was especially able on the Turkish mission in reply to Mr. Livingston. But the great question of that session of the Senate was upon the doctrine of Protection, raised by a resolution of Mr. Clay.

The contest of parties upon what was called the "Bill of Abominations" of 1828, renewed and continued in 1832, arrayed section against section in the interminable strife between Free Trade and Protection.

The North, with Webster in the lead, was at first for Free Trade; Boston was opposed to the Protection policy. But in a short time the New England and other Northern States invested in manufactures, and their "sweet voices" for Free Trade were suddenly changed. The Southern States were the raw producers of the main staples for export, and their theory was that the consumers of imports paid the bounties of Protection.

After the contest had become embittered, and whilst sore and festering, Mr. Clay came forward with his resolutions distin-

( 119 )

guishing between articles manufactured within and those manufactured without the limits of the United States.  Articles not
manufactured in the United States, except silks and wines, were
to be duty-free, and this, of course, increased the duties upon
articles in the country to the point of protection, and in many
cases to the point of prohibition.  The North had all the shipping, all the profits on ship-building, rigging, and victualing,
and all the profits of freights and bottomry.  This, in effect,
was indirectly a tax upon exports and upon producers of exports
in the South; and now it was proposed to compel that section
to use inferior domestic manufactures, and at the same time to
pay the equivalent of heavy imposts on their consumption to
this monopoly of home manufactures.

Mr. Tyler met this issue with marked ability; his effort was
more than argument, it was prophecy, and an eloquence which
implored like the warnings of a seer against the sowing of this
dragon's tooth, to sprout armed warriors against the peace,
union, and liberties of the country.  It *was* a dragon's tooth,
which caused the South Carolina Ordinances of Nullification,
which called for the Proclamation of Force.  In 1832 the danger was imminent of armed resistance, when Congress put into
General Jackson's hands the power of military coercion.  It
was then that Mr. Clay assumed the attitude of the Great Pacificator.  After doing more than any other man to raise the
storm, and hazarding civil war for Protection as a part, and
major part, of his American system, he had the Machiavelian
tact to claim the blessing and the praises due to the peacemaker.  Mr. Tyler alone had the honor of voting against the
Force Bill, while Mr. Clay, who raised the demon, got the credit
of exorcising him.  He would have pressed Protection to a
conflict of arms, but that he knew that Jackson, his worst enemy,
would win all the popularity of preserving peace.  He therefore made peace by a compromise of legislation, graduating a
reduction of duties by a fixed scale, and a set time, and by
classifying the articles subject to impost.

The presidential election of 1832 came in the wake of Nullification and the Force Bill.  And by this time, the begin-

ning of the second term of General Jackson's administration, the Democratic party had split into factions, and was divided against itself. Mr. Van Buren had won the favor of the hero, just as the jackal wins the good will of the lion. He was called the "Mistletoe politician, nourished by the sap of the hickory-tree." He had bred strife between General Jackson and Mr. Calhoun, who was Vice-President during the first term of the administration. He had wielded the influence of what was called the "Kitchen Cabinet" and the "Petticoat Pet," and was nominated for the Vice-Presidency in 1832 by the National Convention, though the Democracy of Virginia voted for Philip P. Barbour.

At this time the Democracy became divided into — first, the Van Buren faction, called the "Locofoco" party, whose motto was, "To the victors belong the spoils;" secondly, the Calhoun faction, the Nullifiers; and thirdly, a portion of the old Madisonian Democracy, who opposed both Locofocoism and Nullification; and the opposition to the second term of Jackson's administration soon consisted of—first, the National Republicans of the Clay and Adams party; secondly, the Nullifiers; and thirdly, that portion of the Democracy called the "Awkward Squad," which was opposed to Nullification, but which opposed Locofocoism also, and was disaffected to the administration by the removal of the public deposits from the Bank of the United States.

It was out of these elements that the "Whig party" was formed in 1839–40. They could not unite in 1836.

But the issues raised by South Carolina on the tariff of 1828 and her position in 1832 presented the dangers of civil war in the conflict of Nullification and the Force Bill.

Mr. Tyler sided with Nullification, and voted alone against the Force Bill, whilst Virginia opposed both. That issue brought us into Congress in 1833. Then, for the first time, we formed the personal acquaintance of Mr. Tyler.

On the doctrine of Nullification we differed. We considered it a gross departure from the true faith of State Rights, and as tending to crush them and to bring strict construction of the

Constitution into discredit. We lived in the same congressional district, and we found him and Upshur, Parker and Coke, and every leading politician on both shores of the Chesapeake, espousing the new faith. We were thrown into the breach and elected to Congress.

Taking sides with Nullification was the leading error of Mr. Tyler's life. In this he departed from the true State Rights faith of Virginia, of which Mr. Madison was the exponent, not in going towards the extremes of Federalism, but in following the lead of the South Carolina school of State Rights and remedies, on the opposite extreme, equally destructive of all rights and all remedies.

Nullification, as promulged and attempted to be enforced by South Carolina, is a very different doctrine or faith from that taught by Mr. Madison and the Virginia Legislature from 1798 to the triumph of the principles of Virginia in 1801.

In the first place, the category of cases in which Mr. Madison applied the doctrine of State Rights and remedies was far different from the class of cases involving any question like that of a protective tariff. He applied it to such cases as those of the Alien and Sedition laws, involving fundamental principles of republican freedom,—the primary and essential natural rights of man, such as the right of residence and freedom of speech and of the press. The ordinances of Nullification were applied to questions of mere political expediency. Whether a denizen might reside unmolested in the country as long as he observed the laws, or a citizen might write or speak and publish freely, without incurring the penalties of sedition, were very different subjects of legislation from that of whether, under the general power to regulate commerce between the several States and with foreign nations, Congress might lay a tariff of duties, excises, and imposts in such a way as to yield protection as well as revenue. It is the plain distinction between cases involving rights which are inviolable, inalienable, and universal, and those which, in the sense of expediency, may exist or not, or vary or not, according to policy, or compact, or convention. Mr. Madison applied it in cases of *last resort* for the conservation of inalienable rights, and Mr. Calhoun applied it in cases of governmental policy and expediency.

But, as applicable to any class of cases, Mr. Calhoun, in fact, changed, and, as we think, essentially perverted, the true doctrine, and this caused it to be misunderstood and misapplied, until it was brought into disrepute and was finally overthrown, if not forever destroyed.

## I.

The leading *fact*, not *theory*, on which State Rights are founded is this: That the States, by the Revolution of '76, became free, sovereign, separate, and independent States.

## II.

That the Articles of Confederation did not in any degree or respect change or in the least impair this individuality and sovereignty of the States.

## III.

That the Constitution of the United States, to which the States were parties and of which they were the creators, did not impair the original and separate sovereignty and independence of the States. It formed only " a more perfect Union" of individual States, but preserved their separate identity. The Union was a union of individuals, and the individuals were *States*, assuming the *plural, not singular*, name of the United *States*,—united to act, to certain ends and for defined purposes, by common means of nationality, but not merged in that nationality; *united*, but not *consolidated*, within the bounds of defined limitations of power. And while sovereignty was *original* in the States, whatever power was allowed to be exercised by the Federal government was *derivative* only,— derived from the *States*, delegated by them and to be exercised for them equally, according to their joint will as expressed in their written Constitution of the United States. *State power is not Federal power at all; but all Federal power is State power*, delegated by them and for them as their joint power, but still their power, to be used for their union.

## IV.

That the Constitution or covenant of Union was *federative*, founded on a fœdus of faith to and with *States*, the mutual contractors to act, each for itself, as to all State affairs, and to act in union with each other as to all *specified* and *delegated* cases, and reserving all powers not granted; each State being still sovereign, exercising all powers not granted themselves, and all granted powers by a common government of their own creation.

## V.

That the Federal government was to be confined in its operations to the powers granted by the States, as its creators, and to be limited *by special prohibitions*, and by the general rule that powers not granted were withheld from the general government, because reserved to the States.

## VI.

That in deciding all issues, whether the limitations of the grants of power were violated either by the common Federal government of the Union, or by the individual States, there was and could be but one common arbiter; that the Federal government could not decide, in cases of last resort, either for itself or for the States, and much less could any department of that government so decide. The only arbiter was *a convention of the States*. If that was not allowed peacefully to adjust dissensions, then the only rule was the ultima ratio of sovereigns. Thus far, Nullification concurred in the tenets of Mr. Madison. But in the next and main principle of State Rights it diverged fatally from the true faith. It made the States irresponsible, instead of being judges for themselves on their individual State responsibility to each other. Thus:

## VII.

That in the last resort "each State for itself was the judge of the infraction as well as the mode and measure of redress."

Here the departure from the true faith of State Rights began. Mr. Madison laid down the rule as *relative* only, whilst Nullification contended that it was *absolute*. Mr. Madison announced the position that each might judge for itself, but not without responsibility to each and all of the other States; that each might judge for itself of the infraction, but that resistance to a law passed within the constitutional limitations was as much an infraction as was the passage by Congress of an unconstitutional law, and that each might judge for itself of the mode and measure of redress; but if one might judge that resistance to the law was her mode and measure of redress, another might judge that enforcement of the law was her mode and measure of redressing the infraction of, or punishing resistance to, the law.

## VIII.

The laws passed in pursuance of, or in accordance with, the Constitution were undoubtedly the supreme laws; but whether passed in pursuance or in violation of the Constitution was a question admitting of different tribunals for decision, according to the nature of the question and characters of the parties.

In cases within the jurisdiction of the courts of the United States, between citizens and persons, or States and States, involving personal or corporate municipal rights, the Supreme Court of the United States was confessedly the tribunal of last resort as to parties to the suits in court.

Until the decision was made in such cases, between such parties, to suits within the jurisdiction of the Federal courts, all parties had to receive and act upon and abide by the Acts of Congress as valid; but the Supreme Court might, in such cases, between such parties, decide that they were invalid, unconstitutional, and void. These decisions operated civilly *in personam* and *in rem*, but *not* on *political issues*.

But by far the most important cases at issue were political cases, and not cases either of law or in equity for the courts. The Supreme Court itself had at the very beginning eschewed the power of deciding who politically was right or wrong. At the very beginning of the nineteenth century, and before the Supreme Court had taken this judicial ground for the sake of the Judicial Department, it left the political jurisdiction to the Legislative and Executive Departments, according to its assignment and distribution by the Constitution, to be controlled finally by the elections of the people, or by the conventional powers of the States. And this was salutary and safe, and practically wise and good, so far as pertained to mere municipal questions affecting persons and corporations as such. But it was inadequate and without power either in the case where the sovereign *bodies politic, the States,* interposed and contested the constitutionality of laws affecting their political rights, or where they contested the jurisdiction of the Supreme Court as to the political issues between the sovereign parties to the Federal compact, affecting the compact itself. When they did interpose, a mere municipal department of the Federal government, the Judiciary, could no more conclude them by decision than Congress, another mere municipal department, could conclude to bind them by *legislation.* This would have been to set up mere municipalities, the Judicial and Legislative Departments of the Federal government, over their sovereigns and creators the States or the people, the sources of all power.

The clause which declares that the Constitution of the United States, and the treaties and laws of the United States made in pursuance thereof, shall be the supreme law, could not justly be interpreted to have any other than a municipal, not a sovereign, sense or meaning: that they were to be supreme within the limitations of the Constitution was to be decided only by the conventional powers of the States. It would have been absurd for the Constitution to forbid the Federal government, or either or all of its departments, to violate it, and then to give to the Federal government or either of its departments the power to decide whether it had violated the Constitution or not, for that would be to give the power to declare its violations supreme, and to enforce them on States as well as on persons and property, without regard to constitutional limitations. So long as the cases were ordinary cases, of no vital and fundamental political importance, involving only municipal rights of persons or property, the laws of Congress were to be deemed valid, until decided otherwise by the Supreme Court, or when decided by that court to be valid, and in either case were supreme. But in plain, palpable cases, involving gross infractions of the Constitution, and sovereign issues, and the political powers of government or its departments, State or Federal, in cases where the States were in conflict, the only tribunal was that of a convention of the States.

This doctrine was most conservative and peaceful. Nothing else could or can preserve and perpetuate constitutional federal republicanism. And nothing can better illustrate this than the late Confederate war with the United States. Could it, would it, ever have begun, and raged on as it did for four years, had this theory of political philosophy prevailed and been pursued? If, when the conflict became imminent, Congress, instead of assuming to decide political and fundamental and sovereign questions, and to clothe the Executive with the power of proclaiming war, and using force to coerce States and their people to submission, had construed the Constitution as obliging them, mere fiduciaries, to call together the sovereign States in convention, does any reflecting man suppose that there could or would have been a war at all?

If a convention of the States had been obliged to be called before Congress could have passed another Force Bill, and before a President could have proclaimed its execution by arms, the States would have obeyed the dictates of patriotism, peace, and humanity in readjusting dissensions, and reuniting in harmony of action, just as, amidst the same sort of dissensions, they were at first united by the wisdom of such men as Washington, Madison, Edmund Randolph, Alexander Hamilton, Charles Cotesworth Pinckney, Franklin, and their compeers, in 1787–89.

Assembling together, delay and deliberation, debate and personal attachment and private influences, postponement of unnecessary issues, and compromise and concession, would have infallibly kept the peace, and saved the blood and the treasure, the honor and the liberty, of the Union !

But the theory of consolidation made the Federal government supreme, without and above the conventional power of the States ; substituted Federal for State sovereignty; converted the two words *"United States"* into the one word *"Congress,"* and the plural word *States* into the word *Nation ;* repelled the idea of the *Union of States,* and acted upon the forbidden idea of a numerical majority of the people.   Already inflamed by the violent interest to set up an unwritten higher law above the limitations of the Constitution; with the powers of mischief already in hand; with but a fragment of State and popular representation seated in the Houses of Congress; acting *ex parte*, and a part for the whole ; seizing arms, Congress and the Executive rushed into the war suddenly, without delay, without convention, without giving the people time to deliberate, against the protestation of some of the original thirteen States, and ravaged the country by war, revolutionized the whole theory of republican constitutional freedom, and changed the government into a national, congressional oligarchy and military imperialism.

But the chief safeguard of the Madisonian doctrine of State sovereignty, and State Rights and remedies, under our system of State and Federal governments, called " compositive," with very little meaning, by Mr. Wheaton, was the protection it afforded and insured to the persons and individual citizens of the people against the despotic dogmas of treason, forfeiture, confiscation, and military commissions, according to the common law ideas.

In case a convention of States was called, as a political tribunal of last peaceable resort, to determine questions as to the compact, and failed to compose the conflicts of States about what the Constitution was or should be made, then each State had the right to judge for herself of the infraction, and of the mode and measure of redress, and whether she would remain in the Union as made or construed by the majority of States, or secede from the Union and resume her separate independence. It was not pretended by the Virginia school, as we have said, that this right was absolute, but only that it was relative.

Thus, to take a case where the weaker States insisted upon the execution of a law passed by Congress, as the Act of 1793, to enforce the provision of the Constitution requiring the rendition of all fugitives from labor from one State to another. The same rule would favor Virginia or South Carolina in recovering a slave, in that case, as would favor the New England States or Pennsylvania in enforcing a tariff for protection. Resistance to a constitutional law by a State was as much an infraction of the Constitution as the passage of an unconstitutional act by Congress. The Act of 1793 was decided to be constitutional, and universally acquiesced in by every State of the Union for forty years, and had been solemnly asserted as valid and binding by the Constitution, and adjudicated upon by the judiciaries of the States, as well as by the Federal courts and judges. At last, several of the States, Pennsylvania among others, attempted to prevent or obstruct its execution within their limits. Good faith required that there should be such a law; it was plainly valid; but some States declared that there was a higher law which forbade them to aid in its enforcement. They went further, and not only forbade assistance by their citizens or officers to its execution, but declared certain acts of slave-owners in pursuit of their rights under that law to be feloniously criminal, and bound their authorities to arrest, prosecute, and punish them for attempting to take their fugitive slaves under the Act of Congress. They left the United States officers and agents, judges and marshals, alone, without a posse to execute the Act of Congress. A slave-owner pursuing his fugitive was liable to illegal arrest, trial, and infamous punishment for doing what was lawful under the Constitution and laws of the United States. Instead of having his lawful property restored to him, he was liable to be imprisoned

9

in a penitentiary. This was nullification, remaining in the Union and nullifying its laws. The Southern States contended that the Northern States could not nullify the laws of the Union; that if Pennsylvania, for example, judged the Act of Congress for recovering of fugitives from labor unconstitutional, and passed ordinances forbidding its execution within her limits, she might so judge and act, but not without just responsibility. Her judgment and action alike related to sister States as well as to herself. If she might judge the law unconstitutional, the sister States, each for itself, might judge it constitutional; if she might judge the act to be an infraction, they, under the same rule, might judge her resistance to it, or nullification of it, to be an infraction; and if she might judge her mode and measure of redress to be by nullification of the act, they, in like manner, might judge their mode and measure of redress to be by enforcement of the act.

And this mode of enforcement would be by using the powers and means of the common government to act on persons resisting the execution of the law. If the slaveholder, pursuing his fugitive slave, had been seized and imprisoned under the State law, he would have applied to the State judges for a writ of habeas corpus; and if they were sworn, as in South Carolina, by a test oath not to execute or enforce the law of Congress, he would have applied for the writ to a Federal judge, whose duty it was to issue it to the Federal marshal; and if the sheriff, or the executive and militia of the State, had opposed his authority, and he could not execute the law, he would so have certified to the Federal judge, and he in turn would so have certified to the President of the United States, who, under his oath to see that the laws were faithfully executed, would have been bound to call out the army or have a body of militia to execute the laws, but as auxiliary only to the civil authority of the Federal courts, not as an act of *war.* And the same rule applied, *e converso,* against South Carolina resisting a tariff, as it did against Pennsylvania resisting the fugitive slave laws of the Union. Thus the rule was relative, and not absolute; and under a *relative* rule South Carolina essayed to nullify laws

absolutely within her limits, without responsibility to her co-
States.   It was vain, and exposed those of her citizens, who
obeyed her ordinances and came in collision with Federal authority, to the pains and penalties of treason.  But Mr. Madison
avoided that error of construing the rule of State Rights.   He
pointed to the remedy of secession from the Union.  If violations
of the Constitution were palpable and gross, if oppression and
inequality were avowed and practiced, if good faith and justice
were set at naught by even a convention of the States, each
State might judge for herself whether she would abide in the
Union or resume her separate condition as a State.  In that attitude of State sovereignty, if assailed she would be " a belligerent," not a " rebel ;" her citizens would be "*inimici non hostes,*"
not "*hostes non inimici ;*" the case would be governed by the
"*jus belli,*" absolute, if you please, but the citizens would be
saved from the treatment of traitors ; the laws of *war* only, and
not of treason, would apply.   The act of the State would be
revolutionary, but the revolution would be one of a *conflict of
States*, not a conflict of citizens or subjects with government.
The State would be responsible to the States remaining in the
Union, but the mere municipal Federal government would be
no longer the common agent, and she would be free from its
authority, and would be amenable only to a convention of the
States, though a convention of the States might act through
the Federal government.   In no case would the State be irresponsible, but she would be responsible to the convention of
States, not to the Federal Congress, or Executive, or Judiciary,
or all combined.

The State could not be prosecuted for treason, nor could her
citizens ; she could only be forced by the other States to submit
to their equal right to judge of infractions and of the mode and
measure of redress, and her citizens would be covered by her
shield of sovereignty.

This, we repeat, called forth most wisely the conventional
power of States,—first, to judge of the infraction and of the mode
and measure of redress ; and, second, and at last, to judge as to
the propriety of the enforcement or repeal of the act resisted or

of the question of peace or war—of winning back the seceding State with amity or driving her into submission by subjugation. The true theory was that the Federal government, in such a case, could interpose no further than to call a convention of States, and that for it to interpose as judge and executioner of a State would be to assume at once and forever powers wholly inconsistent with the limitations of the Constitution and with public law and liberty. These were our views in 1832–33, and we regret that they were not those of Mr. Tyler. He sided with Nullification. The members of the Senate in opposition to the Force Bill, all but him, left their seats when the question was taken on its passage, and he, therefore, voted alone against it. Though in error as to the theory, he was right as to the policy of not voting for that act; and of no vote of his was he so proud as of that vote, to the last hour of his life.

Thus Nullification, with its untenable position of an absolute rule of State Rights, afforded General Jackson the opportunity of establishing the maxim, "The Union must and shall be preserved," and of appealing to Congress for the law of force to be executed by the Federal Executive to coerce a State into submission to the acts of Congress for the mere collection of duties and the regulation of commerce. He had always been a Democrat of the Strict Construction school. His model of a statesman, senator, debater, and politician had always been the celebrated William B. Giles, of Virginia, whose political faith and practice would have guided him to the measure of a Force Bill by Congress, without an appeal first to a convention of all the States; and he had countenanced Georgia in her barbarous nullification of the treaties and laws of the United States, in the cruel execution of the Indian, Tassels, against the notice of the Attorney-General (Mr. Wirt) and the orders of the Supreme Court of the United States, and in her lottery laws, by which the lands of the Cherokees, then a Christianized tribe, which had always been a faithful ally of the United States, were gambled away amidst horrid scenes of rapine and blood; but, then, his favorite, Mr. Forsyth, of Georgia, was his Secretary of State; and, in the case of South Carolina, the opponent of his invasion of Florida whilst it was a Spanish colony, and of his hanging Arbuthnot and Ambrister, Mr. Calhoun, was to be punished and crushed. This was the precedent, sanctioned by his example and by his immense popularity, which overthrew the maxim of Madison, that neither the Federal government nor any of its departments was or could be umpire between the States, and established the supremacy of the Federal Congress, and the Executive. From that time forth the State Rights doctrine, first perverted and misapplied by Mr. Calhoun, and then directly assailed by General Jackson, began to decline and seem impracticable. Congress passed its Force Bill against persons resisting the execution of the laws of the collection of duties, and President Jackson ordered the commander-in-chief of the standing army, General Scott, to enforce their execution. He obeyed the order with alacrity and effect.

Nothing then prevented a conflict by arms but the " Compromise Bill" of the tariff of 1832–33. This example and precedent bore heavily upon the after-issues of 1860–61, as we shall hereafter see, and as we have grievously felt.

# CHAPTER VII.

## THE FIFTH DECADE, FROM 1830 TO 1840.

THE measure which commanded the attention and drew forth the abilities of Mr. Tyler in the Congress of 1831–32, besides the Force Bill, was the bill to modify and continue the act incorporating the Bank of the United States. In every form he voted for amendments, offered by various senators, to weaken and restrict the powers of the Bank, as to its currency; as to the power of Congress to alter or modify its charter; as to the rate of interest on its loans and discounts; as to the amount of bonus to be paid; as to the right of the States to tax its branches; as to indefinite postponement; and, finally, he voted against the bill, on its engrossment and on its passage.

When one reflects upon his course, in 1812, censuring Messrs. Giles and Brent for disobeying the instructions of the legislature by voting for the United States Bank charter at that

( 134 )

early day, and when one sees him repeating his opposition to
the power of Congress to charter a Bank of the United States
in 1819, and finds him again, in 1832, opposing a recharter in
every part and in the whole, in detail and on the final vote;
and when one looks to his after-course, his votes and speeches
in Congress in persistent and uniform opposition to the constitutionality of a Bank charter by Congress, the wonder is,
not that he vetoed the Bank charters submitted to his approval
as President, in 1841, but that any one ever should imagine he
would or could sign and approve a charter for a Bank of the
United States, and that any one should have assailed his consistency on account of his vetoes. In no matter of his public
life was he so consistent as in his course on the subject of
chartering a Bank of the United States.

The bill of 1832 was vetoed by General Jackson, and his
veto of the Bank endeared him to the Democracy, and drew to
him nearer than ever the advocates of State Rights and Strict
Construction. Mr. Tyler was among the most zealous supporters of the Bank veto of General Jackson, though his vote
on the Force Bill, afterwards, separated him forever from the
then administration.

Mr. Tyler was re-elected by the legislature of Virginia to
the Senate of the United States, to serve from the 4th of March,
1833. He had sustained General Jackson in vetoing the United
States Bank charter, and he had in his speech on the Force Bill
suggested the mode of compromising the conflict of Nullification
with the tariff for protection, and, of course, sustained Mr. Clay
in his great measures of pacification, the Compromise Bill of
1832–33. This again put him farther apart from the administration, for General Jackson avowedly desired the opportunity
and pretext to crush South Carolina, and to hang Mr. Calhoun and his comrades for resistance to the tariff. The compromise measures prevented civil war and withheld the arm
of force

But General Jackson was not contented with vetoing a bill
for chartering the United States Bank anew: he was determined
to wage war upon the then existing Bank. Between the ad-

journment of Congress in March and its meeting in December, 1833, he determined upon removing the moneys of the United States from the keeping of the Bank.

Mr. Duane, his Secretary of the Treasury, declined to obey the orders of the chief Executive to remove the public deposits. General Jackson dismissed him at once from the Cabinet, and appointed in his stead Mr. Taney, who did believe that the interest of the United States required that the public moneys should be withdrawn from the Bank, and, consequently, withdrew them. The question of power was raised in the Senate, whether the Executive, in this mode, could assume control over the custody of the public treasure, and whether the Secretary of the Treasury was an officer of the executive or the legislative department of government, subject to the power of the President or of Congress.

The Senate, by a decisive vote, censured the President as "assuming to himself power and authority not conferred by the Constitution and the laws, and in derogation of both," and condemning the reasons assigned by Mr. Taney for the removal of the deposits. Mr. Tyler voted for this resolution of censure, not as on a question of "bank or no bank," but upon the ground that the Executive had no power to assume the custody and control of the Treasury of the United States without authority of an act of Congress, and without reason of probable danger or loss of the public moneys. On presenting a memorial against the removal of the deposits from the people of the city of Richmond, he said, "The memorialists look to Congress for relief. They ask not for a renewal of the Bank charter, but for the introduction of some stable *financial system;* not one depending on eccentric will; not a treasury resting on agents appointed by the President, liable to be displaced at his pleasure, holding their existence but as the breath of his nostrils; fleeting and ephemeral as whim or caprice, passion or political motives, might make them; but resting on law, not to be changed but for high reasons of state policy, approved by the wisdom and sanctioned by the experience of Congress."

This position took no departure whatever from his constant

and uniform opposition to the charter of the United States Bank.

As to the removal of the deposits, the only question with him before the country was, " Whether Congress or the President was charged with the keeping of the treasury."

This resolution of censure was passed by the Senate, and General Jackson immediately hurled back defiance by sending his memorable protest, which the Senate declared to be a breach of its privileges, and refused to place upon the journal.

At once the work of expunction began which hurled senators from their seats in order to fill them with the pliant and supple tools of executive power to draw black lines on that journal around that resolution which dared to censure President Jackson!  Mr. Benton gave notice immediately of a Hannibal-like vow never to cease in his efforts, so long as he had a seat in the Senate, until the resolutions of censure were stricken from the journal.  He fulfilled the vow most fatally by expelling such men as John Tyler and Benjamin Watkins Leigh, of Virginia, and Hugh Lawson White, of Tennessee, and introducing expunction partisans in their places, until the indelible black lines were drawn !

Mr. Tyler especially became obnoxious to Mr. Benton.  The Committee of Finance of the Senate had been ordered to inquire into the affairs and condition of the United States Bank, and Mr. Tyler had made a full and able report from that committee, which was attacked by Mr. Benton in his characteristic vein of "Big Bully Bottom."

Mr. Tyler killed his assault by dignity, decorum, and courtly contradiction.  In reply to the charge that he was a partisan of the Bank, and that the report of the committee was "an elaborate defense of the Bank," he said, " *I am opposed, and have always been opposed, to the Bank. In its creation I regard the Constitution as having been violated, and I desire to see it expire;* but I should regard myself as the basest of mankind were I to charge it falsely."

· He was at this session elected president *pro tempore* of the Senate ; and one of his last acts was to vote against the amendment made by the House of Representatives to the Fortification Bill, placing three millions of dollars at the discretion of the President to provide for anticipated difficulties with France on account of her debt of only five millions due the United States. The failure of this bill was afterwards made one of the pretexts for which Judge White was instructed out of his seat in the Senate by the legislature of Tennessee. But Mr. Tyler's seat was the first to be vacated by instructions to vote for Mr. Benton's expunging resolution. North Carolina's legislature had first instructed her senator, Mr. Mangum; but he had refused to obey or to resign; and in February, 1836, the legislature of Virginia was induced to instruct her senators to expunge the resolution of the Senate of March 28, 1834. The then governor, Mr. Tazewell, declined to transmit the instructions of the legislature to the senators of Virginia in Congress. They were sent by the presiding officers of the two houses of the General Assembly. The General Assembly of Virginia had at previous sessions condemned the expunging resolutions, and the presentation of the resolution of the legislature to the Senate of the United States had caused Mr. William C. Rives, then the colleague of Mr. Tyler, to resign his seat in the Senate, and Mr. Leigh had been elected in his place, as if expressly by command of the legislature to oppose expunction. When instructed in turn by the legislature to vote for the expunging resolutions of Mr. Benton, Mr. Leigh wielded the fact of his previous instructions and his election to fill the vacancy caused by the resignation of Mr. Rives, with great effect. He refused to obey or to resign, and wrote a very able letter justifying his course and reconciling his previous authorship of the doctrine of instructions with his then determination to resist to the uttermost an extreme, plain, and palpable violation of the Constitution. Mr. Tyler took a different course. He consulted with his friends, and he announced that he had always held and maintained the right and power of the legislature to instruct, and the duty and obligation of the senator or representative to obey or to resign, to be absolute and 'imperative; and his friends, particularly Judge White, advised him that he had no election, and it was most politic to resign. He was very reluctant to separate in his course from Mr. Leigh. We were requested to confer with the latter, and did so, and we regret to say that but one member of the Virginia delegation in Congress, within our knowledge, did him the justice and kindness to confer with him. He was ready for the interview. He had already written his letter of response to the legislature, and was, as he always was, fully prepared. He read it to us, and made it the text of hours of commentary. It confirmed our opinion of him, that he was one of the greatest and noblest of the men of his day.

If Virginia could have been embodied and impersonated, and placed where she could have heard and seen him, her instructions to him to vote for the expunction would have been torn into tatters and scattered to the four winds of heaven.

A man of striking manly beauty, with hair of silky, soft, chestnut brown, floating in curls imperial as those of Jove when Olympus shook with his nod; a strong gray eye, which glowed as he breathed forth his inspiration of intellect and heart; a finely-chiseled mouth, expressing the most delicate taste and sweet benevolence; and a nose and chin of manly fortitude:—one could but inwardly exclaim, when looking at him and listening to him, " *Os homini sublime dedit.*"

His comments were sad and sweet in the extreme. His hymn of love to Virginia was exquisitely tender:—his mother, how high and holy in his reverence of her no tongue could tell; and how exalted he held her dignity. He could not see her defiled, and would not aid in degrading her at the footstool of tyranny, even though a tyrant demanded her prostration, and much less would he give way to the prostitution of her to the uses of mere minions who aspired to promotion by superservility to power, even if the President did not desire or demand the sacrifice of her self-respect. But he knew it was in vain. He foresaw and predicted the issue. The Congress would bow basely before a strong and popular Executive, and the moment a Jackson was gone from place, would itself become the tyrant oligarchy of the country. The Constitution would not protect against executive popularity, nor against congressional servility or tyranny. He counted the recreancy of the Senate then as the culminating-point of the reign of the Constitution, and almost portrayed the very course of events which have followed. But he was still urged to resign, and his severance from Mr. Tyler was deprecated; he regretted this too, and insisted that he had an understanding with Mr. Tyler to act in concert, and disclosed a personal motive controlling his own course,—that when North Carolina had instructed Mr. Mangum, her senator, to vote for expunction, he (Mr. Leigh) had counseled him to neither obey nor resign; and having given that advice to his friend, he could not in honor fail to pursue the same course himself. When reminded that Mr. Tyler had given no such counsel, and he could not expect him to obey it, he then said they would have to take different courses. With this he was never content. He always—very unjustly (we think)—complained that Mr. Tyler did not sustain him, forgetting that Mr. Tyler was free from any such obligation as that of Mr. Leigh to Mr. Mangum, and that Mr. Leigh was as much pledged to go along with Mr. Tyler as the latter was pledged to go along with him, Mr. Leigh. So it was, they were obliged to separate. Mr. Tyler could not, and would not, obey the instructions, and, in accordance with the consistency of his whole life upon the doctrine of instructions and obedience or resignation, he resigned his seat in the Senate of the United States on the 20th of February, 1836, and on the 29th of the same month addressed to the Speaker and members of the General Assembly of Virginia a letter of great dignity and strength, giving his reasons for not obeying their instructions, and for resigning his trust into their hands.

This sent him back to private life, but not to obscurity; nor did it diminish his usefulness or prominence for promotion. A singular revolution of events and parties soon brought him again conspicuous for the highest trusts. He had served three years of his term from the 4th of March, 1833, and Mr. Rives was elected to fill his unexpired term until March 4th, 1839.

This brought Mr. Rives and Mr. Leigh into contrast in the

Senate. The contrast was one of high lights and deep shades. The subject was one involving constitutional law, a history of parliament, the limitations of executive power, the guards of legislative power, the freedom of debate, the independence of the separate departments of government, the dignity and duty of the Senate in respect to its proceedings and records, and the learning of philology. As a constitutional and civil lawyer, as a historian, as a logician, as a patriot, jealous of power and sensitive to any encroachment upon limitations guarding the rights of legislation and the freedom of resolutions and laws, as well as of debate, and as a scholar and rhetorician, no man compared with Mr. Leigh in the argument on the topic of expunction. He was a purist in his Anglo-Saxon, and his speech was, in its style, equal to that of the Elizabethan age of English literature, not surpassed by the "well of English" of Dean Swift. His figure of the silkworm spinning its cocoon from its own bowels, as applied in this debate, is a fine specimen of the use of rhetoric's tools, and his illustrations of the verb "to keep," of its meaning *in continuando*, "to keep a journal," show how necessary is the knowledge of the meaning of *words* to a knowledge of laws and to the preservation of liberties. From every source of written language he proved the power of that verb. He went to the Ten Commandments, to the Old and the New Testament, to standard profane writers, to prose and poetry, to prove that it had a peculiar strength of meaning, always conveying the same idea of preservation—preservation as the thing was—and continual preservation ; and in winding up a paragraph of citations of its use, he said, " And, Mr. President, in that catechism which I learned at my mother's knee, I was taught ' to keep—to keep—to keep' my hands from picking and stealing, and my tongue from evil speaking !"

He was not a vehement orator in tone, but was most earnest in utterance and manner. He had a soft, clear, flutelike voice, but it was not loud. He carried no audience by vociferation or violent action ; but he trickled, as it were, gently upon his hearers, and they were held in mute attention by a murmuring music, his eye looking more than he said, and his speech and bearing glowing with a genial integrity of thought which put opposition to blush, it was so clear, so simple, so pure, so generous, so just, and so warm with manly honor and feeling.  Every word was right in the right place, his accent and pronunciation were precisely correct, and the modulation of his voice was natural and sweetly touching.

He was a small man, yet in speaking seemed large, so elevated was he by his theme, and so gallant and game was his mien.   He was lame, one leg shortened, and wore a cork sole on one of his boots.   When about to be emphatic, he usually caught his left wrist in his right hand and sank back on his lame leg, pausing to poise himself, and, as he rose to the climax of what he was about to utter, would bear upon his sound leg and rise on it with his hands free.   This attitude was not always graceful, but always excited sympathy in his hearer for his infirmity.   It was thus he uttered the sentence about "keeping his hands from picking and stealing, and his tongue from evil speaking."   He dropped back on his lame leg, his left wrist in his right hand, paused and settled himself,—in that pause fixed his eyes on Thomas H. Benton with an intense gaze,—began low, uttered softly as far as the words "my mother's knee," raised his voice at the words "I learned," and, pronouncing the words "to keep" three times, each time louder and louder, he rose upon his sound leg, loosed his wrist, and putting forward both his hands, exclaimed, "My hands from picking and stealing, and my tongue from *evil speaking!*"

A pin might have been heard to drop on the floor of the Senate; there sat Mr. Benton, swinging back in his chair, his eyes looking up to the wall, patting his foot, and Mr. Leigh's eyes fixed on him for some seconds, which seemed hours. Breaths were drawn when those eyes were taken off of him. It was the touch of Ithuriel's spear, and the cravat of Chapel Hill was revealed as plainly as the "toad squat" was shown to be Lucifer himself.

Mr. Leigh was a debater of the senatorial order.   Had he been earlier in the Senate, as long as Clay, Webster, or Calhoun, he would have been the master there, with all three present. The longer he wore it the brighter and higher-mettled was his steel. He was an "intellectual bully," but never meant to be personal in debate. Every one thought that, in the instance just related, he meant to be personal to Mr. Benton; but he did not so mean.

This was proved afterwards. We were present at the drawing of the black lines. The clerk of the Senate, Asbury Dickens, rose to go after the journal to bring it in to do execution upon. It was brought and laid upon the desk before him; and just at that moment every senator opposed to expunction, except Judge White, rose from his seat and began to move out, Mr. Benton making the most derisive and scornful exclamations as they made their exit. A man in the gallery cried aloud some disorderly response, when Mr. Benton exclaimed, "Bank ruffians! bank ruffians! Seize them, sergeant-at-arms!" The man was immediately arrested, and brought before the Senate. As soon as this disorder was quieted, the clerk opened the journal at the page of the resolution of censure; it seemed to resist the opening, the back was stiff, and it shut together again, until pressed open wide, and the page so held as to lay upon it the rule by the straight edge of which the black lines were to be drawn. We could not but imagine the book of the journal as resisting the violation. It seemed like a living victim on the altar of sacrifice, and the scratch of the pen alone was heard in the awful silence which prevailed when the gall of party bitterness drew its lines in the blackness of darkness around the freedom and independence of the Senate. The moment was one of intense interest, and was disturbed by Mr. Benton rising from his seat, and ostentatiously congratulating persons in the lower gallery on the triumph of his resolutions of subserviency to the worship of a man who despised and denounced him. He was boisterously moving from man to man, reaching out his hand, until he came to the Hon. Baillie Peyton, of Tennessee, who waited his expected offer of a touch with such a countenance of contempt and detestation that he shrunk back, desisted from his gasconading, and resumed his seat. Peyton was just about to denounce him as a Chapel Hill thief, unworthy to denounce strangers as bank ruffians, when, fortunately for himself, he turned away.

The next morning Mr. Webster requested us, as a witness of the scene, to prepare a description of it, which was done; and, after the adjournment of that session of Congress, we portrayed it at a dinner in Norfolk, in a speech which was published in full in the *Richmond Whig* of the time. In order to describe the apparent effect of Mr. Leigh's eye upon Mr. Benton when quoting the catechism taught him at his mother's knee about "picking and stealing," we said that a short time before we had visited the exhibition of the French painting of Adam and Eve; that we thought we had found it obnoxious to a severely just criticism; that Adam was reclining on the soft sward of Paradise, and whilst Eve was resting by his side, whispering temptation in his ear, the serpent coiled around the tree of Life was breathing the *visible influence* of evil upon the golden ringlets of her hair. The influence was painted: it was visible and tangible. This, we thought, was not the work or design of a master. It was French exaggeration; the French had never been poets or painters; none but a French artist, we thought, would be so poor in invention as to attempt to *paint an influence*. It was not so much exaggeration as the poverty of art. But we admitted, afterwards, that the scene of Leigh looking at Benton, when illustrating the duty "to keep" a journal continually as it was, as the catechism teaches "to keep our hands from picking and stealing," corrected and contradicted our criticism on the painting of Adam and Eve. An influence could be seen and touched. We had seen it, and it had touched Thomas H. Benton. We had seen the look of Mr. Leigh upon him when he quoted the catechism. The bright strong eye lighted a flame; that flame went forth like a sword to the man at whom it pointed, and pierced him to the dividing asunder of the joints and the marrow,—it was visible and tangible and could be painted; and if the sword or spear of the angel might be seen to touch the toad, so artistic license allowed the mist or miasm of evil to be seen, felt, and painted. Mr. Leigh, on reading the speech, of his own motion addressed a card to the Richmond press, saying that, whatever might have been the inference of his audience, he did not think of any personality to Mr. Benton at the time, and that if he had so meant he would have expressed the meaning, as his wont was never to insult any one but in unmistakable and direct terms. The first time we met him afterwards we told him that the inference was so strong that he alluded to Chapel Hill, when looking at Benton, whilst making this quotation, that it seemed impossible he could mean otherwise. He was hurt, and again protested that he meant nothing personally offensive whatever.

At all events, he totally overthrew every champion in the debate, and Mr. Rives was not even straw on the horns of an ox in comparison with him. He was an Ajax Telamon anywhere in debate, but too honest, mentally and morally, for political life. We shall always regret that he did not follow the example of Mr. Tyler and resign.

It is necessary here to pause upon some points in General Jackson's administration during the last years of his two terms. The two major topics with him in the latter part of his reign were the election of his successor and the annexation of Texas. On the question of demanding the five millions from France, he had been peremptory in his tone, and no council of Cabinet or friend could mitigate or temper his demand.

On that subject he had himself dictated the very language he would employ in uttering a threat direct to Louis Philippe. The Cabinet consulted to change the phraseology. Mr. Forsyth, then Secretary of State, was adroit in language, and wisely, he thought, changed the paragraph which the President had dictated. The change in words was but a shade different in meaning; but he sought to make the message more diplomatic in terms and more conformable, of course, to peaceful and courteous national intercourse. It was in vain. When Mr. Andrew J. Donelson, the President's private secretary, brought to him the proof-sheets of the message, Mr. John C. Rives, of the *Globe*, was present.

Mr. Donelson read, whilst the general walked the room, pipe in his mouth, smoking, and the printer the only attendant. All

10

was quietly listened to until the reader came to the passage
relating to the five millions debt due by France.   Mr. Donelson
was evidently desirous so to read the paragraph on that subject
as to avoid notice of the change in words which had been made.
General Jackson at once paused in his walk, stopped, and
said, " Read that again, sir."   Mr. Donelson then read the
passage distinctly, and General Jackson was instantly roused,
saying, " That, sir, is not my language ; it has been changed,
and I will have no other expression of my own meaning than
my own words."

He immediately and vehemently had the change erased, and
his own language, even more strongly importing a threat, inserted, heard the message read through, and then placed it in
the hands of Mr. Rives, forbidding him to let it be seen in his
hands, or to let it pass out of his hands, until after it was
printed as corrected and until permission was granted by him,
" at his peril."

Thus the message was made what it was, which literally
wrung the five millions from France.

He was wiser than his Cabinet.   His absolute dictation
won at once what their diplomacy would have been years in
obtaining.

But he was not always absolute in his dictation.   He was
not so in respect to the annexation of Texas.   That darling
project of his policy conflicted with another more darling, the
election of his successor.

When we went to Tennessee in 1828, we found Texas an en-
grossing subject of interest to the Southwestern mind.   Archer
and Austin were forerunners there, and had made contracts of
settlements with Mexico, which, drawing a population from the
United States, were rapidly filling Texas up with democratic
settlers, and Mexico became alarmed.   She began to apprehend
exactly what soon afterwards happened, a war with Texas and
its subsequent annexation to the United States.

This caused her to commence a series of acts arbitrarily re-
scinding the contracts of Austin and others, seizing their acquisitions, and persecuting and oppressing the settlers from the

United States, who had, without their fault, been tempted by Mexico to seek homes in Texas. This aroused the friends and kindred of former fellow-citizens of these settlers in all the Southwest. " Off to Texas !" was the cry,—to assert the right of settlement there by contract, to protect the pioneers there already, and to take that fertile province from a despotic and semi-barbarous power, degraded by a mixture of races, white, black, and copper-colored, of whom it was said, "They are a nation whose men are all bandits, and whose women are all harlots !"

At the first commencement of the Nashville University, which occurred after our arrival there, a youth, William Wharton, whose father was a Virginian, was graduated, and delivered an oration which marked him as a man of great promise. He was the pride of the Rev. Dr. Lindsley, who then presided over that Alma Mater of many another distinguished alumnus of the West.

Wharton delivered his salutatory, and immediately went off to Texas to join Dr. Archer, also from Virginia, the first military leader of the Texas Revolution, and became, as was predicted for him, a distinguished soldier and legislator, and finally was made legate of the revolution to the United States. He died young, but lived long enough to accomplish his first purpose in life, and to fulfill a most urgent promise he made when begging us to join our fortunes with his own, to tear Texas from despotism, in order to annex her to the United States.

An older but not a better man than Wharton was soon obliged to leave his adopted State for her good. Samuel Houston was then the governor of the State of Tennessee. He had been a popular pet, but his life was one of most dissolute habits. He became a candidate for re-election to the office he held, but General William Carroll, one of the heroes of Jackson's campaigns, the comrade of General Coffee on the night of the 22d of December in front of New Orleans, was his competitor.

The contest, it was thought by Houston and his friends, would be very doubtful at least. It would certainly have been bitter, for General Carroll denounced Houston in unmeasured terms.  He said on the streets of Nashville that Houston was a coward, that at the battle of the Horse Shoe he—then a private in the ranks—was struck by a ball in the arm, and "blubbered so that General Jackson ordered the calf to be sent to the rear ;" and he spoke without reserve of his habits unfitting him for his place.  Houston, then advanced in life, spent in dissipation, and still suffering from a seton in that wounded arm, sought to strengthen himself and insure his election by an alliance in marriage with one of the most popular and influential families in Middle Tennessee, residing near Gallatin.  A sweet and artless daughter of that family was, in her flyflap bonnet, at a village school.  She was captivating, and her heart had already caught the flame of the love of a suitor whose youth was suitable to her own.  In that coy state of young girl's first love, the eye of the ogre fell upon her.

Her family was sought by Samuel Houston from which to select a victim, not of his love, but his selfish electioneering for influence to save him in office.  Poor, innocent, injured victim ! —the family were flattered by the governor, and she was torn from her youth and her pure, natural, maiden love to become the victim of his jealousy and his heartless, selfish ambition ! The connection was so unnatural and so repugnant to public sentiment that it brought down upon the monster a chivalry which drove him from the seat of power which he defiled.  Her champions placarded him on the public square of Nashville for every crime in the calendar which could deprive him of any pretension to be above a brute.  General Jackson's gallantry alone aided him.  He had been one of his soldiers, and was one of his political adherents, and Jackson was never known to desert a friend !—he had to be servile to him, but he would serve him ; but he did not excuse his conduct, and advised him to resign his office and leave Tennessee, to join the revolution in Texas, giving him, doubtless, instructions then as to the conduct of the revolution.  He was to be made its leader, with the influence of General Jackson, then President elect of the United States, to back him.  Houston at first affected a mind diseased, and put on the white-tanned skin of a pied heifer, and actually wore it on the streets of Nashville until he left the State forever.

General Jackson was a deep and far-seeing politician. He made especial use of Houston. The revolution in Texas went on, doubtfully enough, until it reached the critical point when President Jackson was to interpose the sword of the United States. How was that to be done? None other than General Jackson in the Presidency would have thought of his way of violating the laws of neutrality. He suddenly declared that the boundary usually known to geography and to treaty as the line between the United States and Mexico was not the true line, and, by his organ, the *Globe*, stated that Mr. John Quincy Adams, being Secretary of State at the time the boundary with Mexico was fixed, had, out of his old grudge to the interests of the valley of the Mississippi, betrayed the United States, and agreed to a boundary too far east by several leagues of territory; that the river Sabine was not the true boundary, but that the Nueces was the true boundary. In protecting the border of the United States against aggressions from belligerents on either side of the civil war in Mexico, he would order General Gaines to array his army for border protection with its front on the western line, which he avowed he knew to be the true line of neutrality. This is necessary to be known to save Houston's reputation from the reproach of cowardice at the battle of San Jacinto. He was instructed by Jackson not to fight Santa Anna a decisive battle until he reached the front of Gaines on his pretended line, but to retreat across it, and then, if Santa Anna should pass it, Gaines was ordered to repel him by the arms of the United States. Houston was retreating under this secret understanding with General Jackson. His officers and men were anxious to fight, conscious that they were able to conquer, and were indignant when Houston, at San Jacinto, still ordered retreat. Two by two and ten by ten, they refused to retreat, and, against orders, turned to fight, Houston's motives being misunderstood. They fought and whipped the enemy, and Houston, it is said, was wounded in the tendo-Achillis by his own men. He did not order the battle, and was wounded by them under a mistake of his motives and in ignorance of his instructions. This prevented the success of deep-laid strategy.

In the House of Representatives, in the Congress of the United States, there was a vigilant observer of the contest. John Quincy Adams, of Massachusetts, had watched the contest in Texas and the pretext for the new boundary. As soon as General Jackson assailed him, he was prepared to meet the assault. He gave a bunch of keys to a colleague in the House, and told the House that when he was Secretary of State, under Mr. Monroe, he had to fix the boundary of Mexico; that he had called to his assistance General Andrew Jackson, who advised him that the true boundary was the river Sabine, and that he had caused him, Mr. Adams, to adopt that line; that there was a note or memorandum of that interview between him, Mr. Adams, and Andrew Jackson, made at the time, in his escritoire at Braintree, Massachusetts, describing it particularly; that it was in a certain bundle of papers, labeled as described by him on the floor of the House of Representatives; that he had given the keys of that escritoire to a colleague to be forwarded to a responsible gentleman in Boston, who was requested to examine the escritoire at Braintree for the paper; that its contents would show on its face that, on a certain day, he, Mr. Adams, had consulted with General Jackson as to the true boundary of Mexico, and that General Jackson's own advice had been noted, and was one of the vouchers for his, Mr. Adams's, conclusion as to the selection of the Sabine. He said that if there was no such paper found as described, or that, if found, it did not sustain his statement, he would consent to submit to the reproach cast upon him in respect to the Mexican boundary; but if such a paper was found, with the contents as stated, he would submit it as evidence that the accusation against him was false.

In due time the return to this search arrived in Washington, and fully sustained the statement of Mr. Adams. It showed his extraordinary memory and great care of memoranda. It sustained his statement beyond all ordinary tests of evidence, and he made a most triumphant speech in the House of Representatives, showing his fidelity to his country in the discharge of this duty. He had just taken his seat, when we happened to be passing it. At that time we were, personally, very friendly, and he even showed to us occasionally that we were a favorite. As we were passing, he called out, as Frederick the Great did to some distinguished general, " Come, sit by my side ; I had rather have you on my side than opposed to me."

The seat which adjoined that of Mr. Adams being for the moment vacant, we took it; and then perhaps occurred what will better illustrate the characteristic differences, or rather contrasts, of Adams and Jackson than any labored description could possibly do. Mr. Adams said, "Andrew Jackson is a bad man, and so are you !"

" I am sure, Mr. Adams, that you do not call me to your side to insult or reproach me, but rather to give me instruction. What do you mean ?"

" I mean," he said, "that you have some bad principles,—as that one man may hold another in bondage. You are bad so far as your principles are bad. But I especially mean to say that Andrew Jackson is a bad man because he has no principles at all, and is therefore worse than a man with bad principles." He then went on to say, " When I was Secretary of State, under Mr. Monroe, Andrew Jackson invaded Florida, and hung Arbuthnot and Ambrister. He was arraigned for that conduct before the Cabinet of Mr. Monroe. I alone defended his course, and put him on the high ground of international law, as expounded by Grotius, Puffendorf, and Vattel, and his conduct was justified by Mr. Monroe and by Congress. He was justified in doing right by the highest authorities on the laws of nations. On the contrary, he preferred to plead orders to do wrong, rather than rely on the authorities of the law for doing right. He published a certificate from that old dotard, Johnny Ray (of Tennessee), that he had seen and read an order from President Monroe to him, General Jackson, to invade Florida, which certificate James Monroe, on his death-bed, pronounced to be a forgery. He chose rather to rely on a forged order to do wrong than on the laws of nations to do right.    He said, 'D—n Grotius! d—n Puffendorf! d—n Vattel!—this is a mere matter between Jim Monroe and myself!'"

Jackson was the very man to d—n Grotius, Puffendorf, and Vattel; and Adams was the very man to condemn him for that above all other things as a great malefactor.    Jackson cared only for his justification; but Adams was horrified at its mode.    Jackson made law, Adams quoted it.

Thus it was that General Jackson aimed to annex Texas; but the unexpected victory of the Texans at San Jacinto disarranged his plan of doing so.

Houston's orders were to retreat; but Archer, Felix Houston, Rusk, and Wharton turned and fought, and captured Santa Anna before he reached the lines where Gaines was instructed to repel his advance upon the territory of the United States.

Annexation was thus balked by an accident of arms, and policy forbade annexation by negotiation: the chances of the successor, Mr. Van Buren, might, and probably would, thereby be defeated.    Jackson could not, in the face of the presidential election, risk the effect of that question on the North.

Mr. Van Buren had to be non-committal in order to make his election hopeful.

Thus annexation was postponed for the time.

# CHAPTER VIII.

## THE FIFTH DECADE, FROM 1830 TO 1840.

EVERY intrigue was resorted to for the promotion of Mr. Van Buren's prospects for the succession.

The Kitchen Cabinet, as it was called, had gossiped Mr. Calhoun out of favor and out of the vice-presidential chair; and the last years of General Jackson's administration were devoted to the great end of electing his successor. All the personal influence of the President, and all the magnetic influence of his patronage, were brought to bear on that one leading object. This dominant passion seemed to pervert his will and change his professions of policy and principles, and exposed his administration to every approach and reproach of venality and corruption, and the country to all their dangers. The evil was manifest at once to all his patriotic friends, who before had been his main pillars of strength.

The name highest on the list of Andrew Jackson's friends, which vouched for his ability and fidelity and for his wisdom and virtue, was that of Hugh Lawson White, the Nestor of his day in the Senate, and the Cato of his country. He had been

( 153 )

the dignified, reserved, senatorial counselor of his neighbor and early friend, and had declined every tender of office—promotion could not be conferred on him—after that old friend, under a debt of deep gratitude to him, was placed in power. Hugh L. White, the Senator from Tennessee, was, in fact, more than any other man responsible for General Jackson's "good behavior" in the Presidency. He was sincerely a true and devoted friend of General Jackson, and writhed, as a guardian over the errors of a ward, when he saw him, misled by mercenaries and aspirants, prostitute his power to his passions to defeat his political opponents, and allow his patronage to become the plunder of corruption. No honest guardian of his good faith, no honest partisan of his past policy and profession of patriotic principles, could stand this violation of pledges to integrity of administration. No man had ever been elected so distinctly on a single standpoint of preference as General Jackson had been elected against the evil example of "bargain and corruption." For him in turn to pursue his ambition to elect his successor by permitting corrupt appliances of power and patronage, was especially an unpardonable error. Every friend who loved "Rome more than Cæsar" was obliged by a duty to the country to oppose his designs and the means by which he was promoting them.

His cruel, harsh, and unjust policy of removing the Indians of Georgia west of the Mississippi, in violation of the most solemn treaties as well as of the most sacred rights of humanity; his mercenary policy of administering the public land system; his removal of the public money from the custody of the law, in favor of a combination of State pet banks; his countenance of the use of the money-power of those banks to influence the State elections, as evidenced by the "wool-clip letters" of Reuben M. Whitney, the agent of the Treasury Department; his violent disruption of the pet bank system, to be displaced by the Subtreasury scheme to subject all revenue, all fiscal control, all currency, all circulating medium, all exchange, and all public and private credit to executive dictation, were exertions of power and evidences of purpose but too obviously intended to elect his own successor, and were not to be countenanced or tolerated by honest, earnest patriots, however closely they had been allied to him as his partisans in former contests. This threw off from him all men of the type and tone of Hugh Lawson White, though it bought him "spoilers" enough to more than make up in numbers at the elections for all the honest supporters he lost. He tried all his most winning arts to retain Judge White; but the latter could not be prevailed on either to take Van Buren as a choice for the Presidency, or to countenance the example of a President electing his successor. He could not but see that the example was immoral and vicious in itself, and tended to destroy the integrity of government and the liberties of the people; that it was debasing to the public administration, and so defiled all popular elections as to destroy their freedom. The country could not be safe with such a popular idol in the presidential chair. It was threatening enough, and more than dangerous enough, in the hands of the lion; but how low and how mean would it become in the hands of jackals succeeding! The lion would never prefer a lion, — he always preferred the lower brute for a favorite; and the lower brute was not fit to be king. If a Jackson might elect his successor, the successor was sure not to be a lion,—he was naturally obliged to be a brute of a less noble nature. The election of a successor made everything bend to its baneful purpose, and all the executive departments became hideously corrupt, disordered, and dangerous. Good men of all sections began to abandon the administration and look out for some man on whom to unite in opposition to succession by dictation and corruption.

Unfortunately, they could not then combine on any one man. Judge White could not be flattered to support Mr. Van Buren, and then threats and open denunciations were resorted to, to prevent him from allowing his name to be used as that of a candidate in opposition to Mr. Van Buren. His great virtues had called attention to him as the proper candidate, for the sake of the public good; but there were aspirants everywhere, and their partisans could not or would not unite. Judge White was no aspirant, but when threats were used to intimidate him, his self-respect, pride, pluck, and patriotism, all combined to make him accept a nomination by his native State, Tennessee, in the month of October, 1835. Mr. Tyler's name was placed upon the White ticket for the Vice-Presidency in 1836; and the ticket of White and Tyler carried the State of Tennessee by ten thousand votes in that year, against the mace of Jackson and the strength of Locofocoism.

Mr. Van Buren was elected, but the glory of the Jackson Democratic Republican party had departed, and the party whose motto was, "To the victors belong the spoils," rose, to reign but one term in the Presidency.

The opposition to the succession could not be organized in 1836; but the moment Mr. Van Buren was elected, the elements opposed to him came together, casting aside all past political differences, in order to reprove corruption and reform the administration of the Federal government. Bank and anti-bank men, tariff and anti-tariff men, internal improvement and anti-internal improvement men, annexation of Texas and anti-annexation of Texas men, pro-slavery and anti-slavery men, men of all parties and political creeds, saw the necessity of combining simply upon a pure and patriotic administration of the government, which would guard the public liberties and the laws. The friends of Judge White were the last of the original friends of General Jackson of 1824 and 1828 who came out from the Jackson party; but they were still Democratic Republicans in both the popular and the State Rights sense of that term, as they had been when General Jackson was first elected. The question was, whether they — anti-bank and anti-protective tariff, anti-internal improvement by the Federal government, pro-annexation of Texas, pro-slavery, anti-Federal and anti-latitudinarian, pro-strict construction of the Constitution, and pro-State Rights Democrats of the Madisonian school — could unite with old Federalists, and all their extreme opposites in political faith, in order to crush the Van Buren party of "spoils and corruption."

The first two years of maladministration by Mr. Van Buren, from March, 1837, to March, 1839, determined the question of union or division among men of all political creeds, however variant and dissentient in their principles. They were obliged either to take sides with open corruption, and shamelessly seek a share of the spoils, or else to compromise honest differences of opinion in law and politics, and combine to save the country from the worst dangers of maladministration, the effects of corruption and decay.

The first two years of the Van Buren term were occupied in bringing the odds and ends of old parties into one combined opposition to the "spoils party." It was a new monster, without any principles, and of the worst practices, equally odious to all old parties, however they may have been opposed to one another or divided among themselves. This effort at entire reorganization and combination of old parties and factions made the years 1838 and 1839 notable in political history. The new name of Whigs, a generic name, was then for the first time adopted for the opposition.

Mr. Tyler had, in 1836, retired to private life, and dutifully labored at the bar for the support of a large family; but his fellow-citizens of Williamsburg and James City, where his residence then was, would not permit him to remain in private life. In 1838 he was again returned a delegate to the legislature, and was a member of the House of Delegates when the election of a State senator in Congress recurred in the session of 1838-39.

Mr. William C. Rives had been elected for the unexpired portion of Mr. Tyler's term when, in 1836, Mr. Tyler resigned his seat in the United States Senate. The re-election of Mr. Rives in opposition to Mr. Tyler now came up. There was the second to Mr. Benton, one of the most obnoxious instruments of expunction, arrayed against the victim of expunction, before a legislature in which Mr. Tyler's immediate friends had the balance of power, though they had not the power of election.

The Van Buren faction centered on Mr. Rives, and, to the surprise of Mr. Tyler, a portion of the Whigs were found to back his opponents. The contest continued for days of stubborn struggle and doubt. The wonder was why, after thirty-eight ballotings, neither could be elected, and the wonder still greater was, why Whigs should vote for Mr. Rives! It was solved at Washington City, among the politicians there. The Whig leaders there, Mr. Clay at their head, had coldly calculated that by re-electing Mr. Rives to the Senate, even over Mr. Tyler, they could make him their own, and that by his strength, added to that of the Whig party in Virginia, they could carry that State.

Emissaries were sent to Richmond by the Whig leaders at Washington, to carry out their scheme of treachery to Mr. Tyler. He was then in opposition to Mr. Van Buren; as an opponent of the spoils party, he had been instructed out of his seat in the Senate of the United States, because of his refusal to vote to desecrate the journal of the Senate; Mr. Rives had been found willing to do that deed, and did it; and yet two years afterwards the Whigs were found striving to re-elect Mr. Rives over Mr. Tyler,—the instrument of expunction over its victim!

Mr. Tyler was often afterwards denounced by the Whigs for various acts of treachery, but no one act with which his enemies charged him would have equaled, had the charge been true, this treacherous tergiversation of their own. They were fairly caught in the act, and in their confusion of shame at the detection, *they agreed that if Mr. Tyler's friends, who withheld Mr. Rives's election by the legislature, would yield his re-election, Mr. Tyler should be nominated on the Whig ticket for the Vice-Presidency.* That was the secret of his nomination for that office. It was agreed upon as early as 1838–39.

Mr. Tyler's friends, who had thus far defeated Mr. Rives, would not consent to vote for him, but they left their seats at last, and lessened the number of votes, so that a majority for him was obtained.

Thus was Mr. Rives re-elected to the Senate after expunction, and thus was Mr. Tyler's nomination to the Vice-Presidency secured, during the session of the Virginia legislature, before the nomination of President and Vice-President, at Harrisburg, in 1839. The particulars of that intrigue were never alluded to at the time, and have never before been made public.

It silently worked out its object of defeating Mr. Tyler, but it failed to effect its purpose of electing Mr. Rives to the Senate, and was likely to damage the hopes of the Opposition. During the ballotings the friends of Mr. Tyler discovered the design, and were indignant at the attempt. Judge John B. Christian, the brother-in-law of Mr. Tyler, becoming aware of the Whig game, wrote to a friend in Congress, inquiring whether it could be possibly true that the Whig leaders had sent their emissaries to effect such a purpose. The friend immediately addressed himself in person to Mr. Clay. He informed him of the letter and of the inquiry. At first he declined to answer, denying his responsibility for what any one was doing at Richmond in the matter of the election of senator from Virginia. The friend in turn declined to be put off in that way. He told him he knew that the report had already reached the authors of the scheme; that a certain influence had balked its success; that that influence would continue to do so until it should be finally defeated; that the design to defeat Mr. Tyler by the election of Mr. Rives, was regarded by the friends of the former as the grossest ingratitude to one who had made the sacrifice of his seat in the Senate for the good of the Opposition; that the attempt to elect Mr. Rives over Mr. Tyler, in view of the iniquity of expunction, perpetrated by the one and opposed by the other, of which the one was the instrument and the other the victim, was a breach of good faith, an instance of corruption; that, if it should be effected, it would be at the expense of the Whig party, and very damaging to Mr. Clay's prospects for the Presidency; that if the party gained any friends in consideration of Mr. Rives's election, it would lose more in consideration of Mr. Tyler's defeat; and if he, Mr. Clay, could not explain his complicity in the intrigue, Mr. Tyler's friends should be informed that their apprehensions were well founded and they would act accordingly. He at last consented to enter into explanations. He admitted that he was aware of the attempt to elect Mr. Rives; that he had been consulted as to the policy of so doing; that he had said that he preferred Mr. Tyler's election, if it could be effected, but that, if the party could not elect him, it would be politic, under the circumstances, to do the best the party could, to take Mr. Rives, or any other weapon with which to bruise the head of the serpent of Van Burenism.

The friend replied that the attempt to elect Mr. Rives on this recommendation had alone defeated the election of Mr. Tyler; that it would cause his friends to unite against the nomination of him, Mr. Clay, to the Presidency. Mr. Clay said that it was his chief desire to carry Virginia for the Opposition, and that he, for his part, would prefer to be defeated for the Presidency with the vote of his mother State in his favor, to success with her vote against him; and he had advised the election of Mr. Rives only in the event that it would be most conducive to carrying the State of Virginia for the Whig party; and if Mr. Tyler could be elected, and it was best for the party, he preferred him to Mr. Rives.

This was noted immediately in his presence, the friend commencing the reply to Judge Christian whilst sitting by Mr. Clay's side, and writing at his dictation. When the letter was finished it was read to him, and he approved of it, and from his desk it was taken to the mail. On leaving his seat the friend said to him, " Remember, Mr. Clay, this is your statement, not mine, and I send it to Judge Christian with the sole motive of saving you from the consequences of any suspicion that you are disposed to betray Mr. Tyler."

He expressed an earnest desire that the harmony of the party should not be disturbed, but he was told that he would be held responsible for its breach. The contest still went on at Richmond, and a second and a third time the friend of Mr. Tyler, at Washington, was approached with the request to advise the election of Mr. Rives.

He declined again and again, on the ground that the sin of expunction was unpardonable; that Mr. Rives had allowed himself to be its tool, and had driven Mr. Tyler from his seat in order to take the opportunity of perpetrating a gross and degrading violation of the Constitution, in subserviency to the man-worship of Jackson and the bullying of Benton. At last Mr. Clay and others appealed in such urgent terms that they were told, " The friends of Mr. Tyler will never consent to the re-election of Mr. Rives, the tool of expunction, over Mr. Tyler, its victim, until the party of the Opposition consents to place Mr. Tyler in nomination for the Vice-Presidency, so that he may, if elected, preside over his expunging opponent in the Senate."

To this arrangement Mr. Clay pledged all his influence and exertion, and immediately the friends of Mr. Tyler, at Richmond, were advised to stand out of the way of Mr. Rives, which they did. They could not be induced to vote for him, but, on the calling of the ballot which elected him, they retired from their seats, and were not counted on the ballot, and he was thus allowed to be elected by a bare majority.

Mr. Clay was warned at the time that he was agreeing to an arrangement which might throw him out of the nomination for the Presidency, for the President would hardly be nominated from Kentucky if the Vice-President were chosen from Virginia; but at that time he was not so sanguine of the party's uniting on his name, and if it did so unite, he knew that the lesser would certainly be made subordinate to the greater nomination,—the Vice-Presidency to the Presidency. But Mr. Tyler's friends took the chances, knowing the influences at work against Mr. Clay himself. Those influences developed themselves potentially in the succeeding session of Congress, in 1838–39.

Mr. Webster was undoubtedly opposed to the nomination of Mr. Clay, and his influence was more powerful in New York than it was in New England. Clay's reliance was on the West and Northwest, and he counted for success upon obtaining the influence of Judge White's friends in Tennessee and Virginia. But Judge White himself might still be a candidate. He had been run for the Presidency, in 1836, against his wish; but, having been defeated then, he might deem it his due to be run again when there was a chance of success. Mr. John Bell, the leader of the White and Tyler nomination in 1836, seeing that there was no probability of the nomination of Judge White, was anxious to have him decline in order to make way for his support

11

of Mr. Clay.  No one knew what Judge White would do as to a nomination, whether he desired or would decline it; or, if he declined or did not obtain it, whether he would support Mr. Clay.  We were at the time living at the same house with Judge White, and proud of his intimacy and confidence.  He was one of the best judges of men and things we have ever known, and one of the purest and most exalted patriots who ever served his country, always unselfishly, with a stern virtue and the strongest sense of duty, uninfluenced by fear or favor, but ever touched by the tenderest devotion and affection.  He was grave, taciturn, and laborious, always conscientiously exact, strict, and precise, and abhorred every form of deceit, injustice, or want of ingenuousness.  He committed himself rarely and slowly, but once committed he was immovable as a rock unless convinced of a wrong, and was wholly inapproachable by any indirection or circumvention.  His knowledge of the intrigues going on around him was inexplicable, and the thoughtfulness by which he discerned and resolved them almost awed one as by the presence of a seer whose prophecies were certain to be realized.  He was very thin, tall, and ghostly in appearance, but was physically very sinewy and strong, and had immense capacity for labor.  His eyes were a clear blue, but small, and so deep-set that when he drew his brows over them in thought or conversation they looked like black diamonds, scintillating various sparkling lights; and his lips were so compressed that he wore an appearance not only of firmness but also of constant restraint and self-command.  He was always terribly in earnest, yet at times enjoyed humor, such as that of the inimitable Baillie Peyton, and when he did smile, which was seldom, it was the sweetest smile we ever caught from lip or cheek of man.  He was a great and good man, without fear and without reproach.

One evening in the session of 1838–39 Mr. Clay and Mr. Bell called upon us at our room and at once opened upon their desire and purpose to ascertain whether Judge White expected to be nominated again for the Presidency, and if not, whether he would support Mr. Clay, or whom he would support. They said they came to us because we had better access to him on that subject than any of his colleagues, who desired not to seem as presuming even that he would not permit his name again to be used. They all loved him, preferred him to any other living man, but knew he could not be nominated, and therefore they felt great delicacy in approaching him on the subject. Mr. Clay desired to know his views, and, above all, desired to have his influence. We told him that there was but one way proper in which to approach Judge White. It was useless to attempt it by indirection, or by any circumlocution or circumvention. He had to be approached with the *naiveté* of a little child: one would have to go, as it were, to his knee, look up in his venerable face, with truth and innocence on one's brow, and say, "Judge White, Mr. Clay and Mr. Bell requested me to ask, Will you please stand out of Mr. Clay's way and give him your influence for the Presidency?"

Mr. Clay laughed heartily, and said that he believed honesty was the best policy with Judge White, and he left it to us to take our own way; he was certain it would not be like that of any one else. He was reminded that Judge White was not to be treated like any other man; that if diplomacy was attempted with him, he was so godlike in wisdom and so instinct with virtue that he would divine one's own thoughts before fully fit for his inspection; and that if any arts of address were used with him, he would give a look which no one would wish to meet, but not a word would be got from him. We would see him at their instance, and report in due time.

After tea one evening succeeding this interview, Judge White had retired to his room; we tapped at his door, and were at once admitted. He was at his table, as usual, arranging his papers for the night's labors, but laid everything aside upon our entrance, and, without equivoque or reserve, we told him at once the object of our visit. His face had at times very singular expressions. Whenever his attention was suddenly arrested by some important matter new to him, presenting new aspects, or revealing fully some suspected facts or truths, there would be, involuntarily as it were, a slow contraction of his brow, a close compression of his lips, and a rapid working of his nasal muscles and nostrils, with a hard and audible rapid breathing. He heard us through, as he always did everybody, and quickly this singular expression came over his countenance, and he sat breathing and musing in silence. We rose after a few moments, saying that, having discharged our mission, we would retire. He immediately arose, took us by the hand, and said, warmly, that we could not have done him a greater political favor; and Mrs. White, his good, kind wife, remarkable for her discernment, dignity, and good sense, stepped to the door and added her especial thanks.

We left him to his own reflections, confident that they would be wise and prudent; and in a few days our confidence in him was confirmed. He came, after taking his own time, to our room, and there and then explained his past course and motives, reviewed the then current political events, disclosed his own purposes and resolutions, discussed the politics and prospects of every probable candidate for the Presidency, and opened a vista of prophecy for twenty-five years of the future of the United States, which has since been so surprisingly fulfilled that we never think of him and of that conference without wonder. He reminded us how he had been compelled, by the dictation of General Jackson as to his successor, to allow his name to be used for the presidential nomination in the year 1836. He had never desired the nomination, but had been obliged to accept it, in order to resist dictation and to meet the charge that he was misrepresenting his State and her people in opposing Mr. Van Buren.

He had run, in fact, for Tennessee alone, and Tennessee had amply vindicated his course against every appeal and appliance of Andrew Jackson himself. That was sufficient for him, and he claimed no more. He said that he knew too well the aspirations and machinations of men and parties and factions at Washington, and the probability of events, not to know that *he* had no chance for another nomination, but that even if the chances for it were good, or the best, he had no desire for the Presidency. That he was then an aged man, had lost many of the most precious objects of life, was trying to make his latter days like those of a Christian about to depart to a better world, had no longer any aspirations in this world but to see his country remain free and prosperous, preferred retirement, and was preparing to die in peace, and he must not be deemed or suspected as in the way of any aspirant. That was the solution of the first problem,—he would not again accept a nomination for the Presidency. As to whom he preferred and would give his influence to, that was another question. His own political opinions were well known to all; they were those of a long lifetime, uniformly held and carried into practice in conspicuous places, State and Federal, of a protracted public service. They were consistently and persistently Democratic Republican, of the Jefferson and Madison school; State Rights and the Constitution strictly construed, limited Federal powers for the common purposes of the Union, prohibitions of certain powers to be sternly observed, and popular sovereignty guarded by constitutional laws were cardinal points of faith with him; and the good of the whole country was or should be the chief end of every patriot. Party ends were chief ends of mere partisans. He was no partisan. There was no man likely to get the nomination of the Opposition with whom he agreed in political opinions. He named several spoken of, and said there were several for whom he might be compelled to vote, as opposed to Mr. Van Buren. He abhorred him above all pretenders, who based his claim upon the spoils of party, victory, and patronage, upon appointments to office, and upon jobs to favorites. He named Mr. Webster, and regretted the jealousies rankling between him and Mr. Clay; then Mr. Clay, General Scott, and General Harrison; saying that the latter would get the nomination, and proceeding to state his reasons for the prediction.

He first disclosed to us what was afterwards called the "Triangular Correspondence." New York would control the nomination, and the cards in that State were already stocked. C——, residing in Rochester, S——, residing in Utica, and T——, residing in the city of New York, were to write to one another from the three great sections of the State during the preliminary and primary State nominations. C. to S. and T.:—

" Do all you can for Mr. Clay in your district, for I am sorry to say that he has no strength in this ;" S. to C. and T., the same ; T. to C. and S., the same ; each a professed friend of Mr. Clay, and each to be sorry for his having no chance in his district.

District A was for Clay, but the letters from B and C would show he had no chance in them.  District B was for Clay, but the letters from A and C would show he had no chance in them.  District C was for Clay, but the letters from A and B would show he had no chance in them.  A then would say, " It is useless for us to send delegates favorable to Mr. Clay, for he has no strength in B and C."  B would say the same, " for he has no strength in A and C."  C would say the same, " for he has no strength in A and B."

Thus districts or sections all favorable to Mr. Clay were made to elect delegates who were opposed to his nomination. By this contrivance Mr. Webster's friends were to obtain delegates in favor of General Scott, who was to be made the cat's-paw to defeat Mr. Clay.  But Judge White further predicted that this, whilst it would defeat Mr. Clay's nomination, would also defeat General Scott's.  Scott in this way would get the votes of the New York delegation, and this would bring down upon him the indignation of the friends of Clay.

Thus Clay and Scott would both be defeated, and a *tertium quid*, General Harrison, would probably be the nominee, and be elected.  Judge White begged us to make Mr. Clay understand and guard against this ingenious machination.  He warned him also through us to do all in his power to checkmate this plot of the New York cabal, by having the primary nominations made early in the summer of 1838, as the Triangular Correspondence needed time, and would therefore urge an excuse for postponement until after the Pennsylvania elections in the fall of that year.  But he said the warning would be idle, for the arrangements of Mr. Clay were already intrusted to parties who were co-operating with the plans of his enemies, and of this he could not be warned, because he could not be made to distrust certain of his professed friends.  The primary nominations would be postponed, and his nomination would therefore be defeated.

He regretted this, because he preferred Mr. Clay to any of the others named, yet he could not commit himself to his support, so wide apart were they in politics, unless Mr. Clay would consent to a practical concurrence with him on certain cardinal points in opposition to his heresies of theory. He said the word "Whig" was a generic term, that it was adopted expressly to embrace men of all political opinions,—Democrats and Federalists, National Republicans and old Jackson men of 1824 and 1828, bank men and anti-bank men, protective and anti-protective tariff men, pro- and anti-internal improvement men, pro- and anti-distribution of the proceeds of the sales of the public lands, pro- and anti-annexation of Texas, pro- and anti-slavery men. If Mr. Clay, whatever might be his abstract opinions as to the powers of Congress on these cardinal points, would agree to a practical course upon them, he could and would support him; otherwise he would not, unless compelled by the necessity of a choice of evils. At all events, whether he (Judge White) could support him or not at the election, he would give him his influence for the Whig nomination over any of his known and probable rivals. He illustrated his meaning of practical concurrence on various subjects of theoretical differences between them. A United States Bank to be chartered by Congress, he said, was a settled question. Practically it should be considered defunct until the changes of time or of popular opinion should demand a recharter. That the government was obliged to have a fiscal agent was true, but it was not obliged to have this form of agency. The Treasury Department could itself be organized to perform its own functions of fisc, and currency could be regulated by laws, indisputable in respect to gold and silver and their representatives of private and public credit, and the relations of local State banks could be so modified as to subserve exchange. A national bank in any form was necessarily either a danger of great magnitude or a useless contrivance, a King Stork or a King Log. It would naturally and thereafter forever be either a pet power or an ally of an Executive, and a great curse united with a popular and unscrupulous President; or it would be an antagonist of the Executive and have to be so cautious of a conflict as to be wholly inefficient. Credit, private or public, was a sensitive hot-house plant which could not sustain the storms of party and political strife, and ought never to be exposed to them if it was possible to avoid its exposure. It ought to be organized independent of party politics and their conflicts. For the Whigs to recharter the then late United States Bank would be to bring it directly into the whirlpool of party conflict. If united with the new Executive, it would be corrupting and dangerous, and if Executive power were arrayed against it, it would be made useless, as the then late conflict of Jackson with the bank had proved. True wisdom, then, as well as party policy, required that the Whigs should treat the bank issue as dead, at all events for the next presidential term, and for the future it should be "left to the arbitrament of enlightened public opinion."

On the subject of the tariff, he said that the only pledge he required of Mr. Clay was to adhere to his own plan of the Compromise Bill of 1832–33, to gradually reduce the duties on protected articles, and to approach as near as practicable to a revenue standard, by laying the duties on the unprotected articles.

On the subject of internal improvements by the general government, he demanded that appropriations should cease. The friends in Congress of internal improvements had urged appropriations for them originally, — first, to aid the Territories; secondly, to stimulate the States to construct their own public works. There was no dissension as to the power of aiding the Territories, and the States had been so stimulated to construct their respective works, that they had run into two hundred millions of State debts. Policy required a pause until a future time, when the national and State debts should be largely reduced, if not extinguished.

He utterly repudiated the distribution of the proceeds of the sales of the public lands. They should be made the safety fund to keep the army and navy in continual preparation against foreign war or domestic insurrection and rebellion, and to leave no pretext for rate of duties and imposts which would be beyond any legitimate purposes of revenue.

The annexation of Texas had been avoided during the administration of Mr. Van Buren, and Mr. Clay had already declared against the acquisition of any more territory. Judge White required a pledge on that subject, with a view to preserve the balance of power in the Union between the North and the South in respect to slavery.

As to slavery, he trusted to Mr. Clay's known views and his being a senator of a slave State. He knew he would oppose the abolition of slavery in the District of Columbia, and would do his utmost to pacify the agitation of the whole subject of abolition. He required pledges on five cardinal points only, and said that though Mr. Clay was a latitudinarian and the great leader of the American system, yet, if he would commit himself to a practical course on the subjects named, he would give him his influence for the nomination and for his election.

This conference was fully and faithfully reported by us to Mr. Clay, and he did distinctly make the pledges required of him by Judge White. He emphatically indorsed his views in respect to the recharter of the United States Bank, the tariff for protection, and the subject of internal improvements.

This, in turn, was reported to Judge White, and he then urged the importance of having a Democratic Republican and Strict Construction candidate put upon the ticket of the Vice-Presidency, as the Vice-President might have the casting vote of the Senate. John Tyler was the man he preferred; he had been consistent throughout his whole life; had been nominated on the ticket with him in 1836; had been expunged from the Senate; and the pledge had already been made to place his name on the ticket for the Vice-Presidency in order to elect Mr. Rives to the Senate in 1838.

Alas! already the same fate was ordained for Judge White himself. He had offered his resignation to the Governor of Tennessee in the fall of 1838 on account of bad health, but it was refused. The legislature of Tennessee became Locofoco in the winter of 1839, and at once set about instructing Judge

White out of his seat in the Senate. They passed certain instructions to him, and among others was one to vote in favor of the "Sub-Treasury." At once he responded in a letter, of September 5, 1839, characterized by his purity and wisdom, and causing them to immolate him on the altar of party sacrifice. On the 13th of January, 1840, the Sub-Treasury bill was called up in the Senate, when Judge White addressed the Senate in his own vindication and read his letter of reply to the legislature of Tennessee. It is a master-piece of calm logic, and honest, proud defense; and when its reading was finished he bade the Senate a feeling and dignified farewell. He followed Mr. Tyler's example; he could not obey, but recognized the right of instruction, and resigned. Thus the nation lost its highest exemplar of wisdom, honesty, and purity in public service; and on the 17th of January, 1840, a large concourse of senators, representatives, and private citizens manifested their sense of his worth and of the Senate's loss by a dinner given him in Washington City as a last mark of affectionate respect.

In his speech at that dinner he confirmed what we have here related. His predictions had been fulfilled. The Triangular Correspondence had been successful: the convention to nominate a President and Vice-President had been postponed until after the Pennsylvania elections; the friends of Mr. Webster had used General Scott's name to defeat the nomination of Mr. Clay, and General Scott's nomination was defeated in turn by that of General Harrison, in the fall of 1839. Mr. Clay had been fully warned of the machinations to defeat him, and would not give credence to the friendly caution. He would hardly credit the device and its success to the last. In the very hour of his defeat he was sitting in a room at Brown's Hotel, anxiously waiting to hear of his nomination. He made most singular exhibitions of himself in that moment of ardent expectancy.

He was open and exceedingly profane in his denunciations of the intriguers against his nomination. We had taken two Whig friends of our district to see him; and after they had sat some time listening to him, in utter surprise at his remarks, full of

the most impudent, coarse crimination of others, in words be-
fitting only a bar-room in vulgar broil, of a sudden he stopped,
and turning to the two gentlemen, who were dressed in black
and both strangers to him, he said, "But, gentlemen, for aught
I know, from your cloth you may be *parsons*, and shocked at
my words. Let us take a glass of wine." And, rising from his
seat, he walked to a well-loaded sideboard, at which, evidently,
he had been imbibing deeply before we entered.

Thereupon we bowed and took leave. One of the gentlemen,
after retiring, remarked, "That man can never be my political
idol again;" and from that time to this he has ceased to admire
him. In a short time after that he (Mr. Clay) went across the
Avenue to the parlor of his boarding-house, where he awaited
the arrival of two of his personal friends, on the night of the
nomination at Harrisburg, to bring him the news of the final
proceedings and choice of the Whig Convention.

We went to the depot and got the intelligence of the nomination of General Harrison and Mr. Tyler, and hastened back to
him with the news. Such an exhibition we never witnessed
before, and we pray never again to witness such an ebullition
of passion, such a storm of desperation and curses. He rose from
his chair, and, walking backwards and forwards rapidly, lifting
his feet like a horse string-halted in both legs, stamped his steps
upon the floor, exclaiming, "My friends are not worth the
powder and shot it would take to kill them!" He mentioned
the names of several, invoking upon them the most horrid im-
precations, and then, turning to us, approached rapidly, and
stopping before us, with violent gesture and loud voice, said,
"If there were two Henry Clays, one of them would make the
other President of the United States!"

Trying to bring him to his senses, we replied, "If there were
*two* Henry Clays, the continent would not be large enough to
hold them, and they would not leave a morsel of each other;
they would mutually destroy themselves. You were warned
by Judge White of this result, when it might have been prevented, but you would not take heed!"

"Ah, yes," said he; "you and my old friend Judge White

are like the old lady 'who knew the cow would eat up the grindstone.' It is a diabolical intrigue, I now know, which has betrayed me. I am the most unfortunate man in the history of parties: always run by my friends when sure to be defeated, and now betrayed for a nomination when I, or any one, would be sure of an election."

From that time forward, through the sessions of '39, '40, '41, '42, '43, '44, as long as we remained in the House of Representatives, up to February, 1844, Mr. Clay was excessively intemperate in his habits, and more intemperate in exacerbation of temper and in his political conduct. His scene with General Scott at a whist-table in Boulanger's restaurant, and with Mr. Choate in the Senate-chamber, were but instances of his desperation and of his spite towards those who had defeated his nomination. He at times was inapproachable by his friends, and his foes chuckled at his self-immolation. At once there arose an implacable war, open and declared, between him and Mr. Webster. That enmity divided the Whig party into two factions, on no difference of opinion or principles at all, but purely on personal preferences and partisan predilections. Mr. Webster, it was thought by Mr. Clay's friends, was paving his way for the succession to General Harrison, and it was obvious that Mr. Webster was to have the control of General Harrison's administration.

The defeat of Mr. Clay and the nomination of General Harrison by Mr. Webster's friends, at Harrisburg, determined that programme of the Whig party, even before the election in the fall of 1840, and certainly before the inauguration of the President elect in the spring of 1841.

We must not forget the two great strides of the physical in this marked decade, from 1830 to 1840, — the Telegraph of Morse, and the "Marine Catapulta" of Commodore James Barron, in 1836, from the model of which the idea of the "beaked iron-clad Virginia" was derived.

We presided over the Committee of Naval Affairs in the room at the Capitol, in which Morse had his battery and his isolated wire to demonstrate his discovery, and where Barron exhibited his model of the Catapulta. From that model we, in 1861, from "Rolliston," in the county of Princess Anne, Virginia, suggested to General Lee, by letter, the plan of an invulnerable floating battery, from which the Merrimack was converted into the Virginia. They both have proved how mind can make one material monster overcome and destroy another

# CHAPTER IX.

## THE SIXTH DECADE, FROM 1840 TO 1850.

Campaign of 1840—Tippecanoe and Tyler too—Personations of the Divisions of the Whig Party—Tyler's expressed Opinions during the Canvass—Dismemberment of the Whig Party before General Harrison's Inauguration—General Harrison's Health and Death—Scenes at Washington City—Harrison's Cabinet—"Tyler too" President—What he had to do—The Harrison Cabinet retained—Mr. Tyler's Speech as Vice-President—His "Address to the People of the United States," and his First Message—Fiscal Bank—Veto—Fiscal Corporation—Ewing's Bill—Mr. Clay's Pledges broken—Why—The Ewing, Sergeant, and Berrien Committee's Interview with Mr. Tyler—Mr. Rives's Plan of evading Constitutional Scruples—Mr. Clay's Object to force a Veto—Veto Second—Mr. Tyler's Integrity assailed—His Firmness—Conditions of Peace tendered to him—Mr. Clay inexorable—Congress implacable—The Harrison Cabinet dissolved—Mr. Webster remains with his Credentials in Favor of Mr. Tyler—Disposition to deprive Mr. Tyler of a Cabinet by not confirming any of his Nominees—The First Tyler Cabinet.

THE political campaign of 1840 was in all respects the most memorable ever known to party annals in this country. The *éclat* of General Jackson's name made Mr. Van Buren's election, but could not maintain his administration ; it was crushed by its corruption, and the commingling of all elements of the Opposition. Democratic and National Republicans, Federalists and State Rights partisans, strict constructionists and latitudinarians, Jackson men and Adams men, Clay men and Calhoun men,—all, in a word, united under the motto of " The union of the Whigs for the sake of the Union," and made, in the language of the celebrated orator of Baltimore, John V. L. McMahon, a perfect " avalanche of the people."

The enthusiasm attending the reception of Lafayette in Baltimore in 1824 was not greater than that attending the Convention in 1840 of that city to ratify the nomination of " Tippecanoe

( 174 )

and Tyler too." Raccoon-skins, and log cabins with the latch-strings out, were carried in procession through the land, and General Harrison was elected overwhelmingly by a *feu de joie!* But Mr. Clay, like Achilles, retired to his tent. He chafed under the preference over him of a military chieftain. It was not a military chieftain who was preferred, but Mr. Webster's will had prevailed against him. But the feeling and causes which operated in 1840 were not like those which had operated previously in making Richard M. Johnson Vice-President; it was not a Pop Emmons argument of—

"Rumpsey, Dumpsey,
Colonel Johnson killed Tecumseh."

The feeling was of a sound moral tone, and the leading men of all sects and sections, and the intelligence of the country, united to reform abuses of government and to crush corruption. The motto for every flag was,—

"Tippecanoe!
And Tyler too!"

And in this there was a pointed meaning, intended and expressed. General Harrison was denounced by some as a Federalist, who favored broad and unlimited powers in the Federal government, and for the preference of partisans of that faith he was proposed; but John Tyler was known to be a Democrat and Strict Constructionist of the straitest sect, and to men of that faith he was proposed. In other words, the ticket was expressly intended for

"National Republicans in Tippecanoe,
And Democratic Republicans in Tyler too."

This was known to all well-informed politicians.

Mr. Tyler was put into the Vice-Presidency by the friends of State Rights and strict construction, avowedly for the purpose of casting any tie vote in the Senate of the United States in their favor. During the canvass of 1840 his opponents in the North, hoping to injure his ticket in Pennsylvania, addressed to him calls for his avowals, and he made them without reserve when he could do so with proper self-respect; and if any of his opinions were withheld from the public they were not withheld by himself, but by the leading counselors of the Whig party at Washington City, and they withheld them on the ground that his opinions were universally known to the party and the country to be Democratic Republican and that the calls for them were in bad faith, not to found conclusions upon, but to array votes against him. His opinions were fully known at the Harrisburg Convention, by men who were acquainted with the whole course and tenor of his long political career. He did not commit himself to a Federal party or Federal opinions by accepting the nomination, but the Whig party committed itself to Democratic principles and selected a Democrat to guard them. Even General Harrison had denied the charge of Federalism brought against himself, and pledged himself to strict construction, especially on the Bank question.*

In 1822 and in 1836, General Harrison, in his speeches in the Cincinnati district, in a letter to Judge Berrien, and in a speech at Vincennes, had fully expressed his political opinions; and during the canvass of 1840, his speech at Dayton and his letter to Sherrod Williams committed him to Democratic measures and to strict construction of the Constitution as to the bank, a protective tariff, the expediency of internal improvements by the Federal government, and the veto. As to Mr. Tyler's part, he was too thoroughly committed by the whole of his political course to be doubted; but he was interrogated with scrutinizing opposition, and in every possible form referred to his votes from 1812 to 1813, and from 1832 to 1840, on the right of instruction and the duty of obedience, on the bank and veto, on his casting vote in the Senate upon the latter question, on a protective tariff, internal improvement, and abolition of slavery in the District of Columbia. In his reply to certain citizens of Henrico County, Virginia, Tilmon E. Jeter, Philip

---

* See chapter viii. of his Life, by Abell.

Mayo, and others, dated October 16, 1840, he was explicit in adhering to his past course of opposition to those measures by the Federal government. These answers were repeated in his published letter of the 5th of October, 1840, saying in relation to the bank, " My opinion of the power of Congress to charter a bank remains unchanged" (from opinions acted upon by him in 1819 and in 1832). Again, in a letter to Democratic citizens of Pittsburg, he reiterated his unyielding opposition to the recharter of the bank. He wrote, during the session of 1839–40, from Williamsburg, saying that a meeting of the Democrats of Pittsburg, Pennsylvania, had demanded of him whether he would in any event sanction the incorporation of a United States Bank. He inclosed their proceedings and resolutions, and also his reply, to Washington City, with instructions to submit his reply to the leading members of the Whig party, for *them* to determine whether it should be forwarded and published or not. After examining the right of all citizens to call for his sentiments on public questions, and claiming that the object of such calls should always be to cause the electors to cast their votes intelligently, by enlightening them as to the true opinions of candidates, he expressed the opinion which he ever entertained, " that a Bank of the United States was unconstitutional," and declared that he would not sanction the incorporation of one without an alteration of the Constitution. He then emphatically asked whether, if these were their own sentiments, they would maintain them by voting for him at the polls, or whether it was their object to divide the Whig party by publishing them to the country.

This reply was submitted to the leading Whigs in Congress, and they decided that it would be impolitic to publish it; that Mr. Tyler's opinions were already too well known, through his speeches and votes, to need a response, and that it would be unwise to array them directly against the opinions of many Whigs, perhaps a majority of the party, who were in favor of a bank.

Thus the leaders of the Whig party confessed their *scienter* of what his course would be, and decided that his opinions were too well known to leave a pretext for the charge that he had practiced any concealment or deception. This was after the nomination and before the election. The Whig leaders all knew what he would do. But a large portion of the Whig party, especially the Whig State Convention in Virginia, proclaimed, in their address at Richmond, the exact opinions of Democracy,—State Rights, strict construction, anti-bank and anti-internal improvement and anti-protective tariff, and out-and-out the Democratic Republican tenets,—and pledged General Harrison as well as Mr. Tyler to their profession of political faith. Mr. James Lyons, an eminent lawyer, and a visitor of William and Mary, now living, was the author of the address of the Whig Convention of 1840; and that address speaks for itself.

Thus the opinions of Mr. Tyler were well and fully known to be those of his whole past life, and the Whig party, so far as he was concerned, indorsed them by the Whig Convention and by the election in 1840. There was no rational pretext, no moral excuse whatever, for accusing him afterwards of treachery to the party in being true to himself and his ever-cherished Democratic principles. The party, on the contrary, was treacherous to him, but, instead of crushing him, became divided against itself, and fell *felo de se.*

The election of 1840, we repeat, was decisive; it overwhelmed Van Burenism and the spoils; but then immediately the victorious party became dismembered. It had in itself the seeds of destruction. It was composed, as we have seen, originally of men of every shade of political opinion, and the old Federal element of National Republicanism, the Adams and Clay Whigs, being in the majority, thought it had the right to dictate and prescribe the principles and policy of the administration. But the men who composed that element were divided into the Clay and Webster factions. Mr. Webster was willing to abide by the status of the Opposition before the nomination and election, but Mr. Clay was bent on pressing upon him the extreme measures of the National Republican school,—bank, tariff, and all. This was the motive of the war at first: it was aimed at Mr. Webster rather than at Mr. Tyler. As Mr. Clay was not nominated, he seemed to consider himself absolved from all the committals he had made to Judge White ; and whether he so considered himself or not, or was so absolved or not, he certainly violated all committals he had made practically to adhere to the Democratic policy and principles. Judge White's speech at the dinner given him, on his retirement from the Senate, at Washington, January 17, 1840, alluded to these pledges of Mr. Clay in a way which he and we understood perfectly well. Judge White then said, "Since the respective parties have agreed upon their candidates (Van Buren and General Harrison), I have, among you, said nothing as to whom I should prefer. Upon this subject I do not wish to be non-committal. Neither of the gentlemen named would have been my choice. I would greatly have preferred the distinguished gentleman from Kentucky now near me." (Mr. Clay bowed ; the whole company arose as by one impulse, and gave three deafening cheers. Judge White proceeded : "Upon some subjects he and I did not agree ; but upon some points I disagree with the present chief magistrate also. Most of these points have now ceased to be *practical.* Upon the great subjects now practical I coincide heartily with that gentleman (Mr. Clay), and disagree with the present incumbent. Had he continued a candidate, I would have given him a cordial support."

Mr. Clay himself knew to what Judge White alluded in these remarks, and so did we, as has already been explained. He had committed himself *in limine* to the principles proclaimed in the Whig address of Virginia, drafted by Mr. Lyons. Practically, he himself, if he had been nominated, was to have been "antibank" and Democratic. But, defeated for the nomination, he thought himself again free to press upon his adversaries impracticable issues, and the blows which he aimed at Mr. Webster were caught on the bosses of the buckler of John Tyler.

After the election in 1840, the *disjecta membra* of the Whig party rushed pell-mell to Washington, every man with a raccoon's tail in his hat, and tugged at the string of the latch, out at the White House door, as if sure enough it was a log cabin.

General Harrison himself got to the capital some months before his inauguration, and it cost him his life. He was very infirm, and the excitement was too great for him. He yielded to the " vulgar crowd," was elated by their pressure upon him, and literally sank under a total derangement of his nervous system.

Mr. Tazewell, of Norfolk, had predicted the event of his death, playfully commenting upon the unparalleled luck of Mr. Tyler; but sadly he might have foreseen the speedy fulfillment of his prophecy if he had been in Washington a week after General Harrison's arrival there. He would have seen him in a high state of exaltation, and agitated to a degree which could not but break him down physically and mentally. We witnessed scenes at and before the inauguration of 1841 which it is to be hoped will never be described by either biography or history.

The mode of forming the Cabinet made some shocking revelations, and, in one of the scenes which brought us into immediate contact with General Harrison and the delegations in Congress from the Southeastern States, it was our duty to keep a diary and make a report, which shall never be published, touching the appointments in General Harrison's Cabinet.

The signs of the dismemberment of the Whig party were apparent, and ought to have warned it not to ride like a beggar who had just got a horse to ride. We urged the party watchword of the " Union of the Whigs for the sake of the Union." But no; they were then in power by a hurrah of the people; they, the old-line Whigs or National Republicans of Adams and Clay, had a majority of the party, ruled the caucus, the caucus should rule the party, and the party should rule the country! This rallied the State Rights men and Democrats of the party, of whom Mr. Tyler was one, and we prepared to resist the rush of the host of Federalism which we saw thronging around the new President. Heaven saved him from the fate of Actæon; for, had he lived until Congress met, he would have been devoured by the divided pack of his own dogs.

He was inaugurated on the 4th of March, 1841, and one month thereafter, on the 4th of April, he was a corpse, dying "full of years and full of honors." The Tippecanoe part was gone, but the "Tyler too" part of the Whig party was, by the act of God, left in power. The party was pledged to "Tyler too," but time showed how its leaders kept their faith to him and made good their professions before the election. They scouted their own proclamations and programmes; the majority of the party turned to the Federalism of National Republicanism, and demanded that Mr. Tyler should desert his lifelong faith of Democracy and strict construction, and sanction both a national bank and a protective tariff, and a wilder system of internal improvements than had ever before been dreamed of, until the Northwest got so strong that no party could offer resistance to its demoralizing clamor for appropriations of the public lands. Traitorous to their own nomination, traitorous to Mr. Tyler, with a full *scienter* of what he was pledged to do both before and after his nomination for the Vice-Presidency, the very moment that he became President they forced upon him measures which they knew he could not conscientiously or consistently sanction, and then cried out, "Traitor! traitor!" But we are anticipating.

Immediately after the inauguration of General Harrison we had gone home to the Eastern Shore of Virginia. At the Northampton Circuit Court we heard of the death of General Harrison, and immediately hurried to Washington.

Mr. Tyler needed counsel as to the dangers which environed him. The most momentous questions of public policy were coming upon the administration; the Cabinet had not been appointed by himself, was not intimate with his own political or personal views, and was divided against itself. The great Northeastern question threatened our relations with Great Britain; the question of annexing Texas was fast approaching; the question of land distribution was up for consideration; fiscal relations had to be newly formed; daily the subject of abolition became more and more threatening; and not only was the Cabinet divided between the Webster and the Clay faction, but it was too clear not to be guarded against that Mr. Tyler's Democratic Republican sentiments were necessarily to be brought into collision with the Federalism of the majority of the Whig party. He was advised at once to form a new Cabinet, to hasten a settlement with Great Britain, and, with that view, to retain Mr.

Webster at the head of the new Cabinet, to annex Texas as soon
as possible, to veto any recharter of a United States Bank, any
tariff for protection, and any bill for the distribution of the proceeds of the sale of the public lands. He concurred in every
proposition except that of dismissing the then existing Cabinet.
He was told that he would be obliged to do it at last, and that
it would be most peaceful and politic to do it at once. But his
disposition was always for conciliation, and he dreaded to offend
any one as much as Uncle Toby did to hurt a fly. He endeavored to win the Cabinet by giving its members his confidence,
forgetting that one half of it, for Mr. Clay, was watching the
other half, for Mr. Webster. The Cabinet could not have been
kept together in harmony under General Harrison had he lived.
But it was retained by Mr. Tyler, and the apprehended consequences followed.

On the 17th of March, 1841, General Harrison had issued a
proclamation convening Congress on the 31st of the following
May, to consider sundry weighty and important matters, "principally growing out of the condition of the revenue and finances
of the country."

On the 4th of March, 1841, Mr. Tyler, as Vice-President,
appeared, qualified, and took his seat as President of the Senate,
and in the address which he uttered was heard distinct and
clear the ring of the old Democratic faith which he and his father
before him had ever cherished. His definition of the true con-
servatorial character of the Senate, and of the duties devolving
upon it under the Constitution, as the representative of States,
to carry out *their sovereign will* by which the Federal government had been spoken into existence,—the *equality* of *States* in
this *Confederacy*, "guardians of the institutions established by
the fathers against popular impulse or executive encroachments,
holding the balance in which are weighed the powers conceded
to the Federal government and the *rights reserved to the* States
and the people,"—his prophecy that if ever faction should
seize the Senate, and it should forget its duties, "then would
our political institutions be made to topple to their foundations,"
—and his appeal for "liberty intrenched in safety behind the

sacred ramparts of the Constitution,"—all showed to which part of the Whig party he belonged, and that in becoming a Whig in opposition to Van Burenism he had not ceased to be what he had ever been, a Democratic, Strict Construction, State Rights, Constitution-loving Republican. His very first effort was an appeal against Federalism and for a faithful adherence to the Constitution, and he had repeatedly spoken and voted against violating the Constitution by chartering a Bank of the United States. Thus he was committed from first to last in his political course, when, by the act of God, he was called to take the Presidency. And thus committed to principles, and placed in power, he met the Congress. Before the Congress assembled, he had published an "Address to the People of the United States." He appealed to them to sustain the "wisdom and sufficiency of our institutions under the new test" of the office of President for the first time devolved upon a Vice President.

It was an opportunity for faction to operate and effect great mischief, and he pledged himself to the people "understandingly to carry out the principles of that Constitution which he had sworn to protect, preserve, and defend." He would guard against the concentration of power in his hands, and preserve a "complete separation between the sword and the purse" of the nation. He deprecated the patronage of office to control and keep the public moneys in the hands of the Executive. He deprecated also a public debt in time of peace, and urged economy in the public expenditure, with a view to the smallest revenue to be exacted by taxation only for objects of absolute usefulness and necessity. He urged that all war between the government and the currency of the country should cease. He declared his opposition to the then existing measures of finance, the Sub-Treasury, and recommended their repeal. He promised his sanction to "any constitutional measure which, originating in Congress, should have for its object the restoration of a sound circulating medium," but suggested no measure of his own, because he thought financial and fiscal measures should originate in the Congress. At the same time, he expressly warned the people and the Congress that "in deciding upon the adaptation of any such measure to the end proposed, as well as its conformity to the Constitution, he would resort to the fathers of the *great Republican school* for advice and instruction to be drawn from their sage views of our system of government and the light of their ever-glorious example."

This was directly saying that he would not sanction a bank charter.

Every one knew what were the doctrines of "the fathers of the great Republican school," what he had said and voted during a long congressional and legislative career, and what he had published and repressed before and during the canvass for the Presidency. To demand of him to sign a United States Bank charter was to ask him to sacrifice the symmetrical consistency of his whole public life, violate every pledge which he had made to the people, and break the oath which he had taken to "protect, preserve, and defend" the Constitution of the United States. Yet the Whig leaders, knowing all this, did make that demand upon his conscience and self-respect, and cried out, "Traitor! traitor!" upon him, because he would not consent to be forsworn!

Not only did his address to the Senate and his address to the people of the United States indicate a veto of any United States Bank charter, but his first message to Congress, June 1, 1841, disclosed expressly his antagonism to a United States Bank, to the State banks, and to the Sub-Treasury, each and all, as fiscal agents of the government. As to the first, he distinctly informed Congress that he regarded the people as having sustained the veto; as to the second, it had signally failed; and as to the third, the very last election by the people had decided that it should be overthrown and something better' than either system be substituted by Congress. What that substitute should be, must be left to Congress, as belonging to the legislative province.

He promised to concur in such a system as Congress might propose, "expressly reserving to himself, however, the *ultimate power of rejecting any measure which might, in his view of it, conflict with the Constitution*, or otherwise jeopard the prosperity of the country; a power which he could not part with even if he would, but which he would not believe any act of Congress would call into requisition."

Thus warned, and thus appealed to, not to press any measure upon his power to veto, the Congress held the cup of a " fiscal bank" to his lips, and endeavored to make him drink its very dregs, and, failing in that, made him endure all the bitterness of unjust and unmitigated abuse for exercising a virtuous constancy with a Roman firmness, which should have excited naught but respect and admiration.

But there was a double mistake made in respect to the character of the man. One faction of his enemies, really desiring a bank charter, supposed he was wanting in nerve, and that he would be afraid to meet the odium of those of his party who clamored for a bank; and the other faction, Mr. Clay at its head, fearing that he might succeed in having submitted to him a constitutional measure to manage the fisc, the currency, and the revenue better than any system yet tried, and that he might be a favorite in the election of 1844, were determined to extort from him a veto of a United States Bank charter, in order to make him odious to a majority of the Whigs. And if they did not fear the rivalry of Mr. Tyler, they did fear that of the chief of his Cabinet, Mr. Webster. They were afraid of one or both; and therefore Mr. Clay chose to forget his pledge to Judge White, to "abide by the arbitrament of an enlightened public opinion," which had signally sustained General Jackson's veto of a United States Bank charter.

Mr. Tyler had submitted the measure to Congress, and the Senate called upon Mr. Ewing, the Secretary of the Treasury, to present a plan by means of which the fiscal concerns of government might be managed and the currency of the country regulated. Mr. Tyler had submitted no plan of his own to Congress, for the reasons already stated, but formed a general outline of a measure which, while restricted to the special purposes of the fisc, would, without being a bank with power of discount, regulate the exchange, check the over-issuing of the State banking system, regulate currency, and protect the public credit and finances and revenue against the dreaded fluctuations and shocks of the money-market and of commerce; and this plan was within the powers expressly granted of coining money and regulating the value thereof, and of regulating commerce between the United States and foreign nations, and between the several States. In a word, his idea was that of an exchequer, of purely governmental use and purpose of the fisc and of revenue, incidentally only regulating the standard of value for private and individual trade and commerce. These views he presented to Mr. Ewing, who faithfully consulted the President, the Cabinet, and the best minds in the Congress and in the country. He presented his plan, which, however it may have been objectionable to Mr. Tyler, was never fairly considered. It was smothered in a committee, and a charter for a national bank, under the name and style of a "Federal Bank," was passed, and vetoed by the President. The veto treated the measure as one proposing the recharter of the United States Bank. Mr. Clay had obtained the desired veto, and sought to adjourn and make up the issue of bank or no bank; but the devotees of the recharter of the bank resisted his movements, and endeavored to circumvent the President's objections by another mode of disguising their favorite measure.

They called the thing by another name, that of "Fiscal Corporation," and affected to make it conform to an exchequer,—to something created by government for its own uses alone, those of finance and revenue. Every attempt was made to persuade and drive Mr. Tyler into the sanction of this modification. They rated his intellect so low as to suppose that the name "*bank*" was his dread, and that his scruples might be overcome by adopting the term "corporation"—not regarding the distinction as a weight against their wishes. The power of incorporation was the very power which he denied. The government might act by officers, appointed or elected, or by agents already created or existing, or might exercise its legitimate, granted powers by them; but could it *create* agencies to combine political powers and uses with individual and private powers and uses? That was what, from the first Cabinet of Washington, had been debated between statesmen, down to the year 1841.

Thus, relying upon Mr. Tyler's supposed softness and pliancy, the name of "Fiscal Corporation" was adopted by the friends of the bank in this last effort to obtain a charter. So far as constitutional principles were concerned, there was, in fact, no difference between the two measures. A caucus committee of several eminent men, among whom were Mr. John Sergeant, of the House of Representatives, and Mr. Berrien, of the Senate, was appointed to confer with Mr. Ewing, the Secretary of the Treasury, and with the President, on this measure.

In the mean time Mr. Rives, who had sustained Mr. Tyler's first veto, brought his influence to bear upon the consideration of the second or Fiscal Corporation bill. Mr. Rives had formed a theory of creating a bank for the District of Columbia, under the local power of Congress over the district, making it the central and controlling depository of the public money, and enabling it to exercise all the influence of the other plans upon exchange and currency, on the principle settled in the case of the Bank of Augusta (Ga.) against Earle.

His arguments and persuasions for awhile staggered Mr. Tyler, so far as to cause the President to call some select friends to meet Mr. Rives in conference with him as to Mr. Rives's plan of gratifying the Whigs by a measure reconcilable with constitutional requirements.

Mr. Rives was exceedingly cautious in opening his views at this conference, but at last gradually explained them fully before any remark was made or any objection was urged against them. Mr. Tyler was strongly impressed by the ingenious plan of Mr. Rives; and this occurring at the time when Mr. Ewing, Mr. Sergeant, and Mr. Berrien were waiting upon the President to ascertain how, if at all, the first bill might be remodeled and modified into a second which would obtain his sanction, the President did attempt to reconcile the plan of Mr. Rives with that of the Secretary of the Treasury as changed by Mr. Sergeant. It was at this precise juncture that the misunderstanding occurred between Mr. Tyler on the one part, and Mr.

Ewing, Mr. Sergeant, and Mr. Berrien on the other part, as to
what modifications would meet the President's approval.   This
result was apprehended, from what was known of the bill drafted
by Mr. Sergeant and of the plan of Mr. Rives.   We knew that
the President would submit for consideration by the Whig committee the compromising modifications suggested by Mr. Rives,
and that they could not be reconciled with scruples as to the
power of Congress to incorporate a bank.   It was not a question
of mere " discount and deposit," but one of constitutional power
of incorporation ; and a " fiscal corporation" was a very different
thing from a local bank of the District of Columbia, with the
resulting power of exchange.   As soon as the committee left,
Mr. Tyler communicated to us the result of his interview with
them,—Messrs. Ewing, Sergeant, and Berrien.   He informed
us that he had submitted to them certain modifications, founded
on the suggestions of Mr. Rives, and that they were to draw a
bill in conformity thereto, and to submit the draft to him, as a
plan of compromise.   We assured him that such was not the
understanding of Mr. Sergeant ; his idea was that the President would be content with much less modification than that
which he really intended.   Mr. Sergeant, who had charge of
the second bill, would insist on the power of incorporating
banking privileges coextensive with the United States ; and
with that as a foundation principle, he, the President, notwithstanding the details of modifications, would at last be called
on to yield his scruples as to the constitutional power of Congress to create a bank.   The President was surprised that any
one who had conferred with him could mistake his views or resolves in respect to the question of power.   We assured him
that the Whig leaders were determined to have the power conceded by him, or to force upon him the odium of a veto ; that
Mr. Clay desired the latter, in order to remove both him and
Mr. Webster from all rivalry for the next presidential term,
and that his leading friends, Mr. Sergeant especially, cared
more for the concession of power to create a United States
Bank than they did even for the success of their favorite
candidate for the Presidency, Mr. Clay ; that Mr. Sergeant

would insist on the concession of power to have the bill approved, whilst Mr. Clay would insist upon it to have the bill vetoed; that to incorporate a bank would be to violate the pledges and committals of the Whig party and of himself for his lifetime; but, if he had modified or changed his views, we urged upon him in that case to follow the example of Mr. Madison, in 1816,—to waive all constitutional scruples and to sign an efficient charter; that it was not less impolitic than inconsistent to approve of any "mongrel scheme" like that even of Mr. Rives, and the "Fiscal Corporation" bill was nothing but a United States Bank in disguise, as to every constitutional objection to it, whilst it was encumbered by provisions seemingly only to avoid the question of constitutionality, which would make it inefficient; that if he would sign an act of incorporation at all, he would do himself most justice by signing an efficient charter which would be most useful both to the government and to the country. He concurred fully in these views, and requested us to see Mr. Sergeant at once and to say to him he wished him explicitly to understand that he would sign no bill which conceded the power in Congress to create a national bank in any form,—that he would accede to any plan which might be agreed upon within the pale of the Constitution, but that he would not be held committed to the bill of the "Fiscal Corporation" unless it was modified so as to remove the constitutional objections. This was on the day before the bill was submitted to the House of Representatives, and on that day the message of the President was delivered to Mr. Sergeant. He was informed fully of the President's views, and they were explained to him distinctly,—that he did not wish to be considered as committed to the bill which Mr. Sergeant had in charge, and, if he was so understood, he desired the mistake to be corrected before it was reported; that he could not consent to sign the bill in the form in which it was last presented to him. Mr. Sergeant received the message without uttering a word of comment; he simply acknowledged its receipt, made no inquiries, bowed, and went to his committee.

The next morning the "Fiscal Corporation" bill was reported

by him to the House, and was immediately acted upon without debate.    He himself was not allowed to explain fully the reasons for changing the title of the bill from "Fiscal Bank" to "Fiscal Corporation" before the hammer of the Speaker fell upon the debate, and the bill was rushed through both Houses. Then the war upon Mr. Tyler became appalling: he was dared, as it were, not only to withstand the clamors of the Federal Whigs for the United States Bank, but to go counter to the understanding he had had, as was alleged, with Messrs. Ewing, Sergeant, and Berrien.   John Tyler's intelligence and integrity were then tried to the uttermost, and he proved himself firm as truth itself to the Constitution, looking fully in the face dangers enough to appall any man not fortified by virtue, as he was, and which assailed his personal honor and veracity as a man, as well as blasted every political hope he may have had in the party which elected him.   The bill was passed on the 4th of September, 1841, and on the 9th of the same month he returned it with his second veto.

He paused for consultation, but had no Cabinet advisers who concurred with him.   He had to confer with friends outside of his Cabinet, and, after a final conference, instructed a friend, who was familiar with all his views and all the facts as to the preparation of the second bill, to prepare his second veto, which was done in his presence, and which, with but few modifications by himself, is that now among the public archives.   The veto thus prepared was then submitted to the Cabinet.   He expressed the most anxious solicitude to meet the wishes of Congress, avoiding all constitutional objections; he deplored the want of time to submit a definite recommendation of his own, and had occupied his mind in the most anxious attempt to conform his action to the legislative will; and he most respectfully submitted, in a spirit of harmony, that the measure should not at that time be pressed upon him, but that the whole subject should be postponed to a more auspicious period for deliberation.   While this veto message was being considered, he received an intimation from the Whig leaders that if he would not disturb any member of his Cabinet, the bill might be postponed to the regular session of

Congress. One member of the Cabinet who retired, did not desire to do so, and complained that he was forced to retire by the personal demands and influence of Mr. Clay. At a meeting of the members of the Cabinet, all except Mr. Webster, to determine upon their course, Mr. Clay was present, and demanded of them to resign. The matter was seriously debated ; Mr. Bell, of Tennessee, was opposed to the retirement, and desired that the subject of the bank might be postponed, on condition that in the mean time no hostile movements should be made on the Cabinet; and Mr. Crittenden himself, supposed to be most under the influence of Mr. Clay, playfully inquired whether he might not in honor remain until the stock of wines he had laid in was consumed; but Mr. Clay was inexorable. And while the second veto was pending before the Cabinet, the President submitted to them that he should announce to Congress his abnegation of all pretensions to, or aspirations for, the succession, and his resolve to retire at the expiration of his term, and every member present protested against any such announcement; yet he added to the veto this memorable paragraph : " I will take this occasion to declare that the conclusions to which I have brought myself are those of a settled conviction, founded, in my opinion, on a just view of the Constitution ; that, in arriving at it, I have been actuated by no other motive or desire than to uphold the institutions of the country as they have come down to us from the hands of our godlike ancestors; *and that I shall esteem my efforts to sustain them, even though I perish, more honorable than to win the applause of men by a sacrifice of my duty and of my conscience.*"

The Congress was implacable: the Whig leaders " held the second cup of bank or no bank" to the President's lips; he would make no compromise of his principles, would sacrifice neither his duty nor his conscience, would make no bargain in respect to retaining his Cabinet, but fearlessly vindicated himself from the aspersion that he was governed by ambitious motives, or that he was false and treacherous, and put "the applause of men" behind him in his defense of his "settled convictions, founded," in his opinion, "on a just view of the

Constitution ;" and in twenty-four days from the 1st, he sent to Clay, " with a Senate at his heels," and to King Caucus, with Congress under his reign, his second veto !

This proved potentially that he was no " nose of wax," but a firm, immovable lover of the Constitution, a fearless patriot, a wise and sagacious statesman, and an honest man. The Harrison-appointed Cabinet at once, under the force of Mr. Clay, dissolved. From all this intrigue, Daniel Webster alone kept himself grandly aloof; he had naught to do with Mr. Clay's cabal; his own opinions were unmoved as to the power to create a bank, but, knowing Mr. Tyler's convictions and scruples to be as unmoved, he could not, with proper respect to Mr. Tyler or himself, advise him to violate the consistency of his whole life by approving a bill which deceitfully and cunningly professed only to evade constitutional objections and conscientious scruples. He knew that the blows were intended by Mr. Clay and his friends for him as well as for Mr. Tyler, and they had won the mutual confidence and admiration of each other; and he kept the bickerings of cabal and caucus and the clamors of party factions away from him, knowing that the country had great affairs to be administered, and he calmly and dignifiedly attended, among other great measures, to the settlement of the Northeastern Boundary question with Great Britain. The rest of the Cabinet retired, knowing full well that if they had not bowed themselves out they would have been shown the door. It was a mutual separation between them and Mr. Tyler. It was a cordial union between him and Mr. Webster; that itself is the highest credential of Mr. Tyler's integrity against all contradiction. Webster manfully remained by an honest President, and sustained him by his example against all aspersion and persecution. It was one of the sublimest actions of his great life. He, too, made a sacrifice in remaining despite the clamor of the major faction of those who concurred with him in opinion upon a bank against Mr. Tyler. The policy of Mr. Clay was to separate both Mr. Tyler and Mr. Webster from the great body of the Whig party, and the expectation was that the two standing alone could not make up another Cabinet, and that both would have to retire from the task of carrying on the government. How he "reckoned without his host" events immediately showed. There were ready at hand new men, unhackneyed politicians of the best caliber, far superior in qualifications to those who had retired. Webster himself remained the same Daniel Webster; Abel P. Upshur, John C. Spencer, Robert Wickliffe, Hugh L. Legaré, and Walter Forward (?) were called, as it were, from their homes in the country. Not one of them was *blasé* with Washington City politics, parties, factions, or feuds. Such a Cabinet before or since has never been formed in the United States, for either natural powers or cultivation in law and letters, and for experience in the applied science of government. Each was mighty, and it is hard to say which was mightiest; each was a full peer of Webster, and we would like to know another Cabinet of which that can be said.

13

# CHAPTER X.

THE SIXTH DECADE, FROM 1840 TO 1850.

Of Mr. Webster's public life nothing need here be said. His private intercourse was even more attractive than his position as a statesman was commanding. He was, when in the right mood, the most genial of companions, and his conversation was more delightful and instructive than his speeches or orations. On one occasion we went into the Senate-chamber, and were standing alone in the lobby, listening to some dull debate; he was sitting in his usual place, not occupied, and hardly attending to what was going on, but thoughtful, and, as was his habit when musing, pulling one of his ears. It was a singular idiosyncrasy; and we often asked ourself, Is there any sympathy between his ear and his brain? Does the friction of the one excite the other? If so, what an electric ear his must have been!

As we were looking at him, he caught our eye, rose immediately from his seat, came to where we were, and took us by the arm, saying, "Come here." There was a map of the United States hanging behind the Vice-President's chair, to which he led us and inquired, "Where do you live? Show me the spot." We pointed to the spot of the Eastern Shore, on the Virginia coast,

( 194 )

opposite the Metompkin Inlet. "Well," said he, "do you ever shoot curlews and will—will—willets?" We replied, "Yes." He then descanted on the habits of those birds, and the times of their migration. He said that, at the proper season, his custom was to shoot them, off Nahant, perhaps, and that, according to his calculation of climate and distance, about two or three weeks after he began shooting them there they migrated to the Virginia coast. "Now," he said, "remember, that if you see any crippled ones down your way after about that time, they are my birds." This was said with a magic geniality, and, without waiting for our reply, he asked, "Where did your ancestors come from?" We told him that our blood was half English and half Scotch,—all our paternal ancestors came from the North of England, and most of the *præpositi* had been clergymen; that the only marked man among them we had heard of was Sir William *Wise*, distinguished for his wit, whom Henry the Eighth had knighted for gratifying his spleen against the French by saying, when asked what the phrase *fleur-de-lis* meant, "It means French lice, sire." He laughed, and then gravely told us his reason for asking who our ancestors were. Near his father's residence, along the New Hampshire coast, dwelt an English pensioner, an old ex-warrant officer of the British navy, a bachelor, alone in a small fisherman's cot, named *Daniel Wise*. That his name was no *lucus a non lucendo*, for he was a very Daniel, judge indeed of most things, and especially of men, and was exceedingly good and wise by nature as well as by name; and was the best master of a boat, the most cunning in fishing craft and tackle, and the most inveterate fisherman he ever heard or read of, Izaak Walton not excepted. Mr. Webster, when a boy, was devoted to fishing, and thus won the heart of "Uncle Daniel Wise," who taught him to fix his hook and line and bait, and always fondly took him with him in his boat, whenever he was allowed by his mother to venture out upon the water. That it was in this fishing companionship with this naval pensioner of England, who had, of course, sailed around the world and seen all parts and all people, he had first learned the love of geography and navigation, and the knowledge of the manners and customs and costumes of the different countries and people of the world.   " Uncle Daniel" was a great observer, thoroughly informed of everything he had seen wherever he had roamed, and was well read in geography and history, and instead of "spinning mere sailor's yarns," told him sober tales, curious and wonderful, but never shocking truth, or decency, or common sense.   His own private history he would never give him, but never tired in narrating the stories of his travels.   This first excited his *fervor animi* for knowledge, and drew him by a pleasant attraction to seek her treasures.   He regarded this old man, thus communed with alone, as the Nestor of his youth, and described him with childlike affection.

"Did you ever know him, or have you ever heard of such a man of that name ?"   His description made us know, and want to know more of him at once, but we regretted that we had never known or heard of him before, and that we could not claim a kinship with such a character.   He was dead many years before, it seemed, and we could never compare genealogies with him.   This little incident first drew us near to Mr. Webster, socially, and we were grateful afterwards for any opportunity to hear him talk in the same strain, when he was in the mood to do it, with his heart as well as with his tongue.   At such times we preferred listening to his narrations to reading Scott's best novels ; so simple, pure, and touching was his genial pathos ; his eyes were "great, pathetic eyes," oxlike, beaming generous, genial thoughts, gracious and great.   Clay in comparison with him, socially, was what Tom Marshall called him, "a sublime blackguard."

Abel P. Upshur was born on that peninsula land of Virginia, the Eastern Shore,—"the land of the pine and the myrtle." He was in his youth the leader of the great rebellion at Princeton College.   His mother was a sister of Colonel Thomas Parker, called "Hangman Tom" by the Tories of the Revolution, who was captured at the battle of Germantown, in Mathew's regiment ; and when Earl Harcourt rode along the line of rebel prisoners, ragged and worn and drooping, asking each what his occupation had been, Lieutenant Thomas Parker stood erect, and, when his turn came to tell who and what he was, replied to the question of the Earl, saying, "I am as my father before me was, a *gentleman*, and be d—d to you! Who are you?" The Upshurs were of a similar stock of "loyal gentlemen."

Old Dr. Smith, to the day of his death, we are told, never failed to speak of Upshur's defense of himself and his comrades for their rebellion at Princeton as one of the finest displays of argument and eloquence he had ever heard.

After his college career Upshur studied law in the office of William Wirt, and became imbued with his manners and learning. He first settled in Richmond and practiced his profession there; but, with a view to obtaining a seat in Congress, he moved to Northampton, on the Eastern Shore, his native county, and, failing to be returned to the House of Representatives, in Congress, being beaten by Mr. Bassett, he was afterwards elected to the House of Delegates of the legislature of Virginia. There he became highly distinguished as a debater and orator of the first water. His speech upon what was called the "Marriage Bill," to repeal the laws prohibiting a man from marrying the sister of his deceased wife, was a signal effort of art and learning in debate; and during its heat, when the celebrated General Blackburn, of Bath, rather indecorously and sardonically hinted that "*our Abel*" had interested motives in the repeal, because the Eastern Shore people, isolated as they were, had been obliged to intermarry among themselves, and that some of his own kindred probably required the legalization of their marriages, Upshur was aroused, and there are persons now alive who speak of his reply as one of the loftiest tone of eloquent invective,—pointed, clear, cutting, and yet in perfect ornate order. His retort was painfully polite, but went through and through his adversary, and, as he left him prostrate on the plain, he rose above him to a height inaccessible to most men.

His forensic displays in encounters with his great rival, Thomas R. Joynes, the father of the present distinguished Judge Joynes, of the Court of Appeals, were splendid. T. R.

Joynes was a master in his way, and Upshur was greater only in oratory. Joynes was a mathematician, quick, powerful, always to the point, reticent, cautious, and over-laborious. He could almost multiply nine figures by nine figures in his head, and as quick as thought could give a true statement of any proportion in the relation of numbers, and, always practical, addressed himself to common sense. Upshur was more highly cultivated, more ornate and graceful, a metaphysician, scholar, logician, and rhetorician. It was a treat to see them fence on any subject, great or small. A scene of more than common moment occurred between them in the trial of the Gibbs brothers for maiming one Hargis. The case was a romantic one, and is well remembered on the Eastern Shore, having the most peculiar state of facts, which were all fully developed on the trial,—a mistress and family of children, a marriage in respectable life among strangers in another State, the bringing home of the lady-wife, the first visit to church of the couple after marriage, a scene there of the mistress breaking upon the new-married couple in the procession of church-going people and tearing the lace shawl from the shoulders of the bride, that followed by the two youngest brothers of the groom, of eighteen and twenty years, severely switching the woman for her audacious assault, that followed by her brother's attempted vengeance upon the youths, and their stabbing and cutting the man nearly to death and inflicting permanent wounds, bringing them within the statute of mayhem. For this a prosecution was instituted against the two youthful Gibbses. Paramour and mistress, husband and wife, brothers and sister thus commingled in a strange confusion of crime, were all in the survey and scenery of the case, and the defense gave Upshur full scope for all his powers.

Joynes prosecuted with all his keen precision, presenting everything in perfect array for the Commonwealth, summing up, first, the whipping of the Magdalen, and contrasting her affront to the bride with the brothers' wrong to her, and her brother's attempted vengeance upon them with their vengeance on his sister, defiled by their brother, leaving their crime against him naked and without excuse, their youth only excusing the cowardice as well as guilt of the *two* stabbing the *one*. The prosecution was thought unanswerable. But by the time Upshur rose to the height of his argument there was a whirlwind revolution in the minds of the audience and jury. Patrick Henry never carried with him the passions of the people with more irresistible force. He had made the marriage relation his study in discussing the Marriage Bill before the legislature, —its holiness, its mystery, its refinement, its purity, its purpose, its delicacy of trust, its exalting and cleansing effect, and its sacred inviolability in the sight of God. And this he put before the jury with a power and rapture of thoughts and figures which made them feel as they had never felt before towards holy wedlock. Then upon the crime which assailed and shamed holy wedlock, in a crowd, at a church-door, he poured out such wrath as carried away every father and brother. The paramour himself had not been attacked, but the blameless bride. The youths had been merciful; they had only switched the bold, bad harlot, and only stabbed, instead of killing, her avenger, who was seeking vengeance for the mere switching of a sister, when he had never sought vengeance for her *defilement*. The whole feeling was carried back against the prosecutor, Hargis; and the two Gibbses were acquitted with acclamations.

After a short practice at the bar he went upon the bench, proving himself not a "Nisi Prius" prig, but a large, comprehensively-profound jurist. He was a member of the State Convention of 1829–30 to amend the Virginia Constitution of 1776. He advocated, most erroneously, the mixed basis of representation, population and property combined, and lived to confess his error. Leigh was the Ajax of that heresy, guided by that miser of aristocracy, John Randolph of Roanoke, but Upshur was the author of the one surpassing speech which carried the question. His law rival, T. R. Joynes, was also a member; and of the two Mr. Randolph said, "I had expected the ancient rights and charters of Virginia to have been defended by the Taze-wells and Trezvants of the south side of the James; but, whilst they have been supine and silent, the fishermen of the

Eastern Shore have proved to be the champions of all that is sacred to this Ancient Dominion.   Our defense has fallen upon that 'figure of arithmetic' of Accomack (Joynes), and that 'figure of rhetoric' (Upshur) of Northampton."

Upshur's review of Judge Story's theory of constitutional law fixed his fame.  He was no longer an asteroid, but a planet. He was in full vigor and known to honor and to fame when persuaded to take the place of Secretary of the Navy in the first Cabinet appointed by Mr. Tyler.  His messages are models of state papers, and beautiful blocks in the monument of his fame.   The morning after his first report was sent in, Hugh S. Legaré stopped us to inquire why that gentleman, Mr. Upshur, had not been sent up before by Virginia to magnify her rightful claim to a race of pre-eminent men.  When told that the reason was that the mother State of the greatest men had so many like him she could not send all her jewels at once, he said that he had read his report once, and that it was so pure in its style, so perfect a model of what a message ought to be, that he had read it twice before rising from its perusal.

He was killed at the catastrophe of the Princeton, in 1844, while Secretary of State.   Had he ever been sent to the Senate of the United States, he would have been universally known and appreciated at his full worth.   Had he been in the place of Robert Y. Hayne, in the debate on Foote's Resolution, it is doubtful whether Daniel Webster ever would have been called the " Great Defender of the Constitution."   He was a finer rhetorician and orator than Webster, and a closer logician,—his style purer and his power of expression clearer.   He had all of his momentum and more activity.  Mr. Tyler's administration brought his abilities into view, and that itself is no little praise.

Of Mr. Spencer's private life we know but little.   He had been known and distinguished in the public councils.   He had served with Mr. Tyler in Congress, and he knew his worth. He was a man of quick and active mind, penetrating and practical.   He knew well all the politics of New York, and was an adept in the ways of Wall Street.  He was Secretary of War, but was best qualified to manage the finances.

Upon the retirement of the Harrison Cabinet, Mr. Webster retained his place as Secretary of State; and Mr. Forward, of Pennsylvania, for the Treasury, Mr. John McLean, of Ohio, for the War, Mr. Upshur, of Virginia, for the Navy, Mr. Wickliffe, of Kentucky, for the Postmaster-Generalship, and Mr. Legaré, of South Carolina, for the Attorney-Generalship, were nominated and appointed in September, 1841. Mr. McLean declining to resign his seat on the Supreme Bench, Mr. Spencer was nominated and appointed in his place in the War Department in October, 1841, and from the War he was changed to the Treasury Department in March, 1843; which place he resigned, owing to a difference with the administration on the policy of annexing Texas. He was succeeded in the Treasury by Mr. George M. Bibb, of Kentucky, in 1844.

Mr. Wickliffe was a man of great Western reputation, distinguished alike for his legal learning and his fine, manly judgment in all matters of politics and government. He remained in his place until the end of the administration.

As for Mr. Legaré, he had not his equal for the Attorney-Generalship in the United States. His life was one of study in the best schools at home and on the Continent of Europe. He was diplomat at Brussels long enough to enable him to dive deep into the civil law, and had at home been a reviewer of the highest order. He was grandly classic, and equal to the originals of his studies. He was a Greek article in language, and a votary of the masters in literature. He had been rudimentally taught, and had followed his rudiments down to supreme practice. His Life has lately been published by his estimable sister, with all a sister's partiality, but truly, according to his real merit and worth. We regret only a passage in the review of his biography by the "Southern Review," vol. vii., number 13, of the date of January, 1870. It says, "All who have studied our history must remember how unpopular was the administration of Mr. Tyler. It seemed to have a upas power of blighting every reputation which approached its shadow. Legaré alone lost nothing by his association with it. On the contrary, his fame steadily increased. The President, in the midst of his distracting cares, learned to rely upon his Attorney-General for counsel and assistance. These were always frankly given, and thus a friendship was gradually established between them. Upon the withdrawal of Webster from the Cabinet, the duties of the State Department were confided to Legaré *ad interim*. He showed his diplomatic skill by conducting to a successful conclusion the Ashburton Treaty, or at least that portion of it relating to the long-vexed and dangerous question of the right of search."

Mr. Tyler's administration was *unpopular* for a time. The party which elected him was false to its professed principles, and tried to cover their own treachery by clamoring treason against him; and the party which he had aided in crushing came not, of course, to his assistance, but chuckled that their opponents were guilty of suicide, by ostracizing for the time their best men and by preventing the best of measures, the credit of which they might have secured. Every question that the administration disposed of was of the highest importance, and was managed with the utmost ability, yielding the richest fruition. The administration added to the reputation of every member of its counsels. Did not Webster and Upshur and Spencer and Wickliffe gain reputation as well as Legaré? What reputation was ever blighted by the shadow of an administration which wisely and well settled the Northeastern Boundary question, the Caroline question, the Bank and Tariff questions, the Southwestern Texas question? — which overthrew its revilers and revived Democracy, crushing both old Federalism and Locofocoism?

As contrasted with any administration since, who would not have it installed again, with all its purity, independence, integrity, and intellect? It had, it is true, no aspirant of its own for the succession, and had no candidate in the field for the Presidency, but it utterly demolished both of the corrupt parties which endeavored to sully its fame and to obstruct its honest efforts to maintain the best measures for the good of the country. The clamor raised against it was but for a day, and is a part of history only.

Every reputation which it is said to have blighted now looms high above the cloud of dust from the dirty arena of Whigs divided against themselves, or of Locofocoism taking vengeance at the time. The parties and factions of the hour Mr. Tyler put behind him as our Saviour did Satan. There were others more distinguished than Mr. Legaré, though as a lawyer he was entitled to be ranked with William Pinkney himself. He was worthy of Mr. Tyler's administration, and it was worthy of him; but it was not he who conducted the Ashburton Treaty to a successful conclusion, for that work especially belonged to Mr. Tyler himself and to Mr. Webster, who did not retire from the Cabinet until it was essentially concluded; Mr. Legaré took upon him *ad interim* the mere winding up of what was already concluded, and Mr. Upshur actually finished it. This is said not in order to detract from Legaré, but to prevent an undue compliment to him at the expense of the reputation of others. His reputation needs no such compliment, and were he alive we are sure he would decline it.

Mr. Webster, as we have just remarked, retired from the Cabinet only when the work of the Ashburton Treaty was concluded. That was a question which it was due to the Northeast, his section, that his master-mind should manage; and when he saw clearly the end of it, he magnanimously retired to make way for a Southern statesman, when the time came to take up the next most important matter of foreign relations,— Texas.

This Cabinet proper of Mr. Tyler's administration was first disturbed by the retirement of Mr. Spencer; then by the retirement of Mr. Webster, and afterwards by the death of the lamented Legaré. He accompanied the President to Boston, to attend the Bunker Hill celebration, and disease fatally seized upon the sigmoid of his viscera. He died at the residence of Professor George Ticknor, of Harvard University, in Boston, June 20, 1843. His death was a national loss; but he had comrades in the Cabinet who were his equals, and such as he would have considered fully competent to take the Attorney-Generalship or the Department of State. Mr. Upshur took the place of Mr. Webster, and Mr. Nelson the place of Mr. Legaré.

The second session of the Twenty-seventh Congress, the session of 1841–42, was marked by measures alike violent and disgraceful, and by the most acrimonious and unscrupulous factious proceedings of the Opposition.  The interval between this session and the called session of the summer of 1841, instead of softening the asperities excited by the vetoes, only heaped up fuel for the flames of the regular session.  The message was calm, temperate, uncomplaining, unreproachful, and wisely addressed itself to the highly important public business then calling for harmonious action, and requiring great care and skill in the conduct of the country's affairs at home and abroad. Some matters of state were even threatening to the national peace, yet Congress converted itself into a committee of the whole to consider nothing else but " how," in the language of the ogre of Whig politics, " to head John Tyler."

The message brought to the consideration of Congress the very critical questions between the United States and Great Britain, growing out of the affair of the seizure of the steamer Caroline in 1837, the case of McLeod, the forcible seizure of Grogan, the protection of the territory of the United States against invasion at all hazards, the protection of the flag of the United States in the African seas, and the Northeastern boundary between the United States and Canada.  The boundary and relations with Texas were also presented ; the Indian war in Florida; the finances ; moderate counsels were recommended in revising the tariff of duties, and the expediency of laying duties solely in reference to the wants of the treasury for revenue was suggested ; the proceeds of the sale of public lands to be applied to diminishing the duties on imports; and the currency and exchange and the fisc to be provided for by the system of an exchequer.

The message fully redeemed the President's pledge to propose a plan for the regulation of the currency, exchange, and the fisc by the proposal of an exchequer.

It was thoroughly elaborated by Mr. Cushing in his very able report of that session, showing its merits as compared with a Bank of the United States, or with the State bank system, or with the " Sub-Treasury ;" that it possessed the qualities of:

1st. A safe and convenient agency for the custody and management of the public funds.

2d. A useful agency of exchanges and collections.

3d. A national paper currency.

4th. For the regulation of the bank paper currency of the States, by receiving it in payment of public dues, and presenting it for redemption at short intervals of time.

5th. The utilization of the public deposits, and of the specific funds of individuals, by rendering them the basis of a national paper circulation.

6th. The bestowment, incidentally, of the business of the treasury, and within the letter of the Constitution, of benefits on the people of the United States.

7th. Not intrusting the control of the public funds, or of the currency, to an irresponsible private corporation.

8th. Not loaning out the public money to private individuals.

9th. Not making, and being incapable of making, any excessive issue, and incapable of suspending cash payments.

10th Conducting the business of the treasury without the necessity of aid from the creatures of the legislation of the States.

11th. Maintaining the legal money-standard by the use of either coin only, or of paper always equivalent to coin.

12th. Being always within the control of Congress to repeal or amend it at pleasure.

This plan of a fiscal system is the very foundation of the present prevailing system, without which the United States could not have been carried through its late civil war. Derided and denounced by the Congress of 1841–42, it was laid on the table, and was not allowed a consideration until its necessity and expediency were developed by the extreme exigencies of the Union. The reasons were obvious at the time, and too plain to be misunderstood. One branch of the Whigs were determined to have a national bank or nothing; the other branch had obtained the veto, and desired to subject the President to the odium of deranging the currency and embarrassing the treasury; and the opponents of the Whigs, the spoils partisans of Mr. Van Buren, sought vengeance, and promoted the confusion of the party which had broken them down. Thus the exchequer was smothered for the time, and the President was left only what Mr. Clay called "a corporal's guard,"—but six members in the House of Representatives, and not a supporter in the Senate, except Mr. Rives.

We had the honor to be captain of that distinguished guard, and have reason now to glory in its eminent triumph; it defeated the bank and crushed both factions of the Opposition. The very next election restored the Jackson Democracy to its pristine purity and power. Thus ended the savage struggle for a national bank. The President's firmness prevailed as to his policy and principles, and he outlived every assault of his enemies, and saw them overthrown by the power of truth. His reputation was not blighted any more than that of Mr. Legaré; both were canonized by their wisdom, moral courage, and integrity.

Other measures during this memorable session excited more vetoes of the President and more venom of party. An act of September, 1841, had been passed, and very improperly approved by the President, to distribute the proceeds of the sales of the public lands among the States. It was carried by State clamor. over the Constitution; the President ever after regretted his approval of it; but it contained a limitation that it should cease in time of war, or whenever the exigencies of the treasury might demand duties for revenue exceeding twenty per cent. ad valorem.

In the year 1842 it was found that government would have to exceed twenty per cent. of imposts, or resort again to the proceeds of the sales of the public lands, and the President sent his message to Congress dated March 25, 1842. He called attention to the finances, showed a deficiency of means from ordinary sources, and urged retrenchment of expenditures, and in preference to laying duties higher than the compromise of the

Tariff question permitted, he recommended the most effectual method of supporting the credit of the States, as well as of the Federal government, by applying the proceeds of the sales of the public lands again to the public expenditures and debt. This was maintained by the clearest reasons of economy and good faith, enforced by causes of no ordinary character, deranging the currency and credit of the States. In the face of this message, Congress passed what was called the "Little Tariff Bill," which not only violated the Compromise act of 1833, but the Distribution act of 1841. This brought down upon this bill another veto, in his message of June 29, 1842.

Congress immediately prepared another bill, revising the whole tariff. The very necessity for the bill proved that the time had arrived to suspend the distribution of the proceeds of the sales of the public lands, as provided in the act of 1841. The effort was to distribute the proceeds of the sales of the public lands with one hand, whilst high protective duties, far above twenty per cent., were laid with the other, at a time when the treasury was seriously embarrassed. There could be no expectation that the President would countenance such profligacy of expenditure in order to give opportunity for sectional or selfish legislation, or such *mala fides* in executing the tariff compromise. But it was an object then to make the veto odious, and the Whig leaders drove the President to the extreme of another tariff veto.

The bill was passed, and on the 9th of August he returned it with his veto. The message was a very able one, and sent in without consultation with his Cabinet. This message was made the pretext of most unauthorized, unprecedented, factious, and false proceedings on the part of Congress. The Constitution provides the manner of proceeding upon the veto. This was meant not only to provide the mode of proceeding, but to prevent the imprudence, indecencies, and intemperance of heated action. All decorum was abandoned, the rule of the Constitution was unheeded, and the most intemperate action was taken.

No consideration of the bill was had by the House of Representatives, but a committee of thirteen was appointed, at the head of which was placed Mr. John Q. Adams, the ex-President, advocate of "light-houses in the skies," the fanatic of abolition, the leading champion of the Massachusetts school of protective duties, and the man most vindictive against the South for its combined opposition to his minority election to the Presidency in 1824, for and in consideration of his "bargain and corruption." The committee was not wholly servile to this illicit action. It made three reports, one by Mr. Adams, full of vituperation, one by Messrs. Charles J. Ingersoll and Mr. Roosevelt, and one by Mr. Thomas W. Gilmer, of Virginia. The reports speak for themselves. Mr. Adams's report was a complaint against the veto,—protesting against the action of Congress being "strangled by the five times repeated stricture of the Executive cord." It recommended a change of the Constitution, allowing a majority of Congress to pass a bill into a law over the veto. Mr. Gilmer's report was a very able one. He was, in early life, a rival and compeer of Mr. Rives, of the State Rights and Strict Construction school, an able and an honest man, firm, laborious, and prudent, whilst bold and generous in chivalric action. He was born and educated a gentleman, had been Governor of Virginia, and whilst in that office was highly distinguished in his correspondence with Mr. Seward on a question of the extradition of a fugitive slave. He was able to stand alone on any committee when his conception of his duty called him to be bold and to act in defense of the right.

The report of Messrs. Ingersoll and Roosevelt sustained him, and, though the majority of ten to three was great, the President triumphed. The Revenue bill was passed without the distribution clause. But the Executive office and its defense as well as his own required of Mr. Tyler decisive remonstrance, and on the 20th of August, 1842, he sent in to the House of Representatives his solemn protest, marked by self-respecting defense and sound reproof. This action, these reports, and this protest have but to be read to place Mr. Tyler above the reproach of all his revilers.

At this session, too, in spite of all malignity, his administration concluded a treaty with England settling the questions of the Northeastern boundary and the right of search. It also concluded the Florida war, and passed an act authorizing armed occupation of that Territory. It settled the disturbances in Rhode Island, and maintained the established law, which ought to have been a precedent for establishing the position that the States were not to be questioned by the Federal authorities as to the supremacy of their established State governments.

It held the true doctrine that the Federal Executive "could not look into real or supposed defects of the existing State government, in order to ascertain whether other plan of government proposed for adoption was better suited to the wants and more in accordance with the wishes of any portion of her citizens."

And it would have been well if Congress had heeded this admonition when it undertook by legislative power to overthrow eleven State governments, and to revolutionize them by congressional restraint and reconstruction.

The action of President Tyler in the case of the Dorr rebellion is a model of what Federal Executive action should be in a case where a State Constitution is disturbed ; and reconstruction of late is its contrast in the extremest degree. The government of Rhode Island was established by royal prerogative, by a charter of a Stuart king, aristocratic in every feature, and a large majority of the citizens subject to its anti-republican features endeavored to hold an election and to establish such a republican form of government as the Constitution of the United States guarantees. But Mr. Tyler adhered to the maxim that he was bound " to respect the requisitions of that government *which has been recognized as the existing government of the State through all time past until he was advised, in regular manner, that it has been altered and abolished, and another substituted in its place by legal and peaceable proceedings, adopted and ratified by the authorities and people of the State."*

How different this from the treatment of Virginia by Congress and a Black Crook Convention !

Mr. Tyler's letter to Governor King, of Rhode Island, of the

date of April 11, 1842, is a fine specimen of the teaching of
the old régime of Presidents in comparison with this age of
congressional usurpation and of Executive proclamations. Nothing could show more fearfully the rapid tendency to the
concentration of all power in the hands of Congress and of the
Federal Executive.

Virginia had a Constitution, the first formed in 1776 by the
fathers who had overthrown kings, which established the first
written bill of the rights of man, and which lasted for fifty-four
years an accepted plan of republican government; in 1829–30
it was made, if possible, more republican and democratic, and
twenty years after, in 1850–51, was still further liberalized by
amendment.  When the late civil war broke out, there was no
question but that she had a republican form of government,
and there was no human authority legally empowered to change
it but her own people assembled in convention within her own
defined territory.  A majority of the people of Rhode Island were
not permitted to change her charter of Charles the Second, for
want of conventional power and form; and yet, since the surrender at Appomattox, a military despotism, exerted by the
Federal Executive and a congressional usurpation in time of
peace, has assailed and annihilated no less than three Constitutions of the people of Virginia, that of 1776, that of 1829–30,
and that of 1850–51, which had all been recognized and received
by the nation as *de jure* and republican for the whole time of the
existence of the Federal government.  Rhode Island's kingly
or royal charter of limited suffrage could stand and must stand,
but Virginia's conventional power of her people was torn away,
persons not citizens were given elective franchise, and the
franchises secured by her organic law were destroyed by the
highest pretension of human power, more than kingly or imperial, a power of reconstruction !  It will be well for those who
are and would remain free to note these high lights and shadows
of human history.  We have marked them by points firmer than
those of pen or pencil, and so will the nation yet, unless given
over to individual blindness, ere they are established canons of
despotism.

There was an evident design on the part of the Clay faction of Whigs to lay a foundation for proceedings of impeachment. Every effort was made, by measures to extort vetoes, by speeches and reports in both Houses of Congress, and by the vilest vituperation of the press, to create such a prejudice against the President as would tolerate impeachment and try him by the animosities of both parties.

This was impossible; his conduct was above impeachment, and his administration such a rock of integrity and intelligence that the waves of partisan proceedings broke against it into mere spray, and the leaders, too wily to risk reputation upon the issue, shrank back from their own designs, made to recoil by the firmness and virtue of a man who feared not and failed not to do his whole duty to the country. The administration was merely dashed by the spray. Providence made the factious Opposition convict itself of its own fatal folly. The Whigs of Mr. Clay's faction had an incorrigible zealot among them who brought impeachment into perfect travesty of itself. The coarse creature could not be restrained by his betters in the party, and he vowed that "he would head John Tyler or die." He gathered together all the garbage of abuse against the President, and heaped it into resolutions of impeachment; but, when stated, when summed up into its worst form, it was so foul, so false, so pointless, so offensive to every sense of good morals and good taste, so utterly bad and badly put, that it completely demolished the impudent and imprudent author himself, and disgusted, especially, the enemies of the President, who desired not to see him so "praised by faint damns" instead of being " damned by faint praise."

In the midst of his conflicts with Congress, and oppressed already, as he was, by his public cares, the heaviest grief came upon him,—the loss of the wife of his youth, who had been the angel of his career for twenty-nine years, who had given him a large family of children, who had graced and crowned his home-life with every blandishment and bliss. She died at the Executive Mansion, on the 10th of September, 1842, beloved by all who knew her sweet, still, silent, unobtrusive worth, and mourned not alone by a husband who devotedly cherished and loved her, and by children who felt her affection like a balm at every breath, but by the friendless, the poor, and the distressed, whom she always turned to relieve, and never forgot amid the splendors of a court and the gilded attractions of her position in high places. The bitterest political opponents of the President, the *Intelligencer* and the *Globe* presses, praised her in obituaries which were not cold or formal, but warm with "the love and esteem of all." Happily, in Mrs. Semple, in Mrs. Robert Tyler, and in Mrs. Waller she left behind her sweet bouquets for the White House, and the President was not desolate in his bereavement. He was prepared for the departure of Mrs. Tyler, as she had, previously to her last illness, been touched by that cold hand which sometimes gently warns of "the last call." Death in any form is terrible, but to the gentle, sweetened by grace, even death is often tender. She was a Christian, ready and assured, and did not suffer, physically, much pain. All the pain her honored husband, her sons and daughters, her friends and neighbors, and the beneficiaries of her bounties, felt, and felt deeply. How worthy she was, how loving and loved, and how honored in life and death, Mrs. Halloway has told in her "Ladies of the White House."

But family afflictions mitigated not the persecutions of the President by the party which elected him to power, violated its own pledges when accusing him of treachery and tergiversation, and the sessions of 1842–43 and 1843–44 but continued the vengeful spirit which scrupled not to assail and oppose every measure he proposed for the public good: it was enough for him to propose, for them to oppose and upbraid. The patience, equanimity, and smiling consciousness of rectitude which composed him all the time of his darkest trials, and kept him firm in the righteousness of his course, were more than any ordinary human virtue. He was calm, cautious, forbearing, forgiving, hopeful, and cheerful all the time, and no bitterness disturbed his placid contemplation of his exact situation and duty. His only weakness was that he could hardly say "no" to a friend, and was ever ready to try to appease a foe. He was unlimited in his confidence to the one, and ever charitable and gracious to the other. He never spoke harshly of his revilers, and often provoked his friends by offering excuses and apologies for them; yet his enemies not only drove him to vetoes, tried to force him to resign, endeavored to deprive him of a Cabinet, and rejected his nominations to places entitled to his Executive confidence in the Cabinet and foreign missions, but actually withheld from him the ordinary appropriations for the expenses of the Executive office.

His private secretary has published to the world that "such was the bitterness of party feeling"—he ought to have said, "such was the bitterness of party leaders"—that "no appropriation was made by Congress either for furnishing the White House or for the office of private secretary, or for the incidental expenses of fuel, lights, doorkeepers," etc. Yet he kept the even tenor of his way, or mildly stood a steady target for every missile of rancor, meanness, and malice. They passed his great soul, his firm virtue, harmless to him, but destructive, deadly destructive, in reaction against the fiendish foes who had no scruples and no shame.

Mr. Tyler's first Cabinet was nominated and confirmed on the 13th of September, 1841.

In March, 1843, Mr. Forward, Secretary of the Treasury, resigned, and Mr. Spencer was transferred from the War Department to that of the Treasury, Mr. Cushing, of Massachusetts, having been first nominated and rejected by the Senate. Mr. Webster, having accomplished his great work of the North-eastern boundary, the settlement of the Caroline and McLeod affairs, and the right of search with Great Britain, resigned the office of Secretary of State in May, 1843. Mr. Legaré was appointed to act *ad interim* in his place, and died June 20, 1843. In July, 1843, the Cabinet was reorganized, three vacancies existing in it at the time, those of State, War, and the Attorney-Generalship. Abel P. Upshur was then made Secretary of State; John C. Spencer was continued Secretary of the Treasury; James M. Porter, of Pennsylvania, was made Secretary of War; David Henshaw, of Massachusetts, was made Secretary of the Navy; John Nelson, of Maryland, Attorney-General, and Charles Wickliffe continued Postmaster-General. At the next session of the Senate, the nominations of Messrs. Porter and Henshaw were rejected, and William Wilkins, of Pennsylvania, was made Secretary of War, and Thomas W. Gilmer, of Virginia, Secretary of the Navy, both of whom were confirmed February 15, 1844. Thus the Cabinet stood: Upshur, of State; Spencer, of the Treasury; Wilkins, of War; Gilmer, of the Navy; Nelson, Attorney-General; Wickliffe, Postmaster-General,—when the awful catastrophe of the "destructive Peacemaker," on board the steam frigate Princeton, occurred on the Potomac River, the 28th of February, 1844. And here we must indulge in an episode.

# CHAPTER XI.

On the 8th of February, 1844, having been nominated and confirmed as Minister Plenipotentiary to the empire of Brazil, we resigned our seat in the House of Representatives of the Congress of the United States. Previous to that time there was a vacancy in the Supreme Court caused by the death of that eminent jurist and patriot, Judge Henry Baldwin. Mr. Tyler requested the place to be tendered in his name to Mr. John Sergeant, of Philadelphia. There was a delicacy and embarrassment in obeying the request, and so the President was informed.

We had some apprehension that the tender would be repulsed, coming from Mr. Tyler, whose course Mr. Sergeant had condemned, through one who had vindicated that course and the good faith of the President. Mr. Sergeant was stern and proud in his integrity, and extremely jealous on the point of honor. Mr. Tyler said Mr. Sergeant was a man of the highest probity and the most distinguished ability; that his condemnation of his course respecting the fiscal corporation arose entirely from misapprehension and misunderstanding, and he honored him the more for acting on an honest conviction, though that conviction was founded on mistake, and was unjust to himself; he knew he was honest and able far above most men, and the country and Supreme Court should not be deprived of his name

( .15 )

and services for any personal misjudgment of himself or his course.   He insisted on tendering him the place.   At the time the tender was made, the great case of Vidal et al. *vs.* Girard's executors was before the Supreme Court.

Originally Mr. Sergeant was the counsel of the city of Philadelphia in that case, and he had at the previous term of the court ably argued, and, in fact, won the case,—mainly on the ground of the decisions of the Pennsylvania courts on the doctrine of charitable uses.   But anxiety was felt concerning the issue by the city, and the decision was deferred, at the instance of Mr. Sergeant in part, in order that Mr. Binney might add his great weight of argument and authority to his own.   Thus time was gained for the deliberate preparation of great minds for the final struggle on the important doctrine involved in the law.   Mr. Binney went to England and conferred with Lord Campbell, in order that he might study and scan the rolls on the doctrine of charitable uses.   He came back thoroughly armed, bringing new armor from the unpublished rolls on that doctrine.   His aim was to subvert the doctrines laid down by Judge Marshall and Judge Tucker in the cases which had gone up previously from Virginia.   Daniel Webster and Walter Jones were arrayed against Sergeant and Binney.   It was the heaviest of forensic artillery duels.   Sergeant had made his arguments most overwhelming on the grounds of Pennsylvania decisions, regardless of the doctrines maintained in cases coming from Virginia. Binney was now prepared to show not only that the doctrines of charitable uses, insisted on by the city of Philadelphia, were those of the State from which the case came, but that they were the true doctrines of the common law and of the State of Virginia, and ought to prevail in every State and everywhere. This was his burden to show, and his work was not supererogatory or vain,—useless to win the Girard case, but invaluable in teaching the sound law of charitable uses.   The case was doubly won, first by Sergeant on the American law, and then by Binney on the English law.   The forensic display in the case was grand on both sides.

Mr. Jones's three points in the case were :

1. The bequest of the College fund was void by reason of the uncertainty of the *cestui que trust*.

2. The corporation of Philadelphia was not authorized by its charter to administer the trusts of the legacy, and no other trustee could be substituted without defeating the intentions of the testator.

3. Even if otherwise capable of taking effect, the trust would be void, because the plan of education proposed was anti-Christian, and therefore repugnant to the law of Pennsylvania. (See Vidal and others *vs.* Girard Ex'rs, 2d Howard, 143, January Term, 1844.)

Mr. Jones said, "A part of this devise would make it a curse to any civilized land. It is a cruel experiment upon poor orphan boys to shut them up and make them the victims of a philosophical speculation," etc.

In his quiet, insinuating, lisping tones, he said, "Mr. Girard had devised mere nourishment for the mind, without care of moral instruction, and the Trustees had expended an immense sum in erecting a temple of marble to the 'unknown God.' The testator had not meant to make the College religiously free, but to make it free of all religion. The orphans needed a fish, and they were given a serpent; bread, and they had gotten a stone!"

All this was taken to be personal to Mr. Sergeant, who was one of the chief counselors of the city of Philadelphia in administering the charity; and the point of Mr. Jones was a poniard to him,—the more so, because he had always admired and respected Mr. Jones as one of the first forensic men of his day. Jones did not seem to be conscious of where or whom his point touched, but whilst he was speaking in front of the judge's seat, Mr. Sergeant was boiling with indignation and wrath in the court lobby, and the moment Mr. Jones was done he took him to the lobby and called him to severe account. Jones was astonished, disclaimed all personality, and calmly remonstrated against Mr. Sergeant's wrath; but the latter was not appeased, and it was feared that some one would have to interpose to prevent serious collision between these two, giants of intellect and champions of argument, but both small in stature. They were finally reconciled, however, though the one was sore under the figure of speech, and the other was sore from the scolding he had got for it. It was rich to see such a scene between two such men.

Again, there was another scene. When Mr. Binney rose to deliver his argument, Mr. Webster, having the conclusion, was obliged, by rule, to furnish him with all his points and all his authorities. This he did with great urbanity, just as Mr. Binney was about to open his address to the court. Jones had been heard, Sergeant had closed, and Mr. Binney had taken a moment to retire to the anteroom of the court, to adjust his personal attire and presence. He was particular about that, and came into the court refreshed by water and smooth from the comb and brush. He was always very serene in his aspect, and, without a forward look, expressed a composed self-reliance. He had just begun, when Mr. Webster rose and apologized for not having obeyed the rule before, and then cited his points and references. Mr. Binney paused to hear him, with his arms folded, and when he was done smiled a sweet smile of indifference, and gently said, with a slight wave of his hand, that he "fully excused his learned brother for his delay of citation, for he would have no occasion to touch a single point, or anything cited by him," and then unfolded that masterly treatise on charitable uses, which his great argument deserves to be called,—a standard of authority now on the doctrines then in debate.

Mr. Webster was taken aback, and staggered.

Mr. Binney was no better lawyer than Mr. Sergeant, but was a far better speaker, and his style was as rich and pure as that of any other orator or writer of English in his day. His eulogy on his professional brother and rival and friend, Mr. Sergeant, is a gem of encomiastic composition. His forte was lucid order, perfectly expressed by the clearest logic and the richest but most severely chaste figure.

Mr. Sergeant's forte was solid terseness, direct to the truth, but didactically dry. Neither was superior to Mr. Jones as a forensic debater, and all three were lawyers of the highest degree, either superior to Webster in the court, but not in the Senate.

The evening after Mr. Binney concluded his great argument, in January, 1844, Mr. Sergeant was visited by us, at his hotel, to deliver the message of Mr. Tyler. Mr. Binney was in the next room. Mr. Sergeant received the compliment with graciousness and evident pleasure; but he hesitated not to decline the tender of a place on the Supreme Bench. Before he assigned his reason he enjoined secrecy during his life, and especially it was not to be disclosed to Mr. Binney. It was that he was past *sixty years of age*, and that he ought not to accept; but he regarded Mr. Binney as being much more robust than himself, considered that Mr. Binney might accept, and *did not wish him to know* that he had declined because he considered himself too old, and requested that the President would make the tender of the place to him. It was tendered to Mr. Binney at once, and, behold, he declined it for the same reason, but begged that *Mr. Sergeant should not be informed of his reason*, and that the place might be *tendered to him*.

Neither, we believe, ever knew the reason of the other for declining.

Mr. Binney said he had once, in the vigor of his manhood, aspired to judicial position,—to a seat on the Supreme Bench of Pennsylvania; but Mr. Justice Gibson of that State had been preferred to him, and that cured his ambition, and he had never since aspired to the bench.

No better instance than this could be given of Mr. Tyler's magnanimity. He knew that neither of these gentlemen approved of his course as President, and that both condemned him personally on the Bank question; but he knew that they were good and great men, and he forgot his own grievances, personally, for the sake of the public good. He was remarkable for his faculty of selecting the right men for the right places, and hardly ever allowed a personal predilection to prevail.

Mr. Binney was among the warmest admirers of Judge

Marshall. He was his critic of the "Life of Washington." The evening he declined a place on the Supreme Bench he naturally conversed on the Girard case and the doctrines it involved. He said that Judge Marshall's decisions on the cases from Virginia were the only authorities he had reason to dread in the case, but that charitable uses were exactly the sort of subject on which Judge Marshall could err; that they were purely arbitrary and artificial doctrines, and required great learning and research, which Judge Marshall had not bestowed, and, great as he was, incalculable as was the good he had done on the bench, he doubted very much whether that good was not largely counterbalanced by his great error, for the want of learning, on the subject of charitable uses.

To return to the catastrophe of the Princeton. We were a few evenings after sitting again with Mr. Sergeant in his room at Gadsby's Hotel, conversing at ease, when the notable waiter on his room, John Sable, black, with moonshine eyes, always smiling and showing his teeth in white contrast with his ebony, entered, smiling as ever, and bowing complacently to Mr. Sergeant and his guests. Mr. Sergeant saluted him, saying, "Well, John, what is the news to-day?" John smiled more winningly still, and bowed lower, replying, "Well, sir, none but very sad, just come this moment,—the Peacemaker is busted, and it is said Mr. Upshur and others are killed and wounded,—the hack is just from the wharf with the news." This was the first announcement to us of the sad event, and was the more shocking from its contrast with John's smiling and bowing. We immediately sprang down the stairway to the street front door. There was a large crowd already gathered, each inquiring of the hacks just driven up, "Who was killed,—who injured?" In the crowd, at the right, we saw the figure of young Abel Upshur, the brother of Mrs. Upshur (she was a Miss Upshur), and as soon as one of the hack-drivers answered that Mr. Upshur, Mr. Gilmer, and others were killed, he burst from the crowd and ran for Mrs. Upshur's residence. To prevent the shock of his sudden announcement, we pursued him in a hack, but he outran the hack, and had already when we arrived stunned Mrs. Upshur, her daughter, and sister. We never saw such dumb and dismal grief. Mrs. Upshur sat tearless, with eyes staring and fixed on vacancy, alternately raising her hands and letting them fall on her lap, repeating incessantly, "It can't be so! it can't be so!" And the daughter, afterwards Mrs. Ringgold, one of the softest, sweetest images of her father, sank in the most piteous moaning for her father, who had cherished her with the fondest devotion and tenderness. We gave to them, and after them to Mrs. Gilmer, all the consolation in our power, took their requests to proceed the next morning to the steamer, there to see the bodies, and retired late at night to reflect on what the administration was to do in filling the vacancies in the Cabinet. We came at once to our conclusions. Mr. Webster remained in the Cabinet until the Northeastern question was settled, and as long as Upshur or Legaré was alive, the Southwestern question was in safe Southern hands; but now that they were both taken away, there was one man left who was necessary above all others to the South in settling and obtaining the annexation of Texas. We need hardly say that man was John C. Calhoun, of South Carolina. But we knew that, for some reason of which we were never informed, the President was opposed to calling him to his Cabinet. It is vain to conjecture the reason, and we are utterly unable to account for the fact, but the fact was known, and that caused us to be guilty of assuming an authority and taking a liberty with the President which few men would have excused and few would have taken. We thought of Mr. McDuffie, then in the Senate, and determined to act through him. The President, in 1843, at the instance of the Hon. Baillie Peyton, had sent our name to the Senate for the mission to France, and the nomination was rejected at a moment when it was the rule of party not to allow him to have any of his own friends in appointments when the Opposition could prevent. Thus, Mr. Cushing, for the Treasury, Mr. Porter, of Pennsylvania, for the War, and Mr. Henshaw, of Massachusetts, for the Navy, were all rejected; and when our name for France was before the Senate, and the doctrine was openly avowed that the President should not be allowed to have his

own friends in place, Mr. McDuffie had met the dogma as it deserved, and denounced it with great cogency and spirit. Our nomination hardly deserved the defense he made, but its natural effect was to draw us to him in personal gratitude for the vindication which it caused in 1843–44 by the confirmation of our mission to Brazil. We determined, through him, to act on Mr. Calhoun, whilst we took unprecedented license with Mr. Tyler. Before breakfast, by sunrise the next morning, the 29th of February, 1844, we visited Mr. McDuffie's parlor. He was not dressed, but came down in his slippers and *robe-de-chambre.* We excused our calling so early by the exigency arising from the catastrophe on board the Princeton, and immediately inquired whether Mr. Calhoun, in his opinion, could be prevailed on to accept the State Department with a view to the vital question of annexation. He admitted the magnitude of the interest involved, and how desirable it was to have it negotiated by Mr. Calhoun, but feared that he would not accept. We then urged him to write to Mr. Calhoun immediately, saying that his name would, in all probability, be sent to the Senate at once, and begging him not to decline the office if his nomination should be made and confirmed. Mr. McDuffie's delicacy towards us doubtless prevented him from inquiring whether we spoke by Mr. Tyler's authority or not, and we made no statement to him pro or con. on that point, but presume he must have supposed that we were authorized to make the request, for he promised to write to Mr. Calhoun at once.

On parting from him we went directly to the presidential mansion to breakfast. At the gate of the White House grounds we met Judge John B. Christian, of Virginia, the brother-in-law of Mr. Tyler, and, when we reached the house, found Mr. Tyler and Dr. Miller, another brother-in-law of his, in the breakfast-room. Mr. Tyler was standing with his right elbow resting on the mantel of the fireplace, and held a morning paper in his left hand, containing an account of the awful catastrophe of the day before. As soon as he saw us he accosted us with tremulous emotion, saying how humbled he was by his providential escape whilst such invaluable friends had fallen from around him, and he turned his face to the wall in a flood of tears. We came to his relief at once by saying that it was no time for mourning or wasting himself in grief,—that the moment called for prompt action and attention to duty, and that his work was pressing and heavy. It was an auspicious time, at least, to nominate for the vacancies in his Cabinet, when the dignity and solemnity of public grief for so great a calamity would shame and hush all factious opposition, and human sympathy alone at such a moment would confirm the nominations he would then make to the Senate. There were too many important affairs to be disposed of in this last year of his term of office to admit of delay. He must subdue his grief and find relief, the best relief, in turning to his tasks. He asked at once, "What is to be done?" The answer was ready: "Your most important work is the annexation of Texas, and the man for that work is Mr. Calhoun. Send for him at once."

His air changed at once, and he quickly and firmly said, "No: Texas is important, but Mr. Calhoun is not the man of my choice."

Aided by Judge Christian and Dr. Miller, we reasoned with him, though in vain, until the bell rang for breakfast. At the table the conversation turned on the calamity of the previous day; and the President gave a minute description of the manner in which by the most trivial circumstance he had been detained in the cabin at the table with the ladies, whilst Stockton, Upshur, Gilmer, Kennon, Maxcy, Gardner, and Benton all went up on deck to witness the trial of the Peacemaker! During the whole breakfast we were exceedingly uneasy, thinking how we should prevail upon him to nominate Mr. Calhoun and justify us to Mr. McDuffie. Of this we were assured, that if Mr. McDuffie's letter reached Mr. Calhoun before a nomination was made, he, Mr. Calhoun, would decline the nomination, and thus waive our committal to Mr. McDuffie; but if Mr. Tyler should nominate before Mr. Calhoun replied, declining, then we would be in an awkward position, as having made an implied committal to his nomination. But "the policy of rashness" saved us, as it had often done before and has often done since, and sent in Mr. Calhoun's nomination. As soon as breakfast was over, we rose, hat in hand, to depart, went with some impressiveness of manner directly up to Mr. Tyler, and said, " Sir, in saying good-morning to you now, I may be taking a lasting farewell. I have unselfishly tried to be your friend and to aid your administration of public affairs, and have, doubtless, your kind feelings and confidence; but I fear I have done that which will forfeit your confidence and cause us to be friends no longer. You say that you will not nominate Mr. Calhoun as your Secretary of State. If so, then I have done both you and him a great wrong, and must go immediately to Mr. McDuffie to apologize for causing him to commit himself, and you too, by an unauthorized act of mine."

" What do you mean?" exclaimed the President, evidently disturbed.

" I mean that this morning, before coming here, uninvited, to breakfast, I went to Mr. McDuffie and prevailed on him to write to Mr. Calhoun and ask him to accept the place of Secretary of State at your hands."

" Did you say you went at my instance to make that request?"

" No, I did not in words, but my act, as your known friend, implied as much, and Mr. McDuffie was too much of a gentleman to ask me whether I had authority express from you. I went to him without your authority, for the very reason that I knew I could not obtain it; and I did not tell Mr. McDuffie that I had not your authority, for I knew he would not in that case have written to Mr. Calhoun as I had requested. And now, if you do not sanction what I have done, you will place me where you would be loath to place a foe, much less a friend. I can hardly be your friend any longer unless you sanction my unauthorized act for your own sake, not my own."

He looked at us in utter surprise for some minutes, and then, lifting both hands, said, " Well, you are the most extraordinary man I ever saw!—the most willful and wayward, the most incorrigible! and therefore there is no help for it. No one else would have done it in this way but you, and you are the only man who could have done it with me. Take the office and tender it to Mr. Calhoun; I doubtless am wrong in refusing the services of such a man. You may write to him yourself at once."

We answered that we would do no such thing, for if Mr. Calhoun was given time to do so he would decline; and we therefore asked that his name should be sent to the Senate at once, when it would be confirmed, and then he could not decline. This was done; Mr. Calhoun's nomination was sent in and confirmed even before Mr. McDuffie's letter reached him. Thus was that great and good man secured to the state, and we had the honor and satisfaction of serving under his wise instructions in the first year of our mission. He was the ablest executive man of his day; his forte was in the Cabinet, not in the Senate. He was pure and simple in heart as a child, and had no equal in mental abstraction. Mr. Tyler never had reason to repent our wayward procurement of Mr. Calhoun's nomination; and neither Mr. Calhoun nor Mr. McDuffie ever knew, so far as we are informed, how it was procured. The honor to Mr. Calhoun was that of having his name sent to the Senate without his knowledge or consent, and of having it confirmed without being informed even that it had been sent in. No Senate would have dared to reject his nomination.

From the White House that morning we went to the steamer Princeton, then lying down the river a little below Alexandria. Our first care was to wait upon Commodore Stockton. He was lying in his state-room, scorched and burnt almost blind; but he was a hero, and could bear physical suffering without a groan,—a generous and noble hero, who felt most the mental agony of having been, though innocently, the instrument of the visitation of Providence. We offered him the solace coming from two of the afflicted families that amidst their own grief they sympathized with him. They and all knew how devotedly he had labored to give to the navy a model ship, the Princeton, armed with the "*Peacemaker*," and how far removed from all blame or reproach his motives were in having on board such an assemblage of dignitaries to witness the trial of his gun, thought to be an assured success, having been thoroughly tested. His

15

eyes were bandaged; but we could perceive the explosion of his feelings, and his bosom heaved as if it, too, would burst. He reached out his hand, which we grasped in friendship for life; and we have now hanging before us a picture of the Princeton, painted for him in New York at considerable cost, and which was very fine until captured and injured in the late civil war.

The "Peacemaker" was placed on the bow of the vessel. The commodore had a splendid collation in the cabin, and, before the gun was fired, had invited all his guests below to partake of his generous hospitality. The ladies and the President were first shown to the table, and the former, being afraid of the gun, kept below and detained the President with them. Those who went up to witness the firing had just partaken of the wine, and parted from the ladies and the President with toasts to the "Commodore and his Peacemaker." The awful scene, as it occurred on deck, was fully described by officers and men of the ship. It seems that there had been a foreboding with some, openly expressed before the accident, that it or something like it would happen. One of the seamen, an "old salt," told us that Secretary Upshur distrusted the gun, and, just before the moment of firing, desired him to place him at a point of safety. The gun was, as we have said, on the bow; the seaman placed the Secretary a little aport, with the foremast directly between him and the breech of the gun. Alas! how singular that, though the "salt's" experience put the Secretary at the very point where injury was least to have been expected, he was struck by two fragments of the torn cast-iron, —by one immediately over the right brow, cutting to the bone parallel with the brow its whole length, so that it fell like a flap over the eye, and by the other on the watch-fob of his pantaloons, breaking his watch-crystal and instantly stopping the hands of the watch. We carefully bore the watch, as it was taken from his person, home to his family, and requested them to mark the time it told, as his pulse had ceased with the tick of the watch when its hands were stopped. His noble head—a finer structure than that of Webster—was crushed by the blow on the brow, and the concussion on his side must have taken away his breath instantly. Stockton, who never knew fear, and who was more than sanguine of the success of his experiment, stood on the port side of the gun, immediately beside or opposite the touch-hole, with Mr. Gilmer, Secretary of the Navy, to his right. Commodore Kennon, Mr. Gardner, and Mr. Maxcy were standing between Mr. Upshur and the port gunwale, Kennon a little aft. On the starboard side Mr. Benton had his hand resting on the bow carronade, and a colored man-servant was leaning his breast on the same carronade. The gun was fired, and the havoc was shocking. Stockton was struck down blind; Gilmer's body, broken and crushed in every part, was driven to the port gunwale on the deck, looking like a wad of blue cloth, he having on a full circle Spanish cloak; two fragments struck the deck between the foremast and the gunwale, and, ricocheting, made an angle around the foremast and struck Upshur as we have described; Gardner and Maxcy were struck directly by the powder-blast and killed outright; Kennon instantly fell, but rose to his elbow, and breathed a few moments in the arms of a sailor; and the breech-pin of the gun, blown obliquely starboard, struck the bow carronade, and the concussion knocked Mr. Benton senseless and killed the ser-vant. The story was that General Jackson always doubted whether Benton had his right mind afterwards.

By the time we reached the ship, the gallant and gentlemanly officers had performed their sad offices well; the dead bodies were bound up with that neatness which characterizes sailors' work, and decently laid out in their clothes, and were ready to be placed in charge of friends. We took the bodies of Upshur and Gilmer in our charge, and saw to them until the last sad rites were performed.

This catastrophe imposed upon Mr. Tyler the necessity of forming his Cabinet anew. He appointed John C. Calhoun, of South Carolina, Secretary of State; John C. Spencer, of New York, Secretary of the Treasury; William Wilkins, of Pennsyl-vania, Secretary of War; John Y. Mason, of Virginia, Secre-tary of the Navy; John Nelson, of Maryland, Attorney-Gen-eral; and Robert Wickliffe, of Kentucky, Postmaster-General.

# CHAPTER XII.

## THE SIXTH DECADE, FROM 1840 TO 1850.

Departure for Brazil—The Calhoun Cabinet—The Last Year of the Administra-
tion, and the Annexation of Texas—Mr. Spencer retires—Election of 1844—
The Triumph of Mr. Tyler's Policy—Comparison with Jefferson's Adminis-
tration—Mr. Tyler's Second Marriage—A Scene on a James River Steamer
—Mr. William L. Marcy; Anecdotes of him and Robert G. Scott, Esq., of
Richmond, Va.—The Sherwood Estate of Mr. Tyler—His Appointment and
Services as Overseer of Roads in Charles City County—His Retirement and
Private Life—Professor Holmes's Slur upon him in the University Series—
What he did in preparing for the Acquisition of California—The Effect of
the Gold-Mines—The Revival of the Missouri Compromise Controversy—The
South dwarfed in the Union.

WE departed for Brazil in March, 1844, leaving the President
with his new Cabinet of able ministers; and it is enough to say
of them that they were the equals of the first Cabinet appointed
by Mr. Tyler himself.

Calhoun was the compeer of Webster; Spencer himself was
in better position; Wilkins was the equal of Forward; Mason
and Nelson were worthy successors of Upshur and Legaré;
and Wickliffe remained the same efficient master of his place.

The last year of Mr. Tyler's administration was chiefly employed in negotiations for the annexation of Texas. The Maine
boundary had been settled by Mr. Webster, and this last task
was appropriately a work for Mr. Calhoun. Spain had regained
her possession of Texas in 1692. A part of it, as far west as the
Colorado, had been claimed by the United States as a part of
Louisiana, in 1818, but by the treaty which ceded Florida to the
United States, in 1819, the boundary of the United States had
been fixed at the river Sabine. By the battles of Gonzalez, the
Alamo, Goliad, and San Jacinto, Texas gained her independence,

and in 1837 she sought admission into the Union. Her tender of annexation was rejected by Mr. Van Buren, though his Secretary of State, Mr. Forsyth, was a Georgian.

Northern jealousy of any more acquisition of territory in the South prevented the Locofoco dynasty from venturing to do what the people of the United States, in fact, demanded. Before he was killed, Mr. Upshur had nearly, if not quite, concluded negotiations with Van Zandt and Henderson, the Texas Commissioners, under the auspices of Mr. Tyler; and when Mr. Calhoun came in, he found Upshur's work entirely worthy of his approval and co-operation, and it took only from February 28 to April 12, 1844, for him to finish what Upshur had left to be concluded.

On the 12th of April, 1844, Mr. Tyler negotiated the treaty of annexation, and it was rejected by the Senate on the 8th of June following. In less than two months this great acquisition was refused by a partisan Senate, 16 ayes to 35 nays, such was the unreasoning malice of a Federal Whig majority with Northern proclivities against a measure so vital to the nation, because it was that of a man whom they were trying to balk in every effort to serve his country. But the wisdom of the President was not to be defeated by so stark mad an opposition. The palm of winning the prize, worth the work of a presidential term, was not to be lost to a watchful President, guarded remarkably by Divine Providence. Notwithstanding Mr. Clay and Mr. Van Buren, on the same day in April, 1844, the one in the *National Intelligencer*, and the other in the *Globe*, both published letters against the annexation of Texas, as "compromising," in the language of Mr. Clay, "the national character, and dangerous to the integrity of the Union;" yet the administration did not expire before, on the 1st of March, 1845, a joint resolution was adopted annexing Texas, and giving to an honest President the only triumph he sought,—that of wisdom and virtue. Mr. John C. Spencer, not concurring in the treaty for annexation, had, in May, 1844, resigned his place in the Treasury, and George M. Bibb, of Kentucky, was nominated and confirmed in his place.

The question of the annexation of Texas controlled the presidential election.

In May, 1844, the party national conventions were held. The Whigs nominated Clay and Frelinghuysen, opposed to annexation; and the Democrats nominated Polk and Dallas, in favor of annexation; the election took place in the fall of that year, and the people sustained the administration of Mr. Tyler by an overwhelming majority for the annexation ticket. Thus the nation itself at last carried the question for Mr. Tyler, overthrowing Mr. Clay " with a Senate at his heels." Such a victory was never obtained by a President without a party. This ended his administration and crushed all his enemies,—the Federal Whigs and the Locofoco Democrats,—the Clays and Van Burens of his opponents and revilers. Victory after victory, success after success, he won, and boon after boon, with countless blessings, he bestowed on his country, with only a corporal's guard at his command, against hosts of numbers and hells of hate. This did not look like a upas-tree which blasted all in its shade! Let us compare his administration with that of the Father of Democracy.

On the 6th of February, 1809, when Mr. Jefferson was approaching the close of his administration of public affairs, and was about to end his public career, the Virginia legislature passed resolutions of eulogy on his course, which showed that he was a favorite son of his mother State; and the best that could be said in his approval, what was said in love and affection for him, could have been said as truly in justice to, if not in favor of, Mr. Tyler.

First. Mr. Jefferson's administration was praised for its pure Republicanism. It was Republican when there was a Republican party, with power to enforce Republican policy. Mr. Tyler's was Republican when there were none so poor as to do Republicanism reverence. It was purely Republican, for it was so from choice and not from any prospects or hope of reward. It was pure as martyrdom is always pure, in contrast with petted power.

Secondly. Mr. Jefferson's administration was praised for

putting aside and behind it all "pomp and state." If Mr. Tyler was ambitious for either, Congress withheld from him all support of either, and he smiled with a relish for the plain fare which was appropriated for his self-denial, not for his indulgence.

Thirdly. The Jefferson dynasty was praised for "patronage discarded." Mr. Tyler was denied in many instances the assistance even of his friends in office.

Fourthly. Mr. Jefferson was praised for abolishing internal taxes. Mr. Tyler deserved praise for diminishing external taxes of the tariff, by forcing the application of the proceeds of the sale of the public lands to the payment of the public debt and the current expenses of the government.

Fifthly. Mr. Jefferson was praised for disbanding superfluous officers. Mr. Tyler was not allowed a number sufficient for either convenience or economy of the public service.

Sixthly. Mr. Jefferson was praised for renouncing the monarchical maxim "that a national debt is a national blessing." Mr. Tyler threw himself into the breach against the distribution of the proceeds of the sale of the public lands whilst the government needed revenue, and whilst the party who elected him clamored for protective duties on importations.

Seventhly. Mr. Jefferson was praised for extinguishing the natives' right to one hundred millions of the national domain. Mr. Tyler extinguished even more of Indian titles.

Eighthly. Mr. Jefferson was praised for acquiring, without guilt or calamity of conquest, the Territory of Louisiana. Without guilt or calamity of conquest, Mr. Tyler acquired the whole of Texas, which the administration of Mr. Jefferson, Mr. Madison, and Mr. Monroe had not only failed to acquire, but had yielded by treaty, and thus he laid the level foundation for the acquisition of the whole of New Mexico and California to the Pacific by necessary and just conquest.

Ninthly. Mr. Jefferson was praised for preserving our peace amidst great and pressing difficulties. He only deferred the war of free trade and sailors' rights to his successor. Mr. Tyler settled every controversy with Great Britain in spite of actual border hostilities, including the Boundary question and the right of search.

Tenthly. Mr. Jefferson was praised for cultivating the good will of the aborigines and for extending civilization to them. Mr. Tyler closed the bloodhound war of Florida and brought that Territory a sovereign State into the Union.

Eleventhly. Mr. Jefferson was praised for teaching lessons to Barbary. Mr. Tyler's method was higher, in teaching lessons to Christian powers in respect to neutral and maritime rights.

Twelfthly. Mr. Jefferson was praised for preserving inviolate the liberty of speech and of the press, "without which genius and science are given to man in vain." Mr. Tyler lived to better purpose, in showing how a pure patriot could steadfastly do his duty to his country and its Constitution and laws and liberty, whilst the freedom of speech and of the press ran riot in abuse of him and of his measures. And he lived to outlive the falsehood of defamation, and the weakness as well as the wickedness of personal and party abuse. His noble triumph was the public good, and his only failure was to aspire to office and to succeed to a succession.

It is pleasing to add that the turmoils and troubles of his public life did not ruffle his temper or wean his affections from the best things in life, the wooing and winning of another pearl of the partnership of love—a good and precious wife. Just before we parted with him for years, in the month of March, 1844, he called for us in his plain coach to ride with him on the Callorama Hills around Washington. We had not driven far before we discovered that his brow was knit into no knots of carking cares of state. He turned aside all allusions to politics, and showed signs of secrets more sacred and tender. His friend Mr. Gardner, of Brooklyn, New York, who was so suddenly killed by the Peacemaker, had, shortly before his death, returned from a tour in Europe, with two beautiful, bright daughters, and they were, and had been for some time, in Washington, young, fresh, and fashioned in all the gossamer wings of the foreign costume of the day. We had always heard that " an old fool is the worst of fools in love-sickness," and he showed the usual signs of its contortions into ludicrous shapes of seeming. He got it out at last that he thought of marriage, and wanted to know our opinion on the subject.

"Well, of course, you have sought and found out some honored dame of dignity, who can bring grace to the White House, and add to your domestic comfort?"

"Oh, no dame, but a sweet damsel!"

"Who, pray, of damsel degree, could or should an old President win?"

He told us; and we uttered our astonishment, by asking, "Have you really won her?"

He replied, "Yes; and why should I not?"

We answered, that "he was too far advanced in life to be imprudent in a love-scrape."

"How imprudent?" he asked.

"Easily: you are not only past the middle age" (he was then fifty-four years of age), "but you are President of the United States, and that is a dazzling dignity which may charm a damsel more than the man she marries."

"Pooh!" he cried, chuckling. "Why, my dear sir, I am just full in my prime!"

"Ah, but has John Y. Mason never told you about an old friend of his, on the south side of the James, rich and full of acres, calling his African waiter, Toney, into council, upon the tender topic of his marrying a miss in her teens? Toney shook his head, and said, 'Massa, you think you can stand dat?' 'Yes, Toney; why not? She is so sweet, so beautiful, that she could make me rise from a bed of illness and weakness to woo her for a bride; but I am yet strong, and I can now, as well as ever I could, make her happy!' 'Yes; but, massa,' said Toney, '*you* is now in *your* prime, dat's true; but when she is in *her* prime, *where* den, massa, will *your* prime be?'"

He laughed heartily at Toney's philosophical observation, but afterwards in seriousness said that he longed for the renewal of his domestic life, and had been fairly caught by the flame of Miss Gardner. We remonstrated that his life was renewed in his children; that he had daughters, lovely daugh-

ters, full of grace, fit to do the honors of the White House, and
some of them were the elders of his intended. What if family
dissent should make domestic jars and his latter days be
troubled?

He had always been too tender to the pledges of his first love
for them ever to withhold from him their filial confidence, or
deny to him his parental authority to judge and act for his
own happiness!

We saw the game was up, and then said, " We see you are
bent upon your last love, with or without counsel, and you have
ever been too lucky for us now to doubt or distrust your fate.
You are going to marry the damsel, and we are not foolish
enough to make two enemies by opposing the passion of the
wooer and the won."

Thus we parted for four years; and on the 26th day of June,
1844, at the church of the Ascension, in New York City, he
was married to Miss Julia Gardner, whilst we were running
with the trade-winds between Madeira and Teneriffe. Had we
known Julia Gardner's virtues, truth, and wisdom, as well as
we knew the beauty of her form, when her intended consort
gave us his confidence, we should have taken him by the hand
and encouraged his steps to her side. She did the honors of
the White House, with bright tact and grace, for eight months,
and then retired with him to his country home, at Sherwood
Forest, in Charles City, doing domestic duty, of wife and
mother of many children, for seventeen years, until his death
left her a widow; and she is still mourning for his loss. She
has returned lately from Staten Island, to live at last where
she ever most enjoyed life and love.

Years after, when we returned from Brazil, in the fall of
1847, we crossed the Chesapeake to Norfolk, on our way to
Richmond. At breakfast, in the National Hotel, whom should
we find at the table but Mr. Tyler and Governor Marcy, of
New York, hurrying their meal to take the same boat up the
James? We greeted each other most cordially, and never in
life did we enjoy a day's travel more than we did that day
with the two to Wilson's Landing, where Mr. Tyler stopped,

and with Mr. Marcy to Richmond. Mr. Marcy was one of the most remarkable men we ever knew. We had known him well during Mr. Tyler's troubles. He was the special intimate of Mr. Gilmer, as Mr. Buchanan was ours, through whom we worked in Congress, with Democracy, for all the measures of the administration. He had a strongly-marked face, with very shaggy eyebrows, which he seemed to train downwards purposely over his eyes, which were very keen, piercing, and observant. His brows seemed to sift his vision, which came into his look like spraying beams of light through meshes of hair. Thus his expression was cunningly concealed whilst he penetrated your thoughts and feelings. He did never exactly smile or laugh, but his humor was rare and dry, and, when he was pleased, the light of his eye scintillated more sparkling through his brow-meshes, and, like Kriss Kringle, he "shook like a bowlful of jelly." To look at him in such a mood was itself humor.

We rose when we reached Wilson's Landing, to see Mr. Tyler off; and whilst his baggage was being removed to the wharf, we observed that he had a double-seated, four-wheeled wicker carriage for small children; it would carry two, and had a tongue for extra draft. "Aha!" said we, "it has come to that, has it?"

Mr. Tyler chuckled, and vauntingly exclaimed, "Yes, you see now how right I was; it was no vain boast when I told you I was in my prime: I have a houseful of goodly babies budding around me, and if you and Marcy will only get off and go up with me to Sherwood, I will show you how bountifully and rapidly I have been blessed. They are all so near in age that they are like stair-steps, and the two youngest are so much babies alike that each requires the nurse's coach, and we have to have one with two seats!"

Mr. Marcy's eyes sparkled through the brows, and he looked for explanation. We gave it, and told an anecdote to account for the ex-President's fruitful paternity, and Mr. Tyler went off in the highest spirits, shaking his finger at our raillery, and leaving Marcy shaking the jelly of his humor.

Once afterwards, during the term of Mr. Polk, we had another scene with Mr. Marcy, which showed his curious bent at times. An old friend, Robert G. Scott, of Richmond, a burly, genial, good-natured man, of tender heart and able mind, and a powerful criminal lawyer of his day, with a brusque manner and the voice of a Stentor, was an applicant for the consulship of Rio de Janeiro, whilst Mr. Marcy was Secretary of State. We had advocated the appointment of Mr. Scott, and got the promise of the place for him; but the nomination was delayed until Mr. Scott's patience was exhausted. He had a large practice, and the delay embarrassed him with the doubt of taking new cases. He went on to Washington, and we, happening to be there, went to see Mr. Marcy with him to get some definite recognition of his appointment. Mr. Marcy gave us audience, and Mr. Scott opened the object of his visit, and firmly announced that he was tired at the delay and embarrassed by the uncertainty. Mr. Marcy sedately heard him through, without a remark; but we saw the twinkle in his eye through the brow-sieve, and when the reply to Mr. Scott came it was as we expected,—gruff, dry, hard, and sharp. He said,—

"Mr. Scott, for every bough of the top of the tree of appointments — for the missions plenipotentiary, for example — there are about one hundred applicants; for the middle boughs of the chargéships, there are about three hundred applicants; and for the lower limbs of the consulships, there are about one thousand applicants. Those who are tired of holding on to the upper boughs of expectancy hope to catch upon the places of the chargéships, if they fail to get the highest; and those disappointed in obtaining the chargéships hope to catch on the limbs below them. This will enable you to calculate your chances for a consulship. For the plenipotentiary place but one can be appointed, and the ninety and nine fall upon the chargéships, and thus the applicants for them become multiplied into 399; and for the chargéship but one can be appointed, and thus 398 have to fall upon the consulships, increasing the number of applicants for them by 398, and making the chance of a consulship about as 1398 to 1!"

There he paused and shot his glance at poor Mr. Scott, who, after the first moment, raised both hands, slapped them on his knees, and exclaimed, "Good God, sir! then I may as well go home to my clients, and quit the business of office-begging!" And he was about to rise and bid the Secretary adieu, when Mr. Marcy raised his finger, and said, "But, Mr. Scott, I have advised the President, and I hope the suggestion will be followed, that in my humble opinion *the failure* to obtain the higher offices shall not be deemed a lien on the lower: thus your chance will remain as one to a thousand only for a consulship!"

"Well, well," said Scott, "that chance is not worth waiting for, and I'll go home."

"When you do," said Mr. Marcy, "go to prepare for your passage to Rio, for your appointment is already determined upon." And, as usual, after scanning Scott's joyful surprise, he again shook the jelly of his humor. All this was done gravely, seriously, without a smile, and completely deceived Mr. Scott, who was appointed, and served with honor in the office for several years; and his worthy son succeeded him with like credit.

Mr. Tyler had acquired a very valuable tract of land in Kentucky before he was President, which, in the latter part of his term, he sold for a considerable sum of money, and this enabled him to purchase "Sherwood" estate, on James River; and a summer residence, near Hampton, was purchased out of means of Mrs. Tyler, and he was thus made comfortable for the rest of his life. He laid up nothing from his public life, and but for this sale of land in Kentucky he would have been obliged to return to the practice of his profession after his presidential term expired. His purity was above all suspicion of venality or corruption, and his poverty was proof that he retired from office without a flaw in his integrity, whatever was said of his political course.

Almost all of his leading friends and constituents in Charles City had been decided Whigs, and some of the most influential were bitter against him; but in a very short time he won them

all back to their former fondness for him.   As if to mock his
retirement from the Presidency, and to express contempt for
his course, he was appointed overseer of one of the worst roads
in lowland Virginia.

Instead of resenting the indignity, intended to belittle him,
he was tickled with the appointment, took it cheerfully, ordered
out the hands, very much against the wishes of proprietors, who
had, all their lives, lazily verified Tom Moore's lampoon upon
old Virginia roads,—

> "Ruts and ridges,
>     And bridges
>     Made of planks,
>     In open ranks,
>     Like old women's teeth!"—

and so sturdily set to rights the mortar of clay and the jack-
straws of corduroy that the whole country around rode unjolted
in praise of his industry and skill.   But he worked the roads so
well and so often that he turned the joke upon the jokers, and
convinced his neighbors that he was fit at least for the highway, if not for the high place of the Presidency.   By usefulness,
kindness, utter abnegation of himself, attention to every want
and feeling around him, and cheerfulness, he won all hearts,
and made a social circle in his neighborhood worthy of his
retirement and tender to him and to his memory.

From 1845 to 1855 his life was perfectly private, confined to
his home and his county; but he kept his eye on the prog-
nostics of coming events, and was most solicitous ever about
results which he could not fail to foresee.

Here we cannot but notice what is said of President Tyler
by Professor George F. Holmes, LL.D., in a school "History
of the United States," University Series.   He says of him:

"His experience of public life, 'which public manner breeds,'
*was limited*, but *sufficient* when he found himself *accidentally*
at the head of the government, and of a party from which he
differed on the cardinal questions of the Bank, the Tariff, and
State Rights."

We do not know what Professor Holmes calls "experience," if the time and the part taken up by Mr. Tyler in "public life" did not make him experienced, from the bar to the House of Delegates, from the House of Delegates to the House of Representatives, from Congress back to the General Assembly, from the General Assembly to the Council-chamber, from the Council-chamber to the gubernatorial chair of Virginia, from the State Executive to the Senate of the United States, from the seat there to the Presidency of the Senate, from the Senate-chamber back to the General Assembly, from the General Assembly to the Vice-Presidential chair of the United States, and from nineteen years of age to the day of his death! But Professor Holmes speaks of some sort of "experience" which "public manner breeds;" and we do not know what he means by this, unless to say that Mr. Tyler's experience in "public life" was not bred by "public manner." He was always in "public life," and in the highest places where "public manner breeds," and if he had not the largest experience, much less such as was only "sufficient," it must have been because he was inapt to learn; yet Professor Holmes says he was a man of "considerable talents." Yes, of "considerable talents," and a tact hardly equaled by any man of his day, and a judgment so true and successful that John Tyler's luck was proverbial. Public manner added full fifty years' experience to his tact, and made him the President of the United States whose administration compares well with any other, from that of Washington to that of Grant. This slurring notice of such a man looks like some prejudice of the partisan, and not like the discriminating teaching of a professor of history.

Mr. Tyler had during his term appointed Captain Frémont to explore the region of the California Territory, and he claimed the discovery of the "South Pass." He had also sent Captain Ap Catesby Jones to the coast of the Pacific to watch events and operations there. Mr. Polk, his successor, elected as a Democrat and as an annexationist, was met at once by the Mexican war, a natural consequence of the annexation of Texas. General Zachary Taylor was commissioned with the defense of the frontier of Texas, Commodore Conner was sent to the harbor of Vera Cruz with a squadron, and Commodore Sloat had orders to seize California as soon as hostilities began. Mexico declared war in 1846, and the war opened the ball of revolution in America. Its tendency and effect was to change the genius of the United States. The war was prosecuted with enthusiasm and success, and resulted in the acquisition of Texas, New Mexico, and Upper California. This vast domain, and the gold-mines of the Sacramento, changed the whole destiny of the United States by the signature of the treaty of Guadalupe Hidalgo, on the 2d of February, 1848, and peace was proclaimed on the 4th of July, 1848. But the golden fruit was guarded by the dragon; and the immense immigration to America, and the enormous addition of wealth to the treasures of the world by the California mines, revived the Missouri Compromise contention. A Wilmot proviso was introduced, and, though it failed, it commenced the struggle which ended in civil war. Two more free States were admitted, Iowa and Wisconsin, and the beam of the balance of the Union was kicked against the South.

# CHAPTER XIII.

## THE SEVENTH DECADE, FROM 1850 TO 1860.

WHEN Mr. Polk left the Chief Magistrate's chair, in March, 1849, the population of the United States numbered over twenty-three millions, the South having about four millions only of whites.

At the presidential election in 1848 the Democratic party was broken by the nomination of Mr. Cass, and the Mexican war brought upon the nation the chronic curse of a military leader for the highest civil office

General Taylor, the hero of Buena Vista, was elected; Mr. Fillmore was chosen as Vice-President. The President elect was a great "rough and ready" in the field, but ignorant of law and politics, and unfitted for the administration of civil affairs. The conquest of Mexico and territorial acquisitions embroiled the nation in a strife for sectional ascendency, and the crisis demanded extraordinary experience, judgment, foresight, sagacity, and moral courage. Mr. Fillmore had some experience in Congress, was conscientious and laborious, but a man of mediocre talents and timid, and for "Free Soil." Free Soil became the watchword and reply of the Northern masses, and coupled with the maxim of a "majority to rule," began to grow into huge proportions, threatening not only slavery but all constitutional guarantees and limitations. A large portion of California lay south of the compromise line, and yet the administration countenanced the military usurpation, by General Riley, of dictating a "free soil" constitution, and that State was admitted into the Union excluding slavery. Free Soil had presented its first candidate to sow dragon's teeth, and Mr. Clay turned pacificator again, to the detriment of the South, as he had done before in 1819. By his "Omnibus Bill," hashed up into separate measures, in 1850, the military usurpation in California was sanctioned, and that State was admitted as a free State; Utah and New Mexico were made Territories without provision as to slavery; Texas was given ten millions of dollars, and might be made into four States, with or without slavery; the slave-trade in the District of Columbia was abolished; and a law was passed to recover fugitive slaves, and that law was nullified everywhere in the Free Soil States with impunity and without redress. In the midst o this state of things General Taylor died, and the executive office devolved on Mr. Fillmore. He was a federal Whig; tried to carry out the compromise measures of Mr. Clay, but they had engrafted in them a gross error and wrong, the doctrine of Non-Intervention, as it was called by the friends of its author, Stephen A. Douglas, and it was impossible for any President to control or check the excesses of conflict which grew out of them in the Territories.

That doctrine or feature drew the competing settlers together, aspirants against each other's efforts to gain the dominion of the Territories, and disorder and danger were the inevitable consequences.

At the same time the spirit of acquisition of more domain raged; Cuba was invaded by Lopez, and Walker attempted to seize Lower California and Sonora and Nicaragua. The nation in every form began to grow fat and kick. Its materialism became monstrous. The spirit of the times was unbridled and fierce, and excited apprehensions for the public peace. Those apprehensions elected Mr. Pierce in the succeeding campaign, in 1852, over General Scott, of the Whigs, and Mr. Hale, of the Free Soil party.

The Democratic party came again into power, and, amidst every difficulty at home and abroad, for a time, at least, preserved the public peace. It settled all difficulties with Mexico, with Austria, with Great Britain, and with Spain, and made the Gadsden treaty. But domestic troubles increased. Mr. Douglas consummated the causes of territorial disorder and of national discord by his Kansas and Nebraska bill, declaring non-intervention by Congress or the United States, leaving the settlers to accept or reject slavery, and abrogating the Missouri Compromise. This was called "Squatter Sovereignty," and it had its Jack Cades without number. This caused the fixed formation of what is called the Republican party.

The first threatening movement was that of the assembling of delegates from seven Southern States, at Nashville, in the year 1850, which sat from June to November. This convention failed to do anything but to start the remedy of secession.

In 1854 the Kansas-Nebraska bill was passed, and it hastened the conflict.

The government was made, by the principle of non-intervention, to renounce its functions of protection to persons and property in the Territories; they were left to the stronger hands of border struggles for a majority, and to all the fraud and force of unprincipled and unpatriotic adventurers on both sides. With a judicial blindness unparalleled in human history, the South was induced by Mr. Douglas to back this bantling of his, worthy only of a demagogue, who concealed his real desire for Free Soil by fathering a measure seemingly intended to defeat it. The South was first duped and then subdued by it; but the Republicans, led by men of the sagacity of Thayer and other leaders like him, took "non-intervention" at its word, and made it work out the destruction of slavery and the loss of every

Territory to the South. Both sections were arrayed, and tried to obtain the first ground of occupation; the question was, "Which squatter shall be sovereign?"—and the first battle-ground was Kansas. The slave State of Missouri, contiguous with that Territory, was a first advantage for the South; but the Free-Soilers were well ordered in their action, operated in solid concert, with vastly greater wealth and the largest population; they formed immigrant aid societies, and rapidly hastened forward squatters furnished not only for settlement but for aggression or defense by arms. The "Blue Lodges," on the other side, were zealous in the use of opposing means to the designs of the immigrant aid societies, and thus a border war was actually enacted by Congress to carry on a free sectional fight, and it raged for the time with all the rancor and venom which ought to have been foreseen by men of wisdom, or divined by men of good moral instincts. Fraud, force, ruffianism, cruelty, arsons, murders, corruption of elections, reigned unbridled, broke up settlements and plundered or destroyed villages, and unregulated warfare skirmished and marauded, seized and captured, *ad libitum*, whilst "non-intervention" caused the strong sovereignty of the United States to stand by and look on without raising an arm to protect the weak or shield the right.

This ravishment of the frontier spawned that fanatic, as much sinned against as sinning, John Brown of Ossawattomie, who was the special protégé of Gerrit Smith, and the forerunner of civil war.

Whilst Governor of the State of Virginia, we foresaw what would be the result of these orgies of misrule, and tried to avert it. One legislature in Kansas, in July, 1855, passed very strong laws for the maintenance of slavery, and the Free-Soilers, in October of the same year, at Topeka, formed a Constitution excluding slavery.

The administration of General Pierce used military force, and this roused the non-interventionists to excessive resistance, until the Topeka legislature was dispersed by military force, in 1857. And out of these border troubles the tickets for the next ensuing presidential election, in 1856, were formed: the Democrats ran as their candidates Buchanan and Breckinridge, the Whigs and "Know-Nothings," combined, ran Mr. Fillmore as their candidate, and the Free-Soilers, John C. Frémont.

In 1854-55, this new organization of Know-Nothings had overrun the Northern States, and was arrested only in Virginia. It was the most impious and unprincipled affiliation by bad means, for bad ends, which ever seized upon large masses of men of every opinion and party, and swayed them for a brief period blindly, as if by a Vehmgerichte! At the foundation of it were the plans of Exeter Hall, in Old England, acting on Williams Hall, in New England, for a hierarchical proscription of religions, for the demolition of some of the clearest standards of American liberty, and for a fanatical and sectional demolition of slavery. Federalism, in the form of Whiggery, seized upon it unscrupulously, as an instrument with which to bruise the head of Democracy; but in all its forms it was hideous and revolting, and had only to be exposed to shock the moral sense of every sound patriot. The task of exposing it fell to our lot, and we spent a year in its destruction. But the snake was "scotched, not killed." Our effort was to revive the popular and Democratic party, and it was successful for the time in electing James Buchanan President of the United States, in 1857, and in postponing civil war for four years.

Mr. Buchanan came into office in 1857, with great difficulties of administration to be encountered; but still, if they had been met with nerve, and stern reliance upon the love of peace, order, and right, they would have been subdued. It was not too late to save the Union as formed by the Constitution, and the country from the blood-guiltiness of civil war, which broke down all the barriers against unlimited power, and all the guarantees of civil liberty. He ought to have seen that slavery was no longer the question; the real question was, "Shall the Constitution of the United States survive, or shall non-intervention leave it exposed to the wrong and violence of the brute force of a majority on the border?"

He ought to have seen that this applied not only to the Territories, but also to the States; not only to the slavery of the colored race, but also to the constitutional freedom of the white race; that it was not a sectional question as to which side of Mason and Dixon's line should prevail in the new settlements, but whether the States themselves should continue to exist as united under the Constitution, or whether the war-power, necessarily forced into action by non-intervention, should be allowed to supersede the civil laws and institutions, Federal and State, of the Union. In a word, he should have intervened to "keep the peace." But he was hesitating and timid, and an event which occurred upon the very first day after his inauguration alarmed him out of his propriety. The Supreme Court of the United States, on the 6th of March, 1857, decided the "Dred Scott case," that a negro was not a citizen of the United States, and that the Missouri Compromise was unconstitutional. This added fuel to the flames of excitement, and opened all the territory south of 36° 30′ to the immigrant aid societies to increase the Free-Soil States, and this especially caused Mr. Buchanan to be too cautious and temporizing in his policy. The Kansas troubles descended to his administration, and he was not courageous enough to meet them manfully. The Topeka Constitution was rejected by Congress and the administration; in fact, Mr. Buchanan himself gave countenance to the iniquities of the pro-slavery Constitution of Lecompton, in November, 1857. That Constitution was a fraud, gross, palpable, and tyrannical, and the Southern settlers were as guilty in this attempt at usurpation as the Free-Soilers were in the Topeka attempt. Having been active and efficient in the nomination and election of Mr. Buchanan, we urged upon him most earnestly the justice and policy of setting that Lecompton outrage aside, and of protecting the purity and freedom of the territorial elections; but in vain. He could not be prevailed upon to interpose for the right, and allowed the struggle to go on, until the people of Kansas, after rejecting the Lecompton fraud, finally adopted their Constitution of Wyandott, in July, 1859, and were admitted into the Union, January, 1861. It was about this period of the highest inflammation of the cancer of Kansas that the raid of John Brown upon Harper's Ferry took place, in 1859. He had been outraged in Kansas, his home had twice been invaded, one of his sons had been driven to madness by cruelty, and his youngest son had been butchered; and he became frenzied to the extreme recklessness of the raid, which capped the climax of aggression, and let slip the dogs of war for the time, and blew a bugle-blast from a gallows platform of convicts, which resounded from one end of the continent to the other, and roused every evil passion for the conflict at the next presidential election. It is due to ourself to say here that we did our full duty in that trouble. We had prepared beforehand for the worst, and hesitated not a moment to call out the militia to enforce the laws and to preserve the peace. A portion of the militia had anticipated our action, and kept the marauders hemmed in until the regular forces captured them. The President, fearing that our action would be too decisive if allowed to reach the scene in time, hastened Colonel Lee (Robert E.) forward with a squad of marines, and he gallantly captured Brown, and a worse man, Mitchell, killing twelve, including one of Brown's sons, with the loss of one marine. We should have reached Harper's Ferry from Richmond with several volunteer companies before him, but were stopped purposely, it was thought, at Washington City, in order to give Lee time to do the service by the United States troops, without the interposition of the State authorities. This was Mr. Buchanan's only act of intervention, and it was a false step, vain and too late. We had urged him to interpose in time to prevent the extension of the trouble beyond the Territories; we had spent months of labor in endeavoring to expose the destructiveness of the Douglas doctrine to the South, in a treatise upon State and Federal Relations, addressed to a friend in Alabama, and published it at considerable expense in Richmond; the lamented O. Jennings Wise had, by his pen, in the *Richmond Enquirer* and by pamphlet publications, endeavored to convince the South of the Lecompton fraud and non-intervention error, and of the apprehended consequences of both; and every effort was made to prompt Mr. Buchanan to perform his duty of protection to the whole nation. But he failed to do aught but capture John

Brown, and that only applied the fuse to the bomb-shell of civil war. He and Mr. Douglas split the Democratic party; the Whigs were demoralized by the Know-Nothings, and the Republican party was aggrandized in numbers from all factions in the North; it had already the pulpit and press and public schools and the chief wealth of parties in the North; and it is rather a wonder that Abraham Lincoln was not elected by a larger vote than that of 180 out of 303 electoral votes in the contest of 1860.

Three Free-Soil States had been added—Kansas, Oregon, and Minnesota—during the administration of Mr. Buchanan; the population of the United States had increased to thirty-one and a half millions, and the white population of the States which seceded was about five millions only. A majority of fifty-seven electoral votes was small in proportion to this state of things, and the presidential canvass convulsed the whole nation. The election itself was not the cause of the convulsion or of the revolution. The causes had accumulated from 1819. The Southern States felt compelled to secede from a sense of safety. Slave property was not all that was involved; it was, indeed, as nothing when compared with what was involved in the issue of that election. The whole theory of the government was involved in that fatal word *construction*, which the South foresaw would gain a prefix which would make it "*reconstruction*." The Constitution had already constructed a government, which government had construed it into " construction construed," and every man of sagacity saw that this was what we now endure — "reconstruction." Physics prevailed over metaphysics. The progress of the country had been so rapid and immense as to change the entire character of our population. Moral philosophy and constitutional law had fallen before steam and telegraphs and railroads and territorial acquisitions and unprecedented immigration. Free Soil was a majority, and a majority brooked no limitations to its will. Nothing would be any safer than slavery would be. Slavery of the colored race would be destroyed, and the freedom of the white race would lose all its guarantees against the abuses of a majority.

Such was the course of events which rushed us into civil war. The South itself was not united upon secession. A large portion of our people desired total separation ; but a number of respectable and experienced thinkers deprecated secession, saw no necessity for it, but instead much weakness in it, and counseled to "fight in the Union." And this brings us to scan the part which Mr. Tyler, then in his retirement, took in the contest.

We looked to his opinions with great hopefulness, knowing his remarkable tact and talent for a suggestive policy. His counsel was that of forbearance and peace. He was a sincere lover of the Union, but devoted to the States and their rights. He relied with great faith on the wisdom and strength of the constitutional provisions for the common protection, and trusted in the patriotic motives and common sense of the popular mind for our escape from impending dangers. He urged a " Peace Convention," and, we believe, was mainly instrumental in getting up that which afterwards met at Washington. He was active in urging the legislature and Governor of Virginia to call upon the States to assemble in order to avert the present dangers, and to amend the Constitution of the United States so as to prevent like crises in the future.

Virginia made the appeal for peace in vain. Her call was not met by all the States, and its failure emboldened the Northern majority to insist upon their extreme measures. The fact was, the time was already lost for preventing war. The exodus had come. There was no compromising the question of slavery, and its violent abolition would necessarily destroy all the constitutional moorings of the country. Thousands in the slaveholding States would never have risked one drop of blood for the inglorious privilege of being masters of slaves ; but they dreaded the thought of being dwarfed in the Union, and being made slaves themselves by a host of new-comers to the continent, who were not imbued by the spirit of our fathers, or the spirit and understanding of our institutions. The fate of the slavery of the colored race was sealed, and it could not secure any guarantees for the future ; and if the Constitution could be set aside and violated in respect to the right of slave property, it could be as to any right or possession whatever. The Federal Congress and Executive and Judiciary were combined against slavery, and of course would unite on all the means to abolish it, however much they invaded the sovereignty and equality of the States in the minority of the Union. And the Free-Soil States themselves had already defiantly broken the faith of the Federal compact. We were willing that Mr. Tyler and others should make the overture and attempt at peace, but from the moment of the Lecompton fraud, and the Kansas wars, and the John Brown raid, we began to prepare for the worst. We looked carefully to the State Armory; and whilst we had the selection of the State quota of arms, we were particular to take field ordnance instead of altered muskets; and when we left the gubernatorial chair there were in the State Armory, at Richmond, 85,000 stand of infantry arms and 130 field-pieces of artillery, besides $30,000 worth of new revolving arms, purchased from Colt.

Our decided opinion was, that a preparation of the Southern States in full panoply of arms, and prompt action, would have prevented civil war. The story is told, and still believed by some, that Mr. Floyd, whilst Secretary of War under Mr. Buchanan, distributed a large supply of arms to the Southern States. The story is a doubtful one; but, if true, it is certain that none of the arms were supplied to Virginia; and the misfortune of this State was, that her whole militia system had been destroyed by an unprecedented dereliction of duty and by the folly of her legislature. A prompt, bold, defiant, armed attitude would have prevented war, we repeat; but the peace policy prevailed in Virginia; whilst the Cotton States were bent on what they insanely imagined would be peaceful secession,— mistaking Cotton for King, or for even money or credit!

In a lecture delivered before the Maryland Institute for the Promotion of the Mechanic Arts, on the 20th March, 1855, at Baltimore, Mr. Tyler, in speaking of the pacification by which the Force Bill of General Jackson's administration had been rendered harmless, said, " At another day that same flag [the

Palmetto, of South Carolina], as it waved in full glory over the plains of Mexico, caught the gaze of an admiring world, and impressed, as I trust, upon the heart and mind of America the principle that, in differences of opinion that may and will spring up between the States, the last counselor should be the pride of power, and the last mediator should be force." And he concluded that lecture by saying, "Rome, in her day of power, claimed to be the mistress of the world, and Alexander wept that he had no more worlds to conquer; and yet neither the one nor the other looked down from their height of power upon possessions more extensive or more fertile than those which we enjoy. I mention these things not in a spirit of vain boasting, but for a far different and more interesting purpose: it is to induce a still deeper impression of love and veneration for our political institutions, by exhibiting our country as it was, and is,—and will be, if we are true to the great trust committed to our hands. I listen to no raven-like croakings foretelling 'disastrous twilight' to this confederacy. I will give no audience to those dark prophets who profess to foretell a dissolution of the Union. I would bid them back to their gloomy cells, to await until the day shall come, which, I trust, will assuredly come, when this great republic shall have reached the fullness of its glory. I will not adopt the belief that a people so favored by Heaven will most wickedly and foolishly throw away 'a pearl richer than all their tribe.' No! when I open the book of the Sibyls, there is unfolded to my sight, in characters bright and resplendent and glorious and vivifying, the American confederacy in the distant future, shining with increased splendor,—the paragon of governments, the exemplar of the world. If I misinterpret the prophecies, let me live and die in my error. Let it rather be thus than awaken me to an opposite reality, full of the horrid specters of strong governments, sustained by bristling fortifications, large standing armies, heavy burdens on the shoulders of industry, the sword never at rest in its scabbard, and the ear deafened ever by the roar of cannon. No! leave me for the remnant of my days the belief that the government and institutions handed down to us by our fathers are to be the rich legacy of our children and our children's children to the latest generation. If this be a delusion, let me still embrace it as a reality. Keep at a distance from me that gaunt and horrible form which is engendered in folly and nurtured in faction, and which slakes its thirst in the tears of the broken hearts and appeases its appetite on the blasted hopes of mankind."

Alas! he did misinterpret the prophecies; the gods loved him too well not to grant his prayer, and did not let him live to see "the specters of strong governments." He was taken away from the touch of subjugation,—he never tasted the bitterness of its ashes. His heart was not broken; he died in hope, and was never forced to see the "gaunt and horrible form" of that despotism of Congress which has destroyed the Constitution, States, laws, and liberties of the people of the United States. He was too much for forbearance, peace, and compromise; and that state of mind of most leading men in Virginia caused us to be found unprepared for inevitable war. Yet these same men, when forced to resort to an ultimate mode of preventing coming calamities and redressing past or preventing future wrongs, were those who betook themselves to secession rather than to the wiser remedy of "fighting in the Union." They did not and could not foresee in time that they "must fight," and blindly persisted in believing that "secession might and would be peaceful." It was a delusion causing war, and war unprepared for. If they had seen that the war was inevitable, they would have prepared for it; and if at the very beginning they had been prepared for it, and had first "drawn the sword instead of blowing the horn," there would have been no war. That was the first advantage in the idea of "fighting in the Union." The prompt, prepared attitude of war would have brought about a peaceable adjustment, which would have sheathed the drawn sword in the interest of the Union, without a drop of blood. This was the only hope of peace, and this would have made peace, unless war, in the eye of Omniscience, was the only means of abolishing the slavery of the colored race in the country. And if it was the only providential means of God to compel the exodus of the negro race from bondage, yet, if we had been ready and prepared for it, we might have enforced terms which, while they yielded the emancipation of bondmen, might have saved freemen of the white race from chains, and might have preserved the Constitution of the United States, the rights of the States, and the liberties of all the people.

But with them, Mr. Tyler among the rest, unfortunately, to " fight in the Union" was to fight with halters around their necks,—was treason. This was the great error of the Southern leaders. It did not proceed from cowardly or selfish motives. They thought themselves morally bound to assume the attitude which would most effectually preserve their constituents from the personal consequences of penalties, forfeitures, seizures, and confiscations. Their error was in supposing that to fight in the Union would be rebellious, and that to secede would make the war intergential. In the first case, they conceived, we would be rebels,—*hostes ;* in the last we would be enemies,—*inimici non hostes.* This, we repeat, was a great error, both of judgment and of law.

In point of judgment, their declaring themselves absolved from the obligations of the Union would not make them so. Success alone in arms could do that; and if their enemies succeeded in arms, the conquerors would not fail to treat them either as enemies or as rebels, or as both, as they might elect. But they thought themselves safer from the halters of treason by seceding, in case their enemies should succeed. It was in vain urged that there was a greater danger threatening them than that of halters,—the danger of the application of the absolute rules of the *jus belli,*—of confiscation of the property of persons, and of the annihilation of States, and the other operations *inter gentes* " *vi concitate belli ;*" that the *jus belli* was an absolute rule under the laws of nations, and knew no limitations; whilst the rule of Confederate or United States in conflict, without a separation or secession, would be governed by the law of internal sovereignty, the Constitution of the United States, with all its guarantees, limitations, prohibitions, and restrictions.

Blockade and non-intercourse, for example, would be a very different thing under the law of external sovereignty, the law of nations, from what it would be under the law of internal sovereignty, the Constitution of the United States; and we could claim all the benefits of existing organization in the post-office, in the custom-house, in treaties with foreign powers, and in the eminent domain. This was urged in vain, and could not be understood. The halter of treason hung before their eyes and turned them away from their true policy.

In point of law we urged the true views of our compositive system of government, a constitutional Union of separate and independent States, before and since the war, in vain. The courts of Virginia and the United States, since the surrender, have been as wild in their decisions respecting our political law as were the Confederate leaders before the war began. They have made the late conflict of the States of the Union a perfect nondescript revolution,—internal, external, intergential, civil; having fixed rules and exceptional; absolute and relative; international and intra-territorial; under municipal and prize; under the constitutional law and under the international law; mixed, confused, arbitrary, and whatever dictation on the one side and servile fear on the other may prescribe or accept.

We often conferred with Mr. Tyler, especially upon what that law was. He always admitted the truth of our views, yet, like others, would not agree to their adoption and application.

# CHAPTER XIV.

## THE SEVENTH DECADE, FROM 1850 TO 1860.

The Essential Rights of States—The Original Condition of the several United States—What Change did the Constitution of the United States make in their Sovereign Condition?—The War-Power of the United States—War-Power and the Power to Repel Invasion in Constitutional Contrast with the Powers to execute the Laws and to suppress Insurrection—The Prohibitions to the States—The Error of Secession—Instances of Insurrection and Rebellion—A State defined—The Primary and Secondary Elements of a State—The Conflict of States never an Insurrection: of these States, it is Internal or Civic War, governed by the Law of Internal Sovereignty—The States invaded, and their Duties in the Case—*Inimici non Hostes*—Dorr's Rebellion.

OF all the absolute and conditional rights of States, the most essential and important, and the first, is the right of self-preservation. This is not only a right with respect to other States, but a duty with respect to its own members. It necessarily involves all other incidental rights which are essential as means to give effect to the principal end. Among these is the right to require the military services of all its people; to levy troops; to maintain a naval force; to build fortifications, and to enforce and collect taxes for all these purposes of self-defense. And the exercise of these absolute sovereign rights can be controlled only by the equal, correspondent rights of other States, or by special compacts, freely entered into with others, to modify the exercise of these rights. Such is the received law, as laid down by the best modern authority, the "American Elements," I may say, of Wheaton.

To these preliminary principles the fact must be added that, prior to the formation of the Constitution of the United States, such were the rights of each and every State of this Union, among other independent, sovereign States of Christendom. Vir-

ginia, for example, undoubtedly had the right of self-preservation and of self-defense, with all the incidental means; and it is
also equally true that she as a State prompted and promoted
the formation of the Constitution of the United States expressly
to create "a more perfect Union," for the very purpose of enabling her more effectually to protect and defend herself, and to
protect and defend each and all of the States, and to preserve
the rights and liberties of all.

Then the question arose, How far did the formation of the
Constitution of the United States modify or restrain this absolute sovereign right of self-defense and self-preservation in the
several States of the Union?

The Constitution gave charge of the "*common* defense" to
Congress.

To Congress was granted the power to *declare war*, grant
letters of marque and reprisal, and make rules concerning captures on land and on water; to raise and support armies, and to
provide and maintain a navy; to make rules for the government
and regulation of the land and naval forces, and to provide for
the calling forth the militia to execute the laws of the Union,
suppress insurrection, and *repel invasion*, and for organizing,
arming, and disciplining the militia, and governing such part of
them as may be employed in the service of the United States;
but the States were to appoint the officers, and to train them
according to discipline prescribed by Congress.

Now, it is palpable that such of these provisions as relate
to *war* and its means and incidents, and to "repelling invasion," apply only to "foreign war," or war *inter gentes*. And
it is equally plain that whatever force of armies or navies, or
"captures on land and on water," or "calling forth the militia"
against our own citizens it authorizes, are not for the purposes
or ends or uses of *war*, but were authorized for two purposes
alone, and those domestic and internal only,—first, *to "execute
the laws;"* second, "to suppress insurrection."

War, to make it valid, must be *declared*. No *war* could be
declared against the States of the Union or against their citizens by the Congress of the United States.

It was folly to imagine that Congress would be so unwise and artless as to declare war against secession. It would have been at once to acknowledge the fact of a separation and the right to secede. It was obvious that Congress would proclaim an insurrection to be suppressed, and would call forth forces to execute the laws; that it would declare no war; and that it would in any event, with or without secession, operate on individual citizens *in personam,* and hold them accountable for treason and amenable to its penalties. There could be nothing gained to the citizens, then, by secession, and the whole prestige of the Union would be lost to the popularity and probable success of the Confederacy. The Constitution and Union were the best and only guardians of the people against the dangers and trials and halters for treason.

By the Constitution, Congress had no power to declare war against any State or States of the Union, but, on the contrary, was rather restrained from so doing. The militia, or military or naval forces, could be called forth for no domestic or home purpose except either " to execute the laws" or " to suppress insurrection ;" and there were restraints upon that power even, since the States alone could appoint militia officers and train the militia. *Foreign* war and the *repulsion of invasion* stand in the Constitution in pointed contrast with " the *execution of the laws*" and " the suppression of insurrection." War and invasion apply to the territory and rights of the nation as against foreign powers only. The execution of the laws and the suppression of insurrection apply to the internal sovereignty and its powers respecting its own citizens and States. No government has the power of making *war* upon or invading its own territory or people. It is absurd even to suppose that the States in forming the Constitution ever meant to give, or ever did give, the power to Congress to make war upon and invade them. Congress was given the power to wage war and to repel invasion, to protect the States and their people against foreign powers ; and it was given the power to execute the laws of the Union and the States, and to suppress insurrection against the authorities of either the States or the Union.

17

The Congress could not make war upon the States or their people, or invade them ; but yet internal and intra-territorial war is expressly provided for in the tenth section, third paragraph, of the first article of the Constitution, which provides, " No State shall, without the consent of Congress, lay any duty of tonnage, keep troops or ships of war *in time of peace*, enter into any agreement or compact with another State, or with a foreign power, or engage in war, unless actually invaded, or in such imminent danger as will not admit of delay."

This conditional and limited, or contingent, prohibition to the States proves that, without its inhibition, each State would have retained all these powers unlimited ; and it shows that the States may now exercise them all " *in time of war*," and that it leaves in each State still the power to lay tonnage duties, to keep troops or ships of war *in time of war*, to enter into any agreement or compact with another State, or with a foreign power, or *to engage in war, when actually invaded, or when in such imminent danger as will not admit of delay.* Thus, on the contingencies named, each State had reserved the power of war, internal or external, against any State or States in the family of nations at home or abroad. Each State, in given exigencies of invasion or imminent danger, had retained her power of self-defense and of war, not only as against foreign states, but as against sister States or their common agent, the Federal government.

And the very object of this reservation is so plain that the effect of its omission would have been to expose a State to the necessity of passive submission to wrongs and inequalities in the Union, and her citizens to the dreaded danger of halters for treason. Her reserved right to declare war, at home or abroad, when invaded or in imminent peril, retained to her as a State the sovereign right of self-protection, and to her citizens as a people the shield of her sovereignty against treason, its infamy, and its penalties. Each State, as one of the principals to the compact of the Constitution, might well be expected to retain such a power ; but she could not rationally be supposed to have ever given the power to her own creature in part, the Congress, to declare war upon her and to wrong and invade her without the right of redress. Thus, there was *a power of internal war*, but that power was not in Congress; it was in the States, and retained by them. And this right of the States, to protect themselves against actual invasion and from imminent danger not admitting of delay, necessarily made each State the judge of actual invasion or of the imminent danger, without delaying for the consent of Congress, on her responsibility as a State to her co-States and to the Union. It was the right of the conflict of States, for cause, with each other·or with Congress, in cases of actual invasion or of imminent danger not admitting of delay. It was the right of civil war between States, with each other, or with the Congress or Federal Executive, to redress wrongs in the cases named, as well as with foreign powers or with the Indian tribes. It was a right under the Constitution, and there was no necessity to secede in order to save citizens from halters. The error of secession was, as has since been proved, that it could not save the citizens from the accusation of treason, and that it gave a pretext for applying the absolute rule of the *jus belli* against the States in respect to personal rights and to property. It could not insure the safety of the citizen, and would annihilate the State rights by the rule of war *inter gentes*, and it has annihilated them. To avoid the halter of treason it ran the State into the vortex of the *jus belli*. If each Confederate State had remained in the Union, and declared war for actual invasion and for imminent danger not admitting of delay, her individual citizens, who took up arms under her laws for her defense, could not have been made to answer for her acts, except as enemies in war, not as *hostes* chargeable with treason and felony. The States in the conflict of revolution were responsible to one another, and their rights were *relative* only, not absolute, in the Union; but the individual persons who were their subjects and citizens could not be made responsible either in person or in property for the acts of their States. They could be held responsible only for their individual acts in violation of the rules of war. If not enlisted in the war, they, still in the

Union, were under the protection of the Constitution; and if in the army or navy or civil service of the resisting or revolutionary State, they would have been entitled to the character of *inimici non hostes*, and could not have been punished as felons and traitors. Otherwise, the compositive system of government of the United States would be the most dangerous and oppressive in the world. The citizen, however innocent and *bona fide* his acts, for or against his State, would be between Scylla and Charybdis, and liable to be punished for treason whether he sided with his State or against her. No construction could permit such perversion of every idea of allegiance and protection. Where States are in conflict with one another, their citizens on the high seas are not pirates, and on land are not felons. They are then simply and technically "*enemies.*" "*States*" only are responsible in the conflict of States, either at home or abroad; and, if the general government had the power to call on the citizens of the revolutionary State to execute its laws against her and to suppress insurrection, and the State also had the right of war to repel actual invasion and to call on her own citizens to defend her against imminent danger not admitting of delay, then no sane person could risk a residence in the country, the moment a civil war began, because he would be exposed to the penalties of treason, take whatever part he might, either by force or choice. The truth is, the conflict of States can never, in any form, be called or treated as "insurrection." Without the conflict of States, there never can be such a thing as war, either external or internal; and where there is war between States, the persons of their citizens or subjects are treated always as *inimici non hostes.*

Where subjects and citizens unorganized as a State rise up against the sovereignty under which they are protected, and to which they owe allegiance, then and then only can they be lawfully treated as *hostes non inimici.* Belligerency, in its largest sense, means any organized conflict of people in arms in considerable numbers sufficient to exceed mere riot, rout, and unlawful assemblage, in which they have not the sanction or authority

of a State either *de facto* or *de jure*. But mere conflict in arms,
by people who have no sanction or authority of a body politic
called a State, is not *war*. If it is carried on at sea, it is piracy;
if on land, it is felony and treason; but no acts of war between
*States* are either piracy or treason. Their citizens, bound by
force as well as by law to obey the commands of the sovereign
of their domiciles, cannot be deemed traitors; and the States
themselves in conflict cannot be punished for treason. A State
cannot commit such a crime.

The instances of insurrection and rebellion involving treason,
in this country, are numerous enough to illustrate every shade
of difference between them and the war between States in
which no treason can be committed. There are the instances
of Shays's Rebellion in Massachusetts; of the Whisky Insurrection in Pennsylvania; of the State of Franklin in the Territory—
now the State—of Tennessee; of the Hartford Convention in
Massachusetts; of Georgia in the Tassels and Cherokee dis-
turbance; and of the more modern and striking case of the
Dorr Revolution in Rhode Island. In every instance, the case
was where mere citizens and subjects, or individual persons,
numerous and having organization, but wanting the sanction
and authority and orders or form of a State, rose in resistance
against their governments, State and Federal; they were in-
surgents, rebels, traitors, what law defines to be *"hostes,"* as
contradistinguished from "enemies," because there was no
war. Dorr, for example, had full and complete organization;
he had, it was supposed, a majority of the numerical, though
not of the conventional, people to back his truly republican claim
of political rights against an oligarchic King Charles charter,
odious to the ideas of American liberty; and he was, to a great
extent, quietly permitted to bring his organization to the point
of popular revolution against the State. But neither his
nor any other insurrection in our history had the forms and
authority of a State. In no case was there a conflict of States
with one another. A State consists of certain primary and secondary elements of construction and organization, which necessarily give it the power of making war; but no mere associa-

tion of persons, without the attributes of a State, can make war. If they take up arms against their own governments, or against foreign powers or people even, they are alike *hostes non inimici.* But a State cannot be a traitor, or guilty of treason, nor can her citizens be traitors for obeying her mandates. Any organization to be a State must have,—

1st. A territory with defined and acknowledged boundaries.

2d. A people, defined by citizenship.

3d. A people, defined by franchise. The one is the numerical people, and the other is the conventional and constitution-making people of a republican State.

4th. Her conventional people, or voters, are the source of her laws, organic and statute, and they alone possess her conventional power.

5th. Her constitution of government founded and resting alone on her conventional power.

Of these five cardinal and primary elements, the existence and essence of a republican State consist, and on these they depend. They are fundamental and organic, conventional and constitutional. The constitution depends on the convention, and the convention on the franchise, and the franchise on the citizenship, and the citizenship on the defined place and the time of residence. But, in addition to these primary elements, the body politic, called a State, must necessarily have certain secondary attributes, which may be styled most properly *" municipal :"*

1st. A legislative power, to pass statute laws in conformity with her constitution.

2d. An executive power, to execute her constitutional statutes.

3d. A judicial power, to construe and ever vigilantly to guard her constitution, and to decide upon public and private rights and wrongs, according to known and established rules and precedents in cases of judicial cognizance.

These three attributes constitute municipal government. By these a State exerts her powers and acts, but the life of the State and her being are in the primary elements; and these organic and municipal elements combine to form the government of a republican State. Her government is distinct from her sovereignty; the former rests upon her constitution, and her constitution rests upon her sovereignty, which consists in her conventional power. Her municipal government may be driven away from its seat of power, but her constitution and her sovereignty, or conventional power, still remain. Rebellion, insurrection, has nothing but a numerical people, has but mere numbers of persons; it has no territory, no franchise, no conventional power, no constitution, no municipal government of a State. But each and every State of the eleven States in the civil war of the late revolutionary conflict of States in this Union had all the primary and secondary elements of sovereignty, — territory, citizens, voters, conventional power to frame a constitution of government, a constitution of government formed and guaranteed by the United States to be republican, and a municipal government giving laws over an immense space to millions of population, deciding upon laws and rights and wrongs under them, and executing them, and with the reserved power of peace and war, in the categories and contingencies above described.

The plain distinction between the cases of States in conflict with one another or with the Federal government, and the cases of individual persons in conflict with either, was blindly overlooked at the very beginning of the war, and since has been broken down, and despotically on the one side, or timidly on the other, disregarded. It has been so confused by error and ignorance and by usurpation since the war, that our sense has been astounded by the terms "rebel enemies" applied by judges of the Supreme Court of the United States! In other words, or rather to explain the practical and intended meaning of this solecism in terms, they have declared *citizens rebels* and *States enemies*, to hang the former as traitors, and to annihilate the rights of the latter by reconstruction, as enemies subject to the arbitrary and absolute rule of the *jus belli*. They would not observe the rule of law in the case even of the lowest corporation,—that where the stockholders constitute the company, and the managers and officers are their agents, necessary for the conduct and management of the affairs of the company, but not essential to its existence as such, nor forming an integral part, the corporation exists *per se*, so far as is requisite to the maintenance of perpetual succession, and holding its franchises, the non-existence of the managers not implying the non-existence of the corporation.   The corporate functions may be suspended for want of the means of action, but the capacity to restore its functionaries, by means of election, remains.   So a State may, by internal war, by epidemic, or otherwise, lose its governor, the members of its legislature, the members of its judiciary, and all the chief officers or functionaries of its several municipal departments of government, but still the body politic remains, consisting of the five primary elements of a State, and its capacity to restore its functionaries, its mere municipal officers, by means of election, remains.   Ay, and if there be not functionaries sufficient to call forth the conventional people to the polls, then the Constitution of the United States guarantees that each State of the Union shall have a republican form of government, and it becomes the duty of the Congress of the United States— not to assume to make the Constitution for the State, for she has one already ; nor to dictate who shall be her voters or conventional people, for they are already defined by the State Constitution ; but—simply to call forth her voters, already constituted by an existing State Constitution, either to hold a convention of their own, or to elect the functionaries necessary to carry on the municipal government according to the State laws.   All this beauty and harmony and symmetry of our compositive system has been destroyed by the timidity which, before the war, to escape halters plunged into the *jus belli ;* and by the tyranny which, during and since the war, has, to suit its ends as occasion required, used and applied all the laws of treason, insurrection, rebellion, and war in confusion wосre confounded.

The late civil revolution of States, or conflict of States in *civil war,* was governed by a very different rule from that which governs either rebellion or insurrection at home, or even a war *inter gentes.*   And here the wisdom and beauty of the Constitution of the United States, harmonizing State and Federal relations, and the relations of citizens to the States and the Union, rise up to the admiration of all who understand its provisions, and who are just and republican enough to execute them faithfully. States, as we have defined, indestructible in their primary elements, however liable to accident or casualty in their municipal functionaries, having the corporate immortality of succession in their cardinal and vital being; States, as we have seen, which existed before the Constitution of the United States was formed; States, which framed the Constitution of the United States, had the power of war and peace, of making treaties and repelling invasion, before the Union and the Congress existed. And we have seen that their existence and their power of war for self-preservation were not merged in the Union, or in the metropolitan government which makes or executes the laws of the Union; the Constitution, on the contrary, created a "union of States," called the United States. The Union was made by the States, and the States were not *unmade* by the Union. There could be no *union of States* where no States were left to be united. They existed *de jure* before they made the Union, and in making it they expressly excluded the conclusion, that thereby their own existence and powers were excluded, or even merged, in the formation of the Union. The Constitution itself—every declaration, grant, limitation, prohibition, or reservation of it—proves this. They each and all still retained every primary and secondary element of States,—their distinct boundaries, population, citizenship, conventional power and franchise, and their Constitutions, as also their municipal departments of government, legislative, executive, and judicial; as well as all their powers "not delegated," and their powers " reserved,"—especially their power of war in cases of actual invasion or of imminent danger "not admitting of delay."

It was under these independent, ungranted, reserved, and constitutional powers of States that certain States, resolved on resistance, should have declared themselves actually invaded, and that they were in imminent danger not admitting of delay. They could not wait to obtain the consent of Congress, because their invasion was commenced by the Federal Executive, sanctioned by Congress.   For this they should have engaged in war, the war of States with the Federal government and with the op-posing co-States in the Union.   This they had the right to do, under the third paragraph of the thirteenth section of the first article of the Constitution which they had themselves prescribed. This would have been constitutional war, war between States and governments, and this, under our compositive system, made citizens of the States involved in the war *inimici non hostes.* They could not have been held individually responsible for the war, and the government, State or Federal, involved in the war could not have operated upon them in person, except to treat them as lawful belligerents.   This would have been ample protection to them against all prosecutions for treason.   It was war, but not war *inter gentes,* in which international law is the law of sovereignty.   It would have been a civil, in-ternal, and intra-territorial war, and *not* subject to the absolute rule of the *jus belli* of the international law.   In this only would the war have been peculiar, that in our Union of States —called by Wheaton a *Bundesstaat,* a bundle or band of States, or a compositive system of States—the sovereignty was divided into external and internal.   The external sovereignty was merged in the Union, and the supreme law of that sovereignty was the international law; but the internal sovereignty was distributed between the Union and the States; its principles and component parts could be governed only by the law of in-ternal sovereignty—*the Constitution of the United States.*

This civil, internal war, governed by the Constitution of the United States, the law of internal sovereignty, might have its external cases, such as those of blockade, *inter gentes ;* but the general law of the war would be the law of internal sover-eignty.

This view has since been sustained by Vice-Chancellor Wood in the case of the United States *vs.* Prioleau, etc., 1 Jurist, etc. The States, as contradistinguished from the Confederacy, were not and could not be made the subjects of conquest by their own governments under their own law of internal sovereignty, the Constitution of the United States.  The United States might claim Confederate property, but could not claim State property, for the latter would be governed not by the international law, but by the Constitution of the United States, as the law of internal sovereignty. This war had,—

First, its internal cases, involving rights of States and of citizens and their property, such as arrests and seizures on land, and proceedings operating both *in personam* and *in rem*, governed by the Constitution of the United States; and, second, its external cases, such as the prize cases, cases of " prize or no prize," necessarily cases *inter gentes*, involving neutrals abroad as well as belligerents at home. These external cases were governed, of course, by the absolute rule of the *jus belli*. No other cases of the war were so governed. There were, third, a mixed class of cases, contraband in their nature, in which rights were *suspended* only by the war. And internal war could not set aside or destroy the Constitution of the United States or its limitations. The *internal* cases could not be governed by the *jus belli*.

The supreme law of these cases could only be the constitutional provisions—first, of common defense and self-protection, or the national power to preserve and defend its own authority, to keep the peace and restore order; second, to execute the laws; and, third, to suppress force by arms.

This civil war could be proclaimed and prosecuted by the Union internally only to maintain and support the Constitution of the United States. The Federal government was bound to assert and exert its authority for that purpose, and to execute such laws as were made in pursuance of the Constitution. Whatever was necessary and proper to be done by armed force to maintain the Union and to execute its constitutional laws might be done, but no more. No force for conquest, or for any purpose of mere warlike penalty, no power for subjugation, could be exerted; and the moment that the laws could be executed and the authority of the Federal government was established, the powers of war ceased, and civil process and jurisdiction resumed their reign and sway under the Constitution of the United States. This had been too fully discussed and settled by Hamilton, Edmund Randolph, and Governor Mifflin, during the Whisky Insurrection in Pennsylvania, to be misunderstood. Every case, internal and intra-territorial, had to be governed by the supreme law of internal sovereignty, the Constitution of the United States, and the laws made in conformity therewith. The war-power, or military and militia power, of the Union was but auxiliary to the Constitution and laws of the Union. The only limited *jus belli* was the power to execute the laws. There could be no other constitutional or legitimate purpose of the war but to enforce the Constitution and laws of the Union.

Thus the wisdom of our Federal Constitution was exhibited beyond that of any other federation of history.

1st. It left a war-power in the States which shielded their citizens from the crime or penalties of treason.

2d. It saved alike the States and their rights, and the rights of the persons and property of their citizens, in the conflict of States, from the arbitrary and extreme application of the absolute rule of the *jus belli* of international law.

And is it any argument against this clear exposition of our compositive system, to say that it leaves internal war by the States, either as to States or persons, without its penalties?

The reply is, that war of that kind has no penalties but those of war,—its battles, its death, its wounds, its captives, and captures in war. This wise result was intended expressly by the framers of the Constitution—by the States themselves. They wisely foresaw that a minority of States might be wronged by a majority; and the dread of war alone, which could win nothing by conquest and impose no ultimate penalties beyond the effect of arms, might deter a majority from violating the Constitution. If it did not, then the Constitution, *proprio vigore*, would protect the States and their people in fighting for their rights and for its guarantees.

But these views, just and clearly sustained as they are by the laws of nations and by the Constitution of the Union, and ably expounded as they have been by Hamilton and Edmund Randolph, early in our history, and afterwards by Wheaton in his

"Elements," and since the war by Judge Treat, in the Missouri
cases, were all scouted. And so distinctly have they been set at
naught since the war, in contrast with the precedents before,
that whilst Congress claims that persons attached to the Confederacy were traitors, it at the same time claims that by the
rights of war between States it could dictate franchise and citizenship and constitutions of government to States having constitutions already defining citizenship and franchise, in defiance of the law of internal sovereignty, the Constitution of the
United States. In the Rhode Island case, the Federal government deemed itself incompetent to interpose for the people, to
afford them the opportunity of changing the king's charter into
a Constitution, even under the constitutional clause making it
imperative on the United States to guarantee to each State a
republican form of government. So sacred was the principle
then held, that neither the Federal Executive nor the Congress dared to interfere with a State Constitution, to modify,
change, or destroy it, or even to assist the State's own people
to change it for a better. But now, it has been seen that by
act of Congress no less than eleven of the State Constitutions
already existing, and not destroyed by the war or in the least
impaired by it, have been set aside and annulled by statutory
reconstruction, founded solely on the rights of war and the force
of the *jus belli*. The conflict of States has been made, by Congress, internal rebellion, to *hang citizens;* and *external and
intergential war between States,* in order to strip States by the
*jus belli* of the right of self-government.

Some few of us foresaw this, but we were unheeded; and
when the conflict came, Mr. Tyler, after attending the Peace
Convention and presiding over it in vain, for war was then inevitable, unfortunately sided with secession as the mode and
measure of redress, instead of "*fighting in the Union for the
Union!*"

Alas! few at that time could see the great truth, the most
conservative and beautiful in our compositive system, that the
conflict of States in our Union is neither insurrection nor rebellion, but is civil and internal *war;* and being *internal* and

*civil,* it is not governed by the law of external sovereignty, the *jus gentium,* with its absolute rule of the *jus belli,* but by the law of internal sovereignty, the Constitution of the United States; the domestic sovereignty of the States saving individual citizens from the halters of treason; and the law of internal sovereignty, the Constitution of the United States, saving both States and their citizens from the penalties of the *jus belli.*

# CHAPTER XV.

Peace Convention—Virginia's Attitude—Rapid Rush of Events from the 4th of February to the 18th of March, 1861—The Part of Mr. Tyler—His Speech on opening the Peace Convention—Virginia's Delegates disagree among themselves—The Rule in the Case of Hylton *vs.* United States, as to *Uniformity* and *Equality* of Taxation throughout the United States, contended for by Mr. Tyler—Proclamation of the Federal Executive, and its Effect—The Seizure of Harper's Ferry—Secession declared by Virginia on the 17th of April, 1861—What Virginia ought to have done—Mr. Tyler elected to the Confederate Congress—His Death—The Obituaries—His Will.

THE Peace Convention was called by Virginia. She had not as yet assumed the attitude of the Confederate States already seceded, or of the Federal government, or of neutrality. Her first movement was that of a peace-maker. There stood the colossal power of the Union, north, and there the States combined in secession, south; and here was Virginia, the mother of States and of statesmen, midway between the bristling bayonets of the belligerents, her territory and people easily accessible to invasion from either north or south, and she was physically compelled to look to her safety, and morally bound to take which ever side her judgment pronounced to be that of justice, law, and right. She was sure to be "actually invaded," and was already in "such imminent danger as not to admit of delay." Whatever may have been the position of other States, her prompt and decisive action was impelled by necessity and force. She was obliged to take up arms, but did not do so hastily, nor until after she had exhausted her efforts at conciliation. This call for a Peace Convention was mainly the work of Mr. Tyler. He, with Mr. Rives and Mr. Summers, was sent to the convention on the 4th of February, and on the 6th of February, 1861, it met at Washington and

( 271 )

was organized. On the 4th of February, 1861, the Confederate Congress met at Montgomery, Alabama. The Convention of Virginia met at Richmond on the 13th of February, 1861. The Confederate Constitution was adopted at Montgomery, and President Davis was inaugurated, on the 18th of February, 1861. And the Peace Commissioners appointed by Virginia reported back to the governor and legislature on the 18th of March, 1861. Thus, in about forty days and forty nights, this deluge, like the flood which destroyed the world, gathered, and there was no Noah and no Ark to save us !

The part which Mr. Tyler took in the Peace Convention, and in respect to its results, was the most glorious of his life. It alone is a monument worthy of any name. He acted the part not only of a Father of his State, but of his whole country. An Ex-President of the United States, he was made president of the convention called by his State to preserve the peace of the United States, and it was the hope of many at the time that the peace would be preserved. But the convention was too late. If it had been called a year before, or if Virginia had drawn her sword for self-defense at once, instead of delaying or dallying for compromises, war might have been averted. But the State had not drawn her sword, and the Peace Convention sat almost after the clash of arms had begun. From the *National Intelligencer* of Wednesday, February 6, 1861, we extract an account of some of the proceedings of the convention, and the speech of the President elect:

## "THE COMMISSIONERS' CONVENTION.

" The convention of delegates from the several States co-operating with Virginia in the work of national preservation was yesterday organized by the unanimous election of the Hon. John Tyler as its permanent President, and of the Hon. J. C. Wright, of Ohio, as Secretary.

" In selecting by acclamation for their presiding officer the distinguished Ex-President of the United States, the members of this dignified body have conferred an honor which will be as worthily worn as it was gracefully proffered, and the appropriateness of whose bestowal will be recognized by their countrymen throughout the whole land. It was fitting that one who had swayed the destinies of this great people as the Chief Magistrate of the Union should preside over deliberations which have for their object to preserve that Union which our fathers created.

"And as affording gratifying evidence of the patriotic inspirations under which, as its President conceives, this convention of delegates from so many States is called to labor for the preservation of the government, we take pleasure in giving to our readers the subjoined authentic report of the eloquent and appropriate address delivered by Mr. Tyler on taking the chair:

"'GENTLEMEN,—I fear you have committed a great error in appointing me to the honorable position you have assigned me. A long separation from all deliberative bodies has rendered the rules of their proceedings unfamiliar to me; while I should find in my own state of health, variable and fickle as it is, sufficient reason to decline the honor of being your presiding officer. But, in times like these, one has little option left him. Personal considerations should weigh but lightly in the balance. The country is in danger: it is enough,—one must take the place assigned him in the great work of reconciliation and adjustment.

"'The voice of Virginia has invited her co-States to meet her in council. In the initiation of this government that same voice was heard and complied with, and the results of seventy odd years have fully attested the wisdom of the decisions then adopted. Is the urgency of her call now less great than it was then? Our godlike fathers created; we have to preserve. They built up, through their wisdom and patriotism, monuments which have eternized their names. You have before you, gentlemen, a task equally grand, equally sublime, quite as full of glory and immortality. You have to snatch from ruin a great and glorious confederation, to preserve the government, and to renew and invigorate the Constitution. If you reach the height

18

of this great occasion, your children's children will rise up and call you blessed. I confess myself to be ambitious of sharing in the glory of accomplishing this grand and magnificent result. To have our names enrolled in the Capitol, to be repeated by future generations with grateful applause,—this is an honor higher than the mountains, more enduring than monumental alabaster.

"'Yes, Virginia's voice, as in the olden time, has been heard. Her sister States meet her at the council-board. Vermont is here, bringing with her the memories of the past, and reviving in the recollection of all her Ethan Allen, and his demand for the surrender of Ticonderoga in the name of the Great Jehovah and of the American Congress. New Hampshire is here, her fame illustrated by memorable annals, and still more lately as the birthplace of him who won for himself the name of Defender of the Constitution, and who wrote that letter to John Taylor which has been enshrined in the hearts of his countrymen.

"'Massachusetts is not here.' (Some member said, 'She is coming.') 'I hope so,' said Mr. Tyler, 'and that she will bring her daughter, Maine. I did not believe it could well be that the voice which, in other times, was so familiar to her ears, had been addressed to her in vain. Connecticut is here; and she comes, I doubt not, in the spirit of Roger Sherman, whose name with our very children has become a household word, and who was in life the embodiment of that sound practical sense which befits the great lawgiver and constructor of governments. Rhode Island, the land of Roger Williams, is here, one of the two last States, in her jealousy of the public liberty, to give in her adhesion to the Constitution, and among the earliest to hasten to its rescue. The great Empire State of New York, represented thus far by but one delegate, is expected daily in fuller force, to join in the great work of healing the discontents of the time and restoring fraternal feeling.

"'New Jersey is also here, with the memories of the past covering her all over. Trenton and Princeton live immortal in story, the plains of the last encrimsoned with the heart's blood of Virginia's sons. Among her delegation I rejoice to recognize a gallant son of a signer of the immortal Declaration which announced to the world that thirteen Provinces had become thirteen independent and sovereign States.

" 'And here, too, is Delaware, the land of the Bayards and the Rodneys, whose soil at Brandywine was moistened by the blood of Virginia's youthful Monroe.

" ' Here is Maryland, whose massive columns moved into line with those of Virginia in the contest for glory, and whose Statehouse at Annapolis was the theater of the spectacle of a successful commander who, after liberating his country, gladly ungirthed his sword and laid it down upon the altar of that country.

" ' Then comes Pennsylvania, rich in Revolutionary lore, bringing with her the deathless names of Franklin and Morris, and, I trust, ready to renew from the belfry of Independence Hall the chimes of the old bell which announced freedom and independence in former days.

" 'All hail to North Carolina, with her Mecklenburg Declaration in her hand, standing erect on the ground of her own probity and firmness in the cause of the public liberty, and represented in her attributes by her Macon, and in this assembly by her distinguished son, at no great distance from me.

" ' Four daughters of Virginia also cluster around the councilboard on the invitation of their ancient mother. The eldest, Kentucky, whose sons, under that intrepid warrior, Anthony Wayne, gave freedom of settlement to the territory of her sister Ohio. She extends her hand daily and hourly across *" la belle rivière,"* to grasp the hand of some one of kindred blood of the noble States of Indiana and Illinois and Ohio, who have grown up into powerful States already, grand, potent, and almost imperial.

" ' Tennessee is not here, but is coming,—prevented from being here only by the floods which have swollen her rivers. When she arrives, she will wear the badges on her warrior crest of victories won, in company with the Great West, on many an ensanguined plain, and standards torn from the hands of the conquerors at Waterloo.

" ' Missouri and Iowa, and Michigan, Wisconsin, and Minnesota, still linger behind; but it may be hoped that their hearts are with us in the great work we have to do.

"'Gentlemen, the eyes of the whole country are turned to this assembly in expectation and hope. I trust that you may prove yourselves worthy of the great occasion. Our ancestors probably committed a blunder in not having fixed upon any fifth decade for a call of a general convention to amend and reform the Constitution. On the contrary, they have máde the difficulties next to insurmountable to accomplish amendments to an instrument which was perfect for five millions of people, but not wholly so as to thirty millions. Your patriotism will surmount the difficulties, however great, if you will but accomplish but one triumph in advance, and that is, a triumph over *party*. And what is party, when compared to the task of rescuing our country from danger? Do that, and one long, loud shout of joy and gladness will resound throughout the land!'

"The choice made by the convention in the selection of its secretary will be recognized, by all who know Mr. Wright, as an appointment eminently fit to be made; and, this patriotic council having thus auspiciously initiated its deliberations, we may be permitted to hope that its results will not disappoint the just expectations of the American people."

The convention failed. The Virginia delegates did not themselves agree as to the conditions of peace. Mr. Tyler differed widely from his colleagues, Rives and Summers. Mr. Summers contended for extreme concessions, and he and Mr. Rives both blundered egregiously in thinking that the slave States would gain much by accepting a proposition that the Territories should not tax slaves in their limits otherwise than as they should or might tax all other persons. Mr. Tyler showed them that already, by the rules of uniformity of taxation in respect of duties, excises, and imposts, and by the rule of equality as to direct taxes, consisting only of tax on land and the poll tax, the Constitution itself protected the people of all the States and Territories against Federal taxes which were either wanting in uniformity or in equality, as shown by one of the earliest cases decided by the

Supreme Court of the United States, the case of Hylton *vs.* the United States. And to take such a condition as something new for a compromise was to concede that it was not already provided for and guaranteed. In the debate with Mr. Summers before the Virginia State Convention, in March, 1861, on their different reports, Mr. Rives being present as a spectator, Mr. Tyler was very able, though in feeble health. That was, perhaps, the last long effort of his mind on any important and exciting topic, and, though feeble in body, he sustained himself admirably. He was no longer hopeful of peace, and the Federal Executive's proclamation against rebellion and insurrection compelled him to give his voice for secession at once.

The Convention of Virginia had appointed a committee of twenty-one members to deliberate upon the proper action of the convention. Sixteen out of the twenty-one of this committee had at first been opposed to secession, were warmly for the Union, and but five were for resistance by arms in self-defense. The Union majority on this committee was for delay, for compromise, for anything rather than war. They held back their report to the very last, and some of them held conferences with Secretary Seward himself at Washington for some mode of conciliation. We happened to be one of the minority of five, though not favoring secession, but preferring to fight in the Union; and when the committee was compelled to report it was very much divided. It split into three divisions: the majority report eschewed disunion and war; a minority report favored remaining in the Union, but advised armed resistance within its pale, in case of invasion and war, in self-defense, and the forming of a provisional league with the revolutionary States without forming a new and separate government from that of the United States; and then a third division of the committee voted against both the majority and minority reports, and were for immediate secession and junction with the Confederate States government at Montgomery. Just as these reports were made, the proclamation of the President of the United States was hurled like a bolt of war into our midst: instantly all differences ceased, and the resolution of secession was adopted at once, with but few dissentients, who retired from the body.

The effect of the proclamation was to cause this not well-considered action. But for it, it is thought that a better course than that of secession would have been taken. But, besides the Executive proclamation, there was another cause of rather too hasty action. During the early and latter part of the session of the convention the secessionists were accused of getting up sensational reports and rumors. It was known that the government at Washington had ordered and commenced the preparation of Fortress Monroe, at Old Point Comfort, for the purpose of invasion, and there were daily rumors of other preparations of the President and Congress for aggression. These rumors were sneered at and slighted by those opposed to secession, as Democratic telegrams, until, at last, the announcement was made to the convention that a portion of the citizens of the Valley of Virginia were marching in force upon Harper's Ferry to capture the arsenal and arms of the United States at that place. The secret history of that important event has never yet been divulged, and may never be until this generation, at least, shall be laid in the dust, but the materials are well preserved. The event was electric in its effect of fusing the Virginia Convention into one mass of secession. The proclamation at Washington and this event at Harper's Ferry found their *dénouement* in the Declaration of Secession by Virginia on the 17th March, 1861. Then was the time for a mediatorial armed neutrality on the part of this State, to say to the North, "Hold back!" and to the South, "Give up" their slaves in order that their masters may remain free!—then was the time, if Congress would proceed to force submission, to have formed a provisional government merely, with an alliance or compact of States, for defense within the pale of the Constitution and the Union. But the rush of Virginia to secession from the Union, and to a junction with the revolutionary States into a separate Confederacy, with a President and Congress, under a permanent, fixed form of government, accelerated by the proclamation and by the seizure of Harper's Ferry, had begun, and there was

no stopping it short of the extreme to which it went, of disunion and of war. The Harper's Ferry seizure and the affair
of the Gosport Navy-Yard were nearly cotemporaneous, and
then the war commenced in deadly earnest.

After the Declaration of Secession by the convention, Mr.
Tyler went home to his constituents, in the Charles City district, and declared himself a candidate for a seat in the House
of Representatives of the Confederate Congress, and was elected
by a large majority over two formidable opponents. He came
to his work with a zeal, life, and energy hardly to be expected
at his period of life, being then seventy-one years of age. In
1861 he had overreached his threescore years and ten; yet his
intellect was as bright as it had ever beamed on deliberative
assemblies. He served actively and with the admiration of
his compeers, a Nestor in their counsels, beloved and heeded
by all, until he was stricken down in his harness of civil service, hopeful and hard-working to the last,—a lover of the
Union until he found it was to be the instrument of destruction
to State Rights and civil liberty, and then its enemy only in
the sense of defense against the aggression in its name upon
those for whom it was intended to be a shield and buckler.

We have purposely, and for good reasons, omitted at this opportunity to publish the history of the seizure of Harper's Ferry
and of the powder-magazine at Norfolk; but there is one incident which occurred early in 1861 which we may relate without
danger to any person, and the truth of which is due to a dead
patriot, whose name we have already tried to do justice to, and
due to the art of naval war, which he eminently contributed to
promote. James Barron was not only the inventor of the
metallic blocks and the ship ventilator of our navy, and the
best instructor upon the time and mode of cutting and preserving ship timber, but his genius caused the construction of the
iron-clad steamer, the *Virginia*, for the Confederate defense.
He was dead long before the Confederate war, and his idea of
the *marine catapulta* lived after him.

For the several years between 1833 and 1844, when we
served on the Committee of Naval Affairs of the House of

Representatives in Congress, James Barron was continuously urging upon that committee his invention of an impregnable steam propeller armed with a pyramidal beak on the water-line. He could never obtain an appropriation for the experiment. It was deemed visionary. He offered to place his model under the guns of Fortress Monroe, and to perish with it if it could be penetrated and sunk. He had nicely tried the maximum penetration of coast and ship guns of all calibers, and then calculated the thickness gained by an inclined plane, with a view not only to impenetrability, but to the angle of ricocheting shot. Four feet thickness, perpendicular, for example, when inclined, became six or eight or ten feet, according to the angle of inclination towards the horizontal. The form of the model, then, from stem to stern, and from side to side, above water, would be a terrapin-back at a very acute angle of incidence to a shot fired from a ship's gun deck; so acute that the shot would, especially by solid oak, be deflected upwards, and could never perforate the sides or upper works. He proposed to carry one heavy stern and one bow gun, and four starboard and four port guns, all in iron casemate port-holes. But his most offensive armor was the pyramidal beak. The ship, braced and samsoned abow by all possible inner appliances, was given a cut-water of the greatest strength, sheathed with iron, and the beak was made solid to it, and bearing not on the ribs of the bow, but impinging altogether upon the keelson, continuous as possible with it. The upper side of the beak was made to commence on the water-line, and descended in several steps, so that the end would be under water just deep enough to strike upon the counter of the enemy's ship, and the lower side of the beak was nearly horizontal. The object of the pyramid was strength, to impinge under the water-line, and, above all, when the beak penetrated, to prevent the enemy's ship from hanging on it and carrying the bow of the propeller down with her in sinking. He calculated exactly the momentum of his model at any given rate of speed, showing that no kind of ship then known could bear the concussion of his beak at even three miles an hour rate of speed. He was a master-mechanic and draughtsman, and presented his memorial and model in the most demonstrated formula. Being the only one on the committee, we believe, who gave him an ear of attention, he presented us with his model, and we had it at our residence when secession was declared by Virginia.

We signed the ordinance of secession, and returned to the county of Princess Anne, ill, before the convention adjourned, and witnessed the vandal and cowardly destruction of the navy-yard at Gosport. The Pennsylvania ship of the line had fired the morning, noon, and evening guns in the harbor for years, and her broadside was pointed upon the town, shotted; and a merciful Providence alone prevented her balls from riddling that portion of Norfolk where the laboring and poor people chiefly resided. The fire from the sail-lofts fortunately fell upon the middle of her decks and burnt them through, so as to lower the breeches and elevate the muzzles of the guns before they became so hot as to explode, and thus the broadside of shot passed over the town, doing no damage. The guns boomed with a muffled sound, as if smothered partially by the water in the sinking ship. It was ominous; it was the knell of either the Union or of liberty, and can never be forgotten by those who heard it with enough of divine grace to hope to forgive the craven incendiaries who lighted the torches of the glaring conflagration! The burning of the Gosport Navy-Yard and its abandonment was the most dastard and disgraceful devastation of the war. They were frightened by a ruse of Mahone, rattling his empty cars up and down the railroad and alarming the cowards with the apprehension of the rapid movement of considerable bodies of troops. They were not self-possessed enough to distinguish the sound of empty cars from that of loaded cars. But the result of their fears caused every thought and sense, as well as every feeling, of the Confederates to be aroused. Our wits went to work at once, and the model of Barron came to our mind. We immediately, by letter, described it to General Lee, and the tender was made of six hundred acres of pine and oak, in four miles, by water, of the Gosport Navy-Yard, with a steam saw-mill already cutting timber at

the spot. He was informed that Barron especially recommended that the draft of the steamer should not exceed ten or
twelve feet of water. General Lee was then in State command, and had State means only; but, through him, doubtless,
the Merrimack was raised and converted into the Virginia iron-
clad. Commodore Barron's ideas were not carried out in her
construction. The naval architect did not calculate accurately
the weight of masts, spars, rigging, and upper works taken off,
compared with the weight of iron sheathing put on, and the
consequence was that when launched the hulk stood out of
water several feet higher than the sheathing reached down the
sides. This was remedied by ballast, which made the vessel
draw eighteen feet of water, in order to dip the sheathing below
the water-line. Then, too, the beak, instead of being pyramidal
or inclining on the upper surface, was made horizontal on the
upper and inclined upwards on the lower side. This caused it
to break in sinking the Congress and Cumberland frigates. We
have a cane made of its live-oak wood, and were told it was
perhaps as large a solid piece of it as was left unfrasseled by
the concussions. We witnessed the fight with the Monitor
and Merrimack, and the great fault of the Virginia was that
she drew too much water and was an unwieldy "*wave-wal-
lower.*" But it was a grave error ever to have blown her up.
There was no necessity for it, and the pilots agreed in that
opinion. Enough ballast could have been thrown out to gain
five or six feet in her draft, and she might have been taken to
the mouth of the Chickahominy, and would have prevented all
approach from below, and all crossing of the James at Harrison's Landing.

# CHAPTER XVI.

Death of Mr. Tyler—Proceedings of the Legislature of Virginia—Pr *eedings
of the Confederate Congress—The Citizens of Richmond did him Homage
and Sepulture at Hollywood Cemetery, where his Remains lie; and Honor
was done his Memory even in Baltimore at that Hazardous Time—Item in
his Will touching his Burial.

AT the time of his demise Mr. Tyler was a member of the
provisional, and member elect of the permanent, Confederate
Congress.

On the 18th day of January, A.D. 1862, at the city of Richmond, after a short illness, in the full possession of his mental
faculties, conscious that death was near, calm and collected, he
bade this world farewell, and departed this life with dignity and
without fear, perfectly composed, a firm believer in the atone-
ment of the Son of God, and in the efficacy of his blood to wash
away every stain of mortal sin.

He was by faith and by heirship a member of the Episcopal
Church of Christ, and never doubted Divine Revelation. He
was an honest, affectionate, benevolent, loving man, who had
fought the battles of this life bravely and truly, doing his
whole great duty without fear, though not without much unjust
reproach ; with a genial soul, glowing with good will to man,
and reverence to God, and so righteous that his worst enemy
on earth might well pray, "Oh that my latter end be like his !"

He had forgiven all his foes long before he died, and did them
more than justice whenever he spoke of their despiteful usage
to him. In the last scenes of our intercourse with him in the
convention which declared secession, he passed in that body a
eulogy on Henry Clay, so undeserved from him upon one who

( 283 )

had, in the Senate of the United States, so fiercely denounced him, that we could not refrain from reproaching him privately for uttering even what was truthful in the encomium. But for this charity and this forgiving temper and disposition he was richly and rarely rewarded. No man in all history ever so out-lived calumny and all enmity of others as he did. When he left his fellow-men he left nothing in their hearts and memories but admiration and veneration of his character, and the remem-brance of the good deeds he had done. And his good deeds were not "interred with his bones." They are now living in the policy his Presidency pursued.

Immediately on the day of his death, the General Assembly of the State of Virginia took obituary action.

### SENATE.

### "DEATH OF PRESIDENT TYLER.

"The President laid before the Senate the following communi-cation from the Executive :

"EXECUTIVE DEPARTMENT, January 18, 1862.

"GENTLEMEN OF THE SENATE AND HOUSE OF DELEGATES,— John Tyler departed this life at his lodgings, in this city, after a brief illness, at twelve o'clock last night. Mr. Tyler has served the people of Virginia with ability and distinction, in various public positions, for almost half a century. He has served in the General Assembly, on the Executive Council, in the House of Representatives of the United States, as Governor of the State, Senator in Congress, Vice-President and President of the United States, member of the State Convention of 1829–30 and the Convention of 1861, and at the time of his death was a member of the Provisional Congress, and a member elect of the Permanent Congress, of the Confederate States. His ser-vices have been important and valuable ; and in all of these posi-tions he has fully met the public expectations. The loss of such a man, at a time when his talents and experience are so greatly needed in the public councils, is a calamity greatly to be deplored. Well may the people of Virginia and the Southern Confederacy mourn for the loss of one not less distinguished for his manly virtues than his brilliant career as a statesman.

"Respectfully,

"JOHN LETCHER.

"On motion of Mr. Dickinson, of Prince Edward, the communication was laid on the table and ordered to be printed.

"A message was received from the House of Delegates, communicating resolutions commemorating the death of Hon. John Tyler. The preamble and resolutions were read by the clerk of the Senate, as follows:

"The mournful intelligence of the decease of John Tyler, after a brief illness, has cast a gloom over this General Assembly. The sad news will spread throughout his native State with painful effect. It will be heard throughout the Southern Confederacy with deep and abiding sorrow. He has filled a large space in the history of his country. Heaven has blessed him with length of days, and his country with all her honors. He has secured, we believe, a blissful immortality.

"For the page of history his fame is destined to occupy, it is proper briefly to recount the many offices he has filled. From youthful manhood to green old age, he has served his country faithfully, as a member of the House of Delegates, where his ripening intellect displayed the promise of usefulness, and attracted attention; as a member of the Executive Council, where his wholesome advice lent wisdom to authority; as the Governor of this Commonwealth, where his administrative powers gave efficacy to law, and his execution of the will of the people, expressed by their representatives, was rendered pleasant by kindness and courtesy; as a member of the first convention called to amend the State Constitution, in which body his ripened experience gave his counsel the force of wisdom and prudence; as a member of the House of Representatives of the United States, standing firm amid the rage of party spirit and remaining true to principle and to right; as a Senator representing this State in the Senate of the United States, in which he shone conspicuous for his strict adherence to constitutional obligation and for his manly defense of the rights of the States and the honor of the country; as Vice-President of the United States, presiding over the deliberations of the Senate with dignity and impartiality, preserving the decorum of a body that then was a model for legislative assemblies; as President of the United States, when the national honor and reputation were acknowledged unimpeached and unimpaired in every land, and the powers of the earth looked up to the new government as an exemplar of morals and of power worthy of respect and imitation. He thus, step by step, ascended to the eminence from which he surveyed his country, peaceful and glorious, and calmly retired in dignity to a private station, happy in the contemplation of a bright career, happy in a refined and prosperous home, happy in the circle of family and friends.

"His State called him again into her service. She was to be assembled in convention to resist oppression, and to withstand a galling tyranny against which her best men chafed. His services were invoked to aid in maintaining the high position she had heretofore occupied. He came from his retirement. He advised separation in peace, or war to vindicate her honor. He was again selected a commissioner to tender to the government at Washington the terms upon which Virginia would remain united with her former sisters. He was honored with the presidency of that Peace Conference. His manly appeals for justice were uttered and unheeded. He returned, and recommended separation and independence. His advice was taken. It became necessary to form and establish another government for the new Confederacy. He was appointed by the Sovereign Convention of Virginia a member of the Provisional Congress. While occupying a conspicuous place in the eyes of the Confederacy, and the new government was assuming its permanent basis, he was elected by the people a member to the first House of Representatives of the Confederate States, with a fair promise still of usefulness, to stamp his wisdom upon the enduring monuments of a new national existence.

" But it pleased the Almighty to check his career, and take him to Himself.

" Such is the brief outline of the career of John Tyler. In private he was the perfect gentleman, the warm-hearted, affectionate, social, and delightful companion ; it may be said of him, his kind hand ministered to the wants of the distressed.

"*Resolved*, By the General Assembly, as a testimonial of a nation's sorrow for the death of a great and good man, that a joint committee of the Senate and House of Delegates be appointed to confer with a committee of the Congress of the Confederate States, to make arrangements for his funeral and burial.

" *Resolved*, That, with the consent of his family, his remains be deposited in Hollywood Cemetery, in the city of Richmond, near the remains of James Monroe, and that the Governor of this State be authorized to cause a suitable monument to be erected to his memory.

"*Resolved*, That these resolutions be forthwith communicated by the Speaker of the House of Delegates to the Congress of the Confederate States, with a request that they concur therein.

" Mr. Branch, of Williamsburg, said that as he had the honor to represent a part of the district in which the deceased had lived during a long life of public service, he moved the unanimous adoption of the preamble and resolutions which had come from the House.

" Mr. Robertson, of the city of Richmond.—' I cannot permit the occasion to pass without saying a few words to express my sense of the merits and virtues of a deceased friend. On my way to the Capitol this morning, I learned that John Tyler, late President of the United States, had paid that debt which, sooner or later, must be exacted of us all. It was my good fortune to be acquainted with him, I may say intimately, from early life, dating from my college days. I have known him in all the walks and through all the relations of life. It were needless for me to recount the attributes of his character, his integrity, his high attainments, his devotion to his country. I am not accustomed to the language of eulogy. Fortunately for me, and fortunately for my friend, he needs none. The high places of trust which he has received through his whole life, commend him to the hearts of all.

"'Sir, if there was any one trait that marked his character more than another, it was his firm devotion to those principles which carried the American people through the war of the Revolution, and to the same principles which, I hope, will before long carry us through the struggle in which we are engaged. I need not speak more fully of the many high offices which he has filled. They are too well known to be repeated. His acts and his character are identified with the history of our State and country, and are known in Europe. I am confident that no dissenting voice will be heard upon the passage of these resolutions. It is in consequence of my representing this district that I felt it incumbent on me to make these few remarks.'

"Mr. Dickinson, of Prince Edward, had not intended to have uttered one word on this mournful occasion. He had not even heard of the illness of Mr. Tyler till he was startled (while on his way to this chamber) with the sad announcement which filled him with sorrow and surprise. 'Deeply sympathizing in the just tribute to his memory, which these resolutions so appropriately propose, I should be untrue to the promptings of my own heart, and unfaithful in reflecting the high appreciation in which he was held, by those whom I represent on this floor, if I failed to unite in expressing my own grief and theirs. Unlike the venerable senators who have preceded me, I am too young to have been admitted to the relations of personal intimacy with the distinguished and lamented dead, which they enjoyed. And yet from my boyhood it was my privilege to know and regard him as a friend and political guide. As a public man, I have been accustomed to look to the principles which governed his career with more than ordinary respect.

"'I am untaught, sir, in the language of eulogy; my heart is too full to attempt it on this sad occasion. Nor is it necessary that I should. Our illustrious friend, by a long life of usefulness in the public service, extending through a period of half a century, in every dignified position, from a seat in this Assembly to the Presidential chair, wrote his own eulogy in his country's history. By his talents and attainments, his unyielding integrity and elevated devotion to principles, his lofty and ardent patriotism, happily blended with those high qualities of public and personal purity, which dignified and adorned his character, he has erected in the hearts of a grateful people a monument which will long be cherished as a national treasure.

"'Identified with the history of the country through a long and eventful life, mingling as he had done in the stirring scenes of party strife, it was his happiness to outlive the animosities and heart-burnings which they engendered, and to be universally regarded in the calm eve of his life as a patriot statesman. Thus favored, he has gone to his last account. A patriot and a statesman has fallen, and a nation mourns his loss. He fell where he ever stood, foremost in the ranks, battling for the best interests of the country which he loved with the affection of a pious son. These tidings will thrill with painful interest throughout this young republic, in whose service he has fallen at the post of duty.

"'But, sir, there is another, a narrower and a holier circle, within which this afflictive stroke will fall with peculiar heaviness—where those gentle and endearing traits of private virtue which so eminently adorned his character, shone with unusual luster. I would not intrude too soon upon the sanctity of domestic grief to mingle my tears with theirs; yet I cannot fail to remember that their grief, though more poignant than ours, is yet common to us all. Like them, we too will cherish his memory with all that warm affection which his life inspired.

"'I trust, and feel assured, that these resolutions will command the unanimous assent of the Senate.'

"Mr. Collier, of Petersburg, and Mr. Isbell, of Jefferson, also spoke. We regret that we have not space to add to the above even the substance of their feeling and eloquent remarks upon the character and services of the subject of the resolutions. It was evident that, in the tributes that were thus paid, it was the aim of the several speakers to rest the merits of the distinguished statesman upon the single and appropriate language of justice and truth.

19

"The committee nominated on the part of the Senate to meet the committee on the part of the House, to carry out the object designated in the resolutions, consisted of Messrs. Branch, Robertson, Collier, Isbell, Newman, Johnson, and Wiley.

"After the announcement of the committee as above, the Senate adjourned.

### HOUSE OF DELEGATES.

"The House met at 12 o'clock, Mr. Collier in the Chair. Prayer by Rev. Dr. Moore.

"The Speaker *pro tem.* presented to the House the following communication from the Governor:

"EXECUTIVE DEPARTMENT, January 18, 1862.

"GENTLEMEN OF THE SENATE AND HOUSE OF DELEGATES,— John Tyler departed this life at his lodgings, in this city, after a brief illness, at twelve o'clock last night. Mr. Tyler has served the people of Virginia with ability and distinction, in various public positions, for almost half a century. He has served in the General Assembly, on the Executive Council, in the House of Representatives of the United States, as Governor of the State, Senator in Congress, Vice-President and President of the United States, member of the State Convention of 1829–30 and the Convention of 1861, and at the time of his death was a member of the Provisional Congress, and a member elect to the Permanent Congress, of the Confederate States. His services have been important and valuable; and in all of these positions he has fully met the public expectations. The loss of such a man, at a time when his talents and experience are so greatly needed in the public councils, is a calamity greatly to be deplored. Well may the people of Virginia and the Southern Confederacy mourn for the loss of one not less distinguished for his manly virtues than his brilliant career as a statesman.

"Respectfully,

"JOHN LETCHER.

" Mr. Barbour arose, and said that the mournful fact communicated in that message marked one of the events in our national
history.  It would be unjust for him to enter into a eulogy
upon the deceased statesman.  That man was the last great
link that connected the generation that made the first immortal
revolution with the generation that made the present one.
Through all that lapse of time John Tyler stood high in the
honor and confidence of the people of Virginia.  His name has
become historic.

" In conclusion, Mr. Barbour presented a series of joint resolutions in reference to Mr. Tyler's death, which were unanimously
adopted.  (The resolutions will be found in our Senate report.)

" Mr. Newton, of Westmoreland, said that, unprepared as we
all are by this event, he still felt that he must offer his tribute
to a dear friend and an illustrious statesman.  John Tyler was
no ordinary man.  He was truly a great and illustrious one.
It might be said of him, as was said of another illustrious man,
' He has sounded all the depths and shoals of honor.'  There
was no office that he had not filled with honor.  Though he
(Mr. Newton) had been sometimes alienated from him in the
turmoil of political life, he had ever been ready to testify to his
worth and purity of purpose.  Mr. Newton adverted to memories which such an occasion as this, in this hall, brought flock-
ing to his mind.  When he first entered here, John Tyler was
Governor of the Commonwealth.  He looked around in vain for
those who then filled these seats.  They were all gone.  He
looked towards the seat where the Chatham of Virginia was
wont to sit muffled in his flannels, or leaning on his crutch
(William B. Giles), and he could imagine he almost saw him
now, hurling his thunders at wrong and oppression.

" Mr. Newton called over other names of departed Virginians
who distinguished this room when he first came here.  Their
absence brought up mournful feelings, and served to teach us
the shortness of life.

" Mr. Robertson, of Richmond, said that he was impelled by
feelings he could not repress, and would not repress if he could,
to offer a few words.  But he felt deeply pained to know that,

so suddenly called on, the tribute must be imperfect and utterly inadequate to the occasion. It was but a few minutes only since information had reached him of the death of Mr. Tyler, and in that brief period it was impossible for the mind even to have reviewed the many and illustrious series of his services, or to have catalogued the multitude of his virtues. He would not attempt the hopeless task. But he might be permitted to signalize the rare benignity of his nature, that embraced all in the folds of his love, and in time attracted the love of all with whom he came in contact; for it mattered not how far men differed from him in opinion, or blamed or approved his course, still there was that in him which attracted all who approached him. He thought he had never known a man so universally attractive and winning as John Tyler, nor one whose heart was more open to every genial and kindly affection.

" As a statesman, his career had been eminently distinguished. In that highest part of it, as President of the United States, he administered our affairs with great ability. In that part of it, in particular, which concerned our foreign relations, and to which other nations mainly look for an estimate of a public man, his administration was a brilliant success. It may compare for wisdom, energy, and an enlightened perception of our foreign policy, with any, even the most brilliant, of the administrations that preceded it. I rejoiced, therefore, that he still lived to shed in the eyes of the world that just weight and dignity to the cause of the South, reflected on them by his participation in our councils. I had even looked to his carrying into a yet higher sphere than that to which he had already been called, the advantages of that trail of glory as a statesman which, seen afar off by the nations, could not but reflect a certain luster on the new government now undergoing those heavy trials which every people must meet in asserting their independence. But the hope and all of that future connected with Mr. Tyler's name, on earth, is past. Mr. R. would not pursue his remarks further. He was too sensible how far they fell short of what his wishes or the merits of the subject demanded.

" Mr. Anderson, of Botetourt, added his tribute to the exalted worth of the great man who had just left us. It had been his pleasure to have had a long acquaintance with John Tyler. He had entered public life when Mr. Tyler was a prominent states- man before the country. When he was but a youth, he had first formed an intimacy with him ; and never had an acquaint- anceship been more delightful. He had never met a man of more winning manners. He united all the highest social quali- ties. No statesman had been called to higher stations. No one had spent so much of his life in the service of his country. His career is an example for our young men. Notwithstanding the infirmities of age, he put on his armor and stood forth in the front ranks of the defenders battling for their country's rights. He did not doubt that the news of his death would sink deep in the hearts of the people throughout the length and breadth of the Confederacy. He hoped and believed that he was now in a more blissful world.

" Mr. Laidley could not let the occasion pass without respond- ing for the younger members of the House. On their part he would say that John Tyler's life would serve them as an ex- ample worthy of emulation, and that the story of his virtues should be handed down to their children's children.

" Mr. Jones, of Gloucester, said that he came from the same section that gave John Tyler to Virginia. He had known him in childhood ; indeed, he might say he had been raised with his children, and in his intercourse with him he almost looked up to him as a father. In his college days he had received the same fatherly encouragement and assistance. He felt, therefore, that he knew him well enough to say that in every community in which he lived he was without an enemy. All loved him as a friend. In his social relations he was no less esteemed. He would not speak of his career as a statesman. As time advances, his name shall grow brighter, until time shall be no more.

" The Speaker appointed the following committee under the resolutions :

" Messrs. Barbour, Robertson of Richmond, Hunter, Blue, Jones of Gloucester, Mallory, Sanders, Newton, Anderson of

Botetourt, Sheffey, McCamant, Rives, and Grattan.   He also appointed Mr. Barbour to report the resolutions to the Senate. " The House then adjourned."

On the Monday following, the 20th of the month, the Confederate Congress took action.


## "THE LATE EX-PRESIDENT TYLER.

### " PROCEEDINGS IN CONGRESS.

"At the close of the very appropriate tribute by Mr. Macfarland, published in the *Whig* of yesterday, Mr. Hunter, of Virginia, rose, and said:

" 'I rise to offer my tribute of respect to the memory of the deceased.

" ' As has been well said, the name of John Tyler, now passed into the possession of history, has an order of its own in that great sanctuary.   Its sojourn is over.   Nothing can now dim its luster as it passes down the tide of time.

" 'It is said, sir, there is something in the story of the humblest life, which, if rightly told, will afford food for profitable study.   With how much of interest, then, do we turn to the contemplation of the lives of those who have been martyrs of their kind, who have left examples for the imitation of posterity; of those whose voices have been the most persuasive and convincing in. council, and whose shout, like that of the king, has been most potent in marshaling the hosts !

" 'Among the public men of our day, John Tyler has been one of the most marked and distinguished.   With him disappears the last, save one who now sits in this chamber, of those great men who adorned the Senate of the United States when I first entered upon public life with him.   We shall bury the last of the line, the illustrious line of Southern Presidents whose names have connected us with the highest honors of the Union from which we have just parted.   Does not this deepen the sense. of our separation as we see one by one pass away, not only the material links, but the ties of personal association which bound us to those whom we have lately left?

"'No man, Mr. President, has more fully completed the circle of honors which were opened to the aspirations of our public men than John Tyler. Scarcely had he attained his majority when he was sent to the House of Delegates in Virginia. After a service of a few years there, he was successively elected a member of the Executive Council, a member of the House of Representatives of the United States, Governor of the State of Virginia, Senator of the United States, Vice-President of the United States, from which, by the death of General Harrison, and through the operation of the Constitution, he was elevated to the Chief Magistracy of the land. Nor, sir, did his career end even there. When secession began and presaged the storm which is now sweeping over the land, he was sent to the Convention of Virginia, and by that body to the Peace Congress, over the deliberations of which he presided; thence to this Congress, and afterwards was elected by his constituents to the House of Representatives of the Confederate Congress, soon to assemble in this place.

"'But, full as was his life of honors, it was not more distinguished by them than by its achievements. From the commencement of his public career, he distinguished himself in whatever body he was serving, and by his eloquence and, ability won an honorable place in the estimation of all with whom he associated. An advocate of the doctrines of the State Rights school of Virginia, he for the most part adhered to those doctrines with consistency throughout a long and arduous career. Few men exerted themselves more to preserve the Constitution of the United States. He was among the first of our public men who, with the great Calhoun, declared that "the Constitution and the union of the States was one and inseparable." From the period of the Nullification controversy, from the time when he gave his solitary vote against the Force Bill in the Congress of the United States, to his last appearance in Washington at the Peace Conference, he declared the Union and the Constitution must live or perish together.

" ' He exerted his utmost powers to preserve the Constitution and the administration of the executive affairs of the United States. Forced to choose between the desire to gratify the wishes of his personal friends, who had elevated him to the office, on the one hand, and a sense of constitutional obligation on the other, he determined finally to sacrifice the friends with whom he had been associated. From that time forward it was his lot to administer the affairs of the nation, over which he presided in the midst of the severest party struggles the country had ever known, without the cordial support of either great political division by which the people were then divided; and he had to discharge his high duties in the face of such difficulties as had never been encountered by any of his predecessors. But, in despite of that spirit, he called around him some of the ablest intellects of the land,—Webster, Upshur, Legaré, Calhoun,—who aided him in one of the most successful administrations which appears in the annals of American affairs.

" ' It was this administration that added Texas, an empire, to the Confederacy; and it was this administration that successfully accomplished the Ashburton treaty between Great Britain and the United States. It was in this administration that Mr. Calhoun, in his celebrated letter to Mr. King, for the first time made a public demonstration in favor of the right of the slaveholding States to respect and protection; and it was this administration which gave a final and fatal blow to the United States Bank. But prominent, sir, as was this administration, it was, perhaps, not so distinguished as his closing career. He had already reached the year of threescore and ten, when he was called from his retirement to aid in making up that great issue of human destiny which is now being submitted to the arbitrament of trial, as it is said, between nearly a million of armed men. True to the life-long professions of the past, his first effort was to preserve the Constitution, and, if possible, to save the Union with it; but, when disappointed in that hope, none was more determined than he to cut loose his native State from its perilous connection with enemies in disguise—none more resolved to make common cause with the South and take whatever might be the consequence of the act.

"'We all know he threw himself into the cause with his whole soul. Gentlemen here present will testify to the truth of what I say when I affirm that to the last he devoted himself to it with a courage that did not quail, with a hope that did not falter, and with a purpose that held out to the last extremity and relaxed not to the end.

"'Mr. President, it may truly be said that with John Tyler there has fallen a great man. I know, sir, that the death of any good man is the cause of grief to the friendly survivors; and yet I feel I do not err when I say that my deceased colleague was as fortunate in his death as in his life. As a soldier on the field of battle falls, he fell at the post of duty. A life, when it was full of years and honors, passed away. He left us before age had bowed his form or dimmed the luster of his intellect; when the future course of his life was about to promise him more of pleasure than grief. To-morrow we shall deposit him beneath the sod of that soil which he loved so well—on the beautiful banks of the James, where his slumbers will be soothed by the sound of its falling waters. Day after day, in the years yet to come, the morning and evening shadows shall lend a silent and varied charm to the scene; and when'her hour of struggle is over, Virginia, as she leans upon her bloody spear to contemplate the past, and beholding the rising glories of her day, will lift her gauntleted hand to brush away the tear for the loss of him who, in the decline of life, exhausted his dying energies in her behalf, and staked his life, his fortune, his reputation upon the result, which will bring her safety and honor. Sir, she will embalm his memory in her best affections, and hand it down to her generations yet to come; and their children's children will transmit his honored name as an inheritance of princely value—an heirloom which has already run through more than two generations of distinguished men.

"'But it is not my purpose, sir, to draw a portrait of this great man. His is a character which men will choose to study themselves; and they will seek it in the monuments of his own creation rather than in the testimonials of his friends; but perhaps, sir, it will not be deemed as usurping the historian's place, were I to say of him, he was kind and genial in all the relations of private life, and that he used the gift of the eloquence with which he was so highly endowed, in the public service, and not for selfish purposes; that his faculties for usefulness seemed always to rise to the level of the demand upon them; that he was most able to discharge his duty under the most difficult circumstances, and that he served his native State with a love and fidelity which are beyond all praise.

" 'Mr. President, is there no useful lesson which we ourselves may draw from this occasion? Is there nothing in it that will deepen our sense of the uncertainty of human life and the instability of human affairs? Within how short a period has death sent its summons in our very midst? Does not this impress us with the utter worthlessness of the span of life allotted to any one of us, unless we use it for the purpose of preparing for another and better and more enduring state? Do not the scenes passing before us impress on us still more forcibly the sublime truth, "The duties of life are to be preferred to life itself"?'

"Mr. Rives, of Virginia, then spoke as follows:

" 'I should be wanting, Mr. President, to my own feelings, if not to the memory of our departed friend, were I not to claim the privilege of an older and longer acquaintance with him, perhaps, than any other member on this floor possessed, to add a few words to what has been already so appropriately and eloquently said by my honorable colleagues. It is now somewhat more than half a century since, a school-boy in the ancient city of Williamsburg, I first made the acquaintance of Mr. Tyler, then a law student of our common Alma Mater, preparing to enter upon the career of active life. It was thus given me to observe the whole progress of his orb in the heavens, from its first appearance above the horizon, through its meridian brightness and splendor, to its final and serene setting in the western sky, which we are met this day to commemorate.

"'As a young man, when I first saw Mr. Tyler, he was distinguished by the same blandness and courtesy of manners, the prepossessing address, and the graceful and captivating elocution, which we have all seen displayed by him in this hall. These qualities, the sure passport, in a government like ours, to popular favor and public distinction, bore him through a succession of public employments. As soon as he was of age, he was elected by his native county of Charles City to the House of Delegates of Virginia. His first session in that body was, if I mistake not, in the memorable year of 1811–12, which witnessed the bold measure of the declaration of war made by the United States against Great Britain; and the young legislator became thus closely identified with that high-spirited generation of American statesmen, who, succeeding immediately to the great men of the Revolution—the conscript fathers of the Republic—continued, for thirty or forty years after them, to conduct the affairs of the Union with a patriotism, ability, and success worthy of their noble sires.

"'In the different representative assemblies of which Mr. Tyler was successively a member, he was brought into contact with the highest intellects of the age. In the legislature of Virginia, he was a member of the House of Delegates with Littleton Waller Tazewell, Benjamin Watkins Leigh, Charles Fenton Mercer, Robert Stanard, Philip Doddridge, General Blackburn, and many others of the most gifted spirits of this ancient commonwealth. In the House of Representatives of the United States, he was contemporary with Henry Clay, William Lowndes, John Randolph, Henry St. George Tucker, John Forsyth, Louis McLane, and a host of other distinguished men who then illustrated the national forum. Being generally the youngest member of the body to which he belonged, and emulous of distinction, he was stimulated to the highest exertion of his powers by the living models of excellence with which he was surrounded, and his mind was thus kept in a perpetual progress of development and expansion.

"'Trained and formed under these auspices, he proved himself to all the various and arduous posts of public duty

to which he was called by the favor and confidence of his countrymen. In the highest of them all, he gave an honorable proof
of the elevation and magnanimity of his character, bringing into
the leading Executive Departments the most towering talents
of the country, to aid him in the administration of the government. The selection of such men as Webster, Calhoun, Legaré,
Upshur, and Spencer proved how far he was above the operation of any unworthy sentiment of jealousy, or fear of being
overshadowed in the public estimation by his official advisers ;
while his personal management of several of the most delicate
questions of his administration—I refer more particularly to his
broad and comprehensive treatment of the question of the
annexation of Texas, and the firmness with which he upheld the
cause of constitutional republican government in Rhode Island
against the outbreak of an unlicensed democracy—attested the
large and matured statesmanship he had himself acquired in
the schools of practical instruction in which he was bred.

" ' But this is neither the time nor the place to enter upon a
discussion of the merits of Mr. Tyler's administration of the
Federal government, when, by a sudden and unexpected dis-
pensation of Providence, he was placed at the head of it. No
one would more earnestly have deprecated the revival of forgotten controversies than himself. Among the qualities which
most eminently and honorably distinguished him was an habitual
kindliness of disposition, and a generous appreciation of others,
even of those who were his political enemies and opponents.
It was about two years ago, in this city, on a public and memorable occasion, he did himself the highest honor by a warm,
spontaneous, and manly tribute to the character of a great man
and deceased patriot, who had stood toward him in the attitude
of a powerful and declared opponent.

" ' In reviewing the eventful life of Mr. Tyler, we are led,
almost irresistibly, to apply to him a descriptive epithet by
which the Romans were accustomed to express a quality that
ever inspired their confidence and admiration. By that epithet
—*felix*—they did not mean to designate a person who was
merely fortunate but one who, by a happy combination of well-

tempered attributes, knew, in a measure, how to command or propitiate fortune. This sentiment was embodied by them in a maxim, tersely expressed by their great satirist—*nullum numen abest, si sit prudentia.* Thus it was with Mr. Tyler. By a rare union of prudence, good sense, and good temper, set off by the natural gifts of oratory and a persuasive address, he won the hearts of the people and commanded the favors of fortune; and success waited upon him in every step of his public career.

"'Delegate in the legislature of his State, representative in Congress, Governor, Senator, Vice-President, President—he "sounded all the depths and shoals of honor;" and in every trust he acquitted himself to the satisfaction of his constituents. After having filled with honor the highest offices of the government of the Union—which sank, at length, under the degeneracy and corruption of the times—he lived to take a leading part in the establishment of a new Confederacy for the South, which had all his affections and all his hopes; and as a member of this House, he gave his anxious labors to the great cause of securing and perpetuating the structure.

"'His duties as a member of this body engaged his deepest solicitude. Unwilling to withdraw himself from them for a single day without the proper and formal sanction of the House, he said to me, the day before the fatal termination of his disease, that, if he should be compelled to go home to recruit his health, as he should probably find it necessary to do, he wished me to apply to the House for leave of absence for him. A far higher authority, the great Governor of the Universe, has granted him that leave of absence—not from this hall merely, but from all sublunary concerns henceforward forever. He now rests from his labors; but he has bequeathed to us the rich inheritance of his patriotic example and of his counsels.

"'This second admonition of the transitory tenure of human existence, with which, after so short an interval, we have been visited in this hall, reminds us most impressively that "the paths of glory lead but to the grave." But still it is not permitted to us to repine. "One generation passeth away, and another cometh; but the earth abideth forever." Here, while we continue, we have our allotted work; and as those who have gone before us have labored and toiled, so must we, in our turn, toil and labor, to carry forward the great schemes of Divine Providence in the moral government of the world; and if we do so in humble submission to the will of Him who ruleth the destinies of men and nations, we, too, shall have our reward.' "

The citizens of Richmond did honor to his remains in more than usual form of respect and reverence; and, in those dangerous times, when men in Baltimore dared hardly whisper in bated breath the name of a rebel with respect, there even tears were not suppressed, and his praise and the grief of mourners were spoken and sobbed out aloud over his departure.

His will had been written more than two years before he died; and several of its passages are so remarkably characteristic of the man that they are inserted:

"My Will. I. In the name of God. Amen. This is my last will and testament, written wholly with my own hand, with my name subscribed thereto, this 10th day of October, in the year of our Lord and Saviour 1859, whereby I revoke and annul all other wills and testaments heretofore made by me.

"II. In the first place, I empower my dear wife to make out of my estate suitable provision for my burial, which I wish to be accompanied with no unnecessary expense. Let the people of this county [Charles City], whose fathers helped me on in my battles of life with a zeal and constancy rarely ever equaled and never surpassed, be invited to attend my funeral obsequies; and let my body be consigned to the tomb in the earth of the county wherein I was born, there to repose until the day of resurrection. My wife will select the spot on 'Sherwood Forest' [his residence], and mark it by an uncostly monument of granite or marble. I desire also that she will cause a suitable memorial to be erected over the remains of my father and mother, at 'Greenway,' should it not be done in my lifetime; inscriptions both for my own and theirs will be found in the paper inclosing this."

In the sixth item he provides, "I desire also that my wife will take good care of my faithful servants, William Short and Fanny Hall, so that their old age can be rendered comfortable."

A question was raised whether he was born at Greenway, in the county of Charles City, or at Warburton, in the county of James City. His will settled that doubt; Greenway was undoubtedly the residence of his parents, and there, too, was the birthplace and home of his nativity. There was the cradle and nursery of his infancy, the play-ground of his childhood, and there were the scenes which caught the first observations and experiences of which he was capable.

In these touching clauses of his will he shows that beautiful *amor loci* which is the foundation of the *amor patriæ*, the ruling passion of his life, the warm, natural poetry of his composition—that poetry which Campbell so sweetly sung :

> "There is a land, of every land the pride,
> Beloved by Heaven o'er every land beside,
> There is a spot of earth supremely blest,
> A dearer, sweeter spot than all the rest."

His land was his country, his State was Virginia, and in death he clung to "the earth of the county wherein he was born,"—his "dear wife" to "select the spot," dearer, sweeter than all the rest, on "Sherwood Forest," and to mark it by an uncostly monument of granite or marble.

As yet his body is interred at Hollywood Cemetery, near the remains of Mr. Monroe. It is due that the State of Virginia shall erect his monument. He belongs to the State. But let the people of Charles City not forget that they were affectionately invited to his "funeral obsequies," and that they will but elevate and ennoble themselves by coming up every anniversary of his birth to pluck out every weed which may intrude near his grave, and to wreathe his tomb with "immortelles."

# APPENDIX.

## COLLEGE OF WILLIAM AND MARY.

It remains only to narrate Mr. Tyler's connection with the College of William and Mary, and to express the interest he took in her welfare.

His Alma Mater is "full of years and full of honors," and has been the mother of instruction to pupils who have given birth to events of the greatest magnitude on this continent.

For an epitome of her history we proudly refer to the "Sketch," prepared by the lamented Professor Morrison, prefixed to the latest published catalogue, entitled "College of William and Mary, 1693 to 1870." But in that epitome there is an important error. Why say from 1693? The college had its foundation before that year. As stated by the professor, in 1619 a large appropriation of land was made to endow a university to be established at Henrico for the colonists and Indians; and it is also true that about the same time contributions were made through the bishops of London to endow a college in Virginia for the Indians, and in 1621 a subscription was made to endow the East India School at Charles City, and land and servants were allotted to it, and that this was all preparatory to the university at Henrico, and that Mr. George Thorpe, a gentleman of His Majesty's privy chamber, came over to be superintendent of the university, and was in 1622, with three hundred and forty of the colonists, including a number of the college tenants, killed by the Indians. But an important error was committed by the professor when he added, "This disaster, followed by the troubles in the mother country (the revolution of 1642), and, at a later period, by the discontent and disorders in the colony, which were produced mainly by the arbitrary rule of Sir William Berkeley, the royal governor, and which culminated in Bacon's rebellion, *prevented any renewal of the attempt to establish a college in the Colony of Virginia till the revolution of* 1688, *which seated William and Mary on the English throne*," etc.

Now, neither the massacre in 1622, nor the revolution of 1642, nor the discontent and disorders in the colony, nor the arbitrary rule of Sir William Berkeley, nor Bacon's rebellion, nor any other cause, prevented attempts to establish a college in the Colony of Virginia till the revolution in 1688. Nearly thirty years before that revolution in England, the "Grand Assembly," held at James City, March 23, 1660–1, passed Act twentieth, entitled "Provision for a College," in these words: "Whereas the want of able and faithful ministers in this country deprives us of these great blessings and mercies that allwais attend upon the service of God; which want, by reason of our great distance from our native country, cannot in probability be alwais supplyed from thence; Be it enacted, that for the advance of learning, education of youth, supply of the ministry and promotion of piety, there be land taken upon purchases for a colledge and free-schoole, and that there be, with as much speede as may be convenient, houseing erected thereon for entertainment of students and schollers." This act was passed in the 13th Charles II. See II. vol. Hening's "Statutes at Large," p. 25.

Again: at the same session of the Grand Assembly, October, 1660–1, 13th Charles II., "Act 35th" was passed, entitled "A Petition in behalf of the Church." "*Be it enacted* that there be a petition drawn up by this Grand Assembly to the King's Most Excellent Majestie for his letters pattents to collect and gather the charity of well-disposed people in England, for the erecting of colledges and schooles in this countrye, and also for his Majestie's letters to both Universities of Oxford and Cambridge to furnish the Church here with ministers for the present and this petition to be recommended to the Right Honorable Governor Sir William Berkeley." See Id., pp. 30–1.

Again: "Att a Grand Assembly held att James Cittie, in Virginia, 23d March, 1660–1, the following order was made in the Government of the Right Honorable Sir William Berkeley, his Majestie's Governor, Mr. Henry Soanes, Speaker:

"Whereas, for the advancement of learning, promoting piety, and provision of an able and successive ministry in this countrie, it hath been thought fit that a colledge of students of the liberal arts and sciences be erected and maintayned, in pursuance whereof his Majestie's Governor, Council of State, and burgesses of the present Grand Assembly *have severally subscribed several considerable sums of money and quantities of tobacco (out of their charity and devotion) to be paid to the Honorable Grand Assembly or such treasurer or treasurers as they shall now, or their successors hereafter at any time, appoint, upon demand, after a place is provided and built upon for that intent* and purpose: *It is ordered* that the commissioners of the severall county courts do, at the next followinge court in their several countys, subscribe such sums of money and tobacco towards the furthering and promoteing the said persons and necessary worke to be paid by them or their heirs, as they shall think fitt, and that they also take the subscriptions of such other persons at their said courts who shall be willing to contribute towards the same. And that after such subscriptions taken they send orders to the vestrys of the severall parishes in their severall countys for the subscriptions of such inhabitants and others who have not already subscribed, and that the same be returned to Francis Morrison, Esqr." See Id., p. 37.

Again: "At a Grand Assembly held at James City, March 23rd, 1661–2, Anoq. Regni Rs. Carol. SCDI 14, Act 18th March, 1661–2, 14th Charles II., was passed to make 'Provision for a College'"

Act 18th, the same as the act before mentioned, passed in 1660–1.

These were the acts of the Grand Assembly, and the orders

of the Governor and Council of the Colony of Virginia, which founded the College of William and Mary.

We see—1st, that it was founded for the service of God.

2d. For the supply of the ministry of the Established Church of England, and that it has always, from the beginning, been made the handmaid of the holy religion of our Lord Jesus Christ.

3d. That it was begun and established for the advance of learning.

4th. For the education of youth ; and

5th. For the promotion of piety.

We have no doubt that it was founded by the bishops of London, and was called " The College." It was appropriated for by the Grand Assembly in lands, subscribed for by the government, Council, burgesses, and contributed to by the Crown, subscribed to by the county courts and parish vestries, and by private individuals largely, and doubtless, under the regular clergy of the Church of England, was the only college where any regular, liberal teaching was had for those of the colonists who could not send their sons to the schools of the mother country. It had no name but *"The College,"* and could not have had the name of William and Mary until after the revolution of 1688. Its charter and regular endowments were obstructed by the revolutionary and disturbing events both in England and in the Colony ; and it had no charter until the General Assembly begun at James City, the tenth day of October, in the fifth year of the reign of William and Mary ; but it had endowments and was begun as early as 1660–1.

That the college existed prior to 1693 is clearly implied by

" Act III. October, 1693—5th" William and Mary,

which was an act ascertaining merely " the place" for erecting the College of William and Mary, in Virginia. The preamble of that act recites the charter:—That their Majesties had most graciously pleased, upon the humble supplication of the General Assembly, by their charter, being dated the eighth day of February, in the fourth year of their reign, to grant their royal license to certain *trustees*, to make, found, erect, and establish a college, *named* the College of William and Mary, in Virginia, at a certain place within their government, known by the name of Townsend's Land, and *theretofore* appointed by the General Assembly. And Townsend's Land, *previously appointed as the place, was substituted,* by the Middle Plantation, as *the place* for erecting the college to be at that place erected, and built as near the church, then standing in Middle Plantation Old Fields, as convenience would permit. (See 3d H. Stats. at Large, p. 122.) That place is now the spot of "William and Mary."

The Grand Assembly in 1660-1 had enacted "that land be taken upon purchases for a College and Free Schoole, and that there be, with as much speede as convenient, houseing erected thereon," etc. And at the same session of October, 1661, a petition was enacted by the Grand Assembly to the King for his "letters pattents to collect the charity of well-disposed people in England for the erecting of colleges and schooles." And the orders made at the session of the Grand Assembly, at James Cittie, the twenty-third March, 1661, by the Right Hon. Sir William Berkeley, show that the Governor, the Council of State, and the burgesses of that Assembly had subscribed considerable sums of money and quantities of tobacco; to be paid out of their charity and devotion *to the Grand Assembly, or such treasurer* as they should then, or thereafter, appoint, upon demand, etc.; and the commissioners of the county courts were, at *their next following courts,* to subscribe sums of money and tobacco to be paid by them or their heirs,—and their subscriptions, and those of private persons and of the vestries, were to be returned to Francis Morrison, who was made custodian of the funds. Again, the act of 1660-1 was repeated in the act of 1661-2. Now, is it likely that, under these acts and orders of the colonial government, Governor, Council, and burgesses, especially urging "speede," and prompted by the bishops and clergy, both in the colony and in England, no college, or school, was provided without a charter? The act of 1793 attests that Townsend's Land had previously been selected for

the site of the college, which, as yet, had no name.  The seat
of the government was at James Cittie, and Townsend's Land
was on, or near, York River ; and could it be there was no
school called " The College" at or near the capital of the colony,
at James Cittie, from 1660–1 to 1693 ?  Townsend's was changed
to Middle Plantation, and Sir William Berkeley had contributed
to the college, notwithstanding his answer to the inquiries submitted to him by the Lords Commissioners of Foreign Plantations, in the book of Escheats of the General Courts, etc., 1665 to
1676.  The changes in 1693 were merely from private contribu-
tion and subscription to a public corporation, and from a custodian for the colonial government to regularly constituted trustees.  The Grand Assembly and the council had commended
the plan of the college " to Sir William Berkeley, the royal governor," and he had favored the order and promoted the subscriptions, notwithstanding his prejudices against free schools and
printing.

The twenty-third inquiry submitted by the Lords Commissioners of Foreign Plantations to Sir William Berkeley, governor,
in 1670, and answered in 1671, was, " What course is taken
about instructing the people within your government in the
Christian religion ? and what provision is there made for the
paying of your ministry ?"

Answer: " The same course that is taken in England out of
towns ; every man according to his ability instructing his
children.  We have forty-eight parishes, and our ministry are
well paid, and by my consent should be better *if they would
pray oftener and preach less.*  But of all other commodities, so
of this, *the worst are sent us,* and we had few that we could
boast of, since the persecution in Cromwell's tyranny drove
divers worthy men hither.  But I thank God there are no *free
schools nor printing,* and I hope we shall not have these hundred years ; for *learning* has brought disobedience and heresy
and sects into the world, and *printing* has divulged them, and
*libels against the best government.*  God keep us from both !"
(33 2d Hening's Stats. at Large, p. 517.)

This shows how aristocratic was the prejudice of the royal

governor against popular instruction, and how anxious he must have been to establish "a college of liberal arts and sciences"— liberal to the *gentlemen* and very illiberal to the people. His ideas of "*free schools*" and "*learning*" and "*printing*" must have been a forecast of Bacon's rebellion, which five years later drove him from James Cittie, across the Chesapeake, to Old Plantation on the peninsula of Northampton. Here, too, we have the true idea of the modern meaning in America of the words "*the best government.*" Mr. Hening, in a note with an index, says, "Nothing can display in stronger colors the execrable policy of the British government in relation to the colonies, than the sentiments uttered by Sir William Berkeley in his answer to the last interrogatory. These were doubtless his genuine sentiments, which recommended him so highly to the favor of the crown that he continued Governor of Virginia from 1641 to 1677, a period of thirty-six years, if we except the short interval of the Commonwealth and a few occasional times of absence from his government on visits to England. The more profoundly ignorant the colonists could be kept, the better subjects they were for slavery. None but tyrants dread the diffusion of knowledge and the liberty of the press."—*Idem,* p. 517.

There was no charter, doubtless, until the 8th day of February, in the fourth year of the reign of William and Mary ; but we are authorized, we think, in claiming that "The College" was in existence from 1660-61. The charter constituted trustees of a corporation, but the public and private charity existed in the Grand Assembly, holding by the hands of its treasurer for the time being, and by Mr. Morrison, its custodian. The transfer of the charter of William and Mary by the trustees to the president and masters or professors was signed and sealed by James Blair and Stephen Fouace in the second year of the reign of George the Second, the said Blair and Fouace being the only surviving trustees, and was attested by several of the newly-appointed trustees, among the rest by William Gooch, Esqr., his Majesty the Lieutenant-Governor and Commander-in-Chief of the Colony, and Alexander Spottswood, then late

Lieutenant-Governor of the Colony. And this transfer shows that the "messuage" transferred was commonly called " *The College*," that it was situated in the parish of Bruton, in the county of James City, near the city of Williamsburg.

William and Mary, thus consecrated by time, is made illustrious in its patrons, officers, chancellors, rectors, visitors, presidents, professors, and alumni. Dr. James Blair, of Scotland, an Episcopal clergyman, was the first president, and, as Mr. Morrison informs us, he was appointed commissary or representative of the Bishop of London in the colony in 1689. At the instance of the bishop, he came as a missionary to Virginia in 1685. He was appointed president of the college by its charter, and deserves the honor, if not of founder, of placing the institution of learning on a permanent and eminent establishment. His family are still numerous in Virginia, and its members well worthy of the first president of William and Mary. He was a good, great, and eminent man, who had the grace of God and the good of men so strongly in his heart and head, that he was enabled to contend with "powers" combined against his work and to baffle them all. He built up the college from its first regular foundation, and deserves first to be remembered among the first of its patrons, under the authority and control of the bishops of London.

The first chancellors, until 1764, were the bishops of London. In 1764 the Earl of Hardwicke was chancellor. From 1764 to 1776 the bishops of London resumed that office. From 1788 to 1799 George Washington was chancellor. The college held the office of Surveyor-General of the colony, and among those appointed by it to that office were George Washington, Zachary Taylor, the grandfather of President Zachary Taylor, and Thomas Jefferson. No chancellor seems to have been appointed from the death of George Washington until 1859, when Ex-President John Tyler, of Charles City, was appointed; and to the day of his death he felt as honored in succeeding George Washington in that office, as he did in the Presidency of the United States. The visitors named in the charter were *gentlemen* of the highest rank of seventeen counties and of the capital in the colony, and

two of them in London.   Those of 1723 were such as Alexander Spottswood, Governor of the Colony, and Robert Carter,
of Corotoman, Secretary of the Council and their peers.   Those
of 1758, such as the Hon. John Blair, President of the Council,
Hon. William Nelson, and Hon. Thomas Nelson, also Presidents of the Council, the Speaker of the House of Burgesses,
Peyton Randolph, Gent., of Williamsburg, Richard Bland,
Treasurer and Speaker of the House of Burgesses.   From 1761
to 1763, such as Hon. Francis Fauquier; Governor William
Robinson, Commissary; Robert Carter Nicholas, Treasurer of
the Colony; and George Wythe, of Williamsburg.   Visitors
elected after 1763, such as Right Hon. N. Berkeley, Governor of
the Colony; Edward Page, Jr., of Rosewell, Governor of Vir-
ginia; Right Hon. John, Earl of Dunmore, Governor of the
Colony; Benjamin Berkeley Harrison, of Berkeley, signer of the
Declaration of Independence, father of President William H.
Harrison; Edmund Randolph; General Thomas Nelson, Gov-
ernor of Virginia; Thomas Jefferson, President of the United
States; James Madison, President of the United States; John
Marshall, Chief Justice of the United States; Henry Lee,
of Westmoreland; Littleton Waller Tazewell, Wilson Miles
Cary, John Tyler, Senior; William Wirt; John Tyler, Junior,
President of the United States; Right Rev. J. S. Ravens-
croft; Robert Stanard, Senior; James M. Garnett, Robert B.
Taylor, Edmund Ruffin, Abel P. Upshur, George Loyall, Wil-
liam C. Goode, John S. Millson, James Lyons, Right Rev.
William Meade, William Crump, Tazewell Taylor, Right Rev.
John Johns, Hugh Blair Grigsby.

In 1859, Ex-President John Tyler was chancellor and rector;
and in July, 1871, the Hon. Hugh Blair Grigsby, the gentleman,
scholar, and eloquent writer and orator, of the blood of James
Blair, the first president of the college, was elected unanimously
chancellor, and the Hon. James Lyons, the eminent lawyer and
citizen of Richmond, was elected unanimously rector of the
college, to succeed another eminent rector, the Hon. William
H. McFarland, who had removed out of the commonwealth.
The very bursars of the college have ever been gentlemen of

the most favorable standing, and her president and professors such men as James Blair, D.D., William Stith, the historian, Right Rev. James Madison, Dr. John Augustine Smith, Rev. William H. Wilmer, D.D., Rev. Adam P. Empie, D.D., Thomas R. Dew, Esqr., Robert Saunders, Right Rev. John Johns, and Benjamin S. Ewell, George Wythe, one of the signers of the Declaration of Independence, St. George Tucker, Judge James Semple, Judge N. Beverly Tucker, Judge George P. Scarburgh, Rev. Charles Minnegerode, William B. Rogers, and Dr. John Millington.

And a college thus organized and instructed by such men could not but yield the rarest riches of alumni. Before the Revolution there was a long succession of the most eminent colonial men who were proud to be called her sons; and since her brood has been multiplied fourfold without loss of grade. About four hundred different names on her rolls have been put upon the rolls of distinction, and many on the heights of eminence, by her teaching and training. Not only was her teaching after the Oxford order of the *Humanities*, but her training was that of the most refined and urbane *manners*.

Williamsburg was the site of the vice-royal palace, and her court was far more moral than that of Charles II., and quite as ornate in manners. The breeding and cultivation were of the old régime of knights, under the guidance of the Episcopal clergy; and to this day there is a marked superiority of address among the old families and old servants even of Williamsburg over any other people, of town or country, in Virginia. She is so retired and ancient that "Young America" and modern manners have not yet fully abashed her gentle, soft, and polished politeness, as elsewhere—almost everywhere in the land. It is and ever was one of the chief attractions of the sons of gentlemen to her halls of learning and houses of hospitality. No man of his day more kept up that *"ancien régime"* than John Tyler: plain, genial, polished, kind, gentle, affable,— young men were his *protégés* and pets, and he was one of their best models.

A part of the great good he did for his Alma Mater was to

protect her corporate franchise. When there was a strong spirit predominant, and justly so, to break down and annihilate everything like a church establishment, beginning with Patrick Henry's fight against the parsons, running through the latter end of the eighteenth and the beginning of the nineteenth centuries, wringing from Episcopacy the Act of Religious Freedom, and abolishing the glebes and vestries, and making horse-troughs of the baptismal fonts of the Anglican Church, many erroneously urged that William and Mary was part of the establishment,—yea, was the very "red shawl of the Babylonish woman,"—and were for depriving her of her charter, claiming that she was a State or public political institution, and might be abolished. Mr. Tyler nobly stood, among others, by her side, and maintained that, though she had a burgess in the Grand Assembly, and was represented as a municipal corporation in the convention even which formed the State Constitution, which excluded her, for the first time, from representation in the legislature, yet she was founded on private subscription mainly, and stood safely on the ground taken by Mr. Webster in the case of Dartmouth College. There she has stood, and still stands, unassailable ; and it would be sacrilege to question her corporate rights now, after giving twenty-seven of her students to the achievement of American Independence, among whom were a Bolling, a Burwell, a Byrd, two Carters, a Claiborne, a Cooke, a Cocke, a Dade, a Digges, an Eggleston, an Evans, a Harrison, a Mercer, a Monroe, a Nelson, a Nicholson, two Pages, four Randolphs, a Roberts, a Saunders, G. Smith, and Dr. James Lyons (father of James Lyons), names forever to be cherished. Besides her long roll of most eminent divines, lawyers, and physicians in private life, she has given to the country two eminent attorney-generals of the United States, to the House of Representatives of the Congress of the United States nearly twenty members, and to the Senate of the United States fifteen senators, to Virginia and other States seventeen governors, to the country one historian and numberless eminent writers, to the State and the United States thirty-seven judges, to the Revolution twenty-seven of her sons, to the army of the

United States a lieutenant-general and a score of principal and
subordinate officers, to the United States navy a list of paladins
of the sea, headed by Warrington and Thomas Ap Catesby
Jones, to the colleges and University twelve professors, to the
nation three Presidents,—Jefferson, Monroe, and John Tyler,—to
Independence four signers of its Declaration, to the first American Congress its President, to the Federal judiciary the most
eminent chief justice, John Marshall, to the Federal Executive
seven Cabinet officers, and to the Convention which framed the
Constitution of the United States Edmund Randolph, its chief
author and draftsman. In all, she has given to her country more
than two hundred heroes and sages who have been pre-eminently
distinguished in public service and place. These are wonderful
facts, and their number and value, compared with the number
of alumni, show her to be first in fruits, if not first in time,
compared with any other college in America. Counting her
time from 1693 to the present day, the period of her existence
is one hundred and seventy-eight years; from 1661, two hundred and ten years; in a word, for about two hundred years
she has for and during the period of her existence yielded
to her State and country, to mankind and the world, more
than one jewel of the first water per annum, of inestimable
value. Who would see that fountain of truth, of light, of
honor, of law, and liberty fail?

John Tyler, Ex-President of the United States, was devoted
to the task of keeping her full up to the mark of her memories
of the past, and of her high calling for the future; and the Congress of the United States will, doubtless, at its next session,
repair liberally all the damages done by civil war to her venerable walls and to her precious paraphernalia and archives. To
use the eloquent eulogium of John Tyler himself, " Like an
aged Nestor, this institution has stood amidst civil convulsions
which have shaken continents. At the time of its erection it
looked upon a country in the early infancy of settlement, containing a population in all the English colonies which was
not greater than that which at this day is found in the smallest
State of the Union. It beheld that population expanding over

regions bounded by the two great oceans, to be counted by millions in place of the scattered thousands of that early day. It has seen the Colonies shake off the badges of puberty and put on the *toga virilis.* It saw the Congress before and after it had assembled under the Articles of Confederation, and those Articles substituted by the Constitution under which it is now our happiness to live. It re-echoed the words of the forest-born Demosthenes in 1765, asserting the rights of America to be 'natural, constitutional, and chartered,' and in thunder-tones, in after-days, its walls resounded to the words 'Liberty or Death' uttered by the same eloquent lips. Itself an offspring of the revolution of 1688, its sons were the warm and enthu-siastic advocates of that of 1776.

"Under the influence of its teachings, its students threw aside, for a season, their volumes, and girded on the sword to do battle in the great cause of liberty.

"The calm and silver-toned voice of Philosophy, heard within its walls, has been ofttimes hushed by the clangor of drums and trumpets.

"At one time it gave reluctant shelter to the British troops as they passed to Yorktown; and soon after its gates were opened wide to give willing and exultant reception to the troops, with their tattered banners, which followed Cornwallis to his last retreat.

"Its walls were alternately shaken by the thunder of the cannon at Yorktown, and by the triumphant shouts of the noble bands who had fought and conquered in the name of American Independence.

"The boy had gone forth with the surveyor's staff, which it had placed in his hands, into the wilderness of the West, and now returned the hero and the conqueror, and once more stood within its walls, surrounded by the chivalry of France and America, wearing on his brow imperishable laurels, and making the name of Washington famous on the rolls of fame.

"If her catalogue closed with the names of those who belong to the dead generations, might not 'William and Mary' take her place among her sister universities, proudly and rightfully?

But it bears the names of men of living generations, who add to her renown. In the various pursuits of life they perform their several parts. The pulpit, from which are uttered those great truths essential for time and eternity, resounds with their eloquence; while on the bench of justice, at the legal forum, in the State legislatures, in the national councils, in the active marts of commerce, in the pursuits of agriculture, in the tented camps, their names are honored, their attainments respected, and their opinions and examples quoted and followed."

And now the question suggests itself, What has made this mother of minds, not so very prolific in the numbers of her sons, so rich and hardly equaled in the quality of their lives and performances? Our answer is, that she has ever followed the system of the Oxford instead of the Cambridge class of schools. She has ever taught the Humanities rather than Physics; the abstract, not rather than, but as the foundation of, the concrete and practical. She has taught the divinity of Christ, and moral philosophy, and metaphysics, as based upon that divinity; the ancient languages more than the modern; history, rhetoric, logic; the laws of right rather than those of matter; and yet has never neglected mathematics and natural philosophy, chemistry and astronomy, and other sciences. She has especially trained a school of natural rights, and of constitutional law and its limitations; and therefore has given to the world a man, whether Democratic or Federal in politics, the best to draft a constitution, as Edmund Randolph; or to interpret it, as John Marshall; the best to draw a declaration of independence or an act of religious freedom, as Thomas Jefferson; the best to speak his mother tongue, as John Randolph; or to write it purest, as Benjamin Watkins Leigh; and the best to contend in the Supreme Court of the United States with William Pinkney, as Littleton Waller Tazewell; the best to administer affairs of state, as Thomas Jefferson, James Monroe, and John Tyler.

Let William and Mary, then, adhere firmly and persistently to the Humanities. Mammon, the *sacra fames auri*, has harnessed the physical sciences to its car, and is running over and crushing the moral and the abstract. We think it was Robert Letcher, of Kentucky, who said, " Virginia will die of abstractions." His prophecy has been nearly verified by the moral and abstract dying of the *practical* and *expedient* of the age. It is not Virginia which is dying, but the vital being which Virginia gave to the social and political forms of America, which is dying for the neglect and want of the Humanities which her earliest and best schools taught to the State and the nation.

It is a false philosophy, and diabolical, Machiavelian, and mischievous in the extreme, which teaches that anything is *expedient* which is not true in the abstract, *a priori.* Laws, and the principles of laws, and rules, and reasons, studied theoretically and applied knowingly by experience, can alone test what in the end is practical and expedient. Every neglect of those laws and principles must inevitably threaten any system, political, moral, or physical. It may seemingly succeed, temporarily, and pay best for the occasion, but in the end it invariably tends to derangement and destruction. We have written this memoir of men and events for seventy-two years, in vain, if we have not illustrated this truth, best promulged by Paley. If we would be truly practical and do what is ever expedient, we must be true in theory and definite in the abstract. The spirit of this age is to throw aside theory and the abstract, and to apply only what will pay for the time ; and if the free system of government which the sons of William and Mary mainly in part handed down to this generation, is to be restored and perpetuated, it must be by and through the schools and the pulpits, and they will add unto themselves the power of the press. *The very doing of truth* cometh to the light ; and the Humanities alone can teach our children what *truth* is.

Families, fathers, and mothers must carefully nurture the elementary and academic schools, and the schools must foster the colleges, and the colleges must build up the University. We commend, then, to William and Mary a course and curriculum which we think will make her more than ever a nursing mother of our children and of our country and its institutions of freedom. The fear of God and the love of man alone can maintain a republic of equal rights, of law, of order, of peace, and of power. What William Penn said of government is true : "The best system in the hands of bad men is no better than the worst ; and the worst system in the hands of good men is as good as the best." Liberty lives *not in the system of government*, but in the *wisdom* and *virtue* of those who administer it and those who are governed by it. A vicious and corrupt people will not have wise and virtuous governors to administer their laws,—will not tolerate wholesome laws, and will not be governed by them. The governors and governed must alike be trained to wisdom, virtue, and knowledge. The whole or a major part of the people of a republic must be leavened with these essential elements of its life, or it cannot live. And if we would restore the life of this constitutional republic, we must return as quickly as possible to the Humanities, and disseminate them by all means throughout America.

THE END.